a place of
Rage
&
Ruin

BOOK FOUR

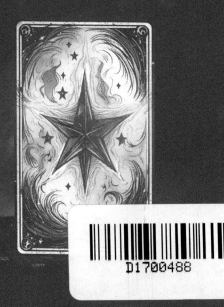

a place of Rage & Ruin

BOOK FOUR

ELLIE SANDERS

Content Warning

Hello dear reader,

You made it past book three. Congratulations. But the question is, has all that darkness and treachery twisted your mind?

There are numerous triggers in this fourth book including; sexually explicit scenes, violence, trauma, grief, and murder,

While book three was descriptively graphic with it's triggers, in this book they will be more sly, more insidious by nature, making you question everything you think you know. Enemies who've been lurking in the shadows, those who you may even have forgotten about, are going to stir, are going to rise.

And the world of Herani will never be the same again....

When they stand behind you, grant them protection.
When they stand beside you, give them respect.
And when they stand against you, show them no mercy.

King Gant's
Lands

King Augal's
Lands

King Callin's
Lands

Camden

King Yannis's
Lands

Ferak Islands

King Hayes'
Lands

One

ALICE

Blood. There was so much blood.

My hand pressed against my mouth, stifling the scream that wanted to tear out of me.

Every drop, every smear shone bright scarlet against the pure white snow and I fought the memory, the reminder of that day so long ago and how my friend had died.

Beside me Jelric didn't move. He just stood still as a statue. Staring at the chaos.

"What the…?" He gasped before falling silent.

But I knew what it was. What all of it was. The strange markings. The charred, butchered remains of what had once been living, breathing, people.

It was a sacrifice.

The air festered around us, the magic hung in the air. Everything about this place felt tainted, poisoned, defiled.

Our soldiers stayed back but I could tell that all of this horrified them just as much as it did us.

So much of me wanted to run, to turn, to flee back to the safety of the woods far behind us and away from this place. Only I couldn't do that, could I? Neither Jelric nor I could. Uther had sent us here for this task, sent us to find out what all this magic was, what it's purpose was.

I forced myself to walk, to move, to take one step after another, feeling that dark magic as it swirled around me, as it whispered into my ears.

I came to a stop and stared down at the mangled face of what I guessed had been a woman. I could just make out clumps of long brown hair, marred with blood and the darkened band of metal wrapped around her throat.

I reached down, touching that broken, crushed skull and like a flash of lightning those last awful seconds, those last horrific moments of her life played in my head like a movie.

"Oh god." I gasped, falling back, landing on my arse.

"What did you see?" Jelric asked, rushing to my side.

"It was, it was," I shook my head trying to come up with the words. "They killed them, all of them, they slit their throats and used the magic in their blood to make the spell."

"What spell?" Jelric replied.

I didn't know. I winced, clenching my fists, trying to fight the memory that wasn't even mine.

"They killed them." I repeated, staring at the seven other bodies. The seven other Fae that had all been collared and butchered. "Who would do such a thing?" I asked but I knew the answer, Magars. They were behind this.

And whatever spell they'd created, what dark magic it was, it had to be powerful enough to warrant the loss of so many Fae.

"Let's go." Jelric said, casting his eyes around as if he expected someone to jump out and attack us.

I didn't object, I let him all but lead me back to the hoard of soldiers who'd travelled with us. I knew my magic could keep us safe but right now all that muscle, all those weapons certainly helped ease my fears of us being attacked, being ambushed.

We rode in silence. Not even the soldiers who'd been so vocal, who'd sung merry songs and joked the entire way here, now spoke. Even the horses were silent, as if they understood the horror they'd come into contact with.

Though neither of us said it, we kept riding far beyond the time we should have stopped to rest. Only once we reached the foothills of the mountains did we finally stop and we were forced to make camp with only the moonlight and our torches to aid us.

I sat beside Jelric, unable to eat a mouthful of my dinner, despite the hunger in my belly. And as I looked around I noted more than one soldier seemed to be in much a similar headspace.

"Have you figured it out yet?" Jelric asked quietly.

I shook my head. "No." None of it made sense. The pattern of the magic was too complex, too dark for me to delve into and read. But I hated the fact that the potential was there, that if I were smarter, more knowledgeable then maybe I would have been able to.

"We should be on our guard." He stated. "Obviously they are planning something."

I sighed, rubbing my eyes with my palms. I hadn't told anyone about the other Fae, about the other Alarin. I'd kept it quiet, kept that information to myself, fearful of what it meant. But now, now it felt like I was being foolish, reckless even.

"I need to tell you something." I murmured.

Jelric tilted his head, studying me. "What is it?"

"There's another, another Alarin." I stated.

His eyes widened, he froze as if he was trying to figure out if this was all some bad joke. "How do you know?"

"He came to Temoor. He tried to persuade me to leave with him." I admitted.

"And you didn't?"

"He's working with the Magars. I'm certain of it from what he said."

He drew in a long breath and as I watched him I could see how weary he was, how much this war, this fight, all of this had taken so much from him too. "It makes sense." He said quietly. "How else would they have so much power?"

"But they collared these Fae, they killed them." I stated.

He huffed, picking up a small stick and tossed it into the fire. "We both know what the Magars are capable of, how ruthless they are."

I guess that was true. They'd destroyed countless cities, murdered millions of people, all in the pursuit of power. What difference would a few Fae lives mean? I wondered for a second if that man had been one of them, one of the sacrifices but something in my gut told me he wasn't. If he was working with them they would know he was Alarin and they'd never have destroyed such a powerful weapon.

"Do we tell Uther?"

"No." He said quickly. "We do not say a word."

"But..." I began.

"To tell him you'd have to admit that you'd met him." He cut across me. "Uther will not reward you for keeping that quiet." I opened my mouth to argue but he continued on. "And he will double down on his position."

"What position?"

"You as an object." He said pointedly.

I narrowed my eyes, wondering if I'd misheard him.

"What good would that do for the other Fae?" He whispered.

"Jelric..."

He glanced around to make sure no one could overhear us but most of the soldiers had kept their distance, as if all that bad magic had put them off being around us too. "I know Guillaume spoke with you."

Of all the things, that had been the last thing I expected him to say. "You know?" I gasped.

"Yes and I agree with him. The Fae are not objects, they're not simply weapons and to regard them as such does a lot of damage."

"You want me to unite them?" I half whispered it.

"I think you can do it."

"But the High King would never allow it. You know him. He has never changed his stance on me, no matter how loyal I am, no matter what I sacrifice or who I save, I am still in his eyes just a possession."

"I know." He replied. "But the High King is not the only one to make the laws of this land."

"Jelric, this sounds like treason." I said feeling more and more on edge.

"It's not." He stated. "We're not talking about usurping his throne. We're not talking about taking anything from him. We're talking about giving a whole race of people equal rights."

"I don't think the High King will see it like that."

"No, probably not but we can make him see it."

"You would help me with this?"

"I think you'll find the majority of the Magi would help you."

"Why?"

"Your magic is different. The way it works, the way it even pulls from the elements. You may be Fae royalty but to the Magi you are a leader too."

I frowned confused by those words. For almost all of my time here it had felt like the Magi were my enemy, that all they wanted to do was lock me away and have me collared. "How can that be?"

"You are magic. Pure magic. Magi channel magic, we read it. We can read what you are even if some of us don't understand it."

Somehow that didn't give me any comfort. "I don't want to be a leader. I don't even want to be their queen."

"You didn't want to be Fae either but look what you have achieved, what you have accomplished since you've come into this world."

"A lot of death and a lot of destruction." I replied thinking back to how only months before I was locked in a cell, bound, half broken, and collared, while people were literally fighting and dying over me.

"But you have saved people too. A lot of people. And now you may be able to save the Fae too. You know what it is like to be collared, to be held captive, but you also know what it is like to be free in this world."

"But I'm not free. I'm still the High King's possession, even now."

"You are freer than any other Fae in this world. So imagine what it would be like to be hiding, scared for your life knowing that one wrong mistake could mean your imprisonment. You could change that for them. You could give them all a life, a place in this world."

I nodded, hoping that he was right. But that scared me too. What if I failed? What if I couldn't do it and all I ended up doing was exposing their existence and leaving them in even more danger than before? It was okay for me, I was safe, comfortable, but the other Fae; if I messed it up would they ever recover?

"How are you doing?" He asked after a few moments of silence. Of watching me getting progressively more lost in my thoughts.

"What do you mean?"

"I mean after Yannis."

"Oh. I'm okay." I said quickly, knowing that that was only partly true. Some days I was. Some days I could barely function beyond crawling out of my bed. The only reason I'd been able to make this journey was because I knew what would have happened if I'd refused; Fain would have packed me up and sent me to Nind to recuperate, and worse, the entire world would have known I was still broken. Still weak. Still pathetic.

No, I'd had to put on a brave face, to pretend because the only way I could protect myself was to project strength.

"And Prince Fain?"

I looked at him, narrowing my eyes. Over the last few months Jelric become more of a father figure, more of a support than I'd imagined but that still didn't make this conversation comfortable. "What about him?"

"How are the two of you?"

"It's complicated." I stated, trying not to bristle. "I feel conflicted. Before I was so focused on him, on us, but now..."

"Now you want your independence?"

"Not exactly," I shrugged. "I just want space to be me. I feel like I've come into this world and it's changed me, altered me so much, I feel like I need to learn who I am now."

"That makes sense."

"I also feel like if I am going to try to help the other Fae then I need to focus on that."

He nodded. "I was thinking about the Prince's powers."

"He doesn't have any."

He gave me a wry smile that made me pause. "What?"

"They didn't tell you did they?" He said.

"Who? Tell me what?"

"When you were taken, when Fain found out, his powers seemed to suddenly manifest." Jelric explained. "Like his magic was responding to the fact yours was bound."

"What?" I gasped. No one had said a thing. No one had even hinted that Fain had done magic. "What did he do?"

"He tore the very ground into pieces. He ripped down the walls of the castles that stood between us and Caraden. And he…" He paused, as if what he was about to admit was too great and he waws worried about how I would react.

"Tell me, Jelric." I murmured. I had to know. I had to hear what I'd created.

"He grew wings."

"Excuse me?"

"He grew wings. After the audience, after he saw the fake you all over Yannis, after you destroyed the walls of Caraden."

I gulped, burying the wave of emotion that hit me as an image I'd buried for so long came rushing back. I could feel that man's hands on me, I could feel the way I'd leaned into his touch, the way I'd welcomed it, even though it hadn't been me, even though it had only been a projection of me.

"Wings." I repeated.

"Great black things. And he flew to the highest tower as if he'd been doing it his entire life."

I didn't know what to say. How to even process that. Wings? Fain had wings? Where were they now? Did they just fold up and tuck away?

"He never told you?"

"We've barely spoken." I admitted. Since we'd gotten back to Temoor I hadn't seen him except in a very few Council meetings and even those I sometimes skipped. He'd spent the greater part of the last two months playing the emissary, soothing the concerns of the other Lesser Kings, smoothing over any cracks that the downfall of Augal, and now Yannis had created in the fragile hold that Uther had over everyone.

In truth, his absence had made things easier.

I'd been able to stick my head in the ground and not deal with our current situation.

What me and he now were to one another.

"What does the High King think about this?" I asked barely able to keep the tone from my voice. No doubt Uther would be pleased. I bet he was dancing from the very rooftops. God, I could see it now; his precious half-brother was giving him everything he ever dreamed of.

"It's not Uther you should be concerned about." Jelric replied.

"Who…?"

"The Council. King Ide. The Magi too, if I'm honest."

"What has it got to do with them?" I snapped.

He let out a half-scoff. "Come now, Alice, you know as well as I why they'd be an issue. King Ide would happily cut Fain down, and the Magi, the Magi fear what they can't control."

"They can't control me." I stated.

"No, and you made it abundantly clear with that so-called execution."

I narrowed my eyes, feeling my anger flare. "What are you saying, Jelric?"

"I'm saying that we need to be careful. Fain is an unknown entity now. Nobody has ever encountered a half-Fae. Who knows what he is capable of." The warning in his voice, the tone sent a shiver down me.

"Why don't you teach him?"

Jelric paused, "Because that went so well with you?" He muttered. "And besides, the Prince doesn't want to learn. He's shown no inclination to develop his powers since we got you back."

"It is his decision." I stated.

"There are mutterings. Whispers."

"About what?"

"Collaring him."

"What?" I snarled. But why should I be surprised? Of course they wanted to do that. Hadn't that been the threat over my head since the minute they'd captured me? Why would it be any different for Fain? "Would that even work?" I asked.

Jelric shrugged. "Who knows. But it would be better not to find out."

I nodded, pulling the blanket tighter around me. The fire was warm enough but when the wind picked it the chill still got in enough to freeze.

"It would be better if he could properly use his magic. A time may come when he needs it…"

"What are you saying?" I asked for what felt like the millionth time.

"You could teach him. Guillaume could teach him."

I shook my head. "If he wants to learn, he can ask, but I won't go to him. I won't…" I trailed off unable to finish that sentence. The thought of spending hours with Fain made me more nervous than I wanted to admit because I knew what would happen. My resolve would break. That bond between us would flare too brightly. And I couldn't have that. I couldn't let that happen. Not when I'd come so far.

"It's just an idea." Jelric said no doubt seeing the look on my face.

"I'll bear it in mind." I murmured before laying down, making it clear this conversation was done.

Two

NISERI

I bowed low, moving into the room ignoring the cry of a retched creature as it twisted and convulsed in the spiral of magic that held him captive.

For a second I felt it, that spark, that memory. My heart leapt, my skin tingled and then the truth came crashing down. That magic was no longer within my grasp. That never again would I ever feel its power coursing through my veins. Never again would I have power.

I snarled, twisting my face into one of fury.

"Well?"

My eyes darted to him, to where he stood not even looking at me. As if, now that my magic was gone, I was no use to him.

"It is done."

"All of it?"

I gulped. "The spell was made."

He turned, fixing me with those purple eyes and then they looked past me, no doubt seeing in the darkness that there was no one else, that I had returned alone.

"The Magi?" He said, though we all knew the answer. If I'd captured the cursed man then he would be here, on his knees, and I would be victorious.

"He got away."

His eyebrows rose. He took a step nearer and that man spinning above our heads dropped a foot in height. "Got away?"

"She was with him." I said quickly, hating that I had to make excuses. Hating that the bitch who'd stolen my ability to channel was now the reason I was about to be punished.

He paused, tilted his head and smirked. "So, she beat you again?" He murmured.

"She didn't beat me." I hissed. "She didn't even see me. Neither of them did."

He snarled. A slash of magic tore at me, ripping me from the ground and I slammed into the stone wall where he kept me pinned in place. I thrashed, I tore at my throat, trying to get the air in but nothing got past his grip.

"I gave you very clear instructions." He said. "I made it clear the Magi needed to be removed from the equation."

"I tried." I gasped. "I tried."

"You failed me." He snapped. "You failed me again."

"I couldn't beat her. And to let her see me, to risk being captured…"

He narrowed his eyes like he knew I was manipulating him but we both knew the truth too. If the damned girl had seen me she would have dragged me back to Temoor, back to the High King and we all knew what would have happened then. They would have tortured me until every tiny secret spilled out and they realised who was really behind all of this.

"If you gave me back my ability…" I began.

His lips curled. He dropped the magic, leaving me to slam into the floor.

"When you've earnt it, Niseri." He said.

I lay there, curled up, reminding myself of everything I would get once this plan came off. Once Uther was taken care of and that girl, that girl finally learnt her place.

He turned his back on me, stalked to where the man was still crying out. "You Magi." He said. "You think that because the universe blessed you with a little power, you are equal to us."

He scrunched his hand into a fist and the man's body curled up, his limbs shattered as his bones bent into impossible angles. "This is a lesson for you Niseri. You should be grateful of what you are being taught."

"I am grateful." I said quickly.

He let out a laugh, cruel, cold, as menacing as the look in his eyes. "Sure you are. You're just as grateful as Sig, here." He said before he sent a flame of hellfire and the man began screaming again.

Three

FAIN

"Well?" Uther said as soon as they walked into the room. They'd only been gone a week, had obviously ridden hard to get there and back so soon, and we could all see from the state of their clothes that the elements had not been kind to them.

I couldn't help but stare at Alice, my eyes, my heart, my damned soul transfixed by her as she all but crept into the room. I hadn't seen her in more than a month, she'd skipped the last Council Meeting before I'd set off for King Morre's lands. Her hair had grown, she'd put on weight too and she looked all the better for it. Our bond stirred and I was quick to bury it, quick to silence it, afraid that the reminder might send her running again.

"You could at least let them rest." I muttered beside Uther.

"It was the Magars." Jelric said as he sunk into the nearest chair.

Alice blinked staring at up me like I was some sort of ghost. "When did you get back?" She asked quietly. Nervously.

"Just after you left." I replied.

She sighed, sinking into the one next to Jelric and I couldn't tell whether her head was lost in what she'd witnessed or whether she was simply exhausted from the ride.

"Here," I said, handing her a drink and she took it, giving me a small smile of thanks, before dropping her gaze once more.

"Eight of them were burnt. Sacrificed." Jelric said. "Out on the hinterland."

"For what purpose?" Uther asked.

Jelric shrugged while Alice screwed her face up. "It felt off." She murmured. "It felt like there was some other purpose to it but I couldn't sense what."

"It was dark magic." Jelric added like we didn't already suspect that.

"It was a ritual of some sort." Alice said running her hands across her face like she was suddenly exhausted.

"Let's continue this tomorrow." I said glancing at Uther.

"It's fine." Alice said looking across at me with that streak of defiance. "I'm fine."

"Tomorrow will be a long day." Ridley muttered like we didn't all know it.

"I want to double patrols. Have the Sanatorium alerted…" Uther began.

"No." Jelric said quickly. "We do that and the Magi will panic. Rumours will spread…"

"Then what do we do?" Uther snapped back.

"I will speak with them. I will ensure those who can be trusted are aware and the others can continue as they are. Ignorant. Harmless."

"No Magi is harmless." Alice muttered under her breath and I heard the bitterness, the old pain from a wound that was very much festering.

I gave her a look of sympathy, at least I tried to, only she looked away, taking a gulp of her drink like she wanted to drown all of it, all those memories.

"Have your spies said anything?" Ridley asked Jelric.

He shook his head. "Not a word. They've been suspiciously quiet."

Uther got up, paced the room while we sat there, waiting for whatever words of wisdom he had. From the corner of my eyes I saw Alice stifling what must have been a fifth yawn.

"Let's call it a night." I said. All this could wait. Whatever shit the Magars were up to I highly doubted they'd do anything between now and sunrise.

"Agreed." The High King said.

Alice got to her feet, walking quickly out the door but Jelric rushed to catch up with her. He whispered something in her ear and she sighed, nodded then left without a backwards glance.

I watched her go, watched her shadow disappear around the corner and then she was gone while it had taken everything in me not to run after her, not to follow her.

"She'll come back." Ridley said quietly.

"It's been months now." I said before I could stop myself.

"And look how far she's come. How much she's healed."

I shook my head a little. I wasn't sure if she would heal enough. After everything she'd been through, what if she couldn't heal anymore? What if this was it?

"You need to woo her." Ridley said.

"What do you know about wooing women?" I scoffed.

"Look at Mira. She didn't want anything to do with me after the whole Lida thing. After Indi's death and now..."

I smirked. Maybe Ridley was right. Maybe I did need to woo Alice, to charm her. I'd tried the distance thing. I'd given her as much space as anyone could need and while that had done her the world of good, now it felt like there was something else going on, something I couldn't put my finger on, that was stopping her from coming back to me.

"Maybe you're right." I said. And besides, it couldn't hurt to try.

Four

ALICE

I woke with a lump in my throat.

I knew today would be hard. I knew today would be long. And in so many ways I wanted to hide here, hide and pretend none of this was happening.

It was Prince Hal's birthday and the last full day he would be here before he was sent back to the safety of Nind.

Since returning, I'd spent hours with him. Hiding away. Masking the loneliness inside myself with his company. And it had helped, he had helped. He'd taught me about Herani, about the geography, the history, at least as much as an eleven-year-old boy could know.

And after today that lifeline would be gone. Would be severed.

I sighed, forcing myself up. I knew I was being selfish, that his status and tradition demanded that he be somewhere safe, but I couldn't understand why he wasn't allowed to just stay here.

And I knew he felt the same.

Cait had tried to soften the blow, throwing a huge party for him with today being the final celebration.

When I walked into the new Great Hall even I paused in wonder at all she'd achieved. She grinned back at me.

"Is it okay?"

"Okay?" I repeated. "It's incredible."

Great ribbons hung from the ceiling in bright, multicoloured fabric. Bright gold stars were strewn over the tables and floor like confetti. A band was setting up in the corner and right in the middle, as the focal point, was a huge pile of presents, all wrapped and waiting.

"Prince Hal will love it." I said.

"He better, I've been up all-night sorting this." She replied.

"Why didn't you say? I could have helped."

She shook her head. "You'd just got back. And I had the servants to help."

"You mean Uther wasn't here, putting this all together?" I teased.

She let out a laugh. "Not bloody likely."

As the doors opened we both turned. I stepped back, into the shadows, partly to allow Cait to have her moment, and partly because all these people, all this attention made me want to suddenly flee.

A mass of people crowded in. Prince Hal pushed his was through rushing to the front.

"Me," He shouted as he looked around. "This is for me."

"It is." Cait grinned. "Your final day."

I wasn't sure if he actually heard her. His eyes were too busy soaking up the mountain of presents. One by one he tore into them, discarding the ones he found boring, the pouch of gold, the books. As he began trying to work out a puzzle box that Jelric got him, Cait whispered in his ear that he had more presents, that he should unwrap them all first.

I grinned watching them while the crowd seemed to fade away and the band played a happy enough tune.

And then I felt eyes on me. I looked up, seeing Fain stood the other side. Quickly I moved, inserting myself between Hal and Cait because right now the last thing I wanted was to talk to him. I felt too emotional. Too on edge.

Hal grinned up at me before throwing his arms around my waist. "It's my birthday." He said full of glee.

"You're almost all grown up." I replied.

He pouted. "I am grown up. Father says after next year I can stay with him. That I won't have to leave anymore."

I smiled, stroking his hair. "You will like that." I said.

"I want to be here. To stay now."

"Hal…" Cait began but King Callin stepped up and we all fell silent.

"Crown Prince Hal." He said bowing. "In honour of your birthday I have a present for you…"

"Which one?" Hal interrupted and I had to cover my mouth to stifle my laugh.

"It is outside." Callin explained as he glanced at me and smiled. "It was not suitable to be inside."

Hal frowned. "Is it a horse? A bigger horse?"

"Why don't we go and see?" Cait said placing her hand gently on Hal's back to direct him.

"Yes." Hal cried before shouting at the top of his voice. "Everyone out. My present is outside."

The mass of faces fell quiet and for a second I wondered how far these people would go, how far they would bend to the whim of a boy, simply because of what his title was. Hal all but marched out the door and Cait was there, right on his heels, keeping him in check as best she could.

As I watched those hundreds of people make their way out I realised I was no longer alone. "Are you stalking me?" I asked.

Fain smirked. "What would you say if I said I was?"

I laughed, turning, taking one step and then another, putting distance between us because this proximity felt dangerous. Felt intimate. And the way my skin reacted, the way my magic pulsated was enough of a warning for me to heed. "Perhaps I need to put a hex on you."

"Hexes are for Magars." He said quietly.

"Sounds like I need to learn some new tricks then…" As I went to go he was there, back beside me and just the smell of him stole my breath.

"Not new tricks." He murmured, studying my face, no doubt seeing that heat rising in my cheeks.

"Let's go find the others." I said, forcing myself to have some semblance of control. Forcing that bond that connection to just still, to quiet. "It's your nephew's birthday, don't you want to be celebrating with him?"

"What I want and what I have to do are two very different things."

I frowned. "What does that mean?"

His lips curled. "Keep charming me and maybe you might find out, Little Fae."

I gulped, recognising what this was, that this was dangerous territory, that he was flirting and worse, I was flirting right back. I dropped my gaze, picked up my pace, anxious to get back to where everyone else was. "Come on. You'll miss King Callin's gift."

"I'm sure it'd be worth it."

"It won't be. I gave him the idea." I stated before walking away from him.

When we walked into the gardens I felt Fain tense beside me. Ahead the tiny train was puffing smoke up into the air as it circled around and around a fountain.

"What is it?" Fain asked.

"It's a train. We have them in my world. It's one way we get around. King Callin had his Magi's make one and he thought it would be a good gift for the Crown Prince."

Fain frowned, "But I thought you didn't have magic in your world?"

"We don't." I replied. "It works with an engine. I can't really explain it but it's not magic, it's just engineering."

"Is it safe?"

I heard the concern in his voice, the worry, as we watched Hal clamber into the tiny open carriage right behind the engine.

"It's safe." I said.

Cait clambered in behind him and Hal hollered for me to join them so I quickly took the opportunity to escape once more.

Five

FAIN

She practically ran from me. Across the grass. All the way to where my nephew was.

As I stood there, watching them, it was hard not to feel frustrated. How could I mend this when all she did was avoid me?

"How's the wooing going?" Ridley asked coming up beside me.

"Maybe I need some tips." I said gratefully taking the glass of firebrand Ridley offered.

"The Mighty Prince Fain?" He teased. "Needs some tips from me?"

"Don't you start, it's bad enough all the women who call me that." I muttered.

"And yet.." Ridley stopped, obviously biting his tongue before he put his foot in it.

"And yet what?" I snapped.

He smirked but didn't answer. "It's not just what you say it's what you do. You need to spend time with her, get her to trust you again."

"How do I do that if every time we're alone she practically runs away from me?" I half-snapped.

"Make time, create times when it's just the two of you. Take her out."

"Take her out where?" I scoffed.

"The gardens, go for a ride…"

I frowned remembering how we'd used to do that, used to slip away, used to disappear, just the two of us, before everything had gotten complicated. Before the world had imploded and I'd turned into everything she despised.

"It worked with Mira."

"This isn't Mira." I muttered.

"No, but the principle is the same." He replied. "You need to remind her what you had. The good times. What she's missing now and that you're not just going to give up."

"When did you become such an expert with women?" I asked.

"Maybe I always have been and you just never noticed."

I snorted at that, knocking back my drink. I knew I was brooding, making this about me, being selfish on a day that should have been about my nephew, but that constant aching need that was our bond meant I couldn't switch off. I couldn't forget, not for a second.

As I watched Alice, I wondered how she was able to. How she could ignore the throb of it, ignore the dreams, ignore everything.

When night finally came we were all ushered to the very walls of the city, told to stare out and wait.

I stood in the darkness, feeling the cold spring breeze chill my neck and for a second I wondered where Alice was, if she had a cloak on, if she was coping with all this socialising.

A spark, a flash of magic shot into the sky. It crackled, it fizzled and then it exploded into a technicolour cloud of wonder. I blinked wondering if I had imagined it.

And then another spark shot up.

And another.

The crowd around me gasped in shock. Hal squealed with delight.

I stared, mesmerised by the magic, by the vibrance, as it continued on and on.

And then I realised she was back, beside me, watching me once more with the ghost of a grin on her face.

"What is it?" I asked.

"In my world they're called fireworks." She said.

I looked back, seeing as another one exploded covering the sky in sparkles of red. "How do you create that without magic?"

"It's a chemical reaction." She explained. "But we have cheated a little."

"How so?"

She shrugged, watching the display with as much rapture as I had. "We couldn't figure out how to do it properly so some are real and some are magic."

"Who's we?"

"Guillaume, Jelric, and I."

"The dream team." I murmured as she chuckled.

"I wouldn't go that far."

"It's pretty impressive." I stated.

"Thank you Prince Fain." She dropped a curtsey, that grin spreading more across her perfect lips.

I stared at her, fighting the urge to reach out, to hold her, Gods, just to touch her prove that she was there. As her face flushed she looked away and I caught Ridley's eye as he gestured silently for me to do as he'd instructed.

I rolled my eyes, turning my back to him. "What are you doing tomorrow?" I asked her.

"Not much beyond saying goodbye to Prince Hal. Why?"

"I want to spend some time with you." I said quietly.

Only she didn't react with joy, with surprise. She recoiled, taking a tiny step back, her eyes widening with what was unmistakably fear.

"I didn't mean to scare you." I said quickly.

"I just…" She fell silent staring at her hands.

"Don't worry about it. Forget I said anything." I muttered before turning, before forcing myself to walk away, to give her space. Telling myself over and over that I was an idiot, a fool, and that I should have known it was too soon, that she wasn't ready. Hell, she'd spent the entire day hiding from me, fleeing me, what other outcome did I expect? That she'd just swoon and say yes, and everything would be fixed?

Gods, I was an idiot. A damned, stupid idiot.

But all the while that bond flexed, it tensed, it felt like a dagger right through my heart turning more and more to agony with every step I took away from her.

"Well?" Ridley said as I passed him. I didn't reply. I just glared at the ground and carried on walking.

Six

ALICE

I pulled the cloak tightly around me, feeling the warmth of it keeping out the chill. Every time I thought spring was about to arrive it turned cold again and today seemed to be no exception.

Ridley moved ahead, checking over the soldiers, making sure they were all prepared for the journey. Somewhere out by the city walls Mira was waiting and I hoped she wasn't too cold either.

Prince Hal finished hugging his father, Prince Fain, and then Cait. As he ran up to me I knelt down so that he could give me a huge hug.

"I'm going to miss you." I said quietly.

"Me too. But you can come visit me."

"If your father allows it." I replied, tightening his cloak, fixing the brooch that held it in place.

"Please ask him." He said earnestly.

"I promise I will." I stated. "But we'll see you in the summer."

"I'll be even bigger by then."

"I think you will be." I laughed.

"I'll be as tall as you. As tall as my Uncle even."

I glanced around to look at Fain. "Perhaps you will be." I said catching his eye.

"Come on Princeling." Fain said stepping forward. "The soldiers won't wait forever."

"Maybe they should." Hal muttered before allowing Fain to lead him over to where his horse was waiting.

"Be good for Lord Ridley." Fain said as he helped him up.

Ridley signalled for everyone else to mount up and after a nod to the High King they set off. Hundreds of them, with Hal's banners flapping merrily in the wind as they went.

I stepped back, watching them go, with that awful pain in my chest, feeling like the summer was so far away, that I didn't know how I'd make it.

The High King turned, taking Cait's arm and they walked back into the castle.

I didn't need to look to know Fain was behind them, that he'd followed them without a glance at me.

I guess I should have felt relieved.

That he wasn't there, pressurising me. Only I knew that wasn't his intent. That every time I'd needed him to back off, he had.

But that didn't stop the guilt. And it didn't ease the hollowness, the hunger, the bond that I tried so hard to ignore.

So I snuck away quickly, not wanting anyone to see how close to tears I was. I'd meant what I said, that I would miss Hal, that his absence would truly affect me. I'd allowed him to help fill the emptiness in my days, to distract me from the darkness that seemed to twist around me whenever I was alone.

And now he was gone.

And so too was Mira. She'd packed her things and was no doubt meeting up with Ridley and the rest of the group at this very moment. Though she had been the one to suggest it, I hadn't hesitated to agree. Afterall, she and Ridley were sort-of back together and I didn't want his absence to cause further heartbreak. They'd been through enough.

As I climbed the city walls, I could feel the glances of the few guards on duty but no one spoke, no one approached, no one stopped me.

I let my feet carry me, let my mind travel as I moved further and further from the castle and around the to the edge of the cliffs. The further I got the more damage I saw. I guess they prioritised fixing what was closest, what was most visible. My feet found debris, bits of broken rock, and arrows too. All reminders of what this city had endured.

And with every step I took, the wind felt less oppressive and more liberating, more revitalising even.

Ahead, I could see the broken remnants of a lookout tower. Another damn reminder, only a bigger one. I gritted my teeth making a snap decision to climb it. My feet crunched with every step, I had to use my hands to haul myself up where parts of the stairwell have collapsed entirely. When I got to the top I wasn't all that convinced of how safe the structure was but as I stared out at the sea that seemed to go on forever, I didn't really care. I think if it did collapse I'd happily fall onto the rocks below and meet my fate.

My legs sort of sank at that.

They gave way under me and I stumbled, falling in a heap onto the hard, wet, stone.

Even now, despite being here, being alive, having fought for every second of this, I still in so many ways would have preferred death.

My tears streamed down my cheeks and I didn't stop them. I just hung my head and let them fall, as wave after wave of sorrow hit me.

This place felt more of a prison, more of a tomb than ever. And if I was honest I knew part of that was my own making.

That my own head couldn't or wouldn't believe that I was out, that I was free, and instead, I was now torturing myself with the memories of it.

I gulped, pulling on my magic, reminding myself with that burst of power that I was in control, I was free. I sent a blast of it, sent it soaring out and watched as it skimmed the waves before it finally disappeared under them.

"I am free." I said quietly.

The wind carried it, stole the words away.

"I am free." I gasped louder.

Another blast of magic, a brighter one shot from my hands. I sent it higher sent it soaring into the sky where it vanished into the clouds.

I could feel myself trembling. I could feel the sea-spit soaking into my clothes but I didn't want to go back, didn't want to return to that castle, to those walls again. So I wrapped my cloak around me, huddled against the elements, creating a fire that burned bright blue as I sat there, as I sobbed, as I let myself feel every awful emotion that twisted inside me.

Seven

ALICE

It was dark.

Without the fire, the only thing illuminating my rooms was the moon itself, shining brightly through the window. I paused, staring at it, like I hadn't watched the sunset and it's rise barely hours ago.

I was so cold now my teeth chattered hard enough that I was afraid they'd break.

Deciding the best way to get warm would be a bath, I went to run one, and then I sat, in that same dark, depressive state until it was full enough to get in.

The heat of it immediately soothed my bones. I sunk down, under the surface, half tempted never to come back up. Except then they'd find my naked body wouldn't they? Long after I was dead, they'd have to haul it back up.

I think that thought alone was enough to stop the notion from truly taking root.

I scrubbed my skin more out of instinct. I washed my hair too, washed out the smell of the sea and the salt of the air that had smothered me for hours.

When I was done I wrapped myself in thick blankets and sat beside the empty fire place, staring into the darkness. I needed to eat. A voice in my head told me that and yet I couldn't bear the thought of doing it, of sending for food, of having to smile and open the door as a servant brought it in, all the while knowing that it would almost certainly taste like ash when I tried to eat it.

No, better to starve, better to let myself only eat when I was so desperate for it that the taste made no difference.

I don't know when I fell asleep. These days sleep felt like my biggest adversary. Because with sleep came the nightmares.

Nightmares of Rebecca, of Yannis, of Sig too.

Of all three of them torturing me, hurting me, forcing me to use my magic against my friends. Forcing me to kill with it.

I shouldn't be here.

I knew that.

Even as I continued onwards, taking silent steps down moonlight corridors.

I didn't know the way but something in me seemed to know which turn to make, which stair to climb, exactly the path that led to his door.

And when I knocked it sounded so loud, as if I might wake the entire castle.

Only the door didn't open. Nothing happened.

I knocked again, knocked harder. How was it possible that he didn't hear? Was he even in there? Perhaps he had left again, had disappeared off under his brother's orders. I shook my head, trying to bury so many muddied thoughts.

"Alice?"

My breath hitched, my heart thumped so loudly as I stared up at him.

"Alice, what's wrong?" Fain said, all concern, all worry.

"I, I…" God, I hadn't thought this through at all. Perhaps I'd still been half asleep when I made my way here but now, now I felt wide awake. Horribly, horribly awake.

He glanced behind me, as if expecting to see an army about to steal me away, and then a look of relief flashed across his face as he realised no such army is there. He ushered me in, shutting the door.

God, this was a mistake. The thought kept repeating in my head as my eyes darted about his room. As it sunk in that this was everything I've been avoiding for months. Him. Me. Alone.

That bond, that cursed, blessed, bond twisted and it was all I could do not to let out a moan.

"I shouldn't be here." I mumbled. "I shouldn't have come."

"But you did." He said gently, reasonably, as I stared at his chest, my mind registering that he was topless. That I could smell him right now.

"I, I should go." I squeaked making for the door and he grabbed my arm, spinning me around.

"Do you actually want to go?"

I stared at him, feeling that contradiction even more. No, no so much of me did not want to, and yet I knew this path was deadly for me. Deadly for the Fae.

"Sit down, let me get you a drink."

I let him lead me over to the couch, let him pour me a drink and downed it like it might put some sense into me. I couldn't look at him. I could feel my cheeks flushing with embarrassment. I could feel my body trembling with how intimate this all felt.

Fear and panic were melding together and right now my head was screaming at me to run like that scared little girl I always reverted to.

"Talk to me." He said gently.

"I'm sorry, I shouldn't have come." I muttered for what felt like the hundredth time.

"Alice, what's going on?"

"I should go." I said getting up and he grabbed my arm pulling me around, forcing me to face him.

"Not until you tell me what's going on." He growled.

I guess he had a right to be angry. If he'd treated me the way I'd been treating him, I'd be angry. I'd all but pretended he hadn't existed for months. I'd all but pretended what we were meant nothing to me. Was nothing to me.

I crumbled. My tears streamed down my face, even as I wiped them away. "I can't do this." I sobbed.

"Do what?"

"This." I hissed. "Stay away from you. But I have to, I have to."

He frowned, shaking his head, "Why?"

"I'm afraid." I whispered.

"Of me?" He asked.

How could I answer that? How could I admit what was going on in my head?

"Alice, if you don't talk to me, I can't help."

"I know that." I muttered. But he couldn't help me anyway. Not really. Not with what I was trying to achieve.

I sunk back into the couch, burying my face in my hands. "And I don't want him in my head anymore."

"Who?"

"Yannis."

His arms enveloped me. I knew I should have pushed him away, should have been more resilient but I wasn't, in this moment it was comfort that I needed. It was him that I needed.

"It's okay. He's gone. He can't hurt you now."

"But he's still there. I can still feel him, touching me." I muttered into his chest, hating that right now I could see Yannis's face while I was in the safety of Fain's arms, and all the while trying not to breathe in his scent and yet devouring it all the same.

"He can't hurt you anymore." He stated. "You made sure of that. You made him pay."

I wished my body would believe it. I wished my head would too. I wished that every time I closed my eyes my mind would remember not the horror but that moment of victory, that one second when I beat him, not all the hours, all the months of it being the other way.

"You're going to get through this. It's going to get easier." He said. "You're a fighter Alice, and day by day, you will fight your way out of this."

I wanted to believe that too.

I pushed myself up, forced myself from his arms. It wasn't just me that I had to fight for, was it, all this time I was wallowing in my own self-pity when there were others out there, others who'd probably suffered far worse than I had.

"What is it?" Fain asked.

"Nothing."

"You think I don't know?" He said. "You think I can't tell there's something going on?"

"I can't be around you." I said avoiding his gaze. "I don't know how to be around you. How to act."

"What do you mean?"

"Every time I look at you I just want you to hold me, but when you get close it just scares me so much and then I just push you away because it feels easier than facing it." I confessed.

"Why am I scaring you?"

I looked away, feeling that shame in my cheeks and not wanting him to see it. "Because I know what you want." I said so quietly, hoping he wouldn't hear.

He frowned, "Alice, what do you think I want?"

I looked back at him and swallowed before thinking it to him because I couldn't say it out loud.

"Are you being serious right now?" He growled. And I felt it, I felt that anger through our bond. "It's not all about that. About sex. I don't look at you and only think of that."

"I," How could I explain it, how could I explain that fear that had taken root so deep in my heart, I could barely breathe without it seeping into me.

"Is that really what you think?"

"I don't know what to think anymore." I said quietly, feeling ashamed of myself.

"I love you." He stated. "My only concern is to make you happy and to help you heal. If that's all we ever have from now on, and you're happy with that then that's enough for me."

He may say that but my head, hell, even the bond between us told me otherwise.

"Is that why you feel conflicted?" He persisted.

"How do you know about that?"

He tilted his head, tucking a stray strand of my hair back behind my ear and that simple touch was enough to make my heart race.

"I can feel it. I can feel your emotions through the bond. I've done my best to subdue it, to ignore it, to give you space and freedom but it's still there, simmering beneath the surface."

It was wasn't it? I couldn't deny it. I couldn't pretend that I didn't feel it. Every second I'd spent in this room, it's felt like it's been growing more intense. More out of control. This thing between us feels ready to devour me entirely.

And yet I can't let it. I can't be that person anymore.

I dropped my gaze, hanging my head. Pain and confusion taking over, as I whisper the words. "I don't know what I want anymore."

"With what?"

"With us." I said. "I'm not the same person I was. I've changed so much I don't think I even know who I am and I'm worried if I go back to you, to what we have then I'll just become the old Alice again. The Alice that built everything around you and I can't be that, not anymore."

He drew in a long breath, sitting back, as if physically trying to give me space. "Do you still feel like I'm smothering you?" He asked.

"No. It's not you. It's not anything you've done or are doing. I just…" I screwed my face up and buried it in my hands. I felt so damned exhausted, exhausted from the mental gymnastics that I was constantly playing just to get through every second of the day. "There are things I need to do and if I'm with you, it complicates it."

"What things?"

Shit. Why did I say that? Why did I admit that?

"I can't tell you." I muttered and he rolled his eyes in irritation. Not that I could blame him.

"I can't help you if you don't let me in." He stated.

"I'm trying." I snapped before I could stop myself and then I felt a wave of guilt, that he was here, being so reasonable, and I was acting like a bitch, behaving like a bitch. "I'm sorry I didn't mean to.."

"It's okay. Just, talk to me. Tell me what it is."

"If I tell you, you have to promise to keep it secret."

"I promise."

"Even from your brother? Even from the High King?" I persisted, searching his face for any hint of betrayal.

"What's going on?" He asked, his tone changing completely.

"Do you promise, Fain?"

"Alice, tell me what it is."

I looked at him, wishing I'd kept my mouth shut. Only it was too late. "There are people who think I can somehow get all the Fae out of hiding. Bring them together. Unite them."

"What are you talking about?" He asked narrowing his eyes.

"They want me to be their leader. Their queen if you will."

"My brother would never agree to that."

"Don't you think I don't know that?" I retorted, jumping to my feet. "But they think I can. They think I can somehow give them autonomy, give them equal rights."

"Alice, that's not possible."

I was pacing, going back and forth, as all that fear overtook me. I couldn't let them down. I couldn't just give up like this all meant nothing. "What do I do?"

"The most any Fae will have is what you have."

"But Guillaume has more. He is free to leave." I replied.

"Guillaume is a very rare exception. My brother will not grant that to anyone again."

"So, you're saying it's hopeless then?"

"I'm sorry, Alice. I know that you want to help them but you can't. It can't be done."

Silent tears slipped down my cheeks. Grief, that's what it felt like, grief and mourning, for a life that these people, these other Fae would never get.

I had royal blood. Alarin blood. And yet still I was nothing in this world. The Fae were nothing.

"I think I need another drink" I muttered feeling that all too familiar defeat sinking back into my bones.

Fain got up, poured me another glass of that amber liquid he liked so much and passed it over. I winced as I sipped it but the alcohol helped, even if the taste burned my throat.

"Who's been talking to you about this?" He asked.

"I'm not saying."

"Is it Guillaume?"

"No."

He sighed shaking his head. "Whoever it is, you can't repeat it. To anyone. Ever."

"Is it treason?" I asked. Jelric had said it wasn't. He'd made that more than clear when we discussed it.

"It's as close to it as you get."

I swallowed.

"My brother would see it as such. He sees the Fae as his. To go against that..."

"I know. I just thought..."

"You can't. You can't even think about it."

I nodded hearing the warning in his voice and then took another gulp of the firebrand fighting back the urge to cough.

"Is there anything else?" He asked.

"Anything else, what?" I replied confused.

"Anything else on your mind?"

"No." I said before putting the glass down. Ignoring the flash of guilt about the fact I was hiding something from everyone. Something big. Something so big it scared me. There was another Alarin out there.

"I can't drink that." I murmured.

He smirked, "If I'd known you'd be stopping by I might have gotten a better drink selection in…"

A laugh escaped me, feeling like it broke through all the tension that had coiled inside me.

"Alice, I love you, and I want you to be happy. I know things went wrong before I left and I know I was responsible for that but I'm trying to show you that I've listened, that I've changed."

Changed. We'd both changed. Both been forced too. He wasn't the same man who'd walked away all those months ago, he wasn't the same man who'd surrounded me with an army of soldiers claiming he was just keeping me safe.

But then I wasn't the same woman who'd walked down those steps and surrendered to Yannis, I wasn't the same woman who had entered this world, who had been burned by it, cut by it, collared by it.

As I looked back at him, as I heard those whispers in my head about needing distance, about not letting myself fall back into what was easy, I knew that right now we were both miserable. Both tormented by this. My actions weren't making anything better. They were making this worse.

"Maybe we can start over?" I said quietly as that bond between us flared up hotter than ever. "But slowly."

"I can do slowly." He said taking my hand.

I nodded, staring at where we were now touching, where my skin was aflame. "I've kept you awake far too long."

"If it's helped then it was worth it."

I smiled, nodding, hearing the sincerity in those words. Seeing him, talking this through had helped.

"Do you want me to walk you back to your room?"

My eyes met his. "Can I stay a little longer?" I asked not yet ready to leave him, and in truth, not yet ready to face the monsters I knew were already waiting for me back in my own room.

"You can stay as long as you like." He said before leading me back to the couch.

I WOKE, SEEING THE PALE HINTS OF FIRST SUN STREAKING THROUGH the gap in the curtain. I was still in his rooms. On his couch. His arms were around me but they didn't feel constricting.

I don't know when I'd fallen asleep but clearly I had.

I watched Fain for a moment, seeing how peaceful he looked.

And then quietly, stealthily, I crept from the room, and back out into the deserted corridors beyond.

Eight

FAIN

The Council Meeting went on and on. I sat there, trying to keep my attention on the discussion, on the papers in front of me, but my eyes kept drifting to where she sat.

She looked exhausted though I knew no one else would see it. No, they'd see the magic glow of her skin, the gold of her hair and nothing beyond it.

But I saw.

I saw as her hand shook every time she raised her glass to drink. I saw each stifled yawn that she desperately tried to hide.

And I saw how she reacted when we broke for food. That not a crumb passed her lips as if she thought it was poisoned.

"...Dimolle is now stable. We're almost ready to withdraw some of our troops." Callin's ambassador stated.

"Good." Uther replied.

"What of the land?" King Ide asked looking around, no doubt sensing an opportunity.

"What of it?" Uther asked.

"Well, what will become of it?" Ide replied.

Uther raised his chin, almost daring him to object to the words he spoke, "I will keep it. It will join with my own lands and remain under my rule."

"You have lost a Lesser King. Is it not worth creating another? A new ally?" King Ide suggested as his eyes connected with Highflynn's for the briefest of moments and I wondered if that was their plan, make Highflynn a king and have the pair of them team up against everyone on the Council.

"No. Dimolle will remain as mine. It will be a warning to any Lesser King who might be tempted to follow in Yannis's footsteps."

I felt it, the way Alice's emotions spiked. The way she tensed. Enough of the room turned to look at her and she stared back at Uther, forcing a hard look onto her face.

When the meeting was finally over I got up with everyone else. As they filtered out of the room, I gathered the papers, passing them to a servant to take back to my quarters.

But when I turned I saw her stood awkwardly, chewing her lip.

"Everything okay?" I asked.

"What are you doing now?" She replied catching me off guard.

"I have a few things to sort."

"Oh." Her face fell and I cursed myself for being so blunt. "I was just, I was wondering if you fancied escaping this place for a little bit?" She said quickly.

"You mean the castle?"

"Yes."

Perhaps last night had been more of a breakthrough than I'd realised. When she'd snuck away, when I'd woken to find myself alone I'd convinced myself that nothing had changed, that all of it, all her words had been a mistake. That she'd changed her mind and once more wanted nothing to do with me.

But apparently I was wrong. "What did you have in mind?" I murmured.

Her eyes lit up, for a second they sparkled. "You're sure?"

"Positive."

"Okay, I mean, I just wanted to get out of these walls. Feel the wind on my face again."

"The wind?" I repeated with a smile. "I can certainly arrange that." I held my hand out without thinking and to my surprise she took it. "Let's do some escaping together."

Gods, she was beautiful. As she rode, as she smiled, as it felt like the entire weight of the world suddenly lifted from her shoulders.

We'd ridden far out from the city, far from prying eyes and whispering words.

It was just the two of us. No guards. No one to watch, to observe, to comment. It felt like freedom. It felt like peace.

"We've never done this." Alice said.

"Done what?"

"Just gone for a ride. It's always been for a specific purpose. Some task or other." She stated.

"Can riding itself not be the task?" I murmured.

She laughed, saying something I didn't catch as she kicked her horse into a canter and sped off, leaving me in the dust cloud that followed.

When I finally caught up with her, she was at a standstill, staring back at the city, at the horizon beyond it.

"You look happier." I said before I could stop myself.

"I feel happier." She sighed. "Just being outside those walls makes me feel happier."

"Do you still hate Temoor?"

"Yes. I know it looks different now but underneath it's still the place where my friends died."

I stared back at those crooked walls, at all the obvious repairs we'd had to make. "If you could leave it, where would you go?"

She shrugged. "Probably Nind."

"I wish I could take you back there." I said.

"I bet you do." She smirked before that heat rose in her cheeks. She cleared her throat, dismounted quickly and stretched her neck as if her back was tight.

I tried to look away, to give her space or whatever the hell she wanted and maybe it was the bond driving this, forcing us both to act like this.

Before I knew it was off my horse, stalking towards her, closing that distance the way a monster does their prey.

Only it was her that leaned up, her that kissed me first. She wrapped her arms around me and rocked her hips against my cock as if she were some sort of seductress. As if we'd been playing this game for hours and finally the tension had snapped.

I groaned, grabbing her arse, pulling her on top of me as we all but stumbled into the dirt.

I got lost in the kiss, in the taste of her, in the feel of her against me and then I froze, registering what had been steadily growing.

She was trembling.

That bond between us that had burnt hotter than the sun now felt like it had been doused in ice.

I frowned, opening my eyes, staring at her face and saw the fear for just a millisecond before she tried to brush it off, tried to mask it.

"Do you want me to stop?" I asked her even though I knew the answer.

She shook her head, but her throat bopped.

"You're shaking…"

"It doesn't matter." She said dismissively, and that pissed me off.

"Yes it does." I stated. "You're not ready for this."

"I don't want you to stop."

"Alice…"

A tear dropped from her eye, and she wiped it angrily on her shoulder. "I just want to be normal again."

"And you will be. It's going to take time. You need to listen to your body and trust what it's saying to you."

"And what about the rest of me?" She replied. "Because the rest of me doesn't want you to stop right now."

I sighed, pulling her into my arms in what was meant to feel comforting, "Let's just lay here a while. Just feel the wind and nothing more."

She opened her mouth to reply, to argue, and then dropped her head, gritting her teeth and I felt that wave of sadness wash over her once more.

Nine

ALICE

A week passed. A week where, I'll admit, I did avoid him.

I skipped the Council Meetings, I hid in my room, trying to tell myself, convince myself, that I could be normal. That I was normal. That all of this was in my head and the sooner I snapped out of it the better everyone's lives would be.

I barely ate, I only washed my hair when it got so skanky I had no other choice.

I lost myself in a pit of despair so dark and so deep I wondered if it was even possible to climb out of it.

I knew I looked like shit but there was nothing to do about it. Even the magic glow of my skin couldn't hide the bags under my eyes. I'd spent hours walking through the castle, trying to prove to myself that it was over, until my feet had blistered and I'd practically collapsed in a heap and woke to find myself in a random corridor, late for my lesson, with a stomach growling in protest.

"What happened to you?" Guillaume as I walked, almost gingerly, into the arena.

"Long night." I said because I wasn't yet ready to have an actual conversation about it.

"Oh," Guillaume replied. "Well, it's nothing a bit of magic can't fix."

"It's not a hangover. I just couldn't sleep."

He sighed, nodding, with a look that told me he understood exactly what haunted my nights. "Do you want to skip today?"

"No. Besides that's not very teacher like to suggest it." I said, crossing my arms.

"I was trying to be considerate."

"I don't need any special favours." I muttered.

"Good." He smirked. "Because you're not getting any."

Yeah right, even as he turned his back I could see the bullshit in those words. And then I registered what was so obvious. That there were no wards, not crystals.

"What are we learning today?" I asked, what could we possibly be practising that meant Guillaume didn't care who witnessed it?

"Stormcalling." Guillaume said with a grin.

"Stormcalling?" I remembered that word. He'd said it before, talked about it before. My magic responded, as if it understood the excitement of what it was about to do.

"It's quite complex." Guillaume warned.

"Are you saying I'm not up to it?"

He shrugged. "I guess we'll have to see."

Arsehole, he was baiting me, trying to push my boundaries but right now, this was exactly what I needed. "What does it involve?"

"For one we need to be outside and ideally by the cliffs."

I frowned. "Why did we meet here then?"

"I did send a messenger but you weren't in your rooms."

"Oh." I replied, flushing, but grateful that he wasn't prying any further.

"Come on. I've not got anything else in my diary today so we've got time."

"You're assuming I have time?" I teased as we walked back through the archway.

"What else do you have Alice? Council Meetings? You'd rather spend your day in a stuffy room, with stuffy old men, or be out here, showing all of Temoor your true power?"

I gulped. "My true power?"

He grinned back at me, and those golden eyes sparkled pure mischief as he said, "Just wait till they see."

"You really did mean the cliffs." I stated as we stood, with the castle to our backs and it felt like the end of the world in front of us.

"Stormcalling can be dangerous. It helps that we have the sea right in front of us."

"Is it what I think it is?"

"It's in the name." He replied.

I couldn't help grinning then, because there was nothing quite like stretching my magic, proving it was mine, showing the world that they hadn't taken this, that no matter what they did to me, they wouldn't take this.

"You'll need to really focus this time. Really concentrate on the pattern." Guillaume murmured beside me.

"Got it."

"I'll create the first and you copy it. We'll start small and then build it up."

I nodded, steeling myself for this.

"The bigger we go the further out we should aim. I don't want us accidentally trashing the city all over again."

"Yeah, I don't think we'd be too popular if we did that." I grinned.

Guillaume closed his eyes, and I felt that tingle as he focused his magic. I'd never seen him do that, focus quite like that. Whatever this stormcalling was I realised it was probably the most advanced magic I'd ever consciously drawn on.

"Close your eyes. I want you to feel the pattern too." He instructed.

I shut my eyes, letting the magic wash all over me. It felt like tiny raindrops in the air around us. It felt like tiny whirls of a tempest gradually building, gradually undulating around and around and around.

My clothes started to soak as it dripped down around me. I gasped, stepping back, the rocks feeling like ice beneath my feet.

"You try." Guillaume said. As if he hadn't noticed how close I'd just come to landing on my arse. "Don't make it any bigger though, just copy exactly what I did."

Replicating was easy. I could do that without thinking.

I shut my eyes, only to avoid the spray and within seconds I'd made the exact same pattern.

"Very nice." He said.

I practically beamed back at him at the compliment. He'd said stormcalling was complex but this felt like child's play and I'll admit I was a little disappointed at the lack of a challenge.

"Right now you get the feel of it we need to make it bigger, actually call the storm."

"I'm sorry, what?" I replied, blinking as my lashes dripped down tiny droplets of rain.

"What you did just now wasn't it." He stated. "That was raindrawing. It's useful for a drought. Useful if you need rain for whatever reason but stormcalling is a whole different ball game."

"Right." I said feeling thoroughly confused.

"We start with the raindrawing but you need to then focus on the air. Throw out your senses, throw them out as far as you can because somewhere out there is the remnants of an actual storm…."

I gasped as I realised what he was actually saying. "You mean I'll be calling that in to it?"

"Exactly. Not all magic is pure creation. The more complex you get the more magic interweaves with natural magic, the natural world around us. The greatest magic you can produce won't even come from you. You'll just be manipulating what already exists, using it to your advantage."

"And that's why the Magi can't do it?"

"Exactly. They can only channel magic not interweave it, not meld it with the world."

"Why've you never told me that before?"

He shrugged. "It's hard to explain. I knew it would be easier once you got to this stage, once you could feel the difference."

"Okay." I murmured before looking out over the sea. Somewhere out there was a storm. I just had to find it. It felt like madness and yet I couldn't wait to get started. "Let's do this."

Guillaume nodded, pulling his magic, weaving it around to form what looked like a perfect cloud in front of us. My jaw dropped, I stared at it amazed by how it was just hanging there, floating above the harbour as if it were a totally normal thing to do.

"Now you try." He said.

I clicked my neck, stretched my fingers as if I were about to perform some sort of military operation.

And as I blinked a second, perfectly formed, identical cloud appeared next to the one Guillaume had made.

"This is easy for you isn't it?" He asked, side-eying me.

I let out a laugh. "Is it not for you?"

"No." He said narrowing his eyes.

I turned, frowning, to look at him, "What?"

"Do you realise how frustrating it can be teaching you sometimes?"

"How?"

"Because of your power, because of your ability, you're becoming more skilled every day, things that have taken me years to learn you seem to pick up like it's natural, like you just instinctively know how to do it."

"I don't mean to make you feel like that." I said quickly.

"It's not a bad thing. It shows the control you have now. And the power you're getting."

My stomach dropped at those words. "Guillaume, please don't tell me you're going to leave."

"Why would I do that?" He asked confused.

"That was the agreement, remember." I stated. "Once you'd taught me everything you knew, once you'd helped me gain control, you could leave."

"Alice, I think we're a little past that don't you?"

My eyes widened. "You mean you won't leave?"

"No. You know what I think of you. You know how I see you. I can hardly walk away from my Queen, can I?"

Some queen I made. I hadn't even tried to get my people their freedom and already I was being pushed back at the first hurdle. No, despite what Fain had said, despite his words of caution, I wasn't just going to just write them all off. I wasn't going to just leave them to their fate.

"What are you thinking?" He asked.

"About the other Fae." I admitted. "About how I can help them but I don't even know where to start."

"Let's not go through that now. We're in the middle of a lesson. What should be a hard lesson. Let's focus on stormcalling and if you want, we can talk about it later."

I nodded. "That sounds like a good idea."

"Right," He said as if suddenly putting his teachers face back on. "So, now you've pulled from the elements around, and seeing as that was easy…" He shot me a look that made me laugh. "I want you now to really try. Let's see what you can do."

"You're sure?"

"Why not? You haven't struggled so far."

"So, what do I do?"

"Push further out, feel the elements, feel the energy because out there somewhere is a storm and I want you to pull it to us."

I looked at him feeling both alarm and excitement.

"Pull it just to the horizon remember. We're aiming to do this safely."

"Got it." I said closing my eyes, pushing out my senses, feeling further and further until I found what I was looking for.

It must have been hundreds of miles away and yet I could sense it, taste it, feel the power of the storm. I steeled myself, rooting my feet to the rocks as if just pulling the storm might just tip me over into the water.

And then I whispered my magic into it, weaved it through every drop, wrapping around it like a great web of my own creation.

It was harder than I imagined. The raincalling had been easy, but this felt like I was actually having to put some work in. I kept drawing, feeling as the storm started to move, started to race across the water, covering the miles as if they were only metres.

I laughed opening my eyes, seeing the sunlight disappear and the grey clouds rolling in.

"Careful now. Not too close." Guillaume warned.

I eased off, keeping the storm just beyond the horizon now. Just out of reach.

"Gently does it." Guillaume said but I didn't hear him. I was too focused now. Too invested. I pulled it again, only slightly, feeling as the storm responded to me as if I now had control over the weather too.

"That's enough." Guillaume said.

I dropped my magic, let it fall but the storm didn't stop. Dark clouds formed over the horizon and I gasped seeing the size of it. The storm was huge. Too big. I could feel the wind even from that distance.

And below it, far below it was pulling the sea, dragging it along in one almighty wave.

"Shit." I said feeling my stomach drop.

"I've got this." Guillaume stated moving quickly to block the magic, to force the storm back. But it didn't stop it. It didn't do anything.

As our eyes connected he shook his head, conveying so much in that one gesture.

"Let me try." I said copying the same pattern Guillaume had to stop it but still it had no effect.

"I think we need to make a run for it." Guillaume said.

"Wait, there are ships down there." I gasped seeing where the wave was sweeping them all along.

"Alice…." He said but I didn't hear him. I sprung up, scrambling over the rocks, to get nearer to where the disaster was already looming. Perhaps if I could get close enough then my magic might have more effect.

"ALICE," Guillaume yelled but the wind was now too strong. The rain lashed in my face and I ran feeling the magic in the air all around me.

The storm was almost on us now. Almost at the city. It was now or never.

I heard the rumbling of the thunder, saw the flashes of lightning illuminating the sky even with my eyes closed and instinctively I pulled it to me. I pulled that power. I pulled that wild magic. Suddenly it all made sense, the intertwining, the use of my own magic and the natural magic together.

It washed over me, it flooded through my veins and I sent it out like a massive barrier, throwing the storm back. Forcing it to disperse.

The clouds suddenly vanished.

The darkness suddenly went.

And the sky, it looked an impossible shade of blue.

I looked down to where the ships were now all beached in the harbour, high on the rocks, where the sea could no longer reach them. They looked battered but intact.

I turned looking to Guillaume, seeing that he was soaked to the bone and then I realised I was too. My hair was dripping wet and stuck to my head. My clothes clung to my body in a way that felt uncomfortable at best.

"Sometimes I swear…" Guillaume said as I burst out laughing in relief.

"I would say it was easy but…" I teased.

He shot me a look offering me his hand to help me back over the rocks and I gratefully took it.

As we made our way back I came to a sudden stop, seeing all the faces, all the people along the walls, along the battlements too. All watching us. My stomach churned with unease.

"Did you tell anyone what we were going to do today?" I asked him.

His lips curled as if he knew full well that he'd kicked a hornets nest. "Should I have?"

"Maybe Jelric would have been an idea." I said feeling like we were about to get a serious telling off when we got back to the castle.

"Pfft, do they want me to teach you or what?" He said as I shook my head knowing exactly how this was going to play out.

Ten

FAIN

We were in the midst of a meeting when the Magi came rushing in.

Me, Jelric, and Uther.

And then the door had crashed against the wall and the man had stumbled in, barely coherent.

And now we were stood here, at the gates to Temoor, witnessing what could only be described as an apocalyptic vision.

"Gods," Jelric murmured beside me.

It was incredible. Her power, to witness it in such a way. It stole my breath. It made that bond inside me unfurl in a way I'd felt before. Pride, that's what it was, pure pride at seeing what Alice was capable of.

But something changed, as we watched, as we witnessed that storm growing nearer, as the skies darkened and the rain came down like ice, something changed.

Guillaume was rushing around, yelling.

Alice looked panicked.

And then she ran, right to the edge of the rocks and I feared she would fall in, would collide with all the magic and the storm she'd created and be lost. She threw her hands up, stopping it right before our eyes and the storm disintegrated, it vanished.

I shook my head. Words seemed to escape me.

But as my eyes dropped, I saw those ships, I saw them stranded, thousands of miles from where they belonged and I knew whose they were, who very well could be on them.

"Prince Rayling." Jelric muttered beside me and I nodded. Clearly he knew too.

"Send an emissary." I ordered. We needed to act quickly, clear this mess up before we started a war.

They walked up, soaking wet, half drowned towards the gates.

As Alice looked up, our eyes connected and for a second I saw it, that power gleaming from her skin.

But she eyed me warily, eyed Jelric too.

"Here we go." She muttered and it was all I could do not to smile at that. The old Alice was coming back.

"Alice," Jelric said beside me, sounding almost breathless, as if the magic she had drawn had made him drunk on it.

"Jelric. Prince Fain." She said dropping us a curtsey as best she could in her still soaking dress.

"Let's go." I said smirking.

Her eyebrows rose at that. "Go where?"

"The High King wants a word."

Alice glanced at Guillaume before sighing and following.

"Both of you." I stated as Guillaume narrowed his eyes but followed anyway.

Thankfully Uther's rooms weren't too far from the East Gate but they still left a pool of water as they made their way through the castle.

When we stepped inside we saw Uther stood, with his arms crossed watching us all with an expression I knew only too well.

As I glanced at Alice to give her a silent warning I saw how much she was shivering. Gods, I should have let her get changed first, I should have made sure she was warm. I yanked my cloak off, placing it over her shoulders and ensure it was tight enough to keep the chill out.

She smiled up at me before her eyes darted back to my brother.

"What was that?" The High King asked.

"Stormcalling." She said.

He raised an eyebrow.

"I was teaching Alice to how to use the elements." Guillaume stated. "How to intertwine her magic with natural magic."

"That's a thing?" Uther asked.

"It's quite advanced magic." Jelric stated and Uther looked from his Magi to his Fae.

"If you want her to progress, if you want her to get stronger then you have to allow for some incidences." Guillaume stated and we all heard the edge to his voice.

Uther shook his head enough to show how his mood was as he sunk back into his throne-like chair. "Do you both realise what you've done today?" He asked.

"We called a storm." Alice stated when no one else filled the silence.

"You did more than that. Do you know who you brought with it?"

Alice frowned for a second like she was trying to put it all together. "Who are they? The ships?" She asked clearly alarmed.

The High King narrowed his eyes, looking across at me and nodded.

"They are from the Sea Nations." I explained.

Alice frowned more, clearly not understanding, though I didn't blame her for that.

"They are a country, a sea country more than a thousand miles to the west of us." I stated.

"So, what does that mean?" She asked looking from me to Uther

"It means you've just created a diplomatic crisis." High King Uther stated coldly as she gulped.

"I didn't mean to." She said quickly. "The storm wasn't even that far. It was only a hundred miles or so." She explained.

"A hundred miles? You pulled a storm from that distance?" Jelric asked incredulously and Alice shrugged.

"It was the nearest storm I could find." She said staring at her boots.

"It's pretty impressive for her first attempt." Jelric stated.

"She stopped the storm too." Guillaume said. "She might have brought it in but she stopped it before the ships were smashed. She saved them."

"She wouldn't have needed to save them if she hadn't brought them here in the first place." Uther growled.

"I felt that magic but it was different." Jelric said cutting across him. "It felt different."

"That's because what I did was different." Alice replied. "I pulled the power from the storm, pulled the power from the lightning too and combined it with my own to break it up but it was mostly the natural magic I used rather than my own."

Jelric shook his head as if he'd never heard of such a thing before.

"What is it?" The High King asked him.

"I have never felt such a thing. Never believed such a thing were possible." Jelric half-stammered.

"It is the difference between Fae and Magi." Guillaume said puffing himself up. "Fae can wield the elements, wield natural magic. The more advanced the magic the less the Fae has to draw it, and create it and the more natural it is."

"So, what does this mean?" The High King asked and Jelric frowned before answering.

"It means Alice's powers could be even greater than we thought. Even greater than we had imagined."

I could see that look on his face as he stared back at her, as he realised her potential. She gritted her teeth, fisting her hands, and through our bond I felt that old bitter emotion flush through her. That one of resentment, that feeling she always had when he acted in a way that showed she was still just a weapon and nothing more.

"Can I go? Can I get dry now?" She asked jutting her chin in a show of defiance.

Uther nodded. "But next time you try anything like that, I want us forewarned. I don't like surprises."

She sighed, turning to face me and went to pass my cloak back.

'Keep it.' I thought to her, not wanting her to catch a chill on her way back to her rooms. Her lips curled up in a smile, she murmured her thanks and I watched her go.

As the door shut, Guillaume looked between the three of us.

"How is her training going?" Uther asked him.

"Well. Very well. She is more skilled and more talented than any other Fae I've encountered." He said before he could stop himself.

"Good."

"She has control too." Guillaume continued. "Full control. It won't be long before she has surpassed me."

"And you will leave us?" The High King asked with a quick glance at me. We'd spent many an evening trying to come up with a solution, with a justification for where Guillaume was when he did go because his loss would almost certainly be noted. And what we didn't want was another Lesser King seeing him as fair game and hunting him down.

"With respect, I would like to stay. But on the same terms as before."

My jaw dropped. "Why do you want to stay?" I asked.

"You all know what she is, correct?" He said looking between us.

"She is Alarin. Fae Royalty." Jelric stated before anyone else could.

"That is why I wish to stay. You may see her as your possession…" We all heard the edge to his voice as he said that word. "…but to me, she is my Queen and I wish to serve her here, if that is where she chooses to be." Guillaume said facing the High King again.

I narrowed my eyes looking quickly from Guillaume to my brother. This was dangerous territory, dangerous talk, and I knew then that Guillaume was the one speaking to Alice about uniting the other Fae.

The High King narrowed his eyes too assessing him. "Not many people know what she is, what she truly is." He stated.

"The Magi do. They can read her pattern."

"If they understand it." Jelric said. "Most are not knowledgeable enough to, thank the gods."

"But the point is…" The High King continued cutting across them both. "While she is anonymous, while she is simply 'the Fae Girl' she is safe. Protected. If people knew what she truly was. What she was truly capable of, then there would be an even greater war than the one we had with Yannis over her."

"So, you keep her here to protect her?" Guillaume asked with enough scorn his voice for Uther to bristle.

"Partly." Uther snapped. "She is my Fae and that has not changed. But she is more than that now. She has made herself more than that."

"How do you mean?"

"She has proven herself more loyal than most of my courtiers, most of my Kings too." Uther said, leaning forward in his chair. "The things she has done, what she has sacrificed for not only me but my son too. That cannot be overlooked."

"So why do you not set her free? You know she is loyal to you. She said it herself."

My eyes darted to Jelric, to the way he tensed up, the way he too panicked at those words.

"This is not a conversation for us to be having." Uther growled as his own eyes flashed.

"Come, Guillaume, you are wet too." I said quickly intervening before this turned ugly.

The Fae turned, fixing those strange golden eyes on me and for a moment I thought he would refuse. We stared at one another, still in many ways adversaries, before he dropped his gaze and half-stormed out of the room leaving me to follow.

"I meant what I said in there." He stated as soon as the door shut behind us.

I paused, glancing around to see if anyone was nearby. "I know. It's not the first time you've said it either."

"What do you mean?" He asked.

"To Alice."

His eyes widened. "She told you?"

"Yes."

"And you think it can be done?"

"No." I stated. "Guillaume, listen to me, what you want, what you're trying to achieve, it's impossible. And it's too dangerous for yourself as well as Alice."

"Why? Why is it?" He snapped.

"Because the High King will never allow it. Will never permit it. In his mind the Fae, all the Fae, belong to him. They are part of his right of Kingship."

"But he said he sees Alice as different. As more than just a possession."

"He may say that but he won't act like that. I know my brother. I know what he is."

His eyes flashed again. He took a step closer, narrowing that space between us. "But you know Alice too. How can you just stand by and do nothing while she is still his prisoner?"

"She's not his prisoner. Not anymore. And it's more complex than that."

The look he gave me made me want to punch him. Clearly he thought I was happy about all this, that I was content to keep Alice in this situation.

Something in me snapped. Maybe it was my pride, maybe it was that deep down I knew I wasn't doing enough for Alice. "Do you think I want her living like this? Do you think I don't want her freedom too?"

"Why? You benefit from this arrangement too don't you?" He said sneering.

"What does that mean?" I asked.

"While she is here, while she is his possession, she is prevented from leaving your side. She is practically forced to be with you."

"Is that what you think? That I somehow force her?" My fist slammed into the wall before I could stop it.

"Don't you?" He said.

I could feel it, that magic, that glimmer of it under the surface of my skin. Some part of me was itching to let it out again. "I love her. I have always loved her. I would never do anything that would put her in harm. That would endanger her."

"And yet you left her here, left her at the mercy of Yannis too."

"Do you think I wanted to do that?" I was now yelling, bellowing as my anger took over. "If I could, I would have killed every soldier that stood between me and her. I would have ripped down those walls with my bare hands to get to her. I would have died to save her if it came to it."

Guillaume stepped back, running his eyes over me, that look of disbelief still on his face. "If you love her as much as you say, why won't you help her with this?" He asked.

"You think it is easy? You think that I can simply change the High King's mind on this?"

"You are the High Prince. He is your brother." He stated like it was simple. Like I was just being lazy.

"Guillaume, there are more politics here than you realise, than you understand."

"If you were really felt as you say then you would help her. Or perhaps you're not willing to die for her anymore." He said tilting his head, glaring at me like I was a worthless piece of shit and as he walked away, leaving me stood there, I felt those words, I felt as worthless as he wanted me to feel.

Eleven

ALICE

By the time I got to my rooms even Fain's cloak was soaked through.

I shoved them off me, leaving them in a pile on the floor and rushed to run a hot bath. While I waited I wrapped a thick robe around myself, trying to persuade the fires to get going, but as always my efforts made no difference and in the end I resorted to lighting them with magic.

As I watched the flames flickering an eerie blue light I shut my eyes, thinking about the storm, about the feel of it, the feel of my power too. I had done that. I had created that. In a battle I wasn't sure how useful such a pattern could be but the sheer power I had pulled still made the hairs stand on the back of my neck.

Full control.

Jelric had said it.

Even Guillaume had stated it.

Deep down I knew that was what I had now, and to say I felt invincible in this moment felt like an understatement. I just wished I could bottle this emotion up, to save it and in the dark nights, when my mind got confused, when my head was convinced I was back in a cell with a collar around my neck, I could let it out, I could prove to myself that I was so far beyond that now. So far from that broken thing this world had made of me.

A knock at the door made me jump. With a sigh I went to answer it, knowing that if Mira were still here I'd be able to hide and leave her to face whoever it was.

"What are you doing here?" I asked as Nela all but strutted inside.

"I could ask you the same thing." Nela replied with a smirk.

"What?"

"The leaving drinks?" Nela said folding her arms.

"What?"

She tilted her head, pouting her lips. "You've forgotten haven't you."

And then it hit me. "Oh shit." Nela was leaving. Fain was sending her away, sending her for training so that she could fill the void created with General Gare's death. "I am so sorry." I said quickly. "Things got a little wild today."

"You mean with the storm?" Nela teased. "Well, there's no need to apologise. Just get your glad rags on because we are going out."

For a second I considered bailing. I considered making an excuse. But tomorrow Nela would be gone. Tomorrow I would truly be alone.

I could hear the bath water still bubbling away as it filled.

"Give me two minutes." I said, rushing to turn the taps off.

What I needed right now was not alone time. What I needed right now was not silence, not my own depressive thoughts. It was a good friend and a very strong drink.

I ran to the dressing room, yanking the first suitable dress I saw and pulled it on. My hair was a mess, my skin was a ruddy shade of pink from all the wind and rain but I didn't care. Right now, I wanted to forget the entire day and focus solely on Nela, on giving her a proper goodbye.

We were in what had been the old Great Hall. It's walls had been obliterated in the siege and the Magi's had rebuilt it half with glass, half with stone and it now resembled more of a giant greenhouse than anything else. With the new hall built to be bigger, grander, more magnificent, someone somewhere had had the wisdom to turn the old one into a huge bar.

A band was set up in the corner and the music was blasting around them and people were already dancing.

"The usual?" Nela said as we approached the long glistening glass bar.

"Not tonight." I said seeing Nela frown. "I want to mix it up for a change."

"I like that idea." Nela said.

There was a small crowd waiting to be served but it was moving quickly, and within minutes I was ordering shots.

Only the man stared back at me in confusion.

"Seriously?" I sighed. "Do they not do that in this world?"

"Do what?" Nela asked.

"You know, a shot of super strong alcohol that you drink in one?"

Nela frowned.

"Right, that's it." I said turning back to the barman. "I want two small glasses of your strongest spirit straight. No screw it, I want four but two of one spirit and two of another. If we're gonna do this, we're gonna do this right."

Nela laughed beside me though I couldn't tell if it was because she'd thought I'd actually gone mad. The barman certainly looked at me as if he believed I had but he did it anyway, placing the glasses in front of us.

I picked up the first glass and gave it to Nela who eyed it suspiciously.

"Right so what you do is, on the count of three…" I began.

"You drink it all?" Nela said amused.

"You drink it all." I stated chinking my glass against Nela's. The servings were almost double a normal shot and I knew I was going to feel this in the morning but at that moment I just didn't care.

"One, two, three." I said before necking it back.

Nela gasped. "That was disgusting."

I laughed. "It was just the drink. Try this one…."

"Again?"

"Again." I repeated. If this was a leaving party then I was determined we were actually going to party.

The second tasted only mildly better than the first. I wiped my mouth pulling a face.

"I thought this was a thing in your world?" Nela said.

"It is but the alcohol isn't quite the same. The flavours are off…" I turned looking at all the bottles behind the bar. Surely there had to be some similarities? "Wanna try and find the ones that match the best…"

"You might just be the death of me." Nela laughed.

Yeah, I think she was right there. We shotted another three before I found one that tasted close enough to Tequila to give me an idea. "Right this time we need salt and a lemon."

Clearly Nela didn't expect me to say that from the look on her face. "What?"

"Trust me…"

"I don't think I want too." Nela replied as I got the now very confused barman to pass us some.

"So, you lick the salt, shot the glass, then suck on the lemon." I explained.

"You're having me on."

"I'm not."

"You do it then." She jerked her head, clearly expecting me to refuse.

"Alright." I laughed before pouring the salt onto the back of my hand and licking it.

"You are mad." Nela said as she watched.

"To General Nela." I stated holding my glass up to salute her before downing it. Nela burst out laughing as I tried not to gag.

"Your turn." I said once I'd got myself back under control. I could feel the buzz, could feel the way my movements were slightly off that I was truly drunk now.

"Not a chance." Nela said, folding her arms, pulling a no-nonsense face.

"I'll give it a go." The man to the right of her said and we both turned, realising that around us were a whole bunch of people. All watching. God, how long had they been there? I glanced at Nela and she didn't look bothered at all. Maybe it was the alcohol, or maybe I was just beyond caring now but I decided then not to overthink it.

I clicked my fingers, calling the barman to get another shot ready. As he lay it out on the glass counter I instructed the stranger on what to do. He watched my face, looking so serious, as if this is a challenge he didn't want to fail at.

In one swift movement he licked his hand, his tongue picking up the salt granules, then he knocked the glass back before barely putting the lemon in his mouth. Around us a round of applause exploded, like he'd just won some sort of battle.

"That's not actually that bad." He said.

"That's because you didn't even suck on it." Nela stated, raising an eyebrow.

"Come on, General. Show the troops how it's done." I teased.

The crowd, jeered around us. Nothing like a bit of peer pressure.

"Fine." She huffed. "But I swear this is the last time I'm letting you lead me astray."

"Like hell." I laughed.

Nela poured the salt out, almost suspicious of what the jar contained, and then licked while narrowing her eyes at me.

"You are dragging it out." I stated.

She sighed shotting the glass then practically rammed the lemon slice into her mouth before half choking.

"That was disgusting." She said as I practically fell off the chair laughing.

"My turn." Someone else said before shouting for the poor barman.

"Look what you've started." Nela muttered in my ear as everyone else started to clamour for this 'mystery Fae drink.'

"It's a revolution. A drinks revolution." I smirked.

"I don't think Fae should be allowed in bars. They're too dangerous."

"Come on then. Let's dance." I half-slurred. I was done drinking for a while.

"You want to dance?"

"It's your leaving party. We have to dance." I said, grabbing her arm, yanking her over to where all the heaving bodies were congregating.

"What is up with you tonight?" Nela laughed.

"You're leaving, I'm drunk, and I called a whole god damn storm today and created a diplomatic crisis." I half cried throwing my arms up.

"All very good reasons to dance." Nela said.

I shut my eyes, swaying to the beat. It's so familiar it's like a memory of home, real home. My world. For a second I forget where I am, who I am. I just dance, as if this beat here is all I need to live for.

And then the song ends and a new one begins. I jerk, turning my head, staring at the band as my head does somersaults. "How are they singing that" I asked Nela who laughed at me confusion.

"What you didn't think your songs would catch on?" She replied.

I winced. "In Montefore maybe but here…"

Nela paused, realising that I wasn't joking. "Alice, I don't think you realise how obsessed this entire world is with Fae. You saw them at the bar, they couldn't get enough of your strange drinks. Do you really think people wouldn't want to soak up every little detail about you?"

"But my songs…" In my alcohol dazed head this felt so serious. It felt like another piece of me, another part that this world had stolen and claimed.

"They're not your songs anymore. They're everyone's. You brought them here and now we've assimilated them into our world too."

Assimilated. Was that what they'd done? Maybe I was overreacting. Maybe I was overthinking this. Maybe they hadn't stolen this part of my world but had welcomed it, embraced it.

I glanced around, seeing all the smiling faces. Seeing the way they were all singing those words. Nela laughed beside me before joining in with the lyrics and suddenly it felt like it didn't matter. The weirdness, the strangeness of it because I was in this world now. I was stuck in this world and if people were happy and were enjoying these songs then what did it really matter anyways?

The band finished playing and I grinned as they started the next song. Maybe I was really drunk, maybe I was more drunk than I'd ever been but just the words, just the song made me laugh.

And suddenly it felt like none of it mattered, the hell I'd been through, the torture, the fighting, even the Stormcalling. Suddenly I just didn't care about any of it.

"You could never know what it's like, your blood like winter freezes just like ice…"

I started singing, almost shouting the lyrics as the chorus kicked in. "Don't you I'm still standing better than I ever did…"

"Now you're getting into it." Nela laughed before joining in.

We threw our hands in the air, now full on shouting the words, not caring that people were looking, not caring what anyone thought.

As I looked at Nela, I realised that I really would be losing my last friend tomorrow. Cait was still there of course, Cait had become a really good friend but Nela was one of my first. Nela had been there pretty much since the start and with Mira gone and Indi… I shook my head slightly. I didn't want to think about it now. I could wallow once Nela had left. I could be sad once she had gone because right now I just wanted to enjoy it for a little longer. Pretend a little longer.

By the time we left the bar was practically empty. The dancefloor was deserted except for us two and the pair of us could barely stand from all the alcohol they had consumed.

We stumbled out, our arms wrapped around one another but just as we walked through the doorway I felt someone watching from the shadows.

I frowned, seeing two men who weren't even trying to hide themselves as they openly gawped at us, at me.

I scowled at them, my magic sparking under my skin, and for a second I considered teaching them both a lesson in manners. Only Nela chose that moment to mumble something incomprehensible and all but passed out in my arms and I had to move quickly to catch her.

Using my magic to bear most of her weight, I carried her away.

Twelve

ALICE

I woke feeling like someone had driven a dagger right into my brain and was jabbing at it over and over and over. My tongue felt like sandpaper, I could taste something so close to vomit on the tip of it.

So, I lay there waiting for the sound of Fain's laughter, for him to tease me before going to make a cup of tea and then I remembered; he wasn't there.

He was somewhere in the castle, but he wasn't with me.

I sunk my face into the pillow, burying the wave of emotion that hit me, but as I rolled under the furs, I realised something else. That I hadn't dreamed. Not once. From the moment I'd laid down and shut my eyes. I'd actually slept right through. Like a normal person.

I guess this was a cure wasn't it? I half snorted at that. Some bloody cure. If I became a raging alcoholic, burying my demons with drink at least I'd be able to get some shut eye.

In the room across the hall, I heard a groan that told me Nela was awake. I'd put her in Mira's bed last night, seeing as she didn't have much use for it right now.

With a pull of my magic, I sorted my own hangover and got up to see if Nela was even alive.

She was sprawled out, one leg off the bed, her arms splayed above her head and her face hidden in the gap between the two pillows.

I let out a cackle before I could stop myself.

"You did this." She groaned. "You and your damn Fae drinks."

I smirked, sinking onto the edge of the bed. "They're not Fae drinks. They're just drinks."

"Whatever." She muttered. "How are you so perky anyways?"

"I got rid of my hangover."

"Urgh, of course." She groaned, rolling over to face me. "You're Fae. You can just cure yourself." She covered her face with her hands, as if the poor sunlight was hurting her eyes. "How the hell am I even going to get down to the stables, let alone ride like this?"

"Want me to see if I can help?" I asked.

"With what?"

"The hangover…"

She blinked at me. "What do you mean?"

"I'm not promising anything, and I've not tried it before but I might be able to get rid of it for you." I said.

"If you're joking right now.."

"Give me your hands." I smiled, pretending to be more confident in this moment than I actually was.

Nela practically shoved them in my face.

I pulled my magic, making that same pattern and sent it through my grip into her body. The gasp told me that it had worked.

"I can't believe it." Nela said sounding infinitely better than she had only seconds before.

"I wasn't convinced it would work" I admitted.

"You're an actual hero." Nela said.

I laughed, shaking my head. "Come on. You need to get going or Fain will kick my ass."

She raised her eyebrows, smirking at me.

"What?" I asked.

"Nothing." She replied getting up, grabbing her discarded clothes as if that now forbidden topic of Prince Fain had never been mentioned.

As we made our way down to the stables it was hard not to feel the hard kick of reality. This was really it. Nela was leaving. And I wouldn't see her until god knows when.

I wanted to stall my steps, to find some excuse to make her stay but that was me being selfish, wasn't it? Nela had her future to think of, her own dreams. If I made her stay she'd had to put them all on hold and I wasn't willingly to do that.

"I'm really going to miss you." I said

Nela gave me a sympathetic look. "I'll be back soon. There isn't that much they can teach me that I don't already know."

"Have you told Fain that?" I asked.

"Yeah, but he wasn't convinced."

I laughed in response and then my eyes fell on all the other soldiers waiting. The stable boy, holding her horse that was already saddled up and pawing at the ground in frustration.

"I guess this is it." Nela said spotting them too.

"Take care of yourself." I said giving her a huge hug but not letting her go.

"You too. And don't stop the training. Just because I'm gone doesn't mean you can just give up on it."

I smiled at that. "I won't but I need to find a new sparring partner..."

"You've not asked Prince Fain?" Nela said with a smirk.

I rolled my eyes. "Not a chance."

"All jokes aside I mean it. I know you have magic but it's a good back up." She stated.

"I know." I agreed. "I promise I'll keep training and when you get back maybe I'll be able to kick your ass."

"Just as long as you stay away from my ribs."

I laughed again, shutting my eyes, wishing this hug could last forever.

"You have to let me go." Nela said gently.

Let her go.

That was exactly what I was doing. Letting her go, letting her live her life, to move on. If Indi were here, would she be going with her? Would the pair of them become Generals together?

I sighed, forcing my arms back to my side. Nela gave me one final look before going to mount her horse and signalling to the soldiers around her that she was ready.

"Goodbye." I said hearing the words catch in my throat and hoping against hope that Nela hadn't heard it. I didn't want to be emotional, I didn't want to make her feel guilty because where Nela was going, what she was doing was a good thing.

She deserved it.

She deserved to be a General and there was no way I was going to make her think or feel anything other than that.

But the minute those gates opened, the minute those horses disappeared through them and I was left standing there, all those bitter emotions hit me like a tsunami.

Alone. I was alone now. And I had to somehow learn how to live like this, how to cope like this, how to be in my own space without that fear taking over everything.

Thirteen

ALICE

I hid in my rooms for the rest of the day, telling myself that I wasn't hiding, that I just needed space.

But I knew the truth. In my heart I knew I was lying to myself, fooling myself. I watched the fire burn down to nothing then tried to relight it over and over until I grew so frustrated I pretended that the cold was also good. That it might do something for my soul.

I played my stringlet, but I plucked the strings quietly, as if even the sound of something merry was too much to bear. And I couldn't bring myself to sing any of the words.

Through the window I could hear the wind howling, the weather still felt on edge, was still responding to the effects of magic that had swirled around it. Whatever I'd done had clearly somehow upset the balance a bit and while part of me felt exhilarated by it, exhilarated by my powers I also felt unnerved too.

And as I contemplated my own power my mind flickered to thoughts of the Prince. To what his had become. Jelric had said he'd grown wings, that he had ripped half the land in two, destroying castle after castle to get to me. Such magic, such ability. I gulped, wondering if I could do the same. My hands reached back, touching the skin of my back, what would wings feel like? Would they hurt to flap? Hurt to fly?

I could feel those scars, those reminders of what Sig had done to me. If I'd grown wings I could have flown away, could have flown to safety.

A single tear trickled down my cheek. Stupid. I was stupid. To think such things, to believe that anything would have changed the outcome, that my magic could have saved me.

From the corner of my eye I saw movement. The flicker of something. I turned, pulling my magic, just as something slid under the door.

"What the…?" I murmured getting up, my instincts going into overdrive.

It was a piece of parchment, folded up, sealed with a fancy bit of black wax. I prised it open, and scanned the contents, frowning at the ridiculousness of the cursive handwriting.

As the words sunk in, I hesitated. Was this another plot, another ploy to get me alone? King Ide had pulled that stunt before. I wouldn't put it past him to try again.

And I'd learnt this time.

I'd learnt not to take everything at face value.

'Fain?'

'Alice?' Gods, why did his voice always have that effect? How could he instantly soothe me like that?

'I just got an invite.'

'I know.' He sounded calm. Almost.

'So, it's not a fake?'

The pause felt more dramatic than it should. *It's not a fake, Alice.*

I sighed, wishing in so many ways that it was. That I could burn this paper and stay here, holed up, because the alternative now felt worse. Much worse.

If I don't want to go?

I felt his sigh. I felt his regret too. *My brother would not be happy if you took that path.*

I see.

The High King was playing that card. Was plucking at my strings, proving once again that I was just a puppet for him to toy with.

"Fine." I muttered out loud. "Fine."

He wanted me there did he? He wanted to flounce, and preen, and show off his powerful Fae, but that didn't mean I had to be a slave, that I had to be a cardboard cutout of a person.

I could feel all that resentment, that anger, that bitterness growing, leeching back into my blood.

I would be there.

But I would go on my terms.

Fourteen

FAIN

The room was packed. Every Lord, every damned noble was here, jostling for attention.

Uther stood across from me, with that crown glinting on his head. He rarely saw fit to wear it so the few times he did, it felt more dramatic, more effective.

I sipped my drinking, waiting, though nobody here knew that's what I was doing. Lord Highflynn stood beside me, muttering, murmuring. I thought the man hated me but he seemed happy enough to engage in small talk when he thought it might benefit him.

"Tell me, Prince Fain," He said quietly, "Your brother is not a forgiving man."

"No, he is not." I agreed.

"And yet he saw to forgive you."

I raised an eyebrow, curious as to what supposed wrongs I'd committed in this man's eyes.

"Afterall, was it not your miscalculation that got this city sacked, that resulted in the capture of not one, but two of his Fae?"

I bristled, anger swarming me for a moment before I buried it back down. He was right. It was my fuck up and part of learning, of growing, of being a better person was acknowledging your mistakes.

"What do you want?" I asked.

"Rillon." He said.

"Excuse me?"

"He deserves a pardon."

"Does he now?" I sneered.

"The man was a fool, but he was as tricked as the rest of us. The High Queen tricked him."

I let out a laugh. This was the new tactic was it? Pretend poo Rillon was simply bewitched into becoming a traitor.

"He tried to steal Alice's magic." I growled.

"Not a dissimilar act from what you yourself achieved." Highflynn stated. "Afterall, do you not boast the ability to fly now?"

My fists curled. My anger flared more. He dared to compare us? To act like what Rillon tried to steal and what I was granted by mistake were one and the same? That my entire relationship with Alice was comparable to that one act of barbarity committed by my brother.

But my retort was lost, as was my attention, when the door opened and she stood on the threshold like a very vision of the gods.

Highflynn stared too. Half the room fell silent as she blinked back. Not that I could blame them.

She was wearing a dress of dark, stormy, grey. Her hair was tussled, as though she'd been out fighting the elements again. And I could see the fire in her eyes, I could see the way her magic glowed.

Gods, she stole my breath as I watched her moving into the room, commanding the space around her.

"Here is my Fae." The High King said, beckoning her over to him, as if her presence had no effect on him.

I watched the way she walked, I closed my eyes, sensing the way her magic was there, on the very cusp of exploding.

She looked like she was ready for a battle. She looked like she was ready to fight every person in this room.

Beside Uther stood Prince Rayling and his ambassador. Both of them were openly gaping at her like she really was an oddity.

She tilted her head, fixing them with a stare. "You." She murmured. "You were at the bar last night."

My eyebrows rose, I saw Jelric look across at me in confusion.

The Prince smiled while his ambassador nodded his head.

"This is Prince Rayling. And this is Ambassador Moran." Uther said emphasising their titles. "They were on the ships you brought to our harbour."

"Oh." Alice said flushing a little.

"No harm done." The Ambassador said smiling though we could all hear a slight edge to his voice.

Alice gritted her teeth, glancing between them like she knew they were looking for an apology and she wasn't willing to give it.

"You are not what I expected." Prince Rayling said running his eyes over her as she bristled more.

"What did you expect?" She half-snapped and I'll admit my lips curled.

Yeah, she was in a mood. She'd clearly come here tonight with her talons out, ready to fight, and though the courtier in me knew what the consequences might be, the other part, the magic part, the part she'd created, was already relishing every delicious moment.

Uther's eyes flashed in warning.

A servant appeared announcing the food was ready and Alice slipped from his side, slipped into the crowd, taking the opportunity to escape.

As we all began to take our seats I saw her, huddled with Cait, looking like two conspirators. Cait shook her head, and the jewels in her crown shone against the candlelight. I knew she and Uther had had a blazing row about it. About her being here. About her wearing that crown.

She wasn't his queen. Those were the words she'd screamed at him. Words the servants had pretended they hadn't heard. Words I knew Uther refused to hear.

He'd taken her from the shadows, forced her to sit beside him when she was content to be a nobody and, as the resentment shone in her eyes, I couldn't blame her for feeling it either.

When the last of us sat down, I blinked realising that Alice was now opposite me. Had Uther orchestrated that on purpose? I knew he was meddling, trying to get us 'back together.' He'd spoken enough times of his fear that Alice might take someone else to her bed, and what risks that would pose to him.

It felt like déjà vu.

It felt like we'd come full circle once more.

Did he really think that was where her head was at? Was he so caught up in his own world that he couldn't see how much of Alice's had collapsed around her, how much she was still trapped in her own trauma.

Sex was probably the last thing on her mind. And besides, if she did find someone else, if she chose to be with someone else, that was her concern and no one else's. As much as I hated the thought of it, she wasn't mine, not any longer, I could feel that, I could sense that. She spoke of trying again, but the walls were still up. She still saw me as that arsehole who'd locked her away, and until she saw otherwise, we couldn't move on. We couldn't continue down that same destructive path.

"Prince Fain." She said quietly drawing my attention and I tried not to blink in surprise.

I tilted my head, feeling something flicker in her magic. She truly was feeling feisty this evening.

'You look beautiful.' I thought before I could stop myself.

She blushed. *'At least I'm dry now and no longer a drowned rat.'*

'You didn't look like a drowned rat. And right now, you look like you're about to wage a war.'

She smirked, her eyes glancing to where my brother sat at the head of the table. *'Maybe I am.'*

My eyes darted to him too. Hearing the boasts, hearing the way he was all but claiming Alice's power as his. *'Maybe tonight he deserves it.'*

Her eyes widened. She shook her head a tiny bit. *'Careful, you wouldn't want anyone else to hear those traitorous thoughts, Prince Fain.'*

My lips curled at the taunt. It felt like the old Alice, the confident Alice, the Alice that spoke her mind was back.

And then she said the words that made my stomach clench and wiped the smile right from my face. *'We need to talk.'*

'About what?'

She sighed. *'Your magic.'*

My eyebrows rose. I'd intentionally not said a word. I'd intentionally kept it from her, because it felt like another thing, another dilemma that we'd have to face.

'Jelric told me...'

"Alice..." The High King said pulling her attention away as her words faltered in my head. She looked down the table to where it felt like everyone was now watching her.

"Your Highness?" She said in a tone that sounded ever so slightly insolent.

"Our friends would like to know about your world." Uther gestured as Prince Rayling smiled.

"Oh." Alice replied. "What is it you want to know exactly?"

"What it is like, how different it is from our own?" The Ambassador asked.

"It is different." Alice stated. "Our houses are different, how we dress, even the way we live is different too."

"Do you have kings where you come from?"

She rolled her eyes enough for me to see. "Yes. But we don't have magic."

"Imagine a world without magic." The ambassador said and Alice gave him a smile because we both knew had no idea what magic felt like, that he'd never channelled it, so how could he really feel the difference?

"If you don't have magic in your world, how did you come to be in ours?" Prince Rayling asked.

"Fae are unique. They are transported by the magic from our world that connects to theirs." Jelric explained.

"But how does that work if they have no magic?" Rayling persisted.

"There is magic there, in their world. But they cannot feel it. Cannot use it. It is dormant. To them it does not appear to exist."

"Seriously?" Alice asked him and he nodded.

"Until you reached a place where our two worlds connected, your magic was dormant, but once you were there, it came to life and that's what transported you here."

"Huh," Alice said as if some invisible piece had fallen into place in her head.

Someone else spoke. The conversation moved on but she sat there, her eyes glazed, lost in her head.

I thought about speaking to her in her mind but as she frowned I decided it was better to let her process whatever the hell she was thinking.

Once the meal was finally done, we moved to another room where drinks and tables were laid out for everyone to socialise.

I should have been used to this. I'd spent the who knew how many years playing politics, standing beside my brother and yet as I walked into that room it felt like the inner circle of hell. I could hear the whispering, I could see all the sneaky looks. King Ide and his cronies were all holed up in a corner, conspiring. Half the Magi were weaving their little schemes, ensuring whatever games the Sanatorium were playing would be fruitful for them.

I shook my head, stalking over to get a drink. The wine had been pleasant but I needed something stronger. Something to still the voice that was growing louder and louder as each minute went by.

"...We do not have Fae in our country..." Prince Rayling's voice carried enough for me to hear.

I tensed, listening to the conversation between the three of them. The Prince, the Ambassador, and my brother.

"That is unfortunate." The High King replied.

"And to have such a powerful one, you are very lucky High King Uther." Rayling said, his voice silkily smooth.

Uther smiled, "Alice is very special to us."

"I can see that she would be. But if we are discussing any treaty then we would like all things to be considered within its remit."

"Such as?"

"Your Fae."

I narrowed my eyes, slowly pouring my drink, making a show of being normal. It was obvious what they were asking for, that they too had set their sights on Alice.

The High King narrowed his eyes and I could see the coldness setting in his face.

"I hear you just claimed a great victory." The Ambassador continued. "Wars are an expensive business are they not?"

Uther grunted. But another unspoken promise lingered.

"I hear there is another Fae in this castle. We saw him too on the rocks." Rayling continued.

"Yes."

"To have two Fae. That is very fortunate indeed." The Ambassador picked up so smoothly from where his sovereign left off.

Uther tilted his head as if he were bowing to the compliment.

"Perhaps you could spare one?" Rayling said smiling, the hint of a tease to his voice.

"What do you mean?" Uther asked.

"What the Prince is trying to say is that we would like your Fae as part of the treaty." The Ambassador said quickly.

I don't know how it happened, I didn't mean to look but my eyes connected with hers across the room. Did she know? Had she somehow heard it? That these men were all but bartering over her, right here, in front of everyone.

"Perhaps this conversation would be better finished in the morning?" I said with no idea how I didn't lose my shit in that moment.

Uther fixed me with a look that said he didn't much like my interruption but his treaty be damned.

"Perhaps that is best," Rayling smiled. "But think on what we have said." His eyes skimmed the room, landing on Alice, and the look, the hunger that showed there made me want to slam my fist into his face.

I bit my tongue as something under my skin stretched and grew. I could feel it, something painful, something unhuman tearing through my skin.

I had to get out of here. I had to leave before I lost control of whatever this was. Before I morphed into the beast that was growing inside me.

I stormed from the room. My skin felt on fire. My magic was screaming in my ears. I was burning up, turning into a raging inferno that was about to combust.

I rushed to the window, wrenching it open, feeling the cold night breeze, only it didn't soothe me, it didn't do a damned thing to alleviate this pain.

"Fain?"

I blinked, hearing her voice. Her hand reached up, and as she touched my back all that anger, all that energy, all that rage evaporated as if it had never been there.

I shuddered, realising that whatever had possessed me was no longer in control. As I turned to face her I saw confusion in her eyes.

"Are you okay?" She asked.

I nodded. "I just needed some fresh air."

Her lips curled, her eyes turned pained. "Me too." She murmured.

We stood in silence, waiting, until I finally spoke. "Do you want to leave?"

She looked up at me as if I'd just offered her an actual lifeline. "I've had enough politics for one night."

"Me too." I muttered. "I'll walk you back to your room if you would like?"

She nodded, her face showing relief at not having to endure another moment of that shitfest.

Fifteen

ALICE

My mind kept churning. With every step we took, I just kept mulling over what he'd said, what they'd said.

I didn't know if Fain knew that I'd heard. How I'd managed to keep my face neutral I don't know. But they had stood there, discussing me, talking about me like I was some commodity, some bargaining chip.

My anger twisted more. I expected it from Uther. I'd had years of his treatment but to see it from strangers, to witness it, the looks, the hunger, it made my blood boil.

"I don't want to be part of a treaty." I said before I could stop myself.

Fain tensed. "You won't be."

I paused, looking up at him. Thankfully the corridor was deserted but in truth, I didn't care who heard me in this moment. "You're right. I won't be." I repeated. "Because if I was, I wouldn't comply. I'm not just going to be handed around like some object."

His hands grasped my shoulders, his eyes flashed with an anger that seemed to match the fire in me. "Do you think I would let that happen to you?" He asked.

"We both know you can't stop the High King when he has decided something." I stated, inadvertently twisting the dagger that I knew was there.

He shook his head. "Alice, I promise you, you're not going anywhere."

It felt like more of the same. More of those old empty promises. I gritted my teeth picking up my pace, choosing not to voice it out loud.

Did he see something in my face? Did he sense something through the bond? One minute I was walking and the next he'd pulled me back. "I won't let him, Alice. I won't let him use you like that. If it comes to it…" He trailed off, looking about, obviously concerned we'd be overheard.

"What?" I replied. "Would you fight for me, Prince Fain?" I asked, thinking of his new magic. Did he have enough control to do that? Even if he did, I didn't need him to. I could fight for myself now, and I was starting to believe it was high time I did just that.

"Just like every other time." He said in a tone that seemed so at odds with our current situation.

I blushed, staring up at him. My damned heart was pounding in my chest. Could he hear it? Could he sense it?

His lips curled, suggesting he knew exactly what he was doing right now.

I pulled myself free, making once more for my rooms. Perhaps it had been a mistake to let him walk me back. Perhaps I should have just snuck away. Should have left them all wondering where their precious Fae went.

"Can I ask you something?" Fain asked out of nowhere.

"What?"

"If you were free, I mean truly free, and if you could go anywhere, would you stay here?"

"What do you mean?" I replied confused by the question.

"I mean, if you could, if you didn't belong to the High King, would you still choose to be here?"

I scanned his face trying to put that urgency behind his words into something that made sense. "I don't understand what you're asking?"

"With me." He said. "Would you still choose to be whatever we are right now?"

My eyes widened. I swallowed looking up at him. "Why are you asking me that?"

"Because I need to know something."

"What?"

"If you feel forced. If you feel like, even part of you is with me because of being stuck here."

My heart skittered to a stop. Fear laced my blood like ice. "Why would you say that?"

"So you don't?"

"Of course I don't." I snapped. "You're not forcing me. You're not..." I shook my head trying to fight the emotions now rushing through me.

"I just needed to know." He murmured, sounding relieved.

"Do you think you are?" I asked him.

"No. But Guillaume said it and I couldn't get it out of my head."

I narrowed my eyes. "Why did he say that to you?"

"We were talking about the High King. About the fact that you are his possession. He said it worked in my favour too because it meant you were trapped here."

I clenched my jaw, realising exactly what he was getting at. "He shouldn't have said that."

"He was saying it to defend you."

I scoffed at Fain's now attempt to defend Guillaume. "He still shouldn't have said it. I'm not forced to be with you. I want to be."

"If you ever change your mind. If you ever want to me to stop…"

"I know." I said as my mind registered that we were back. Outside my door. I didn't want to just walk away in this moment, to shut the door after such a conversation, and besides, we had more to talk about. More serious topics we needed to discuss.

"Do you want a drink?" I asked him.

Surprise flooded his face. Clearly he wasn't expecting me to say that.

"Just a drink." I stated opening the door, holding it for him to follow.

And then I saw what a mess my room was in and instantly regretted it.

"Why hasn't Mira cleaned any of this?" Fain asked looking around.

"She's not here. She went to Nind." I said, quickly picking up the pile of dresses I'd left strewn about the place, feeling mortified. Fain's rooms were always immaculate. Mine looked like I'd been burgled.

"What do you mean?"

"She went with Ridley."

He frowned, fixing me with a look. "Why did no one tell me?"

I dumped the dresses in the other room before walking back in like I hadn't just done that.

"Maybe because you're a control freak and you would have said no," I muttered loud enough for him to hear. For him to react. "Drink?" I added going over to where the cabinet was because god knows I needed one now. I could feel his eyes still looking about the place, judging the state of it.

"I'm not a control freak." He said.

I laughed, knocking back a mouthful, then poured another.

"So, you don't have a maid?"

"Nope."

"Alice, we need to sort that."

"No, we don't." I stated passing him a glass and then going to stoke the fire. No matter what arguments he came up with there was no way I was getting another maid. No bloody way at all.

"Why don't you want a maid?"

I sighed, avoiding his gaze. The damned stupid fire wouldn't catch and with Fain watching, my heckles were up, just waiting for him to point out exactly how I was doing it wrong.

"Tell me…" He said and that tone, that gentleness seemed to make all those high walls of mine crumble.

I sunk down beside him, glaring at the smouldering, pitiful excuse for a fire. "Right now, when I shut that door, I know I'm alone. I know there's no one there that's just going to walk in at any moment. That's going to watch me, judge me, react to how I look."

"Why would they react to how you look?"

"Because of the scars." I said without thinking.

His reaction, that look on his face made my eyes well. I wasn't going to cry. I wasn't going to do that. I gritted my teeth, impaling my nails into my palms, forcing myself to be strong, to act strong. "Without a maid it is easier." I stated. "I don't need to care what anyone thinks. I can be free, at least in this room, I can have my own space."

"Is that why you let Mira go with Ridley?"

"A little." I admitted. "I didn't want to separate them, not after everything that's happened. But I also couldn't take the looks, the sympathy every time she saw my back."

"Mira is your friend. I'm sure she didn't mean to make you feel like that."

"I know she didn't, but I still felt it."

"How bad is it? The scars?"

"It's bad." I muttered looking down at my glass as shame rushed over me. My skin had healed completely but those white streaks, they marred my skin, showing every slash the iron blade had made.

"Can I see?" He asked gently.

Panic. Sheer utter panic hit me and I scrambled as if he might pin me down and force the dress from my back. "No. I'm not ready. I don't want you to see it." I gasped.

"It's okay. You don't have too."

I turned my head, unable to meet his gaze. It felt like I was so close to a panic attack. That all my fierce bravado back in front of the High King was so far from who I was right now.

"Why don't we just sit here and enjoy not so impressive fire you've made?" He said.

My lips quirked. I stared at the pathetic fire, all but threatening to go out. Of course, he would tease me about that.

"Why don't we talk about you?" I replied. "About the fact you grew wings."

His eyes narrowed. I could feel the irritation at my words. "Who told you about that?" He asked searching my face for the truth.

"Jelric."

"Of course." He muttered. "Of course Jelric would. No doubt he tried to get you to teach me too?"

"He did mention it."

"You know that's what Uther wants."

I frowned, did he think Jelric was saying that for Uther's benefit? "Jelric isn't his loyal follower anymore."

"Excuse me?" He growled.

I gulped, wondering if I'd misjudged this but I repeated it anyway before adding, "He hasn't been for a long while."

Fain leant back, his neck rolling back over the cushion of the couch seat and he stared up at the ceiling as he processed that information.

"Jelric wants the Fae to be free." I stated.

"Alice," He said in that tone that always sounded so caring, but set my teeth on edge.

"Let's not do this now." I replied. I could see he wasn't ready. That though his loyalty might be turning, right now, he was still too much under his brother's sway and despite what we were, despite what he might say, he wasn't willing to take action.

My eyes cast out to the view, to the window, and the moonlit sea beyond. "I never thanked you." I said.

"What for?"

"This room. This view." I'd kept his note, I'd hidden it away, like it was some treasured possession.

He smiled at me, lifting his hand to cup my cheek. "I knew you would like it."

A voice in my head told me not to do it, but I moved anyway, leaning into him, resting my head against his chest.

And for a moment, for one brief, precious moment I could feel it. The world was silent. The world was at peace.

Sixteen

FAIN

We sat there, not entangled, not truly cuddled up, but close enough to touch. Close enough that our bond flared and my presence alone seemed to give her some comfort.

I don't know when she drifted off. I just remember the way her breathing changed. The way it slowed. I could hear the soft whisper as she drew in breath, then exhaled it again. For a while I stayed there, not moving, letting her sleep, afraid that I might wake her.

And then I worried that she might wake beside me, and that might scare her more.

So I scooped her up as gently as I could, I carried her into her bedroom, and laid her down. She still had her boots on, as carefully as I was able, I undid the ties and slipped them off. Her bedroom was as much of a state as the rest of the rooms. Dresses, shoes, all manner of items were strewn about and I wondered when exactly the place had last been cleaned.

But then it was no concern of mine, was it? If this was how Alice chose to live right now, if this was how she needed it, then who was I to interfere? To judge?

I pulled the covers up, laying the furs over her. The nights were getting warmer. The winter sun was finally turning to spring, but I didn't want her to wake up cold.

With one final glance back, I turned and left her to her dreams, shutting the door, ignoring that old voice in my head that said she'd be far safer with guards. That leaving her so unprotected was reckless, foolish.

But as I walked back to my own rooms, I felt it.

I heard it too.

Her scream echoed behind me. It echoed in my head. And both the bond and my magic flared in response.

I raced back, raced into her sitting room and back through to her bedroom.

My eyes didn't register what they were seeing. My mind went blank as I witnessed what could only be an inferno. Magic, swirling, uncontrollable magic. It spun around, twisted so violently, and right in the middle, right where I couldn't reach her, was Alice.

"Fuck," I hissed. Feeling helpless. Feeling useless.

Deep down I knew she was just having a nightmare but it felt far worse than that. It looked far worse too.

I could go to Jelric, I could even get Guillaume here, if my pride allowed it.

But that Fae part of me took over, my magic took over. I stepped into it as though fear were not a thing. I walked through that rage as if I were untouchable.

Only I felt it, in my soul I felt that terror, and that pain, and that trauma. Everything she had endured and right now, was reliving once more.

I called to her, my voice somehow carrying across the roar. I called her name over and over, hoping she would just open her eyes.

Bits of magic, bits of carnage slammed into me. I grunted, taking the pain, taking the beating because deep down this was what I deserved too. All that time back in Dimolle, I'd convinced myself that I was sharing her pain, enduring it with her, but now I realised how utterly infantile that thought had been.

I didn't have a clue what she'd been through. I didn't have a clue.

My hands reached out. As her back bowed, as another scream passed her lips, I reached forward and I grabbed her in my arms.

She slumped. That magic, that seconds before had raged and revolted, suddenly stilled. And an eery silence replaced it.

"You're alright." I murmured, "You're alright."

She didn't open her eyes, she just lay there, her mouth slightly ajar, her golden hair askew. But that look of terror was gone. That look of horror was no longer marring her features, twisting her beautiful face into something more grotesque.

"I've got you." I said, even though those words felt too much, too complicated, too close to an ownership I wasn't allowed to claim right now. An ownership I had no right to claim considering everything that I had done.

I laid her down back onto the bed, and as her head hit the pillows, she whimpered.

"You're safe." I said. "You're safe now, Alice."

She blinked, her eyes slowly opened and I saw that confusion wash over her as she registered where she was, and who exactly was leaning over her.

"What?" She said, gulping, looking around, her hands clutching at the covers.

I sunk back onto my haunches. Giving her more space. "You had a nightmare." I stated.

Her eyes widened, tears welled in them as she shook her head. "No,"

"You're okay. It's over now."

She drew in one long breath after another, her eyes casting around as if she could sense the magic that had taken over the room. "What did I do? Did I hurt someone?"

"Nothing." I reassured her. "You did nothing."

"But…"

"I heard you scream." I stated. "That's why I came back."

She screwed her face up. "I don't want to go back to using that crystal."

"What crystal?"

"The one Jelric gave me back at Montefore. The one that held my magic when I slept. When I had no control."

"He gave you that?" I snarled.

She hunched up more, looking more defeated as each moment passed. "It helped me then."

"And now?" I persisted.

"Now it would be worse. So much worse." She stated. "Using it, giving up my magic would mean anyone could come here, anyone could…" She gasped the last bit.

"That won't happen." I growled. "And you're not using that damned crystal."

"Jelric will make me if he senses what I've done."

Her voice sounded hollow. I hated the way she was looking like she's giving up, the way a trapped animal does when they realise the cage won't open and that all their dreams are over.

"Where is it?" I asked. "This crystal?"

She lifted her hand, pointed a shaky finger to where a box was over the other side of the room.

I got up, crossing the space quickly, and snatched the thing out. "This?" I asked.

She nodded.

Before she could argue, before she could try to stop me I opened the window and hurled the damned thing out into the sea.

"Fain," She gasped.

"Now you listen to me," I said, sinking back onto the end of the bed, not wanting to encroach too much. "No one is going to force you do anything anymore, do you hear me? You're the one with the power, it's you who gets to decide how you use it."

She scoffed, muttering under her breath but I heard every word. "Like that's really the case."

"It is." I said, standing up, getting to my feet, clenching my fists.

And before she could reply I stalked out, knowing exactly what I had to do to ensure that. What steps I needed to take to resolve all of this.

Seventeen

FAIN

My hand slammed into the door. The guards had already let me through the outer ones, no doubt seeing the look on my face and thinking some catastrophe had taken place.

I heard muttering, movement, the sound of footsteps shuffling as someone got closer and closer.

"What?" Uther snarled, yanking the door open, only his eyes widened when he took me in. "What's happened?"

"We need to talk."

Those four words. Alice had spoken them to me earlier but they'd had an entirely different meaning to what they did right now.

His eyebrows rose. "Do you know what time it is?"

"Do I look like I give a damn?"

He drew himself up, wrapping the rich, velvet robe around himself. "Come then," He said motioning to the couches, as if he had called this audience.

I sat down, not taking my eyes from his for a second. How many times had we had this conversation before? How many times had I asked this same thing?

"This is about Alice." He said.

I blinked back, the only acknowledgement I had.

"Prince Rayling has offered a fine price."

"What?" I snapped, feeling blindsided by that comment, because that was the last thing I expected to come out of his mouth.

He sighed, getting to his feet, walking to where a fireplace was roaring. No doubt some servant or other stayed up all night to tend to it, to ensure that when Uther woke he wouldn't have cold rooms.

"There are bigger things at play." He muttered scowling.

"What things?"

"Our reserves are running low."

"The harvest was good." I stated. "Despite the sacking, we have enough grain and water to last till spring…"

"I'm not talking about food." Uther snapped. "This land, this country, it runs on more than just grain."

"So what…?"

"Gold. I am out of gold."

I blinked again. That was what was needed? "Raise the taxes then."

He scoffed. "From who? The peasants are already at maximum, you think they can afford to pay more?"

"What of the Lesser Kings?"

"Lesser Kings." Uther spat. "Half of them are in arrears as it is. If I demand more, I'll have a revolt on my hands and the last thing we can afford is another bloody war."

"So what are you proposing brother?" I snapped.

"Alice."

"What about her?"

"The Sea Nations will pay. They'll grant us enough gold, enough treasure to replenish our reserves twice over."

"You're going to sell her?" I growled, unable to believe my ears.

"Not sell her. Loan her."

"You cannot be serious."

"I am deadly serious."

I was on my feet, anger and fury pumping through my veins. "After everything she has done for you, everything she has sacrificed…"

"You think this is easy?" He snarled like he even understood it. "You think I want to do that? To ship her off? But what choice do we have? We all have to make sacrifices."

"And Alice is making all of yours." I stated, slamming my hand into the wall.

"Fain," He sighed, shaking his head. "If there was another way, another option."

"There is." I snapped. "You just don't want to see it. It's easier for you this way, you get to fill your coffers, line all those nice big chests in your treasury, without having to face any hard decisions."

"You think this isn't hard?" His hands slammed into me, pushing me back. "You think I haven't laid awake, thinking it over, trying to come up with some other solution."

"What of Augal's lands? What of Yannis's? Both are rich countries."

"Both are floundering." He stated. "This is the only way. The only option. Alice must go. She must."

I pulled a face, curled my fists up but it wasn't my hands that hit him. My magic slammed into him, sending him flying back into the wall.

"No." I said, glaring back at his now crumpled form. "Alice, isn't going anywhere, do you hear me?"

He gulped, trying to get to his feet, and I twisted my hand, keeping him right there, at my feet. At my mercy.

"We don't have a choice, Fain." He stammered.

"Yes, you do." I said. Like hell he was going to make this *our* decision. Like hell he was going to send her away just because it was the easy path for him.

"Alice stays." I snapped. "She stays. Or by the Gods, I will make you pay."

Eighteen

ALICE

I knew the next few hours would be painful. More painful than normal.

The Prince and the Ambassador had been in the city for two days now. They'd spent the entire day yesterday all but locked in a room with just the High King and Fain and though I didn't know what had been agreed I had a horrible feeling I was about to find out.

As I walked in the room, I felt that familiar turn of attention. That familiar movement of eyes, scanning over me. I sighed, going to grab a drink and Lord Highflynn passed me one with a smile. I murmured my thanks, unsure how to take the man. I'd seen him siding up to Ide often enough, but he didn't come across as sleazy, as untrustworthy either.

The High King walked in with Prince Rayling and the Ambassador right behind them. They all looked deep in conversation but I could feel the Prince's curious eyes travel to me and I turned my back, gritting my teeth.

"Don't worry, the Prince will be gone soon enough." Highflynn said quietly beside me. "They've already agreed a treaty. They just want us to approve it."

"Oh." I replied, unsure it this so-called treaty would be a good thing or not. My gut certainly seemed to think otherwise.

As I took my seat my eyes found Fain. He was sat opposite me, looking unconcerned at best.

My face flushed with the memory, with the reminder of how he'd found me the other day. I'd been so careful to keep my nightmares contained, to keep them hidden. Even though I trusted Fain, I hated that he'd seen me like that.

He smiled back at me reassuringly and that spark in me flared.

'Do you know what they've agreed?' I asked, forcing myself to focus, to not feel it, to not dwell on it.

'Don't worry, you're not in it.'

My eyebrows rose. *'You're sure?'*

'Positive. You're stuck here with me.'

'You say that like it's a bad thing.' I teased and he smirked making that damn spark glow even brighter.

Jelric got to his feet, calling for attention. As the room fell quiet, he began explaining the terms of the treaty. Prince Rayling sat, clearly smug with the arrangement but his eyes kept flickering to me enough to make me drop mine entirely.

I listened, I waited, holding my breath, fearing those dreaded words. That I was somehow apart of it, tied to it, but Jelric never spoke them. After the conversation I'd heard between Prince Rayling and the High King the other night, he'd seemed pretty determined to have me written into any treaty so why had he relented with so little?

I frowned, my mind starting to whirl as I contemplated what that meant.

'Why are you frowning?' Fain spoke in my head.

'It doesn't make sense.' I stated.

'What doesn't?'

'The Prince was so adamant.'

'About what?'

'Me.'

His eyes narrowed, but I swore for a second something flashed, a hint of something I barely believed possible. *'You want to know why he gave you up?'*

'Yes.'

'The High King gave him a good reason too.'

'What reason?'

Again, his eyes flashed. And this time I didn't miss it. I didn't question it. Magic. I saw the flash of what his eyes would be if he were truly Fae. My own eyes darted around in panic, trying to see if anyone else had seen, if anyone else had witnessed it. But no one else seemed to be paying attention to us.

'It was you.' I thought back. *'You made him give me up?'*

'I told you Alice, I would fight the entire world to keep you safe.'

I gulped, shutting my eyes, fighting the wave of emotion because god knows I couldn't cry right now. Not in front of all these people. Not in front of so many who would gladly cut me down or sell me for the highest price.

'You're not going anywhere.' He said. *'Anywhere you don't want to.'*

What could I say to that? How could I possibly reply? For the first time he'd actually done something, he'd actually stepped in and stopped Uther. I frowned, unsure what that meant because it did mean something, it meant something big.

'What's wrong?'

I winced, unsure how to reply and then I realised more than one person was now looking between us. Had they realised what we were doing? Did it even matter if they did?

When the meeting came to a close, I got up, needing to escape this space but Uther called me back before I could even get close to the door. So I stood there, gritting my teeth, seeing as everyone shuffled out and curtsied in front of him.

He waited for the room to empty and the door to close before he spoke.

"Your mistake, your error has given me a new ally." He said almost gleefully.

I nodded, not sure how else to respond.

"You have done well, Alice. It may not have been your intention but it will help us greatly and I thank you for it."

"Are they such a great ally?" I asked him.

"Yes. With their help, it will strengthen our forces in this war."

"Then I am happy for you." I stated, unable to keep the edge from my voice.

"Not for yourself?" He asked.

"Why should I be happy? I did not mean to do it and besides, the way I was being discussed at your feast…"

His eyebrows rose. "You heard that?"

"How could I not?"

Was it regret that crossed his face? If it was, I couldn't figure out why. He never usually cared about the way I was discussed. He referred to me as an object more than anyone else.

"Did you think I would give you up? Hand you over to them?" He murmured.

"You said yourself, they are a great ally." I said, crossing my arms.

"Alice, sometimes I think you do not trust me still."

"It is hard too when I am being openly discussed like that." I snapped.

"Like what?"

"Like I'm little more than an object, a prize for you all to claim." I said, clenching my fists.

He winced like my words actually hurt him. "I do not think of you like that."

I scoffed, half laughing at that remark because we all knew that was far from the case. "And yet the other night that is exactly how you made me feel. How you and Prince Rayling made me feel."

He frowned before shaking his head, the ghost of a smile creeping across his lips.

"What?" I asked, not caring if I offended him in this moment.

"I called you a Fire Fae once and the more your powers grow, the more you become one."

My breath caught. Just for a second. That hint that he knew, that he actually understood that part of Fae Lore. But he couldn't, even the Magi didn't know that.

"What is it you want, Alice?" He asked me quietly.

"What do you mean?"

"You clearly want something…"

"What does it matter? You will not grant it to me so it's pointless discussing it." I half snarled.

"Tell me."

I rolled my eyes, looking away, not quite daring to turn my back on him. Though I wanted to. God, how I wanted to.

"You want your freedom?" He murmured and I looked back up at him in total shock that he had said it. Was he taunting me now? Holding that one thing I wanted more than life itself right over my head?

"I have fought for you. I almost died for you, multiple times. I saved your son. I saved your brother too. You know I am loyal to you. What more do you want from me? What more do I have to give?" I asked feeling myself starting to shake as both my anger and frustration threatened to overwhelm me.

He stared at me narrowing his eyes and I could see then that the discussion was over.

With a shake of my head and a quick curtsey, I walked away before I either said something I'd truly regret or worse, I started crying.

Nineteen

ALICE

I t was days later.

I walked along the battlements with Guillaume, waiting to hear what eventful magic he decided to teach me today.

We'd both agreed, without actually saying it, that we'd leave the stormcalling lesson where it was. I had shown I could do it after all, so what was the point in repeating it?

"Today I have a different kind of lesson in mind." He said pointing down to a section of the wall that still needed to be repaired.

"What….?"

"I thought it would be a good exercise in control and precision." He stated.

I screwed my face up, like I wanted to use my magic for that. He took one look at me and burst out laughing.

"Come on, it's not that bad." He said.

"You want me to repair a wall?"

"What is your magic for if not to help others?"

"You've changed your tune." I stated.

"How so?"

"Do you not remember telling me that my magic was not for them? That my purpose was not solely to help them?"

"I haven't changed in that opinion. Your magic is not purely to help them. To fight for them."

"And yet…" I began but he cut across me.

"I'm saying you don't have to be solely focused on them but you can still help."

I huffed. It sounded like semantics to me. "So you want me to repair the wall?"

"Yes. But you need to figure out which stones go where. It's like a jigsaw. A puzzle. You need to put it back together."

"Sounds great." I muttered before getting started, pulling my magic, picking up a large piece and depositing it firmly in place.

Guillaume kept his mouth shut but I could feel his judgement. Clearly he didn't think that piece fit where I put it. I narrowed my eyes, lifting another, pretending that I hadn't noticed.

It took hours. Hours of laying one boulder only to find I needed another. I rebuilt and dismantled it so many times I lost count. By the time I was actually done the sun was beginning to set. I dropped a curtsey and Guillaume smirked.

"Good job, although you took your time." He stated.

"How was I meant to go any faster?"

"I could have done it faster."

'Pfft. Don't make me knock it down and make you…' I thought and he laughed before we both froze.

'You heard that?' I thought and he nodded.

I frowned, feeling my heart race. I knew I'd communicated with Sig in my head, but I'd put that down to anger, to stress, to my magic acting off in the aftermath of everything Yannis related.

"How exactly are you doing that?" He asked out loud.

"I, I don't know." I replied. "I do it with Fain. But I figured it's because of our connection but I did it with Sig too. Before I took his ability to channel from him."

He frowned, obviously mulling something over.

"What are you thinking? What does it mean?" I asked, god what did it mean? Could I do that with every Fae now? Was that another strange talent that I possessed?

"It almost certainly something to do with you being Alarin. When Fae are around each other we build this connection, like our magic weaves together. But your blood, your connection may go deeper than that because of who you are."

"So, you're saying it's because I'm Alarin?" I half gasped.

"Yes. You said you did it with Sig. He's not Fae so it can't just be a normal Fae thing."

Normal Fae. Why couldn't I be a normal Fae? Why did I have to have all this extra, whatever the hell it was? I sighed, rubbing my hands over my face. "Do me a favour…" I said quietly.

"What?"

"Don't tell anyone else about it."

"Who else would I tell?"

I shrugged before looking out at the sea. Would Jelric tell Uther if he learnt? Would Uther even care? My mind suddenly flipped out, doing mental gymnastics as I tried to figure out what the impact of this getting out could be. How it might harm me.

I could feel Guillaume watching me, studying me from the corner of his eye.

"I feel like we need to talk about Fain…" He said.

I turned, nodding. I hadn't exactly planned to bring this up but I also didn't want to just ignore it either.

"You told him, about uniting the Fae." Guillaume said in a way that suggested he wasn't actually asking me.

"I did." I admitted. "I wanted his help. His advice."

His eyebrow rose. His golden eyes flashed. "And what pray did the Prince have to say?"

I shrugged. "That it couldn't be done."

"Do you believe him?"

"Not exactly." I said. "I know *he* believes it but I still want to try. I just don't know how."

"It will take time. It's not something that will happen overnight but I believe you can do it."

I nodded before forcing out the other topic, the heavier one, the one that felt far closer to home. "Why did you tell Fain that you thought he was forcing me to be with him?"

He narrowed his eyes. "Alice, whatever you think you are, however much freedom you think you have, you are still their prisoner. Their possession. And that has never changed."

"But Fain doesn't see me as that. He doesn't treat me like that."

"He may not but has he ever even spoken to his brother about it? Ever even asked him…" He said calmly.

"He can't. He is the High King. You're asking him to commit treason."

"You have done more for him. Risked more for him."

I shook my head. "That was different."

"How so? You went against the High King's orders. You deliberately disobeyed him."

"Because I had no choice."

"And that's the difference." He stated, drawing himself up as if to emphasise his point more. "Prince Fain has a choice. He's choosing to side with his brother over you."

I narrowed my eyes, not wanting to hear it. But it felt true, in my heart, those words felt brutally honest.

"Think about it." Guillaume continued. "I'm not saying this to hurt you, but I think sometimes you are so involved, so intwined with both Prince Fain and the High King, that you cannot see what they are doing. How they are both manipulating you."

Anger, pain, rage, it all flashed through me at those words. Was I being manipulated? Was Fain even capable of that? As our bond twisted enough for me to feel it I knew that it was possible. This connection we'd created, that I'd created, had made that possible.

God, was I really that stupid? I'd never once asked him to help me, never once asked Fain to speak with Uther, and yet should I even have to have spoken those words? Was that even necessary? Surely if he cared for me, if he loved me as he professed, he would have known what I needed, he would have helped without me asking.

It felt like my world suddenly came crashing down. It felt like everything I believed was suddenly doused in doubt.

"I have to go." I muttered, walking away, back towards the castle.

I ALL BUT SLAMMED THE DOOR SHUT BEHIND ME. SHUTTING OUT THE world. But wishing I could shut out the thoughts in my head. Was Guillaume right? Had he ever even spoken to his brother about it? Ever even tried to fight for my freedom? I didn't know but part of me felt incredibly stupid that I'd never even spoken to him about it, never even asked.

I paced the room, slowly growing more and more agitated. It was cold, cold enough to notice and I made a fire if only to distract myself before I started pacing again.

Had Fain ever noticed? Had he ever realised I'd never talked about it? Was he just oblivious or worse, did he think I was naïve, stupid even, for not even broaching the subject? My mind suddenly jumped back to when I'd first arrived, when the High King had ordered his brother to seduce me. That old pain, that bitterness twisted, turning from resentment to fury. Fury to rage.

I shook my head because the Fain I knew, the Fain I still loved, didn't fit with this Fain. It just didn't make sense.

Suddenly I couldn't bear it, couldn't bear not knowing because whatever it was between us, whatever the hell I and Fain were trying to rebuild, I knew it could only work if we trusted each other, if we understood each other and right now, I felt like I didn't know him at all.

I walked, no, more marched to his rooms. Perhaps I should have called ahead, send word through our connection but I wasn't thinking logically, right now it felt like I had a swarm of hornets, buzzing in my head, screaming at me to do something. To actually do something.

My knuckles rapped hard against the solid wood of his door. Hard enough that it echoed down the empty corridor. Hard enough that he would know whoever was knocking was not messing around.

When the door opened, it wasn't Fain behind it. It was Than, one of the Generals on the Council. He did a double take, obviously confused as my eyes widened in shock and then Fain walked out, no doubt realising who it was.

Shit. Double shit. I stood like an idiot staring at him, feeling that rage, that anger, that fury, but with Than there, I didn't know what to say, how to even act.

"Alice?" Fain said frowning slightly like I was the last person he expected to see.

And then my resolve crumbled. Like the weak pathetic thing I always reverted to. "I'll come back later." I muttered feeling the heat in my face.

"It's okay. We've just finished anyway." General Than replied before glancing back at Fain who nodded.

Than called out, back into the room and to my horror two other Generals suddenly appeared. All of them glanced between us, between me and Fain, and then they quickly made their exit while I stood there wishing the floor would just swallow me up.

"Alice,"

I jumped at the sincere way he said it. The loving way he spoke my name. God, maybe I really was a fool.

He beckoned me inside and I walked slowly, trying to gather my thoughts into something coherent, trying to get myself back from the girl who was about to run and hide, and into the one that was going to fight, that would fight, that would stand her ground and show this damned world what she really was made of.

"What's on your mind?" Fain asked, scrutinising me in a way that told me he knew something was seriously wrong.

I gritted my teeth, turning to face him. This was it, there was no going back from this, because once I heard his answer, once he confirmed it, I'd have to decide if it was enough, his actions were enough.

"I need to ask you something." I said, hearing my voice shake. Damn, even my body was betraying me now.

"What is it?" He asked still giving me that wary look, like he knew I was a bomb about to combust.

"Why have you never fought for me?"

"What…?" Fain asked confused.

"With your brother…"

"How do you mean?"

"For my freedom." I snapped as some sort of dam broke inside me. "Why have you never done anything to help me with it?"

"Alice," He sighed. "Do you really think I've not tried?"

I clenched my fists. Unsure how I wasn't totally losing my shit now. "How, how have you tried?"

"After the burning. After the Wash too, with Augal and with Yannis." He stated with an edge to his voice that made my body react, made my stomach twist like it was preparing to really fight. "Alice, believe me. If I could help you I would have."

"You're the High Prince. You're his brother…"

"And it's not enough. Not for this."

I looked away, stepped away. And that dam, that mass of anger exploded. "No matter what I do, no matter what I sacrifice for you all, it's never going to be enough either, is it?" I said so coldly as my voice grew louder and louder. "I almost died for you. And for your brother too." I was shaking, shaking so much I had to clench my fists to try to stem it but it made no difference. "Do you know how many times they beat me? How many times they ripped my back open with that whip?" I could see it, that taunt, that look in Sig's eye after he dragged that iron blade across my face. "Do you know how many times Yannis tried to force himself on me?"

Fain gritted his teeth, his eyes blazed, that magic, that swirl I'd seen before turned into an inferno but he didn't move. He just stood, still as a statue as I continued all but screaming at him as my rage took over entirely.

"Do you realise how much easier it would have been to just give in? To let them win? To let them destroy you and your precious brother?"

"Alice," He murmured, taking a step towards me, as if he might reach out, as if he dared to touch me.

"Don't," I yelled. "Don't you dare touch me." I cried, stepping further away from him. I wasn't going to let him do this, I wasn't going to let him comfort me, confuse me, manipulate me with his so-called love, the way he always did.

Not this time.

"Why are you saying all this now?" He asked.

"Because I realised something." I said as that anger gave way to a gut-wrenching pain. "When I thought you were in danger, I didn't hesitate. I didn't even think about the consequences. But you won't even try for me."

And then I saw it, I saw that snap. I saw the way he suddenly was no longer human, no longer normal. His eyes, his skin, god, all of him suddenly unleashed some sort of power that he slammed into the wall in his own fury. "Do you think I'm happy that you belong to my brother?" He snarled. "That he sees you that way? That he has control over everything you do?"

"You benefit from it too." I snapped.

"I don't view you like that. I don't think of you like that." He said, stepping closer, only this time I knew he wasn't doing it out of comfort.

"That doesn't take away from the facts though does it?"

He jerked his head, his eyes promising bloody murder in a way that should have put the fear of god into me. "And what are they?"

"That I was willing to risk my life for you." I snarled. "I did risk my life to save you and you haven't even tried. You have more of a choice than I had and you choose him. You choose your brother over me."

"You have no idea what you are talking about." He stated.

"No? Then why don't you enlighten me? Go on, show me how stupid I really am."

He drew in a breath like whatever he was about to say, whatever those words were, he didn't want to speak it, to admit it. "It's not my life I'm looking out for here. It's yours."

"Right." I muttered. Another convenient twist. Another convenient way to keep me pliant.

"Do you know what they did to the Fae they had collared? Do you know what happened to them?"

I did know. Cait told me, she told me months ago and I'd buried that information, unable to process it, unable to think on it because it made me feel like a traitor. That I had betrayed my own people by still being here, by willingly helping Uther, despite his crimes.

"...after the attack, after Elynn, they killed them. All the survivors. The High King killed them all because he couldn't trust any of them."

"What does that have to do with me?" I said, wincing at how callous I sounded in that moment.

"Because if I try to free you, if I push too hard, he won't hesitate to do the same with you."

"You don't know that."

"Yes I do. He's done it before. He will do it again. He spoke of collaring you even when you first arrived."

"What?" My stomach dropped at those words.

"I talked him out of it then. I convinced him not to. And now it turns out that you can't be collared, at least not properly. So, what else do you think he'd resort to? It won't matter to him that you saved Hal's life. That you saved my life. He will see it as direct attack on his rule. An attack on his kingship and he won't stand for it."

I gulped, unsure what to say, how to respond. I could still feel that magic, that energy pulsating around him. Magic I'd given him. My own seemed to glimmer, seemed to stir, as if his magic had awoken mine. I could feel it sparking in my hands, I could feel the warmth of it tingling along my flesh. Could he feel it too? Could he feel what his magic was doing? Did he have control right now?

"I lost Elynn." He said quietly. My eyes snapped to his face as my thoughts silenced. "It broke my heart and it took me years to get over it. And then I met you. I didn't mean to fall in love with you. I didn't even want to like you, but I did. And I've already nearly lost you too many times to count. I don't want you to be his possession. I want you to be free as much as you do and if it was just a case of risking my own life, I would do it in a heartbeat as you have done countless times for me. But it's you he would come for, not me, and I can't risk losing you. I just can't."

I blinked, hearing the sincerity in his voice.

"But you did," I said quietly. "You made him change his mind about the treaty."

"That was one time." He growled. "And there is a big difference between selling you to the Sea Nations and freeing you completely."

My jaw dropped. "He was going to sell me?" I growled.

He sighed, shaking his head. "I didn't want you to know that. I didn't... fuck." He hissed, slamming his fist back into that same piece of wall and I saw how it cracked, how it buckled. "I forced him to change his mind. I forced him to do what I want."

"So you could..."

He shook his head. "Not with that. He won't relent on that. I know him, Alice, he has too much pride, he has too much to lose by letting you go."

"But I wouldn't go anywhere." I snapped. "I wouldn't..." His fingers brushed my lips, silencing my words. That magic, that power tingled on my skin, danced along it and for a second I lost myself entirely, forgot where I was, forgot the seriousness of our conversation.

"It doesn't matter, Alice." He stated. "He won't let you go."

"I can't live like this." I cried. "I can't exist like this. I may not be in a cage. I may not be shackled in a dungeon but there is little else different beside it."

"Do you really feel that?"

"Yes. Do you not get what it is like? Do you not see? Everyone looks at me, everyone watches me and all they see is what I can give them, what power they can use for their own means. But I'm not just that. I'm not just Fae. I'm a person too. I have feelings and no one seems to notice that. No one seems to care."

"I care."

I scowled. "Then why don't you do anything?"

"I will." He said, making me pause. "I will, when the moment is right, when I know we have outmanoeuvred him. I will get you your freedom."

Promises. More promises. I didn't know whether to believe him but I wanted to, god, I wanted to. I was so exhausted by all this fighting, so exhausted by simply existing in this world as I was.

"Do you know what I see when I look at you?" Fain asked.

"What?"

"I don't just see your magic, I don't just see your beauty. I see you, the person inside. The brave Alice. The strong Alice. The sometimes-reckless Alice that jumps without thinking, without hesitating. The Alice that sacrificed herself, that went through hell and is still going through it…"

I didn't want to cry. I didn't want to react. But my tears were falling, dropping one by one onto my cheeks and he lifted his thumb, wiping each one away.

"That's who I see, who I love, not the girl everyone else is infatuated with. Not the girl that everyone else stares after and wishes they could have, but the real you. The real Alice."

"How do you see that?" I whispered. I wasn't that brave, strong person anymore, deep down I knew what I was, I was broken, I was damaged, and I didn't know how it was possible to even mend.

"Because I love you." He stated.

A sob wracked through me. All that pain, that bitterness erupted. I buried my face in his chest, and his arms wrapped around me, comforting me in an embrace I so desperately needed.

"I don't know how to be that." I muttered.

"How to be what?" He asked.

"That girl, that person you fell in love with. I'm not her anymore."

He shook his head, cupping my cheek and raising my face so that I had to look at him. "You don't have to be." He said. "I love you as you are now. I love you as you were then. I love each version of you, and every version you become."

"But I'm not strong." I whispered. "I'm broken, and angry, and all I want to do is lash out and hurt this world the way it's hurt me." My eyes widened as I made that admittance. As I said out loud what darkness had been truly swirling in my heart. "I'm broken." I repeated. "I keep trying to heal. I keep trying to be who I'm meant to be. To pretend. But I can't do it. I can't be what I'm supposed to be. And I don't know how to fix myself."

"Alice," He murmured, "There's nothing to fix."

What the hell did that mean? Of course there was, living the way I was, feeling the way I was, that wasn't normal. Nothing about my existence was normal.

"You are what you are right now, and tomorrow, the day after, who knows what you will be. You will change, some days you will be fierce, and some days you will be still, but that is the same for all of us. No one remains one thing, no one remains stagnant. We grow, we adapt. Stop fighting yourself, stop forcing yourself to be something you're not. You're beautiful as you are right now, in all those broken pieces. And when you put yourself back together, when you find your strength, those parts of you, those parts you thought were weak and unworthy, they will be whole. You will be whole."

Twenty

FAIN

I should have walked her back. I should have seen her to her rooms, but I was a selfish bastard and instead, when she'd fallen asleep, I kept her here, kept her in my arms.

And worse, I'd carried her to my bed, wrapped her in my covers, under the pretence that this was what she needed. But deep down, deep down it was what we needed. Both of us.

Sure, I'd felt it, I knew that that magic inside me have soared, that for a moment I'd almost lost control of it.

But as she leaned into me, that riot that was raging inside me had stilled. She had stilled it.

My mind flickered back to the night she'd almost lost control, the night her dreams had set her own magic loose. My touch had calmed her. My presence as stopped whatever might have happened.

I didn't understand it, I didn't understand this bond between us. It felt like it had shifted, altered, adapted.

When Yannis's men had made their play for her and Indi had died, it went into overdrive, I went into overdrive. I became this obsessive controlling, domineering arsehole. That bond brought out the worst in me, and I had let it. I had let my fear, and my panic over losing Alice consume me. But now, now it felt so different, now it felt like it had settled, like it understood what we both needed, how we both had to be to survive.

She stirred, shifting a little, and I loosened my arms to give her more space. Her golden hair was splayed over the pillow behind her. She was tucked in, her hands up by her breasts, curled into my body. She looked peaceful. She looked content.

I shut my own eyes, willing myself to sleep, but my mind was too awake to let me.

And that power, that magic, it still simmered under my skin, like a warning, like a promise. I lay there, listening to her breathing reliving that conversation we'd had, those words, that pain.

I loved my brother. I loved Uther for everything he'd done for me. For all the times he'd protected me, but now, that love was changing. And that fierce loyalty I had for him was changing too. I should have felt guilty. I should have felt bad. But his actions were the reason I felt the way I did. He was driving me away day by day and he must have known that. He must have seen that.

But my fear, Gods, my fear was that I wouldn't just walk, I wouldn't just leave. No, my fear was that this magic, this rage, this whatever the hell was growing inside me would take over and I would do something unforgivable. I would do something irreversible.

That I would kill my brother. I would kill Uther to save the woman I loved.

Beside me, Alice moaned, a soft, almost silent sound but it was enough to tell me she was waking.

She blinked, looking not at my face, but at my body, at the sheets, slowly taking it all in while I mentally prepared for her to push me away, to reject me once more.

Her hand lifted, she brushed her fingers across the scar on my shoulder.

Yeah, I should have put a shirt on, should have slept with one, but I was tired last night, and I didn't think through all of the consequences of my actions.

"Where did you get that scar?" She asked quietly. Her voice cracking ever so slightly from just waking up.

"At Caraden."

Her eyes reacted, the slight dilation telling me that that name set off memories she didn't want to contemplate right now.

"And the one in your shoulder…" I asked. The way she'd slept had twisted her dress so that most of her shoulder was exposed and I moved my own hand to lightly touch where her scar was showing.

"Here in Temoor during the siege. They shot me with an iron arrow. Nela cut it out."

I tilted my head, hearing the lack of emotion in the way she described it. My fingers brushed the sliver of silver on her cheekbone. Another scar. Another pain I didn't know about.

"Sig did that." She said quietly. "Whenever they cut me with iron it scarred."

I frowned, "So your back…"

"They used a whip that had iron blades embedded in it."

Something in me reacted to that. My magic surged for the briefest of seconds. I'd contemplated hunting that Magi down after Alice took his magic, scouring the whole of Herani for him and making him pay for what he'd done. But it hadn't been my place to do it. The punishment had been Alice's to decide, and she'd stated that she wanted him to suffer, to live. I'd forced myself to accept that. To honour her wishes.

"Do you want to see?" She asked.

Surprise must have shown in my face but I nodded quickly.

She rolled over so that her back was now to me, sweeping her hair to one side, not that it was long enough yet to really be in the way.

I moved slowly, giving her time to change her mind, and when she didn't I undid the top of her dress, and exposing only her upper back and shoulder blades while her arms held the fabric and made sure the dress didn't fall away from her front and expose her chest.

"It's bad isn't it?" She said quietly.

Bad? It was horrific. So many lines, so many moments of torture all etched here, forever immortalised in her skin. It was hard to keep my face neutral, to not show the horror I felt. I'd seen men whipped, petty criminals mostly, a few lashes for stealing bread, more for stealing a horse, but nothing compared to what she must have endured. Most men could take ten, fifteen hard lashes before you stopped. But this, what she'd taken, my fingertips brushed her skin, feeling the tiny raised surface were each scar was.

She must have been in agony, she must have suffered days and days of this. My mind flickered back to that pain I'd felt, the way my back had prickled, and I realised then that what I was experiencing was some sort of sympathy pain, that in those moments when I'd forced myself to share her torment Sig had been wielding his whip, he'd been truly torturing her.

"Fain?"

I heard the fear in her voice, the tremor that told me how on edge she was at revealing this to me. Revealing all that vulnerability. I couldn't repay that by showing how I truly felt.

Before I could think not to, I leant forward, placing a soft kiss on her spine, right where the start of one of the deeper scars were.

She gasped in response and her body trembled slightly.

I placed another kiss, then another, leaving a trail across her skin, but going only as far as the fabric allowed.

She rolled over, facing me and as our eyes connected, her hand reached up and she cupped my jaw, no doubt feeling the stubble pricking her skin. My eyes dropped, maybe it was instinct, maybe it was something else but I stared at her perfect pouty lips afraid to make any movements, to do anything that might make her run.

It was Alice who raised her lips, Alice who initiated it, but that kiss, that connection. Suddenly a fire raged in me, my hands twisted around her, pulling her in tighter. My tongue delved into her mouth, seeking more, needing more.

She gasped, she moaned, her body rocked against mine and I knew she could feel it, could feel how mine had responded, how my dick had hardened.

Her dress had shifted, had started to drop. I stared at where the tops of her breasts were now exposed and as if she could read my thoughts she slowly pulled the fabric down.

"Alice," I murmured, afraid this was too much, that this was way too much.

"Touch me," She replied. "Please Fain, please…"

I didn't hesitate. I didn't second guess it then, I held her like she was precious and I trailed more kiss on her skin, brushing my lips against the softness of her neck, the hard line of her collarbone and then down, down to that deep crevice between her breasts.

She gasped more. Her breathing picked up and I listened waiting to hear the sounds of her panic, waiting to hear the words that would tell me to stop.

Only they didn't come.

She wrapped her hands, twisted them through my hair.

I cupped her breast, I brushed my thumb over her hardening nipple and then I lost myself, Gods, I lost myself in honouring her, worshipping her, reminding her of what we'd been, what we could be. I tried to take that pain, that anguish that was coiled up inside her and replace it with love, with pleasure.

She arched her back, she moaned more. Her scent overwhelmed me with every breath I took. Our bond twisted, fused, reset itself.

And then we both froze. Our eyes connected as we came out of that lust filled haze.

Someone was knocking at my door.

I didn't want to answer, I didn't want to let her go but as that moment seemed to fizzle away, and that need in her seemed to die, I reluctantly let her go and slipped from the bed.

I half growled at the poor servant. It was only a bunch of dispatches but the timing couldn't have been anymore shit. I tossed them into the chair, and stalked back to my room.

Only Alice wasn't there, wasn't in the bed anymore.

She was stood, with her back to me, her dress up, over her shoulders and I could sense the way her mood had changed. I cursed myself, cursed my rashness, my selfishness, all of it.

As she turned to look at me, she sat down, like the weight of her trauma in this moment was too much for her to stand.

"I," She murmured, her eyes welling. "I'm so sorry."

"You have nothing to apologise for." I said, sinking to the floor, leaning against the bed beside her.

"Yes I do. I feel like I just keep doing this." She said, wiping her face that was now wet with tears.

"Doing what?" I asked gently.

"Leading you on."

"How are you leading me on?" I asked confused. How was any of this her fault?

"One minute it's okay, one minute I can do it but the next…"

"Come here," I murmured. She crawled into my arms, buried her face in my neck as her body heaved with her crying. "We'll take it at your pace. At whatever pace you are comfortable with."

Twenty-One

ALICE

I paced around the stable block. I was early. Ten minutes early. But I couldn't stay in my rooms.

I'd snuck back through the castle, leaving Fain to whatever joy those dispatches held within their pages. Even now my heart was still racing, and worse, that bond was going manic, was all but screaming in my head to find Fain, to finish what we'd inadvertently started this morning.

Only I couldn't do that. My mind, my body, I knew I wasn't ready for that, and besides, there was still that massive chasm, that issue of Uther, of how the hell we could be something while his brother continued to hold me as he did.

When Cait finally arrived, I could see she was as flustered as I was.

The stable boys all dropped low bows to her and hastened to get the horses ready. Cait barely said a word beyond a murmured thanks, and then she was up, on the large bay they'd saddled up, and was heading out like she needed to put serious distance between us and this city.

I kicked my horse to catch up with hers.

She huffed, shaking her head and then looked across at me.

"What's wrong?" I asked. I'd never seen her so angry, she always seemed so easy going, so relaxed.

"Uther." She snapped. "Bloody Uther."

I tensed, frowning. "If you want to talk about…"

"He's an arse." She half yelled. "An absolute arse."

I bit my lip, glancing at all the people going about their day, who could very well overhear this.

"Let's get out of here." I said quietly. "Head for the hills, then we can talk without any listeners."

She nodded, narrowing her eyes, all but focusing on the horizon as if that was where she would find her freedom. Once we got out of the city walls she kicked her horse into a gallop and I once again raced to catch up with her.

"He never listens." She snapped as soon as we slowed to a walk.

"Tell me what happened." I replied.

"It's not, it's…" She huffed again, "He always thinks he knows best. He always has to have his way."

"He's a King." I stated before that voice in my head told me that that was not a helpful comment.

"He's an arsehole." She snapped. "I made it clear, I made it abundantly clear when I married him that I didn't want to be his queen, that I didn't want to sit beside him, to play politics, that none of that was me. And he agreed but now, now suddenly he's changed his mind."

"In what way?"

She lets out a scathing laugh. "Did you not notice the other night? Did you not see that shiny crown he put on my head when Prince Rayling was here?"

I had noticed. I'd just been too caught up in my own shitstorm to consider the implications of it.

"He says the High King cannot rule without a High Queen beside him."

"Right." I murmured.

"He says, that he can hardly be taken seriously if his wife won't even behave the way society expects."

My eyebrows rose. "Wow."

"And," She scowled. "He wants children. More children."

"Oh shit."

"Yeah." She said. "Everything we agreed, everything he promised, he is going back on."

"I don't know what to say." I said quietly.

"There's nothing to say. The man is a shit. A selfish, conceited, lying shit."

"Cait,"

"Oh, I know," She said laughing almost manically. "I know. I should have seen it. I should have guessed. But my emotions, my stupid, bloody heart told me he loved me and that I could trust him…"

I watched her rant, I watched her expel that anger like a poison that had festered in some wound. She'd gotten down from her horse, had started kicking, punching the air, clearly letting out all that pent up anger that had been building.

When she finally stopped I could see the sweat on her brow.

"You could just do us all a favour and turn him to stone." Cait said, half panting.

I smirked back. "You'd want that, would you? Me to take out the High King?"

She pulled a face. "No, arsehole that he is, I still love him."

"So, what are you going to do?" I asked.

She fixed me with a look, showing that steely determinism I knew was in there. "Oh, I have a plan. He thinks he can manipulate me, he thinks he can slowly chip away, turn me into what he wants. But that's not going to happen. This is my life. I won't become his trophy wife. And I certainly won't be bearing him any gods damned heirs."

"Have you spoken to Fain at all?"

She paused, "I don't want to bring him into it. Especially not after their last argument."

"What argument?"

She tilted her head, "Do you not know? Fain all but attacked Uther."

"Excuse me?"

"He came storming in, in the middle of the night. Uther told me to stay in bed but I could hear raised voices. They argued, Fain lost his temper, and he used magic, I saw him, I felt it."

"You felt it?"

"It was hard not to. Maybe it was a survival instinct or something."

"What were they arguing about?"

"You."

Of course. Of course they were. Suddenly his words made sense. All of it made sense. Uther would never have just relented unless Fain had forced him too.

I stared back at her unsure what to say. But at least I knew now, I knew that Fain's words, everything he had spoken of last night, they weren't just empty promises. He had meant it. He was doing everything he could to help me.

Twenty-Two

FAIN

I walked in behind my brother, trying to present a united front. Today I was here, solely as his Commander, to provide strength to his words.

I knew this meeting would be long, would be tense, would be shit.

Uther sat on his throne, looking around, looking every inch the High King, and the fourteen men looked back at us as if they were ready for war.

"Well?" King Ide said, folding his hands, placing them on the table in front of him.

Only the Lesser Kings and their ambassadors were here. We'd not invited anyone else, because the less witnesses to this the better.

"You are all behind on your tithes." Uther said bluntly.

King Callin blinked. Ide didn't even react. The men representing the other Lesser King's made a serious of noncommittal noises like they weren't sure what the appropriate response was.

"As such I expect all debts to be settled immediately…" Ide spluttered Uther's words. "…And I am further adding interest to this debt as well as raising the tithes for the spring solstice."

Callin's jaw dropped.

Ide sprung to his feet. "This is preposterous."

"Is it?" Uther replied. "Or is it not what is owed to your High King?"

"We paid our debts." He snapped back. "We paid our debts by way of men, horses, ships. You would never have beaten Yannis without our support."

I narrowed my eyes at the statement. They had helped, that was true, but to claim our victory as solely their creation?

"You are confusing two different issues." Uther said. "You are duty bound to fight with me, to provide soldiers, and horses and all that you did. It does not negate the gold you owe."

Morre's ambassador rose to his feet, "If I may, Your Highness." He began. "What you ask for is impossible…"

"Is it?" Uther snapped. "I have given you two years, two years to pay what you owe. Does your King take me for a fool?"

"No, Your Highness," The man said quickly, bowing low as his face flushed.

"Then he will pay what he owes."

"How?" Ide snapped. "How are we meant to produce this gold? You think we can simply magic it out of our arses?"

"If I may?" Callin said before anyone else could reply. "You will have your gold, High King Uther, if that is what you require, but we cannot pay interest. Our countries are already burdened by your taxes, do you wish to bankrupt us all?"

"I wish to balance my books." Uther growled. "Every day you Lesser Kings fail to pay, you put another crack in my treasury. I am not here to subsidise your thrones. My country, my people will not suffer while yours live in luxury."

"Luxury?" Ide repeated. "You think we live in luxury?"

"I know all about the extensive renovations to your castle, King Ide." Uther murmured. "They say the walls are lined with gold, perhaps if you'd been more frugal with your own décor you could afford to pay what is required."

"Frugal?" Ide snarled. "Frugal? I pay a fortune to stay in this fish-stinking city of yours. I pay a fortune to see my soldiers housed and fed, all so they can ride off to fight your wars and you dare speak to me about frugality?"

Uther got to his feet, his eyes blazing. "I am not here to negotiate." He said. "You will pay, or you will lose your thrones."

As he stormed out I sprung from my seat and followed him.

"I'm not sure threatening them was the right approach." I said.

His fist grabbed at my throat, slamming me back into the wall. "No?" He said. "But it worked so well for you, brother?"

I narrowed my eyes, fighting that flash of magic, if I attacked him now I knew this would turn to anarchy.

"Six months." He spat. "That was all she had to serve. Six months by Prince Rayling's side. Only you couldn't stand it, couldn't stand to lose her. Is her cunt that magical?"

I snarled, feeling my anger spike.

"Tell me brother," He continued. "Would you mourn my loss as much as you do hers? Would you care if your actions brought about another war?"

I drew in a deep breath, letting that anger hit me. Yes, I'd been selfish, yes in many ways the treaty had been the easier option for raising gold. But Uther was forgetting one big fact.

"Alice is not a thing to be bartered." I said shoving him back. "She is not an object you can use."

"That is exactly what she is." He snarled before storming off and leaving me to it.

Twenty-Three

ALICE

I stood outside the entrance to the bar, waiting, and growing more concerned by the minute that Guillaume had bailed on me.

When he finally did show I could see he was out of breath, and more than a little flustered.

"Sorry, I still haven't gotten my head around this new castle layout." He muttered. "Every time I feel like I know where I'm headed I end up down a corridor that didn't use to be there and it throws it all off."

"I was worried you were going to stand me up." I replied, brushing his apology aside.

He'd been the one to suggest we go for a drink. I knew he knew that Nela had left. And that Mira was no longer around either. If this was just a sympathy drink then I didn't want to admit it. Besides, outside of our lessons we rarely interacted. As the only two Fae in this city, it felt odd that we kept our interactions solely to an educational one.

"What do you drink?" I asked as we approached the same counter Nela and I had drunk ourselves stupid at months before.

"They have a whiskey drink I like."

I had to fight the urge not to laugh. "I know just the one." I murmured before ordering a firebrand for him and something sweeter for myself.

As we took a seat a vacant table I wondered why we hadn't done this before, just hung out.

"Tell me, what do you miss most about our world?" I asked.

"Many things." He said. "Obviously my family, but simple things too, like just my home, even food."

"Food." I said smiling. "God, what I would give for a curry some days."

He laughed. "Yeah they don't really have anything like that here do they?"

"No, they don't. I didn't even think I was that into spicy food but just a bit of heat would be nice."

"I miss huushuur." He said staring off, as if he was imagining it at that very moment.

"What's that?" I asked.

"It's a Mongolian meat pie. My mother used to make the best ones." There was an edge, a pang of pain to his voice as he said it.

"Do you miss them? Your parents?"

"Yes, but like I said before, I've been here so long now I've gotten used to it. Do you miss yours?"

"Mine are dead too. They died when I was young. All my family is dead."

"You never said anything?" He said as his face reacted.

I shrugged. "I guess it just never came up."

"So, you don't have any family?"

Family. Not technically, but the other Alarin was out there. Somewhere. And as yet I'd not spoken a word of it beyond Jelric. Not dared to consider what all of *that* could mean either. "It's just me." I lied. "It's been like it for most of my life so I'm used to it too."

"Maybe that's why you assimilated here so well, there weren't so many ties to your old world..."

"Maybe." I smiled before taking a sip of my drink.

His eyes cast about, taking in the room, the height, and especially the bar. "How often do you come here?"

I shrugged. "Not that often, especially without Nela and Indi..." I bit my tongue, as a wave of grief hit me but it felt different, easier, as if time had made that pain more bearable. "It's usually livelier than this to be honest." I added.

"I like that it's quiet." He said, clearly not noticing my reaction. "I'm still not that keen on crowds."

"Yeah, but you can get lost in the crowd, here everyone sees us, everyone looks." I stated.

"Sounds like you just need to drink more." Guillaume replied raising his glass.

We both laughed at that. "Now who's the bad influence?" I teased.

"I never said I was going to be otherwise."

"You're my teacher, doesn't it go with the territory?"

"In our old world maybe." He said. "But this place, it feels like anything goes. Besides, I'm not actually qualified to teach."

"What did you do, in our old world?"

"I worked for a vineyard."

I frowned. "And yet you hate wine?"

"The wine here is not the same. The acidity, the grapes..." He shook his head like even the thought offended him.

"I never drank wine really before this place. Not decent stuff anyway." I stated.

"Well, maybe one day I might be able to teach you about that too."

"Ha, I might hold you to that."

"So, this place, they play our songs still…"

I cringed slightly, recognising that the band was just finishing playing 'Hey Jude' in the background. "Yeah. I'm not entirely sure where they learnt it from. It certainly wasn't me but it seems this entire city is obsessed with assimilating our culture into theirs."

"Well, it could be worse. The Beatles aren't a bad band to go for."

"That's true. Although I'm not promising they won't start playing something more cheesy…" I smirked.

He laughed. "If they do I know who'll be responsible."

"Can I ask you a personal question?" I said after taking another sip of my drink.

"Go for it."

"Promise you won't take offense?"

"I promise."

"How come your English is so good? I know French people learn English at school but you don't even have a hint of an accent."

"That's because we're not speaking English." He said with a smirk that made me pause.

"What do you mean?"

"Listen." He replied looking around to the few tables surrounding them. I turned my head focusing on the conversations around me and then I gasped. He was right, it was subtle, really subtle but when I listened hard I could hear it, the syllables, the pronunciation. It wasn't English. It was some totally different language.

"How did I never notice that?" I asked dumbfounded.

He shrugged.

"But how is that possible?"

"It's the magic. When you come here, it changes you. It does something to you so that you can speak their language, understand it. It makes you fluent."

"So what, we can't speak our own language anymore?" I gasped shocked.

"We probably could but we'd really have to focus. It would be hard to do."

"But it would be a cool way to communicate without them knowing."

He grinned back at me. "I think you've already got that one mastered."

"True." I conceded.

"It's also how we can sing, how we are all so attractive too. The magic changes us, enhances our appearance, makes us more desirable."

"Speak for yourself. I could sing perfectly well before I came to this world." I said.

"I thought you were going to say you were attractive too…" He teased making me laugh more.

"So, there's no such thing as an ugly Fae then?" I said.

"I've yet to meet one." He replied.

I sunk back into my chair, sipping my drink more. I doubted we'd be treated any differently if we were ugly. I doubted it would make any difference whatsoever.

Someone bumped into our table. I looked up and as our eyes connected I registered who it was. "Chelsi."

"It's you." She said, before glancing at Guillaume.

He frowned slightly, looking between us.

But that memory, that argument hit me, when Fain had told me that she'd all but used me to get to him, that she didn't care if I'd died in the process or be collared.

Had she been here this whole time? I guess she must have. She must have witnessed the sacking, witnessed everything Yannis put this city through during that siege. No doubt she didn't much care what happened after that either.

"This is the other Fae?" She said looking at Guillaume then back at me.

"Yes." We both said together.

She drew in a deep breath. "Where is the Prince?"

"Not here." I all but snapped.

She grunted, giving me a look that would have made the old me blush. Would have made the old me cower.

"You know he told me." I heard myself saying. "He told me that you didn't care if I was collared."

Guillaume's face darkened, he turned his head, paying more attention now, as if he might just fight her based on what I'd revealed.

"Like you would have done any differently in my position." She said, folding her arms.

I let out a laugh at that. "Oh Chelsi, you have no idea what I would have done because you don't know me. Just like you don't know Fain."

"But I did. I knew him better than you…"

I smirked, some jealous thing inside me twisted but it didn't matter what she said, she wasn't a threat. She never was. Not really. I pitied her, all those months ago, and in a way I still did. She'd told me she loved Fain, evidently that love hadn't faded with time.

She stepped back, throwing one more filthy look and then sauntered off.

As I took a swig of my drink I could feel Guillaume watching me curiously.

"What was that about?" He asked.

"Nothing." I replied. "Absolutely nothing."

Twenty-Four

ALICE

I hadn't seen Fain. Hadn't spoken to him, or passed him by since I'd spent that night in his rooms. Part of me, a big part wanted to reach out, to just talk to him, but what would I say? What was there to say? I'd made things more awkward, I'd made things more weird.

As I lay in bed, trying to sleep, something hit me. A flash, a bolt, something indescribable that was both here, in this room and yet not here at all.

My heart slammed into my chest. Adrenaline coursed through me and, as I scanned the darkness, I knew I was alone. All alone.

I pushed the covers back, slipped from the bed as I called my magic to me. But there was nothing to fight.

Pain. Searing hot pain ran down my back, I doubled over, unable to cry out, and a vision, an image flashed across my eyes

The other Fae.

They were somewhere unfamiliar. Somewhere I didn't know or recognise, but I could feel their fear. I could feel their pain.

Something was attacking them.

And they were trapped, unable to escape it.

I gasped, feeling my panic rising as I saw the scene unfold and then the creature, whatever monster it was turned. It's blood red eyes fixed on me as if I was there, amongst them. I stepped back, stumbled, trying to break whatever spell this was and as it dived at me I let out a blood curdling scream that tore from my throat.

I collapsed against the bed. My body feeling like I'd just fought an entire battle singlehanded.

Wet. Something wet trickled down my skin.

I brushed it with my hand and as I took it away I saw the streak, saw the colour and knew it was my blood. That that creature had somehow wounded me despite me not actually being wherever it was.

But I knew what it meant. In my heart I knew.

I grabbed my clothes, yanking them on as quickly as I could, and then I sprinted out of the room desperate to find Jelric.

The door opened before I could even knock on it.

I stood there, blinking like an idiot, with my hand still raised.

"Alice." Jelric said in a way that suggested he'd been expecting me.

"Did you feel it too?" I asked him and he nodded. "What does it mean?"

"Come in. Sit down." He said but as I walked inside I heard more footsteps behind.

"You both felt it." Guillaume said as he walked in like he'd already been invited.

My heart stunk more. I'd hoped this was all some misunderstanding, some weird manifestation of my nightmares and not actual reality. But if Jelric and Guillaume both felt it then there was no denying it.

"What do we do?" I half-gasped.

"Let's just be calm for a minute." Jelric stated shutting the door and directing us both to a chair.

"How can we be calm? They're being attacked. They're in danger." I cried as panic seemed to overtake me. Panic and guilt.

If I'd done more, if I'd actually attempted to help them, then maybe they wouldn't be in whatever hell they were in right now. Maybe they'd be here, safe and sound.

"Did the other Magi feel it as well? Guillaume asked.

Jelric shrugged. "Perhaps. They may not have understood it. I will speak to those who will have."

"So they know?" I murmured. The Magi now know that more Fae are out there. God, I hadn't done a thing to keep them safe had I, I'd been worse than bloody useless.

Another knock pulled me out of my rapidly spiralling thoughts.

"Who...?" Guillaume asked as Jelric frowned.

The Magi crossed the room, opened the door and I blinked in shock at the man stood the other side.

Twenty-Five

FAIN

Magic. It latched at my throat. It cleaved at my chest.

I woke gasping in the darkness of my room knowing that something had happened. My mind flew into a panic but even as it did I knew it had nothing to do with Alice, I could feel that through our bond.

I scrambled to my feet, scrambled to grab some clothes to cover myself.

And I ran, down the corridors, with my bare feet smashing against the cold stone until I reached Jelric's quarters. But as I crashed into his room I froze.

Alice was there.

As was Guillaume.

All three of them turned to look at me, their faces showing their shock.

"You felt it to?" Alice half-whispered.

"Yes." I said as my heart sunk because whatever this was, whatever had happened, Alice hadn't come to me, she'd gone to Jelric first. She'd sought him out. A flash of betrayal hit me but I buried those thoughts, those emotions. This wasn't about me. None of this right now was about me. "What's happened?" I asked.

"The other Fae." Guillaume said. "They've been attacked."

"Attacked, how?" I replied.

"That is exactly what we are trying to establish." Jelric stated.

I shook my head, walking further into the space. Practically every wall, every possible surface was covered in books. How the servants managed to keep this place clean I didn't know but I suspected Jelric didn't let them in. That he was so precious about his things that he tidied it himself.

I sunk into a chair, looking across at Alice and seeing that pale, fearful expression.

"You want to go, don't you?" I said quietly.

She nodded. "I don't have any choice."

I gritted my teeth staring at the rug. How could we explain this? How could we even try to come up with something to cover what this really was?

"We have to tell Uther." Alice said.

"We can't do that." Guillaume said before I could. "If he knows about the other Fae he will want to capture them, to collar them too."

"Don't you see," Alice gasped. "We're so far beyond that. Whoever is attacking them isn't doing it just for the fun of it. They're doing it to move against us. Against the High King."

"She's right." Jelric said.

"I know I'm right." Alice snapped. We have to do something because if we don't they're only going to come here and then we won't be able to stop them."

"You really want to go to my brother?" I said quietly.

"What choice do we have?" She shrugged.

"If you do this, there is no going back. Not just for the other Fae but for yourself too." I warned.

Her eyes seemed to soften at that. "I know. But like I said what choice do we have?"

Guillaume shook his head. "If we are wrong…"

"Do you think we are?" She asked.

"No."

"Then there's your answer." Alice said getting up.

"You want to go to him now?" Jelric said and Alice nodded.

"We need to move fast. Before it's too late." She stated.

"Fine. I will see to it." He said.

She frowned like she didn't quite understand what he meant.

"You cannot simply walk up to his door and start banging, Alice." I said, slightly amused because we all knew that's exactly what she was planning on doing.

"Where do we go then?" She asked.

"His Council Chamber. I'll have him meet you there…" Jelric said before shooting me a look that said it all. That we could all come to rue this night. That if this goes south, it's coming back on all of us.

We walked in silence. Guillaume ahead, while I stayed beside Alice as my thoughts spun. She couldn't be collared, but would that stop Uther from taking more drastic action? I knew if he did what I would do, what action *I* would be forced to take in return.

Beside me Alice was frowning, as if she was starting to regret her decision.

"There's still time." I murmured.

"Time for what?"

"To come up with another plan. To spin my brother a story…"

She shook her head. "No, Fain. No more lies. No more stories. It's time your brother learnt the whole truth."

I bit back my reply. Swallowed the words that shouted in my head that this was dangerous. That we were playing with fire. Because Alice knew that. She had to know that. And yet she was acting like she didn't even care.

"How do you know it's the other Fae?" I asked. "How do you know this isn't simply some trick?"

"I saw them." She said. "I had a vision, I saw what happened."

"How…"

"I don't know, Fain. I don't understand it. But I know it was real. I know in my heart that it's not a trick."

"Okay." I replied. "Okay."

It felt like Jelric took an inordinate amount of time to get Uther. Alice couldn't stay still. She kept getting up, pacing about, wringing her hands together.

"Come, sit down." I said gently to her but she just shook her head and continued fidgeting.

When Uther finally appeared he just stood in the doorway, watching us all, with his eyes narrowed in suspicion. "What is this?" He asked in more of a growl than a question.

I glanced at Jelric and he shook his head just enough to tell me he hadn't said a word.

"Take a seat." I said, pointing to his chair.

He fixed that gaze on me as he walked over and sat down.

"I need you to just listen until I've finished telling you what's going on." I began before anyone else could.

"Go on." He replied.

"When Alice had the spectral in her, it wasn't just Guillaume that helped her. There were other Fae. A lot of them."

"What?" Uther growled, grasping the arms of his chair as if he was about to jump right out of it in fury.

"Let me finish first." I replied. "These Fae were in hiding. Are in hiding. And now they are under attack."

"From what?"

"We don't know exactly." Alice said and the High King turned to look at her.

"Then how do you know they are under attack?" He asked.

"I can feel it. I've seen it. I can't explain it but it is real." She stated.

Uther scowled before looking at his Magi who nodded enough to show that he agreed with us.

"We have to help them." Alice said. "Because if we don't, whoever is doing this will use them against us. Use their power against us."

"How can you help them if they are in hiding?" Uther asked with a slight mocking tone that only pissed me off more.

"My magic can find them." Alice replied.

Uther folded his arms, glaring more. "So, what are you asking of me?"

"That you let me go. That you let me and Guillaume go and help them and when the others are safe, I will come back to you. Just as I have done before."

Uther's lips curled in contempt. "If I let you go what is to stop you from running?"

"I have never run. I have never been disloyal." Alice said.

"You disobeyed me before…"

"And you know exactly why I did that." She retorted. "But this is different."

"How?" Uther replied. "How is this different?"

"Because for this to happen, it has to be the Magars. It has to be whatever is against you. There is no other explanation."

Uther drew in a long breath before turning to look at Jelric. "You agree with that assessment?"

"I do." Jelric said back.

He grunted before looking across at me. "How long have you known of this? Of the other Fae?"

"I knew back at Nind. I saw them help Alice. And then she protected them all from Niseri." I admitted.

"And you kept this from me?" He growled.

"I did."

"Why?"

"Why do you think? You would have collared them, claimed them for yourself."

"It is my right as High King."

"As you claim it is with Alice, too." I snapped feeling my anger rising more and more. Feeling that power begin to simmer uncontrollably beneath my skin. It felt like someone had put some fire underneath me and I was slowly starting to boil.

"Don't do this now." Alice said cutting across me and looking back at the High King. "I need you to let me go. I need you to trust me with this."

"How can I trust you after you have lied to me for so long?" He snarled.

"I haven't lied. I just concealed part of the truth. But don't you see, this is bigger than me, bigger than all of us. I need to help them. And in doing so, I help you too."

The High King frowned, leaning back in his chair.

"I am still loyal. That hasn't changed and it won't." She stated.

"If I let you do this. If I agree what then? What of these other Fae?"

From the angle she was stood at I could see the way she was clenching her fists, trying to control her anger. "I don't know." She said honestly. "I don't even know if they are alive."

"If they are you have to bring them to me." Uther commanded. "They are also mine by the laws of this land."

"Enough." I yelled slamming my hand down and making them all jump. The table hissed, a burnt imprint remained where I'd made contact and I could see everyone stare at it. I fixed my eyes back on my brother, ignoring the slight fizzle of smoke that now hung in the air. "Can't you hear yourself? Can't you see what you are becoming?"

"And what is that?" Uther snapped.

"Exactly what you were supposed to be fighting. You're so obsessed with the Fae, obsessed with possessing them, with owning them that you're forgetting who you even are. What you stand for. You swore to protect this land. To govern it justly and to fight the Magars but right now, you're just as bad as they are."

"Fain." Alice gasped in shock.

"It's true." I growled. "Have you ever considered how much happier Alice would be if you just gave her her freedom? Because it's not like she's going anywhere. You already know she is loyal. She's already proven herself more times than either of us can count."

"So, what are you saying?" Uther growled.

"That maybe you need to move on from keeping her as you do. Move on from trying to collect all the Fae like they're just pieces on your udo board."

The High King narrowed his eyes, glaring at me, before looking across at Alice.

"Can we just forget about me for a minute?" Alice said. "This is about your war. If you don't want to lose then you have to do this. You have to let me save them. If the Magars capture them, if they use them against us then we don't stand a chance."

The High King looked back between us all, clearly weighing it all up. "You can go." He said. "But when you return you come straight back to me. Not to Fain. Not to Jelric. To me."

She nodded quickly. Relief covering her face.

"Go." Uther ordered, narrowing his eyes at her as he pointed to the door.

Alice gulped, glancing at me as she slipped out the door with Guillaume just behind her.

But I knew Uther wouldn't let me go so easily. I knew now was my chance to truly make my case, that while Alice was gone, while she was away, I could perhaps win her freedom for when she returned.

And as I looked across at him, for the first time I didn't see Uther my brother, I saw only the High King. The man who had captured the girl I loved. The man who had all but enslaved her. In my heart I'd struggled for so long, feeling such a contradiction in my loyalty between Uther and Alice.

But now, now that contradiction no longer existed.

I no longer saw myself as a traitor either.

"You've been keeping secrets, Fain." Uther muttered. "You've betrayed me."

Once those words would have cut right to my soul but now, now they had no effect whatsoever.

"I am loyal." I replied. "But only if you do right by her."

He glared back at me. Slamming his fists onto the arms of his chair. And I knew then that the fight was on. That the battle had commenced. And Alice's very life depended upon me winning this. Winning against the brother I'd sworn to protect. Winning against the man who had in many ways saved me, had raised me, had helped turn me into who I was now.

"It is time, brother." I said. "By the Gods, it is time."

Twenty-Six

ALICE

I couldn't think about Fain. Not now. Even though my mind was panicking about leaving him there, leaving him with Uther, after what he'd said.

Would Uther hurt him? Would he go so far as to lock him in the dungeons, to try to collar him? We'd all seen his magic, seen the way his hands had burnt an actual hole into the wood. I should have spoken with him. I should have taken Jelric's word of caution more seriously because his magic was growing, and it was spiralling out of control.

As that thought sunk in I knew there was nothing I could do about that now. No, I had to focus on the Fae. I had to trust that Fain could look after himself. And hope too that Uther's love for his brother might spare him the kind of punishments I knew he was capable of inflicting.

"Do you know where we're going?" I asked Guillaume as we shoved our packs onto the backs of the waiting horses.

He nodded. "It's a good week of hard riding though."

"I can do that." I replied. "But do you think *they* can wait that long?"

His face looked as twisted with concern as I knew mine was. "We have to see." He said, throwing his leg into the stirrup, and then he was up in the saddle.

God, I hope they could. But everything in my gut told me I needed to be there now. Right now.

We rode all day, pushing the horses harder than I knew was good for them, When we were able to we swapped the horses for fresh ones. Of course we couldn't do it legitimately; if someone were to see us, to see two Fae just out and about the consequences for us could be dire. So we switched them at night, leaving our old ones as replacement.

And then the next day we did the same. Riding practically nonstop. Eating in our saddles, munching on the dried food as if it were a delicacy. But the landscape, the topography, all of it seemed so alien from what I'd seen of Herani so far.

Where Montefore and Temoor had been mainly grassland here heather seemed to cover the ground, turning the entire horizon into a blur of colour.

"Where are we?" I asked.

"In King Rette's lands."

"Oh." I said unsure if that made us safer or not. Another Lesser King. Another man who would no doubt seek to collar us and use us for war. I grabbed my hood, pulling it up over my hair, no one was around, no one was even close but still, I wasn't going to take any chances. And the last thing we needed was to be captured when the rest of the Fae were out there, potentially fighting for their lives.

As night fell, we settled down for another uncomfortable nights sleep. Guillaume had made a fire because we both knew my skills were not anything to rely on. And with our supplies starting to dwindle, I'd figured it would be best to catch our own dinner. Only anything worth eating seemed to be alluding me.

I didn't want to get too far from the camp. I didn't want to stray and end up getting lost because that would just be my luck. But when I saw the rabbit, I paused, deciding it was worth the risk.

I stalked it through the long grass, pausing whenever I thought it might sense me. I knew a part of me was stalling because the thought of actually killing it made my stomach turn just a little. Poor thing was only just trying to survive and here I was, eyeing it up like a Sunday dinner.

When I realised I'd strayed further than I'd intended I, I forced myself to just get on with it and quickly sent a blast of magic to stun the animal. It didn't make a noise as it slumped to the ground. I crossed the distance, picking it up and snapped it's neck in one swift movement, as if I'd been doing it all my life.

But I could feel the warmth of it, the softness of it's fur. Poor thing, it was just it's bad luck that it picked this bit of earth, this patch of grass and our paths had crossed.

I turned, half marching back and then froze as three figures eyed me up. Shit.

The nearest gave me a toothy grin. They all looked like they could do with a good bath, and as I stared at them the one furthest back pulled out what I knew was a dagger.

"What you got there?" One asked, as if we were friends.

"Dinner." I replied.

His lips curled, he glanced at his mates and gave the subtlest hint of a nod.

"I wouldn't bother." I said loudly. "You take one step towards me and I'll make you regret it."

"That so?" The toothless one sneered.

I drew myself up, letting the magic flash in my eyes as a warning. "Turn around, walk away or you won't see the next sunrise."

They exchanged a look filled with hunger. They must have known I was Fae, hell, they could see it just by looking at me and yet they stupidly thought they could best me.

The nearest one took a step, and then another. I pulled my magic, blasting him right off his feet and he landed with a thump, dead before he even hit the ground. The other two paused, for the slightest of moments they paused, and then they ran at me, as if speed might beat my magic.

I took them out. The left, then the right.

As the world fell silent I felt it, that dark, festering feeling creeping into my soul. The last time I'd felt it I hadn't registered what it was. What it meant.

I took a deep breath, inhaling what should have been fresh air, only I could smell the lingering hint of death still spoiling it. I gritted my teeth, understanding hitting me like a ton of bricks. This was why I'd struggled so much after Indi's death. This was why I'd felt I'd changed so much.

Maybe this was also why Guillaume had been so anxious to teach me other magic, other spells, ones that wouldn't simply kill. I guess he understood what such spells did. I guess he knew how it altered your very soul.

When I got back to the makeshift camp, Guillaume he was watching me curiously.

Had he sensed me magic? Did he know that in that short space of time I'd darkened my soul further?

I didn't say a word. I just quietly picked up the knife and began prepping the rabbit, as my stomach growled in hunger.

Twenty-Seven

ALICE

We woke early. Partly because we were anxious to get moving and I'll admit my conscience was playing tricks on me. Making me feel guilty for what I'd done, despite the fact those humans would have happily gutted me if our roles were reversed.

But something in my gut told me today would be worse. That whatever horrors I'd seen so far, today would be another one seared in my head.

We rode in silence, down a long ambling hillside covered in pinky purple heather. The scent of it made me feel almost drowsy, like some magic resided in the plants, and it's sole purpose was to send you to sleep so that you couldn't continue.

When I voiced that opinion Guillaume smirked at me just a little which if anything confirmed my suspicions.

Something in my heart fluttered. My magic seemed to pulsate, like it was on high alert. Did it know? Could it tell where we were?

I glanced around half expecting some invisible shield to drop, for a great magical castle to just appear but there was nothing. Nothing but the rolling hillside and us.

"We're almost there." Guillaume said.

I frowned, staring ahead, blinking furiously.

"Close your eyes. Draw your magic." He instructed.

I did as he bade, pulling enough to let it mingle with the air around me. A mist started to form, started to rise up from the ground. Our horses shied, just for a second but Guillaume simply grabbed my reins and led us on.

And then I saw it. I gasped as it suddenly appeared.

A bridge. A rickety, ramshackle of a thing.

It was strung across the hillside. The end was so marred by the fog that you couldn't see it. Rough rope strands were tied along the sides and through the middle thick planks were laid over thinner ones beneath.

I bit my lip, doubting that such a thing was even capable of bearing the weight of one horse, let alone the pair of us.

Guillaume dropped my reins, nudging his horse onwards and in single file we rode across, as though we had no fear but in my saddle I was trembling, waiting to hear the cracks as the wood beneath me gave way.

As we passed through the mist, the sun shone so brightly I had to squint and cover my eyes. Beside me I heard Guillaume chuckle. I guess he knew what to expect, didn't he?

When I dropped my hands, my jaw dropped in shock. Gone was the heather. Gone was the rolling hills. We were now in the midst of a forest. I could smell the earth, I could smell the bark. The trees were so impossibly tall that as I stared up at them they seemed to vanish into the sky.

"This is it?" I asked but I already knew the answer in my heart.

"Welcome home, Alice." Guillaume said.

My head practically came off at the speed at which I turned to face Guillaume. "What do you mean?"

"This is your home." He stated. "Your ancestral lands. The Alarin's built this with their magic."

"What?"

"This place exists between this world and our own. It is meant to be where we can live, where we can exist in peace, where they cannot touch us."

I blinked trying to register those words. To get any sort of meaning from it all. "But how is that possible?"

"The Alarin's were very skilled with their magic and when Herani turned against them they knew they needed a safe haven. Somewhere all the Fae could retreat to."

The Alarins. My family. My ancestors. They built all of this? I could feel the magic, feel all the intricate patterns of it as it wove around the air. But it felt so complex. So utterly beyond anything I'd ever thought was possible.

I got down from my horse, feeling like I need the earth beneath my feet. My eyes darted about. I wanted to soak in every detail. Every tree. Every sparkle of a spell. All of it. But as I looked I could see something else too; signs of an attack. Charred wood, arrows where they shouldn't be.

A twig snapped behind us. I spun around, pulling my magic, ready to fight.

Guillaume held his hand out, all but blocking me as a man I didn't recognise came out of the shadows.

No. Not a man. A Fae. One of us.

"It's Stephen." Guillaume said quietly.

"Who?"

"He was there when we removed the spectral." Guillaume added like that might help jog my memory but there had been so many Fae there. So many faces. I doubted I'd be able to recall even half of them.

"Guillaume?" Stephen said looking between us like he didn't quite believe his eyes.

He was short, with a mass of ginger hair on his head, and blue piercing eyes that gleamed like sapphires. His clothes looked dishevelled at best. He had streaks of dirt, streaks of blood too.

"Hello brother." Guillaume replied.

"How, how did you get here?" Stephen stuttered.

Guillaume frowned. "What do you mean?"

"We concealed this place. No one should have been able to find us, not even you."

I side eyed Guillaume, waiting for him to respond and he met my gaze before looking back at this new Fae.

"You cannot hide this place from her." Guillaume said. "Her magic would have seen through your attempts."

A micro-expression crossed Stephen's face before he stared at me, almost in outrage. "You brought her here?"

"You were under attack. We came to help." I said quickly.

"Then you're too late." He half snapped. "They've already gone."

"Who?"

"Magars. Magi too. They took almost everyone. Destroyed half the city."

City? There was a whole damn city here?

"How many survivors?" Guillaume asked, keeping his voice neutral but I could hear it, the undertones of fear.

"There's about twenty of us. We weren't here when they attacked. They took everyone else."

"Where are they? The survivors…" Guillaume asked.

"I'll take you to them." Stephen replied before fixing his gaze back on me and very obviously, he hesitated.

"You can trust her." Guillaume stated.

"Are you certain?" Stephen replied, sounding like he very much disagreed.

"I've come to help." I said more insistently.

He nodded but he didn't look convinced.

Guillaume dismounted, taking his reins in his left hand and we followed him, through the trees, along what felt like a pathway carved from hundreds of years of footsteps over it, and all the while none of us broke the building tension. Stephen kept glancing at me, as if he was waiting for me to suddenly flip out and start blasting the entire place with my magic.

When we got to the clearing I all but froze, staring in disbelief at what was in front of me.

"This is it?"

"This is it." Guillaume said quietly, a hint of a smile upon his lips.

It was a city. An actual city. Made from the very trees themselves. I blinked, half believing it would vanish but it was real. As real as everything else I'd experienced.

"How...?" It felt like I could barely string a sentence together.

"Your family. Your ancestors." Guillaume said as Stephen grunted.

"But it's so big." I gasped.

"Come on." Stephen muttered, "You can look around later."

I took the hint, picked up my pace, but my eyes still darted around, taking in the sweeping curves of carved wooden staircases, of turrets that twisted amongst the canopy above our heads. The place had to be capable of housing hundreds of thousands of Fae, but surely, surely there weren't that many here?

When I voiced that opinion, Guillaume said that once there had been, that once we outnumbered the humans five to one but that was centuries ago, long before our time.

I chewed my lip, wondering what on earth had changed, how we, the powerful race, with magic at our very fingertips had been forced to hide while the humans ruled over the entirety of Herani.

Ahead I could see a crowd gathering. They had to be the survivors that Stephen had spoken of. Amongst them was that same ageless, grey-haired woman I'd met last time, the one who'd said they couldn't help me while I was with Fain. I gritted my teeth preparing for more animosity and more suspicion.

Only her eyes widened as she saw me and her mouth turned into a half-relieved smile.

"Welcome back." She said hugging Guillaume the way one would an old friend.

"Hello, Anna." He said smiling.

"And welcome to you too." Anna said turning her attention to me. Her eyes sparkled with a purple I knew to be pure magic and her face was streaked with something that looked a lot like blood.

When my eyes focused on it, she rubbed it absentmindedly. "I've received far worse from this world." She said.

"What happened here?" I replied. "Where are the others?"

"The Magars came. They broke through our defences." She stated. "I don't know how but they knew where we were but they took everyone they could find. Bound them in iron and stole them away."

"Do you know where they went?" I asked.

She glanced at Stephen then back at me. "We have an idea. We can still feel them even though they are collared."

I frowned. "What do you mean 'feel them'?"

"Their connection. When you're around another Fae for a while, your magic melds with theirs, it connects. Once it has happened you cannot sever it."

I blinked, registering that detail. Guillaume had said something similar, the first time we'd mind-linked. Perhaps our magic had melded more than I realised.

"Then why are we stood here?" I asked glancing around. They didn't look like they were in any rush to leave. "If you know where they are, why are we not planning to go get them back?"

"There is no point." Someone in the crowd muttered. "We cannot fight them. We cannot defeat them. They are too powerful. If we go they will simply collar us too."

"That's not true." I snapped, feeling more than a little angry that they weren't even trying. We'd spent the last week exhausting horse after horse to get here and yet these people weren't willing to do anything to save their friends.

"Alice can save them." Guillaume said, catching me off guard, making me turn to stare at him. "Her magic can save them."

"In what way?" Stephen asked.

"She is Alarin. The power she has…" Guillaume trailed off. "Take us to where they are and Alice can get them free."

I gulped, trying to keep a neutral face. Was that true? Surely not, surely I couldn't fight an entire army of Magars? And the thought of killing them, of taking more steps towards my own damnation. No, I buried that fear, forced it back down and forced myself to meet the gaze of the countless Fae staring at me.

I could see some of them questioning it, I could see the doubt in their eyes, but others, others seemed to be desperately clinging to that hope that I could help.

"I can do it." I stated, with no idea what 'it' actually meant.

"Fine." Stephen said.

Anna nodded before clapping her hands in a manner that suggested she was the one in charge here. "Get packed. We'll leave in an hour."

An hour? Was it even possible for everyone to be ready that soon? I didn't voice my opinion but as the crowd hastily dispersed I grabbed Guillaume aside.

"You said my magic could fight them, how?"

The look he gave me made me pause. "They needed hope, Alice."

"Excuse me?"

"They needed something to believe in."

"You lied?" I gasped.

"I bended the truth a little." He shrugged.

"You absolute shit." I snapped as he smirked.

"What else would you have me do? Stand there and agree that it's pointless? Stand there and tell them all to wait for the Magars to come back? At least this way, we die trying."

"I have no intention of dying." I stated.

"Me neither." He replied. "So do us all a favour and make sure your magic is especially effective."

I snorted at the tone. "You really are a shit."

He chuckled but the noise dropped as Anna approached us.

"If we're going to do this then you need better clothing." She said eyeing my dusty leathers. More protection too."

"Protection?" I repeated not sure I was understanding what she was getting at.

"Your ancestors were fighters. They left a whole armoury here, swords shields, even armour."

"What do we need swords and shields for when we have magic?"

"What if they blocked it?" She asked. "What if you were somehow bound, then you'd need a sword. And besides they used iron capped arrows when they attacked us, no magic would've have helped us then but our shields did."

"Yeah I know about those arrows. I got hit by one in the shoulder." I muttered.

"Then you should understand why we have an armoury." Anna stated before jerking her head for me to follow.

Anna had called it an armoury but it looked like an entire warehouse of supplies, all neatly stacked and organised.

"It's not bad is it?" She said beside me.

"It's incredible." I breathed, bending down, picking up a sword from the pile. It felt light, almost impossibly so, and far more manageable than the long ones Fain's soldiers used. I swished it through the air, trying to get a proper feel for it and it practically purred as it moved.

And then my eyes fell on the pile of shields. All of them bore the same strange emblem; red fire, surrounded by a white circle.

My heart seemed to beat louder. Faster. As if it knew what this emblem meant. "What is that?" I asked, pointing to it and trying to keep my finger from shaking.

"That's your family's sigil. The Alarin sigil."

"They have a sigil?"

She tilted her head, studying me for a second with those intelligent eyes of hers. "How much do you know of them, your ancestors?"

"Nothing. Practically nothing." I said quickly. "My parents died when I was too young to remember them. I grew up in a boarding school and all the rest of my family died before I even met them."

I swallowed down the admittance that there was another Alarin out there because I feared how they'd respond to that. How they might decide that that strange man was worth following instead of me.

"…Then I might have something else to interest you." Anna murmured.

"What?"

"A book, an old book, on your family."

My jaw dropped. "Are you serious?"

"It tracks our history from the beginning but as your family is tied to all Fae, it tracks your family line too."

"Can I see it?"

"I'll get it for you but in the meantime, help yourself to anything you might need. I'd recommend some armour at the very least."

I watched her go, waited till I was alone and let out the deep breath I'd been holding. There was a book, a whole history of my family? I knew right now I should have been focusing on the other Fae, the captive Fae, but so much of me wanted to be selfish, to lose myself in all the unanswered questions I'd had since I'd come to this world.

But the other Fae were out there. And we were meant to be leaving in less than an hour. I sighed, turning to appraise the room, where did I even start?

I grabbed a shield, and a sword, putting them by the door. But that seemed like the easy options. Every other weapon felt far too intimidating, and besides, why would I use a crossbow when my magic was vastly superior? I made my way over to where a pile of leathers were all stacked up, only as I eyed them they looked markedly different from the ones I had on. While mine were black, these were a dark brown, with tiny threads of something akin to gold woven through the top in an intricate pattern even my Fae eyes could only just make out. I ran my hand over them and jerked back in shock.

Magic. There was magic in them.

"It's infused with Fae magic." Guillaume said from behind me. "It will protect the wearer from attack."

I raised an eyebrow at that. "Any attack?"

"Think of it like chainmail. If an arrow were to hit it, the magic would throw it off but anywhere not covered would be just as vulnerable."

"Oh."

So much for magic pants then.

"That's why you take the shield, it all works together."

I guess he was right. And it certainly beat what I currently had on.

"Why didn't you ever say anything?" I asked, pointing to that strange emblem so that he'd know exactly what I meant.

"I was waiting for the right time. You were still so new to it all I didn't want to overwhelm you and I knew every time we spoke, I just kept coming between you and Prince Fain. Causing arguments between the two of you. It wasn't fair of me."

"Oh."

"I know how you felt for him, how you feel for him, and I didn't want to do that, I didn't want to force you to choose or even make you."

"Choose what?" I asked.

"Between the High King and your birthright."

I paused, narrowing my eyes. "Why would I have to have chosen?"

"That's the point." He said. "You shouldn't have to choose, at the beginning you were, at the beginning you were so focused on them and were choosing them over everything else. Over your own magic. But now it feels different. Now you have better balance."

I opened my mouth to reply but Anna chose that moment to reappear. She eyed the magic pants still in my hand. "Put those on. Everyone else is ready to leave."

I nodded, glancing at Guillaume before turning my back on both of them.

He thought I had balance now? He thought that I was somehow, what, more in control? With every mile we'd ridden from Temoor, I'd felt my bond stirring, growing more agitated, and at times I'd had to force down the wave of emotion that ordinarily would have sent me flying back to Fain's arms.

It wasn't balance I had. It was necessity. I had to do this. I had to prove this and if I returned to Uther, maybe then he might give me my freedom.

I let out a bitter laugh. God, what a fool's hope. But that's what I was. In so many ways I was a fool to have fallen in love with Fain, a fool to have created this bond, and now, now I was a fool to believe his brother might change, might grow a conscience.

Twenty-Eight

FAIN

The Council was in uproar. I gritted my teeth, looking sideways at my brother who was very close to losing his temper.

We'd barely spoken, barely exchanged any words since Alice had left. He'd said we needed to talk and then, to my surprise, he'd run like a coward too afraid to face me. I knew he was buying time, hoping she would come back with the other Fae in tow, and all of this would be forgotten.

As if I would forget.

As if I would take one look at Alice and be so joyful at her return that I'd forget my loyalty to her. My promises.

"I am the High King." Uther stated, standing up, keeping his voice as level as his temper would allow. "If I choose to send my Fae somewhere, I do not have to justify myself to you."

"But you won't even tell us why." King Ide snapped back and to both our surprise half the Council grunted in agreement.

Clearly the man was growing more allies, had grown more than I'd realised.

"Enough." Uther said. "When she returns then you will have your answer."

King Callin nodded. At least he was being reasonable, but then his focus on Alice was not about power, about greed, the way he looked at her, the way he'd helped her since the whole Yannis thing, sitting beside her at Council meetings, shielding her from the worst of Ide and his ilk. As he met my gaze across the room I couldn't tell what exactly what he was thinking but I knew his thoughts were close to mine.

"Let's call this session to a close." Jelric said standing up and half the Lords and Generals joined him.

I got up quickly, wanting to catch my brother before he could slither away again only a hand grabbed me yanking me back.

"Did your plan to win her back backfire on you, Prince Fain?" Ide sneered.

"What are you talking about?" I growled.

"Come now, we all know you were only fucking her because your brother ordered it. Not that I can blame you, it's not exactly a hard task is it? Anyone of us would have happily taken your place…"

Before I could move, before I could react, Callin stepped between us, putting his hands on my shoulders. "Don't do it. Don't let him win." He murmured in my ear.

I knew he was right, I knew it and yet inside me, something dark, something uncontrollable was already unfurling.

Callin turned me around, tried to get me to move towards the door and away.

"Where is she, Prince Fain?" Ide yelled after us. "Is she in dungeons, chained up, just like Yannis had her?"

"Fain…" I don't know who said it, who spoke my name, whether it was Jelric, or Callin or someone else but that monster inside me exploded. I exploded.

Something shot from my hands.

Pure white, searing hot magic.

Something screamed in my head as I lost complete control of who I was. As I forgot that human side of me and something far more animalistic took over. I slammed my fists into the King, knocking him backwards.

The look on his face was one of pure shock as my magic twisting around him, pinning him up against the stone wall. Only he quickly recovered, he quickly began spewing more hateful words.

"She belongs to your brother, bastard. No matter how much you try to fight it, no matter how many times you try to claim otherwise, she will only ever be his."

"She is mine." I snarled emphasising each word with the pounding of my fists, delighting in the way his body broke beneath my strength. "She will always be mine."

"Fain," Jelric yelled, pulling me off, sending some of his own power into me to force me into submission.

I stumbled back, my chest rising and falling rapidly as I seethed like a thing truly possessed.

Around us half the Council looked on in shock and Ide still hung there, with his face bloodied and bruised. As I looked at all those faces I knew they would use this, twist this, turn this to their advantage. The half-Fae Prince had finally used his power against them and now they would be crying out for my collaring.

I glanced at Jelric and saw the truth of it, that he believed it too.

Without a word, without another glance at Ide, I turned and stalked out of the room. Uther would hear of this soon enough and I needed to be the one to tell him. I needed to get to him first, to ensure this didn't end with me locked up, or worse, executed.

When I found him he was mercifully alone. In his rooms. As if he was still brooding over something.

I walked in, shutting the door behind me and paused as he turned to face me.

"Well brother, it seems you need my help again?" He murmured.

I gritted my teeth, biting back the remark that I had spent the entirety of my adult life helping him, risking everything for him.

"You know they will want you collared for this." He snapped, confirming that he knew, that someone had already informed him.

"I am your Commander." I replied, "Ultimately, I answer only to you."

He let out a snort. "Is that so? I'd say lately you answer only to that Fae girl warming your bed…"

"You really want to do this now?" I muttered.

He crossed the room, glowering at me as he poured out two glasses. "What choice do we have? You've forced my hand on both matters."

"And here I was thinking you were trying to buy yourself time."

"I was, Fain." He snapped. "For both you and me."

I shook my head, not understanding, why would I need time?

"If it is as she says, if there are more Fae out there then my decision will not only affect her, it will affect all of them."

"She isn't lying." I stated.

"And yet she did lie. You lied."

"I did it to protect her."

"Just like you beat the day out of Ide to protect her?"

"He had it coming." I snarled. "The things he said. If anyone had spoken of Cait like that you would have reacted the same."

"But it is not the same." Uther snarled. "Cait and Alice are not the same."

I bit back the retort, snatching the drink from the side and raised it to my lips but just as I went to take a sip Uther let out a deep sigh that made me pause. I could see the deepening lines in his face, I could see the way the bags under his eyes grew darker.

It hit me then how far we'd drifted apart. Once, we spent night after night drinking together, strategizing together but now he felt more like a stranger than the brother I once loved.

"I cannot fight the Council, I cannot always protect you." He said.

"I do not need that." I replied. The Gods knew I could fight my own battles well enough.

"Ide's Magi are already clamouring for you to be collared." He stated.

"Of course they are." I said.

He sighed again, took his drink and walked over to the chairs by the fire. I watched him for a moment before I moved to join him.

"I suppose we should talk of Alice." He said.

"I thought you wanted to wait." I snapped back.

He scowled for a second. "You once again have forced my hand, Fain."

"Give her her freedom." I said. "She has earnt it. The Gods know she damn well deserves it."

He grunted, "I've been thinking about her, about this entire situation."

"And?"

"She says she is loyal, she says she would remain here even if she was free, that she would still fight for me…"

"She would." I replied.

"If I were to release her, I would do it under one proviso."

"And what is that?" I asked, trying to keep my voice level, to not sound as shocked and desperate as I felt.

"That you marry her."

"What?" I growled. Of all the things I expected, it wasn't that.

Ellie Sanders

Uther's lips curled as he met my gaze. "You love her don't you?"

"Of course I do." I snapped.

"If you marry her, I'll give her her freedom."

"That isn't freedom." I retorted. "You'd just be tying her to us in a different way."

"Do you not want to marry her? You've been with her long enough…"

I could see it, the way he was twisting this, manipulating us both. Presenting a situation that seemed so logical, so easy. "I'd want her to have the freedom to choose." I said. "To decide if she wanted to marry and not be forced into it because you're giving her no other option."

Uther grinned more. "Ah, but she does have an option. She can remain my Fae, remain in my possession just as she is now."

"That's not a choice and you know it." I growled. "Would you want that for Cait? You relented with her when you married her, you gave her her freedom not to be a High Queen."

"Cait is a different matter." Uther said dismissively. "I realise now the error in that and slowly I will make her High Queen. So slowly that she doesn't realise it."

"You would be a fool to do that to her." I stated.

Uther narrowed his eyes. "If she marries you then I know we have her loyalty. I know she will not leave." Uther said, ignoring my comment about Cait completely.

"You know she is loyal already. Marrying me would make no difference to it."

"Then what is the issue?" He shrugged. "You love her. Do you see yourself with another woman? A different woman?"

I shook my head before I could stop myself. That bond twisted in disgust. "Of course I don't."

"Then it's a win-win. I get Alice to remain here by my side. She gets her freedom just like she wanted and you get to make her your bride."

"That's not a win-win. Not for her."

He swirled his drink, watching the contents as it caught in the light. "Maybe you should ask her, Fain. Ask her and see what she wants. Perhaps her answer might surprise you."

"I doubt it." I said wondering if he even understood the nature of our relationship right now. How precarious we were. How close we were to crumbling back into nothing. The thought of even broaching the topic put me on edge because I knew what her reaction would be, that she wouldn't blush and smile the way a woman did when she was dreaming of a wedding, no, she would flinch, would recoil, no doubt retreat further from me.

"Now is not the time." I said before I could think not to. "Alice is not ready for such a move."

"You think you know her so well?" He half taunted. "Or is it your own fear telling you she would prefer to be chained to me than married to you?"

I snarled, gripping the arm of the chair as Uther laughed.

And then he lifted his glass as if in more jest and took a long sip. "You will see Fain, you will understand soon enough…"

"Understand what?" I growled getting to my feet.

"That I am right. When she returns, when she brings the other Fae with her, I guarantee she will agree to anything in exchange for her freedom."

"No," I snarled, clenching my fists, trying to get hold of the magic that seemed to swirl inside me. That threatened to take over once more.

Uther got to his feet, half facing me off, but as he took a step his eyes suddenly bulged. His hands clawed at his throat. He started gasping like he couldn't breathe. Like no air could get in.

"Uther?" I cried, moving to him as he fell to his knees. And then I was shouting, yelling for the guards, for Healers. For anyone that might save him.

He collapsed, falling onto the thick fur rug, half-retching as his face grew more and more purple.

"Uther?" Cait screamed, rushing in from behind me. She pushed me aside, grasped his face as her own twisted into one of horror.

A Healer appeared beside her, frantically checking his pulse. "Poison." He whispered.

"What?" I growled, my eyes casting to the drink he'd been consuming barely a minute ago.

Cait crawled across to it, snatched it up and sniffed as if she knew what she was expecting to smell and then her eyes darted to the second glass, the one Uther had poured me, the one that sat untouched on the side.

"Fain?" She said with more than a hint of suspicion in her voice.

"He was fine." I said. "One minute we were talking and then next he just…"

She shook her head, getting to her feet as it felt like the entire room filled with guards. A hand wrapped around me, something snatched around my wrist and, as my senses all but switched off, my mind registered what it was. Iron. Someone had bound me with iron.

I stared at Cait, stared at her in disbelief while a Magi I didn't recognise whispered into her ear.

"Seize him." Cait said.

Before I could react a dozen hands grabbed at me and I knew better than to fight.

She was screaming, wailing, flailing her hands around but that look in her eyes; I knew something was wrong. Something was off.

"What have you done, Fain?" She screamed.

"I didn't do anything." I said back.

She snarled, slamming her fists into me as the guards held me still.

"How could you? How could you? He loved you, he raised you, he would have done anything for you."

"I didn't do this." I shouted back.

She drew herself up, clenching her fists and gave a quick nod to the men holding me. "Take him to the dungeons."

"Cait,"

"Take him." She screamed before running her hands through her hair and half yanking great tuffs of it right from her scalp.

Twenty-Nine

ALICE

We made camp late, having spent the entirety of the day crossing more of King Rette's lands. In my head, a voice kept saying over and over that soon this Lesser King would learn of our presence and I'd once more have to deal with a megalomaniac who viewed us only as a power source.

But then the knowledge that there were more of us, that there were enough of us to put up a good fight, helped me hold my nerve and hold back that old trauma that threatened to raise it's ugly head.

I sat by the fire while Guillaume saw to our horses. We'd opted to walk alongside everyone else while the poor beasts were packed with supplies and weapons.

The further we'd travelled from Temoor the greater that bond between Fain and I had reacted. But now, now it's like it had snapped. Like a wall had gone up and I couldn't feel a thing.

I didn't know what it meant. I didn't understand it. But it made me uneasy.

"It's a lot to take in." Anna said sitting down beside me, no doubt seeing the fraught look on my face.

"What is?" I asked.

"All of this, the Fae realm, your family's legacy, your birthright."

"You see it as that too?" I half whispered.

"Do you not?" She replied.

I screwed my face up, glancing around at the others, at how some were busy setting up tents, others were obviously keeping watch. I could only guess at how long some of them had been here, in this world but surely it hadn't skewed their thinking that much? I took a deep breath trying to figure out how I'd explain where my head was at.

"We're not from here." I said. "None of us are. We didn't live in a world where a king or a queen or some figurehead got to rule over us simply based on who their parents were, what their blood is. I don't see why any of you would want that now, simply because this world operates like that."

She nodded slightly. "I see your point. But perhaps you should see it from ours. Since you arrived, all our magic has changed. It's grown. It's transformed. We knew something had altered it and until we found you that day with the spectral inside you, we didn't understand. But now we do."

"I changed your magic?" I gasped.

"Our magic responded to yours." She stated. "Do you know how long I have lived here, in Herani?"

I shook my head.

"Over a hundred years. A hundred years where I have been tied up, collared, forced to become a weapon and the few years of peace I obtained were destroyed when those Magar crossed into our world and stole my friends from their beds while they slept."

"But what do I have to do with that?"

"We need a leader. We need someone to rally us."

"Oh no," I said quickly. "I'm not that. I can't even look after myself most days."

"But that's exactly what you are. What your magic has made you."

I gritted my teeth staring into the flames. Guillaume had said something similar, months ago.

"What was your plan, once you freed the other Fae?" Anna asked.

I shrugged. "I didn't have one. My only concern was helping them."

"I see." She murmured. "So, you planned on returning to the High King?"

I winced, hating the word that left my mouth. "Yes."

"When you go, I wish to go with you."

I blinked, staring at her as those words made no sense. "Excuse me?"

"I am tired of running. Tired of hiding. Tired of living as I have. I wish to be free."

"I am not free." I said quickly. God, was that what they thought, that I had some life to aspire to?

"You are freer than us. You are protected, you have food and clothes and…"

"A gilded cage is still a cage." I stated. "Do not look to my life and see only the good. Uther keeps me as his weapon. And that's all I am. An object to be used."

She sighed, folding her arms. "I still wish to go." She said quietly. "I am too old to live as I do."

"Have you spoken to Guillaume about it?" I asked.

"No. I've made my decision. I don't want to live my life like this anymore."

"You do realise what you're asking?" I persisted. "You're going against everything you said before, everything you believe.

You said you weren't a weapon. That you couldn't be a weapon for them."

"And it made no difference." She half cried. "They came for us anyway. I have spent thirty years trying to live my way and it hasn't worked. You have been here for a fraction of my time and yet you have lived more than I have."

"I have been attacked too. I have been burnt, beaten, collared, almost drowned. And I've been assaulted, almost raped more times than…" I gasped unable to finish my sentence, flinching at the last words as the heat rush to my face.

Anna gave me a look, half sympathy, half fierce determination. "Have you been happy?"

"Yes." I replied without hesitating. "I've been happy, not always, though."

"I want to come back with you."

I nodded. "I won't say no. It's your choice. But I want you to understand, once you are there, once the High King has you, you cannot go back. There is no return from it."

Anna took my hand squeezing it. "I understand. And I'm willing to pay that price."

I winced wanting to push the point more. Only she understood as well as I what the price was. If she'd been here more than thirty years she must have endured far worse horrors than I had. It wasn't for me to decide. And I knew I'd be a hypocrite if I refused her.

Thirty

ALICE

I stared transfixed at the horror in front of me. We'd spent days cutting further and further south until we'd reached the rugged coastline. All of us felt the pull, all of us felt as we got closer and closer to this particular corner of hell.

"Can you feel it?" I asked, keeping my eyes ahead, not daring to look away.

"The magic?" Guillaume whispered back. As if he was afraid his voice would carry and give us away.

"The Fae. Their pain. Can you feel it?" I replied.

He frowned slightly. "I can't feel their magic unless it is channelled. They're all collared." He stated simply.

"So, you can't feel anything else?"

"No."

"So, it's just me then." I muttered because that feeling had been steadily growing over the morning as we'd gotten nearer and nearer to the island.

I looked down at the waves crashing beneath the narrow drawbridge. The tower was built from the same black rocks as the ones it sat upon, as if it had simply grown out of them and the mist that seemed to hang around the whole island only added to the horror of the place.

"There are Magars in there." I stated. "Not many but enough to be a threat."

"Why would they have brought them here? Why this location?" Guillaume asked.

"You mean the fact it's creepy isn't enough?" I replied as the main gates opened and five riders came out, dressed in long black robes, obviously scouting for something.

We ducked down, hoping none of them were visible from where we hid. "They know we're here." I stated and Guillaume nodded in agreement.

"They can probably sense us. Sense the magic." He replied.

"So, what do we do?" Anna asked.

I looked across at Guillaume wishing my brain could come up with some sort of plan but I had nothing.

"We need to get inside." Guillaume said.

"But they will bind us with iron the minute the see us." Anna stated.

I nodded before running my hands over my face. In my head this had all seemed so logical. Find the Fae, set them free. But how could I do that when I needed to get inside the damned walls? I could hardly walk right up to them and ask to be let in could I?

"We need a plan." Anna stated like that wasn't obvious. I bit back my retort because sarcasm wouldn't help any of us right now.

"We need one soon." I said. If they'd sent scouts out then it was only a matter of time before they found us. We'd left the rest of the group further back along the beach, concealed in a cave that we hoped would keep them safe.

"Let's head back." Guillaume said and we slipped away from the edge, moving carefully to not accidentally knock any debris over the cliff and alert anyone to where we were.

I chewed my lip, trying to come up with something but every idea seemed ludicrous in my head. We couldn't simply march in there. We couldn't attack it, not when they had thousands of collared Fae to use against us. And I sure as hell wasn't going to turn around now and leave them to it because it was too risky for me to do anything.

"We'll think of something." Guillaume said no doubt seeing the look on my face.

"But what?" I replied. "What possible plan can we come up with that doesn't end in our capture or their death?"

His golden eyes flashed. He shook his head looking as frustrated as I felt and continued onwards while I regretted the words I'd just spoken.

He and Anna walked ahead and I let the distance grow, knowing my mood wouldn't help anyone right now. They'd all come here because they believed my magic would save them, that somehow I could do something. But it felt hopeless. No, worse than hopeless.

As I turned the corner to where the entrance to the cave was, I froze. There were horses. Too many horses. And none of them were ours.

I couldn't see Guillaume. I couldn't see Anna.

I ducked back, hiding behind a boulder and my heart sank as those black robed figures I'd watched, came strutting out, with the rest of my group all bound up by their arms like a human centipede.

Someone started yelling orders, a robed man yanked on the rope and all the Fae stumbled, only just managing to stay upright.

I snarled, pulling my magic, sending a blast that knocked the nearest Magar right off his feet.

I knew it was stupid. Reckless. But I wasn't going to stand by and watch them all get led away like slaves.

They turned as one, sending streams of magic back at me which I deflected easily enough. A Magar's power was nothing compared to what I could wield. But they obviously knew that too. One of them grabbed hold of Anna, yanking her by her hair and placed a knife against her throat.

"Stop." He barked. "Stop or I'll slit her throat."

I scowled, wondering whether he'd dare but as he began to drag the knife I saw the crimson drop of blood. I heard the whimper too as Anna tried to pull away but he held her too tight.

"Alright." I cried, holding my hands up. "Alright."

I stepped out, gritting my teeth. A man moved quickly, wrapping iron around my wrist as I gulped.

The Magar holding Anna tossed her aside like she meant nothing and she crashed into Guillaume who managed to keep them both up right. When he stepped up to me, I flinched back only there was nowhere to go.

"You," He said. "I did not expect you."

"No?" I replied, unsure if he actually knew who I was.

He grinned, raising a gloved hand and stroked down my cheek. "King Dray will be most pleased by this turn of events." He murmured only just loud enough for me to make out the words. Only the name meant nothing. I'd never heard it spoken before.

He grabbed my arm, yanking me to where the other Fae were and shoved me back.

"Tie her up with them." He ordered. "We'll drag them all together."

The rope cut into my skin as they bound my wrists. I did my best not to complain considering our situation was about to get much worse.

"I'm sorry." I whispered to Guillaume who merely shook his head.

"You did not do this."

"I brought us here, I…" A sharp smack to the back of the head silenced me.

"No talking." A man snarled.

"Fuck you." I spat back. Like hell I was just going to roll over without a fight.

The man's reacted, he brought his whip back down, slicing it across my face and I felt my lip split as the coppery taste of blood filled my mouth.

"Careful." The other Magar growled. "That girl is Alarin. She's worth more than all the others combined."

So, they did know. My heart sunk at the knowledge. At his words too. That I was somehow more valuable than the other Fae. I dropped my gaze not wanting to look at any of them. God how they must have hated me then.

No one else spoke as we were marched back. No one dared utter a word. All around us was the pounding sound of horses hooves and boots. I tried to speak with Guillaume in my head but the iron around my wrist ensured that couldn't happen.

When we reached the tower half the Fae seemed to collapse in fear. The Magars laughed, making jokes about how they'd soon be resting as they continued to drag us down into the dark depth of that abyss.

As we entered the dark chamber, I squinted, trying to register what I was seeing. The Magar grabbed me, pulling me free from the other Fae and he gripped my face, forcing me to watch as one by one they were hauled across the stone to where chained collars were waiting for them.

"No," I cried, feeling my body shake as I saw them, as I saw the thousands already chained there. I could feel their despair. I could feel their helplessness. They could barley move from how they'd been bound but their eyes were open. All of them were awake, bound, like living corpses.

"What? No more words from your pretty mouth?" The Magar taunted.

I scowled. "You'll see my reply soon enough." I said, as if I had any idea how I was going to get us out of this.

He grabbed the back of my cloak, forcing me to walk right through the middle of them all.

"See what I have done, Fae." He said with a glint in his eye that made me want to be sick.

We had to be far below the tower, as if in the very tombs of the island itself.

"These were your people." He said, as his voice echoed off the stone. "Your Fae. We have taken them from you and now their power is ours to use as we like."

"But why?" I asked, shocked that they had been so cruel. It wasn't even the collaring, but these were people, living people, and they had turned them into nothing more than statues. Entombed them in stone while they were still alive, still conscious.

The Magar laughed. "Do you not understand, Little Queen?" He said quietly. "This is your future now. Come. See the stone I chose especially for you…"

I stumbled as he pushed me further ahead. "You're sick. You're a monster." I cried.

"I am what this world has made me, just as you are." He stated, coming to halt and I realised we were now in the very centre of the cave. All around, the boulders were surrounding us in rings of circles, with the Fae all chained to them and all connected up.

In front of me was a rock shaped almost like a great round table, with a golden collar lying on it that connected to a chain, linking up to all the other Fae's collars.

The Magar let me go and I stared around, trying to calm myself. Trying to dull the horrifying wave of emotion I felt from all the other Fae. He yanked my cloak from my shoulders and it fell silently to the ground.

As he began circling me he closed his eyes, drawing in a deep breath. "I can taste your magic. I can taste your fear too." He said.

"I am not afraid of you." I spat.

"But you are afraid of this." He said picking up the collar off of the stone and holding it to my face.

I swallowed, staring at it in his hand but I bit back the retort. As I met his eyes again and he smiled. He believed he had won now, I could see it. He believed he had me caught.

He pushed me back onto the stone and I let myself fall, half in fear at what was to come. As he climbed on top of me his hand snaked up into my hair and he yanked it to the side before he snapped the collar in place.

I froze, my stomach twisted as that memory, that reminder of the last time I was collared hit me like a ton of bricks.

"You won't be needing this anymore." He said removing the iron.

I glared at him, waiting for the moment I knew was coming. He held his hands up, his magic suddenly holding me as I got to my knees and I gritted my teeth. I knew what was coming now. I knew his next move. He was going to activate the collar.

My eyes darted about, making contact with all the Fae around me. I could see it, the fear, the hopelessness, the despair in their eyes. But that wasn't what I felt. Not in that moment.

Because now I had him.

As he channelled his magic into the collar I pulled my own, intertwining it with his and forced it backwards.

He frowned stepping back slightly, obviously confused by what was happening and I seized my chance. I pulled more. Feeling where my magic and the collar's combined and connected to each Fae around me.

The power, the emotion, all of it almost overwhelmed me and I had to throw a hand out to steady myself.

"What is this?" The Magar snarled.

I grabbed my neck with both hands, clutching the damned collar, forcing it to obey me. I twisted my magic, weaved it into the metal and down along the chains, feeling the way it vibrated, the way it glowed.

One by one I heard the sound of snapping. One by one I knew those collars had broken.

The sound of gasps, of whimpers, of movement echoed.

I got to my feet with my own collar still intact. As I made eye contact with that Magar I snapped the thing in two. It fell but I caught it in my hand, holding it up before dropping it onto the stone.

The Magar stared at me, his eyes practically bulging from their sockets.

"Did you think it was going to be that easy?" I half whispered.

He shook his head, looking around, clearly not believing what he was seeing. He started spluttering, as if he couldn't form any coherent words.

I smirked before jumping off the stone, landing just metres from where he stood. "You thought you could collar me? You thought you could collar all of us?" I shouted, as the anger raged in me, as my voice echoed off the walls.

"This is not possible." He cried out.

I laughed back. "When will you learn that our magic is not like yours? Our magic is greater than yours. We cannot be controlled. And we cannot be collared."

He shook his head, stepping further back from me. I could feel the other Fae breaking the chains that had bound them to the boulders, finally allowing themselves to move after god knows how long of being chained up.

"No Fae can do this. It's not possible." He half cried as the Fae around us started to move closer.

"You do not know what is and is not possible, Magar." I spat.

He opened his mouth to argue, to speak, and I waved my hand forcing his mouth to shut.

"I've heard enough of your words for one day." I said before bringing my hand down and forcing him onto all fours before me.

As he sunk to his knees all the other Fae started to crowd around us. Some were hugging, some were crying. Some were already kicking the Magar and I decided not to step in and stop them.

"You are the Alarin girl." One said.

"Yes." I said not sure how else to respond.

I looked down at Magar again. He was still stuck in the position I had forced him in. A part of me wanted to kill him, to make him pay for what he had done to them all, but my gut told me to not be so impulsive. That he might have information. Whatever he was trying to do, whatever had been going on here, the High King had to know.

"What's your name?" I asked him.

He spat back at me and I sent a blast of magic, forcing his body against the rocks in a position I knew would hurt.

"Your name?" I repeated.

He panted, clearly wanting to refuse but I saw that look in his eyes. One I'd felt month after month. One of defeat. One of submission. "Atran." He snarled.

"Atran." I murmured, conjuring a band out of magic. He flinched as it wrapped around his wrist and I'll admit that made me smile.

"It's not iron." I said. "It won't burn you but it will stop your ability to channel magic." I could see the confusion in his face, that I hadn't treated him the same way he had all of us. "You're coming with me." I stated before turning back to the others. The stench of this place, the horror of it was overwhelming despite the fact they were all free of the chains. "Let's get out of here." I muttered, feeling like I'd never wanted to see the sun, or smell fresh air more than in that moment.

Thirty-One

FAIN

The door creaked open and a stream of light illuminated the cell. I'd been sat in darkness for days. Sat with nothing but my rapidly spiralling thoughts. The iron had burnt a blackness into my skin that was spreading further up my arm with each hour.

But the pain helped.

The pain gave me something to focus on.

"Cait?" I said as the figure stepped into the cramp, stinking space beyond my bars.

She wrinkled her nose, pulling a cloth to cover her face.

The only thing I had for a toilet was a leaking bucket and they'd made no attempts to change it. They'd barely come down here except to check on me in case they thought I could somehow magic an escape.

She stood staring at me, those brown eyes still as glazed over as they had been in Uther's room.

"Cait, you know I didn't do this…" I began.

She took a step towards me, curling her hands into fists. "He's dying because of you, Fain."

"He's still alive?" I gasped. When they'd dragged me out I thought he'd already passed.

"No thanks to you." She spat.

I drew in a sharp breath. This was some trick. It had to be.

"Where is Jelric?" I asked.

Her mouth turned up into a bitter smile. "He won't help you, no one will help you. You're going to pay for what you've done."

I stared back at her, not understanding who she even was. The Cait I knew would never behave like this, would never react like this.

"Cait, listen to me," I said hearing the desperation in my voice. "You need to send word to Ridley, you need to make sure Hal is safe."

She snarled, wrapping her hands around the bars. "Yeah, I do that and he'll know what the real message is."

"What?"

"He's involved too, is he? That's why you sent him, to make sure when the time came he knew that the Crown Prince had to be disposed of. Clear the line of succession for you."

"What the hell are you talking about?" I hissed.

"You did this, Fain. You murdered your brother just so you could steal his crown."

"I don't give a fuck about his crown." I yelled. "You know me Cait, you know I'd never do this."

She let out a hollow laugh. "I did know you once. But you've changed. We've all seen it, we've all witnessed it. That girl's magic changed you. She turned you from a loyal brother into a traitor."

"No." I snarled. How on all Herani did they think Alice was involved with this, that she would do something like this?

"Yes." She said, glaring into my face. "And both of you will pay for your treachery."

I called after her. I raged, kicking against the bars, slamming my body into them but it made no difference.

And as I sunk to the stone floor my mind kept going back to Alice, to wherever the hell she was, to the fear that she'd return and then they'd capture her too. Collar her too.

Thirty-Two

RILLON

Of all the god-awful cities, Temoor had to be the worst. Every time we'd come here, all I could focus on was the stench of rotting fish. The place was shit hole. Not a home fit for a king. For all its strategic position it missed all the majesty, all the drama of Montefore. It wasn't a royal city by any stretch of the imagination.

And yet this was where I would win it all back. I'll admit the irony didn't escape me.

I glanced at King Ide sat beside me on his horse. Gods, how long had I been waiting for this moment? Planning for this moment? Dreaming of this moment?

I glanced at the soldiers all around me. All ready to march in and win me my throne.

"It's time." King Ide said.

I nodded, more to myself before giving the order to advance.

As we approached the city walls we didn't have to hide, we rode right in. King Ide wasn't a threat after all. He sat on the Great Council. He was a key ally to the High King so why would they refuse him entry?

The few that did put up a fight were swiftly dealt with and the rest had been drugged. As we entered the castle itself Lord Highflynn rushed down to meet us, bowing low, his eyes darting from Ide to me.

"Your Highness." He said.

"I take it everything is taken care of."

"The castle is secure." He said standing up, moving to my side as we walked inside.

"Jelric is contained?"

"He has been bound and is locked in his rooms."

"And the bastard, what about him?"

"In the dungeons." Highflynn said almost gleefully.

I smiled, brushing my cloak, noticing the dirt from the ride. I'd have new clothes ordered now, finer ones. Ones that suited my new rank.

"And any sign of the girl?" I asked.

"Nothing your Highness." Highflynn said. "But we have scouts out. And we've sent words to the Lesser Kings. She will find no safe haven with them."

I narrowed my eyes wondering how true that statement was. Until she was in my possession the girl was a serious threat. Who knew what she might do. And besides, we all knew the Lesser Kings wouldn't easily ignore such a chance to make their own moves if she dropped conveniently into their laps.

But we'd had to make our move when we did. Jelric had grown more suspicious. His damned spies had seen to that. And from what Ide had said, my bastard brother's powers were growing by the day. We'd had to take the risk despite the unknowns of the Fae girl.

"Call the Council." I ordered. I needed everything to run as planned from now on. I needed total and complete control.

Highflynn bowed, rushing off to follow my orders and as Ide took a corridor to my right I left him alone to finish securing the castle while I made my way to the High King's chambers.

"This is nonsense. Absolute nonsense." Callin stated, staring back at me like he was the one in charge here.

"We have a signed confession." Lord Highflynn stated waving the paper about. "It clearly states that High Prince Fain ordered him to do it. That the Prince said he would be well rewarded once he was High King."

"This is Prince Fain we are talking about. You know him. You know this is a lie." Callin persisted waving his arms around like the idiot he was.

"Prince Fain has fooled us all." I said. "And very well by the look of things."

"That man is a traitor. The High King ruled it himself." A Lord stated pointing at me.

I rolled my eyes, fighting the urge to laugh. "On Prince Fain's evidence."

"On Alice's evidence too." Callin stated. "You tried to steal her powers or have you forgotten that?"

"I have not forgotten. The girl was very clever. She worked her ways with me first and when that backfired, she stuck her claws into my dear loyal half-brother and now look at him. Because of her, Uther is lying half dead."

"What are you saying?" Someone else asked like it wasn't damned obvious.

"That the girl is behind it all." I said. "You all think she is innocent because of how she looks but she knew what she was doing. She knew exactly how to play you all and she conspired with Prince Fain to steal the crown from my brother."

"This is nonsense."

"Is it?" I replied. "Where is she now huh? Why is she not here? Isn't it convenient that just before Uther is almost fatally poisoned, she vanishes?"

"She is away on his orders. On his request." A Magi persisted.

I clapped my hands together in mockery of those words. "Yes, some mystery errand that no one except Prince Fain and supposedly my brother knows about."

"Where is Jelric?" Callin asked. "If this is true, why is he not here to confirm it?"

I smiled then. Gods it was hard not to. He'd practically paved the way for me. "He has been poisoned too." I stated. "Fain and the girl would have known he could cure my brother and so they made sure that could not happen."

Callin shook his head. "She had nothing to do with this."

"I'm sorry King Callin but you're wrong. They have both deceived you for a very long time. They have deceived us all."

As most of the Council shook their heads, I narrowed my eyes. I'd planned for this. Anticipated this. Most of these arseholes had been there to pass judgement on me, to cast me out and send me into exile, as if I were a mere subject bound by the same laws they lived by. But what they failed to understand was I didn't need them to believe me. In fact, I didn't need them at all, truth be told.

"Perhaps now is a time for loyalty." I declared clasping my hands together. "My brother is mortally wounded and at a time like this we need to protect ourselves from any would be dissenters."

I nodded to the guards, who moved to stand behind everyone who clearly wasn't acting smart. "This Council is dissolved." I stated. I didn't need the Council. Didn't need any of them. I had soldiers. I'd already taken the city. There was nothing anyone could do to stop me now.

As I sunk into that soft, padded throne I wrapped the ermine cloak closer around myself. It was all coming together. I just had one more task to deal with and then I could truly relax.

Thirty-Three

ALICE

There were so many of us. Thousands.

I stood at the top of the hill, staring down at the makeshift camp.

I'd hoped to pass through Rette's lands unnoticed, but I knew we didn't stand a chance now. There were too many of us. God, we looked like an army. And I doubted our presence hadn't already been spotted.

Our travel was slow. Frustratingly so. Some of the Fae were still recovering from the collaring and with the numbers we had, we needed almost constant supplies.

On the one hand I wanted us to get back, to return to wherever that portal was because being there meant we'd be safe, but returning also meant I'd have to leave them, and the way my magic was responding, made my heart soar. It felt like home. These people. These strangers. They felt like a family I'd never had before.

But he wasn't there. Fain. And no matter how whole the Fae made me feel, his absence, his lack of presence felt like it left a gaping chasm in my chest. And the fact that I couldn't feel our bond, that made it worse. So much worse.

I let lout a sigh, quietly walking back down the hill. Guillaume was sat by the fire and the flames of it illuminated his skin, whispering of the magic that simmered beneath it.

"Here." Guillaume said passing me a bowl of food.

Thank god a few of the Fae could cook because the stew we had now was infinitely better than the roasted animals and stale bread we'd been forced to survive on.

"Thanks." I murmured.

"I think if we carry on at this rate it will take at least another week to get back." He stated.

"A week?" I repeated, shocked. I'd hoped for half that time.

"Maybe more."

I shook my head, trying to fight back the wave of emotion that hit me. It was what it was. It did no good to fixate on it.

"How did you break the collars?" He asked after we'd both fallen to silence.

"What?"

"Their collars. How did you do it?"

"They had them all connected. All linked to draw their power into one. When Atran collared me, I pulled my magic and reversed it. I twisted it around and instead of me being connected to the collar it was connected to me. I could then break everyone's collars through the connection."

He blinked, staring at me like he didn't understand what I'd said.

"What?" I asked nervously.

"How, how did you know to do that?"

I shrugged. "I just did. It was like the magic was there for me to read it. To see it."

He frowned, shaking his head and glanced to where Atran was now tied up against a tree and guarded. "What are you going to do with him?"

"I wanted to strip him, take away his ability to channel." I admitted. "But I have to take him to the High King first. To Jelric. They can question him and then decide what to do with him."

"You could take his magic from him and still take him to them." He pointed out.

"I know but it feels like I'd only be doing it in anger and I've already done too much magic like that today."

I stirred my food, took a spoonful and swallowed. In my head saving them had seemed simple but now it all felt so complicated again.

"Anna wants to come back with me. To the High King." I said quietly.

"I don't think she is the only one." Guillaume replied.

My jaw dropped as I looked back at him. "Are you serious?"

"Yes. I think you may well find there's a whole group of us returning."

"But why?" I gasped.

I couldn't understand it. I got that they were scared. I got that they wanted some sort of protection now but it was like they were just jumping into this, seeing Uther as some sort of hero that might defend them when he was still very much the villain in our lives.

"Why do you think?" He replied.

I shrugged not sure how to answer him.

"You don't see what you've done do you?" He smiled kindly.

"Tell me."

"You've united them. You've done exactly what we always talked about."

"All I did was free them from that place."

"No, you did more than that. You've shown them that they don't need to be afraid anymore. That they shouldn't be afraid and that they shouldn't have to hide either."

Before I could answer something caught my attention. I turned my head realising that more of the Fae were watching me now. That they'd been listening to our conversation.

"I want to come with you." A girl said.

I sighed, biting my lip, fighting that same battle in my own head.

"Me too."

My head jerked to the right, my eyes connected with the Fae who'd said it.

"And me." A man said pushing his way through the crowd that seemed to have gathered.

"Stop." I said. "You don't know what you're asking."

"Yes we do." Someone replied.

I shook my head, forcing myself to my feet. "If you come, you have to understand what your life will be." I said. "The High King will see you as his. As a possession. And once he knows you exist, once you walk into that city, there will be no turning back. You piss him off and he will collar you, just as the Magars…" I paused, wondering if I was seeing this all wrong. If I was approaching this all wrong.

We were Fae. We were magic.

"Alice?" Guillaume asked quietly and I shook my head, trying to gather my thoughts.

"Maybe there is another way." I said looking at the man who in many ways had helped me realise what this world was, who had forced me to grow up, to become truly Fae and not just a puppet.

"What do you mean?" Anna asked.

"I mean, we're Fae. We have both numbers and magic on our side." I drew myself up, making my case, after all, if we were going to do this then it was a joint decision. "If we return to Temoor as one, we can demand our freedom. Demand that the High King and everyone else sees us as people in our own right."

"That's possible?" Someone said.

I shrugged. "We decide what is possible. There are over a thousand of us. Our magic outweighs theirs. And besides, they can't collar us all."

Guillaume smiled.

Anna clasped her hands together.

And to my surprise Stephen pushed to the front and nodded. "It's as good a plan as any." He said.

"Then we go to Temoor. All of us." I said.

And together we would demand our freedom.

Thirty-Four

RILLON

Gods, he hadn't changed a bit. They'd told me he was half-Fae. That his magic exploded out of him but as I looked at him now, I saw the same bastard boy who'd stolen my brother's attention. Stolen his love when it should have been mine.

"Hello, brother." I said glancing at the blackened flesh around his wrist. No one was certain that such a half-breed as he would be bound by iron and yet it appeared to be effective enough. It had captured the beast.

Fain frowned trying to hide his shock but I saw it. Oh, how I saw it.

"Surprised to see me?" I smirked.

"What are you doing here?" Fain asked getting up from where he'd been sat in the dirt like the disgusting dog that he was.

"You haven't figured it out." I murmured. "I thought you were better than that, Fain."

Fain narrowed his eyes but said nothing. And as he did I saw it, that hopelessness, that defeat. My heart soared, I let out a laugh because in so many ways it had all been too easy. He hadn't even seen it coming.

"I rule Herani now. I am High King in all but name."

"You are not. Uther still lives." Fain snapped clenching his fists.

I tilted my head, amused by the show of loyalty. "Yes but for how long, brother? There is only so long we have until the poison does its work."

"What are you talking about?" Fain snapped.

"If they cannot find a cure in time, it will kill him." I said almost sadly. Almost.

"You did this didn't you? You poisoned him." Fain stated putting it all together.

I stepped back, holding my hands up. "He is my brother, why would I do such a thing?"

"You won't get away with this Rillon."

I laughed again. "Oh, but I will. It's already done. I have already won."

Fain snarled, grabbing at the bars, snatching at them like he had the strength to rip them from the ceiling. I paused glancing up, making sure that such a thing weren't possible.

"They will stop you. They will see right through you." He growled.

"Who Fain? The Great Council is disbanded. Jelric is under guard and your Fae girl has vanished. There is no one else left."

Fain shook his head. "He is your brother, Rillon." He shouted.

"Yes and look what he did to me." I snapped back. "He had me banished without a moment's hesitation. A moment's thought."

"You deserved it for what you tried to do."

I smirked, folding my arms. "Just as you deserve this Fain. You are no prince. You have never been a prince. You have no royal blood. Your mother was a whore, a five-minute thrill. Uther couldn't see it. Uther was blind to you but I knew what you were. You're nothing. You're worthless and this is where you will remain until I have your head hacked from your body."

"You won't get away with this. They'll see right through you." He repeated, like the stupid dumb brute that he was.

"It's too late, I've already won, Fain. The only person outstanding is the Fae girl and when she finally returns from whatever little adventure you've all sent her on, I'll finally make her pay too."

"She'll destroy you." Fain spat back.

"Not if I collar her first." I said closing the distance between us. "By the time I'm finished with her, she'll wish she was back in the dungeons at Caraden, with Yannis fucking her senseless."

Fain snarled, he slammed himself into the bars as if he could break out. As if he could even try.

"Don't worry brother. Once you're gone I'll be sure to take good care of her for you. Unlike Yannis, I'll take my time with breaking her until she is little more than a slave bending to my every whim."

"I'll kill you." Fain snarled. "I'll fucking kill you."

I turned my back walking to where the guards were now stood.

"Did you hear that?" I said to them, like their opinion mattered. "First he poisons the High King and now he threatens me. Is there no end to his violence?"

The soldiers grunted but I paid them no heed. I didn't actually give a damn what they thought, I just enjoyed stirring the pot.

I glanced back, meeting Fain's gaze through the darkness and grinned. Yes it was all coming together very nicely indeed.

I HAD MOVED UTHER OUT. HE WAS PRACTICALLY DEAD ALREADY SO why did he need to occupy the best rooms?

I stalked into the small room we'd shoved him in, curious to see if he was still breathing, but as I passed the threshold I paused.

Someone was there. I could sense it.

Uther lay exactly as we'd left him. Fully clothed, on top of the bed. No need for a blanket – after all, what did it matter if he was cold? He couldn't do anything about it, could he? And he'd be dead soon enough.

And then I heard it, the soft, almost imperceptible sniff of a cry.

I guess it was time to sort another task. To tick another item off the list.

"Rillon?" Cait said looking up as I walked towards her. Her hair was a mess, her face was wet with tears and her eyes were red from all the crying. She'd always looked immaculate, poised, perfect.

I'll admit I was surprised to see she looked heartbroken. She looked like she actually cared what happened to Uther and that he hadn't just been a means to an end for her.

"I see the glamour has worn off." I stated.

Her eyes were no longer dazed. I didn't know where the damned Magi had gone but that didn't matter now. She was surplus to requirements.

"What?" She said clearly confused.

"What are you doing here?" I asked.

"What do you mean?" She replied screwing her face up.

"I said, what are you doing here?" I repeated, louder, allowing the annoyance to fill each syllable.

"He is my husband." She hissed. "I have every right to be here. To be by his side."

"Get out." I said, folding my arms, rolling my eyes.

"What?"

"GET OUT." I yelled and she froze staring at me like the stupid whore that we all knew she was.

"He is my husband, Rillon." She cried back at me.

I crossed the room and grabbed her roughly by her arm yanking her off her knees and to her feet.

"He is not." I stated. "Uther has royal blood. He is a High King and you…" I opened the door throwing her across the corridor, not caring how she landed and if anyone was there to see. "You are a common whore. A peasant. You are nothing to him. Nothing to any of us."

She whimpered as her face slammed into stone tiles before turning to face me again, with those sad, pathetic, pleading eyes.

"Rillon, please. Don't do this." She said getting up.

"Shut up." I'd had enough of her crying, enough of her begging. She'd played her part. She'd played it very well. For once in her pitiful excuse for a life she'd actually been useful. Too bad she didn't have the sense to save herself now.

"Rillon, you can't separate us. You can't deny what we had." She cried.

"SHUT UP." I yelled. "Uther never loved you. You were a plaything to him. An amusement."

"That's not true." She wailed as the tears rolled down her face.

"I want you gone. I want you out of this castle by nightfall."

"You can't do this, Rillon."

"Yes I can. I'm High King now. If you're not gone by the time the sun is down, I'll have you stripped naked and turned over to my soldiers. Then you'll find out how much of a whore you really are." I snapped before slamming the doors shut on her.

Stupid bitch, did she really think I'd allow her to stay? That I'd ignore her inferior blood all because my brother enjoyed having her in his bed? I made a mental note to have her tracked, to have her quietly disposed of once she was far from the city.

Afterall, she was another loose end I didn't want to unravel.

I walked back to where my brother was. Crouching down to stare at his face.

"You did this." I said after a few moments. "You did this to yourself."

Uther didn't move. Didn't blink. Didn't even show any hint that he could hear me and in truth, I didn't care either way if he could or not.

"I have taken your crown. I have taken your throne." I stated. "You tried to banish me, to erase me from your life, but now I have taken yours from you. Soon that poison will have worked its way through your blood and you will be gone. Dead. I will be High King. I will rule Herani and no one will even remember your name."

My hand slapped across his cheek.

I grinned, striking him again.

I truly had won now, hadn't I?

A cough made me look up. King Ide stood by the door watching. Had he heard what I'd said? I didn't care that much if he had.

"Your Highness." Ide said bowing his head.

"Is it done?" I asked.

"Yes. The army has been purged. There are no more dissenters. No more naysayers. You are High King in all but name."

"Good." I replied. "I want you to go to Nind. Take your men, do whatever you need to do to secure the castle."

"You want me to kill the boy?"

"Not yet. Kill Ridley by all means but keep Hal alive. If we kill him too soon it may threaten our stability."

"We will leave today." Ide replied.

"Don't let me down." I said in a tone that suggested exactly what would happen if he did.

Thirty-Five

ALICE

We changed course, cutting across the dells instead of the mountains now that we were headed for Temoor. As every step we took drew us closer, something inside me fought an internal battle about whether I should have felt happy or concerned at returning.

I knew facing off against Uther had never ended well, but this time, surely, with the numbers we had, we had to succeed.

When Anna came and sat beside me during lunch, I voiced my nervousness and she smiled, taking my hand and reassured me that whatever happened, we were in this together, that we all were united in this.

Something about that at least made me feel better.

But we both tensed when we saw Guillaume rushing up to us with a face full of concern.

"What is it?" I asked.

"Soldiers. Up ahead. King Rette's men." He replied. "The scouts just spotted them."

I gritted my teeth at that. So far I'd met three Lesser Kings and based on how they'd all reacted I wasn't keen on meeting another. Sure, I'd go as far to say King Callin was a friend now but his men had been the ones to introduce me to an iron cage and that memory still hadn't faded.

"Is there any way we can avoid them?"

He shook his head. "Not unless you can make us vanish. They're headed right for us."

"Great." I muttered, trying to remember what I knew of this King. I remembered his face vaguely from Rebecca's memories at the Pavilion when she was pretending to be me but I couldn't think of anything else that would be useful.

"Get me a horse." I said to Guillaume who frowned. "I'm not letting them get within range of the Fae."

He grunted, shouting for one too and as I raised my eyebrows at him he gave me a look that dared me to question him.

We mounted quickly while everyone else seemed to gather together in panic.

"Stay here. And stay as hidden as you can." I said to the rest of the Fae before kicking my horse into a canter.

Ahead I spotted the nervous looking scout and aimed right for him. Guillaume stayed hot on my heels.

And ss we reached the brow of the hill I saw them, moving fast, close enough to get my heartrate going. King Rette had sent a whole garrison. All wearing black armour and mounted on black horses. It looked intimidating but I figured that was exactly the look he was going for.

Apparently he was just as egotistical as the rest of them then.

I came to a halt right in front of them, my horse half-rearing as I yanked on the reins. Their leader eyed me suspiciously and as I glanced across at Guillaume I realised we too must be quite a sight.

Good, I wanted to be just as intimidating to them as they tried to be to me.

"Why are you obstructing us?" I asked.

"We are here to escort you all back to King…"

I shook my head. Here we go, the same attitude, the same behaviour, just a different King.

"No." I said. "We are on the High King's business. You will let us pass."

The man narrowed his eyes. "Not before you meet with our King."

I clenched then unclenched my fists, mentally calculating how many soldiers there were in front of me. Every one of them looked like they were sizing me up.

"You know what we are." I said, letting the magic flash in my eyes as warning. "You are not a threat to us."

"Maybe but you are on King Rette's lands. Surely you did not expect to simply pass by unnoticed?"

I tilted my head in a pretence at amusement. "We are on High King Uther's business. He outranks your king."

"But you will come with us anyway, unless you wish to start a war."

I sighed, glancing at Guillaume. *'What do you think?'* I thought to him.

He pulled a face, clearly not giving a damn if they saw. *'I'm not sure we have much choice. You?'* He thought back.

'As much as I'd like to show him where he can stick it, I'm not sure we do either. Besides, I doubt the High King will be happy that I've started another war for him.'

He smirked while the soldier looked between us trying to figure out what the hell was going on.

"I will go. But the rest of them stay here." I stated.

He opened his mouth to argue and I raised my hand to silence him. "It's that or nothing." I said.

'*I will go with you.*' Guillaume thought to me and I nodded.

'*Eustace, you stay with the others. Tell them to wait. We will return.*' I instructed.

"Half my men will remain here with the rest of the Fae." The soldier stated.

"Fine. But if they harm them…" I began.

"Relax Fae, as you've already stated you can do more damage than we can." He said irritated.

I narrowed my eyes, glaring at him. "Fine. But don't forget it." I muttered before looking at Eustace to tell him to go.

He turned his horse and kicked it into a canter heading back to the others and I watched him go until he disappeared from view.

WE RODE QUICKLY. THE MAN SET A FAST PACE THAT I FELT WAS HALF done just to test us. Not that it bothered me because I was more than used to being in a saddle all day now and thanks to Fain I was used to hard riding too.

As we approached the city, I felt my jaw drop in disbelief. It was nothing like any of the castles in Herani. A wall surrounded the entirety of it that felt made half of stone, half of magic and she frowned, feeling as the pattern and the swirl of it almost made her drunk for a moment.

When I looked at Guillaume I could tell he was feeling the same too.

Within the walls, houses were all laid out on a grid, not mismashed like they were in Temoor and even Montefore. It all felt regimented, controlled. The great castle in the middle wasn't really a castle either. It was more like a huge glass palace. It too was made half of magic, half of real materials and I shook my head in wonder. How long had it taken to build this? How had they even come up with this?

We walked from the stables with what felt like the entire city watching us. I glanced up at the great glass windows that seemed to surround us and saw faces everywhere, looking down at them. I realised suddenly that the two of us must have been quite a sight, both obviously Fae, and both dressed ready for battle.

The entire time Guillaume kept beside me, and it felt half like he was my bodyguard, half my advisor.

'If I say anything you don't agree with, do anything you don't agree with…' I thought to him.

'I trust you.' He thought back, meeting my gaze as we walked.

'It's not about trust.'

'I know. But still. You've got this. Trust yourself, trust that you know what to do.'

I gritted my teeth, nodding and realised the man was looking between us again. Clearly our silent communication was unnerving them and that realisation made me smile. I wanted them all to feel that because they were all far too confident, far too self-assured around the Fae. They had no power, no magic, and yet they had spent their entire lives acting like they were in control. That they could somehow subdue us. Now, I was going to show them in my own way that the tables were well and truly turned.

We were led into what appeared to be an empty throne room.

As I cast my eyes around, it was hard not to get annoyed at the ridiculousness of it. It felt like it was all a show. Another Lesser King flexing his muscles.

Guillaume walked to one of the huge windows and stared down at the ornamental gardens. From the look on his face, I could tell he was just as frustrated by it as I was.

When King Rette walked in he took only a few strides before his eyes fell on me and he stopped. I stared right back at him. Refusing to show any sign of weakness.

Even though I'd seen him before, seen him through Rebecca's memories to see him for myself felt very different. Besides Guillaume and some of the other Fae, he was the first black man I had met. He was huge, not just in height but in muscles too. They appeared to almost bulge out of his clothes despite the thickness of the fabric and the way he held himself showed that he knew the effect his mere presence had on everyone around him.

"No curtsey?" He said.

I narrowed my eyes. "Not when I am forced to your palace." I stated.

Only he smiled as though he was amused. "I doubt anyone could force you to do anything you didn't want, Alice."

My breath hitched. For a moment I felt almost disarmed by the fact that he had used my name and not simply referred to me as 'Fae' like everyone else.

King Rette looked over at Guillaume who had turned, his back now to the window, as he faced him.

"Who is this? Your bodyguard?" Rette asked.

Guillaume gave him a hard stare back.

"Why, do I need one?" I asked back as he looked me up and down in my Fae armour.

"You tell me." He replied, still clearly amused.

"Why are we here?" I asked, getting annoyed by all the games he seemed to be playing.

"Stand your man down and I'll tell you." He said.

"I don't keep secrets from Guillaume. Everything I know, he does."

His eyebrows rose. "Everything?"

"Everything." I repeated more firmly.

"Even your deepest, darkest secrets?" He asked almost tauntingly.

"What do you want, King Rette?" I said.

He stepped closer as if somehow saying his name had drawn him to me under a spell.

I could see the smoothness of his skin, the way the light through the glass reflected off his forehead beneath his closely shaven hair.

"Stand your man down and I will tell you." He said more forcefully.

I sighed, looking at Guillaume.

'I'll wait outside.' Guillaume said in my head.

'You're sure?'

'Sometimes you have to play their games in order to beat them.'

'Spoken like a true diplomat.' I teased.

'Maybe that's what you should introduce me as instead of your bodyguard in future.' He replied.

I smirked. *'I'll think about it.'*

He bowed to me, a quick respectful gesture but the action was not lost on Rette as he watched us with intense curiosity.

As the door shut he stepped closer, almost touching distance from me. I frowned, stepping back, creating more space between them.

"Talk." I said and it sounded like an order. A command.

He laughed, a rich laugh that filled the air and felt more than a little disarming. "You are more than they said you were. More than I expected."

I rolled my eyes at the comment, growing sick of everyone saying that. Sick of everyone acting like I was somehow exceeding their imagined expectations of what I should be.

"What were you expecting?" I replied letting the annoyance sound in my voice. If he thought he could charm me he had another thing coming.

"Not this. I knew you were beautiful. The Fae always are. But you are more than that, more than the simpering girl I met at Yannis's audience."

I scowled, as a flashback, a memory not of my own crossed my mind. "That was not me."

"I heard that, though I didn't quite believe it. The magic sounded too fantastic, too far-fetched to be possible. But now, seeing you, I can see the difference. You are not the same girl."

"You've still not told me what you want, King Rette." I pointed out.

He smirked, appraising me once more. "There are several things I want. Firstly though, you are travelling through my lands. Not just you, but thousands of you. All Fae. I want to know why. I want to know what business you have in my kingdom."

"That is not for me to say. I am here under the High King's orders." I stated.

Something passed his face, some momentary reaction I couldn't read. "You expect me to simply let you all pass by, unhindered, and unquestioned?"

"If you don't wish to be at war with the High King, then yes."

"Are you threatening me?" He asked as his lips curled with amusement again. "In my own palace?"

"No. The Fae belong to the High King. You know this. If you try to stop us then you would be risking his wrath. It's not a threat, it's a fact."

"I will make you a deal then. I will let you pass. I will grant you safe passage through my lands and even give you an escort if you wish..."

"But?" I asked because I knew there was one. There was always a 'but.'

"But you agree to remain here. In this palace…" I opened my mouth to argue and he held his hand up. "..For three days."

"Why?" I half-snapped.

"Why not?" He mused. "It is a simple request? Why would you refuse?"

I stepped back slightly fighting the only too familiar feeling of fear that was threatening to wash over me. "Three days is too much."

"You are that desperate to return to him?"

I narrowed my eyes, unsure if he was referring to the High King or Prince Fain, and I didn't want to show any card that might weaken my hand. "Like I said, the High King gave me orders. How do you think he would react if he knew I spent precious time here with you instead of returning to his side as he instructed?"

I hated the way I was making myself sound so damn obedient, like I really was little more than a lap dog to him. But what choice did I have? And besides, this world was happy enough to twist the rules, to play games when it suited them, why could I not do the same?

He frowned again. "Fine, two days."

I opened my mouth to argue and he held his hand up again. "That is my final deal. You want me to grant you safe passage then grant me what I want too."

I gritted my teeth. "Two days then." I replied feeling like I might have just made a deal with the devil.

"Good." He smiled like I'd truly given him a blessing. "I will have my servants show you to your rooms. I assume your bodyguard will be staying?"

"Guillaume is not my bodyguard."

"That remains to be seen." He replied before walking to the door and holding it open in expectation for me to follow.

Thirty-Six

ALICE

I sat beside King Rette keeping my eyes focused on my plate, trying to ignore all the obvious stares from practically everyone else in the room. Guillaume had been seated only a few people down from me but it felt like he was miles away.

And it also felt like he had been deliberately placed too far for me to talk to, at least out loud anyway.

They had given us both rooms that seemed as ornate and over the top as the rest of the Palace. After making sure the other Fae were being looked after and were safe, I'd washed and King Rette had sent a maid to attend me.

The girl had fussed around and giving me the option of three dresses to wear. While it felt like it was a repeat of King Callin's escapades all over again, these dresses were more like my own, and I settled on a blue one so pale it was almost grey.

And now I was here, eating dinner beside the King, in view of what felt like everyone in the city, as though all of this was perfectly normal.

"Do you eat every meal like this?" I asked him.

"Like what?"

"In front of everyone like it's a grand feast."

"This is not a feast. Besides, the High King dines like this…"

"Does he?" I replied frowning, though I was unsure why I was so surprised. It wasn't exactly against his nature was it?

King Rette smirked at my reaction. "Perhaps you were too much in Prince Fain's company to notice." He said quietly.

I hated the way I reacted, the way my face flushed. "What do you mean?"

"I mean that the High King dines almost every night in the Great Hall, with his Council, with his Lords, but I've been told that his Fae girl rarely attends, except for feasts and only ever at the High Prince's side…"

I frowned more. Is that what everyone thought, that I was hauled up in my room like some lovesick idiot?

"I don't like attention." I said quietly, staring at the cutlery in my hand. "I don't like being watched. I ate in my room because of that. I didn't realise that I missing all this."

When I looked up I could see the confusion in his face. "I think you are an enigma." He stated sitting back in his chair to watch me.

"How so?"

"You don't like attention yet the way you look demands it. You don't like being watched but everything you do makes people want to watch you."

"I can't help how I look." I half-snapped.

"No. I agree with you there. Just as you cannot help that you are Fae."

Something about that tone, made me want to flee. Only I knew that wasn't possible. Not without offending this Lesser King and almost certainly incurring his wrath. I took a mouthful of food unsure how to respond.

"You are their leader are you not?" He asked quietly and my head turned so quickly as I looked at him.

"I…"

"That is how they view you. The other Fae. How they have treated you. My men told me how they were back at dells, and your bodyguard here, he bows to you as though you were a queen. You lead them."

"Yes. But the High King does not…" I trailed off not sure how to answer. "He knows what I am but I still belong to him. He does not recognise me as that."

He tilted his head, studying my face more. "Does it annoy you? Belonging to Uther?" He asked.

"Yes and no." I admitted unsure why I was being so honest though it wasn't like Uther didn't know all of this. "I don't like being his possession. I don't like being viewed as simply an object, a weapon that can be used. But he is better than the Lesser Kings. He at least understands me and he treats me with some respect."

"And you think us Lesser Kings do not?" He asked with a wry smile.

"I have been held captive by two Lesser Kings. One put me in an iron cage and one had me beaten, collared, and tortured. For all the High King's faults, he has never hurt me."

We stared at one another. Him frowning more, as though he was thinking of something he didn't want to say out loud.

"Why did you want me to stay here?" I asked quietly.

"The truth?"

"Yes."

"I wanted to get the measure of you. I have heard so much. And after meeting the fake version of you, I was curious what the real Alice was like."

I swallowed. "That's it?"

"What else did you think?"

I sighed, biting my tongue. My gut told me he was telling the truth and yet it seemed too easy. This was a Lesser King; all they were concerned about was gaining power in whatever way possible.

"We are not all like Yannis." He said.

My breath caught. That old fear flitted through me and I dug my nails into my palms to subdue it. "But you all see me as just Fae. Not a person, just a weapon in your arsenal." I stated hearing the edge to my voice. The venom.

"No. You are wrong there." He replied.

"Am I? You were the one who sent a garrison of your men after us."

"I am a king. Did you expect me not to react when an army of Fae are crossing my lands unchecked and for no apparent reason?"

"We had reason."

"Not that I knew of at the time."

"So, you mean to say that you would have granted us passage if you had known of our journey prior?" I scoffed.

"Perhaps. I have granted you passage now, have I not?" He smirked.

"It is not the same."

"No, this way I get what I want too. Both parties are happy."

"You really only wanted to meet me? That's it?"

He chuckled before taking a sip of his drink. "Perhaps you do not understand it. Perhaps you have not heard all the rumour, the intrigue about yourself."

My eyes widened. "What intrigue? What rumour?"

"Before you arrived no one living had even laid eyes on a Fae. Most people came to believe they didn't exist anymore. And then you appeared, with golden hair, and a fire in your eyes...."

I dropped my gaze, my hand darting to my glass to gulp my drink as it felt suddenly like the room was too hot. Too stuffy.

"...and it was like a match was lit. Every king wanted to have you. Every Magi wanted to collar you."

I scowled. "Why do you all only ever think of collaring me?" I snapped.

"I did not."

"Sure you didn't." I muttered loud enough for him to hear.

"When you arrived, Alice, you were in my lands, you crossed not too far from here. Prince Fain left this very city to take you from Lord Ghosh, to the High King."

How had no one told me that? How come I'd never even thought about where I'd crossed before? Never even stopped to consider it?

"If I'd wanted to, I could have sent an army after him, I could have claimed you for myself, declared war against the High King, just like Yannis did, and you would have been mine."

"I am not a possession." I said coldly.

"No, you are not. Under it all, under all the magic and beauty of you, you are a person."

I frowned more. "Then what are you saying?"

"That I wanted to see the person. Not the Fae. Not the magic. But the real Alice."

I swallowed, trying to calm the panicking race of my heart. "Well, now you have." I said taking another sip and feeling more uncomfortable under his gaze.

"Yes. And I have not been disappointed."

"There is still time. You have one day left, King Rette."

He threw his head back and laughed while half the room exchanged looks. "Then I had better use my time wisely." He said before waving his hands for the servers to come clear the plates.

We walked out into the gardens and it felt like half the court was following, watching, waiting on our every move. The evening breeze felt cool, liberating almost after the stuffiness of Rette's Hall.

I looked back over my shoulder, searching for Guillaume amongst the throng of people. He was just as surrounded as I was, though it looked as though he'd taken a vow of silence and was refusing to engage with anyone.

When our eyes connected he gave me a nod.

'*Everything okay?*' I asked him.

'*Yes. You?*'

'*Yes.*' I glanced at King Rette, seeing that he was watching me curiously. '*Apparently he wanted to meet the real Alice.*' I thought as his low chuckle rumbled out.

'*Good luck with that. Did you tell him the real Alice has a taste for sarcasm and a bad temper?*'

I laughed, unable to stop myself and the King beside me frowned more.

"Are you talking to each other?" Rette asked me.

I blinked, deciding I had nothing to lose by being honest. "Yes. He wanted to check everything is okay."

"But he is not your bodyguard?" He smirked.

"I don't need anyone to fight for me. I can hold my own."

"I'm sure you can." He replied. "You came here in full armour."

My eyebrows rose. "You expected me to be in a dress?"

"I don't know what I expected but it wasn't that."

As we walked further, the people behind us started to thin out, as if the night was drawing them away.

"Tell me about Prince Fain." He said after a few moments of silence.

I narrowed my eyes looking at him. "What about him?"

"Do you love him?"

"How is that any concern of yours?" I asked.

He raised an eyebrow stopping to face her properly.

"Indulge me. I am curious."

"You can keep your curiosity to yourself, King Rette." I huffed, crossing my arms.

He smiled more as if I were charming him when I was pretty certain I wasn't. "I like you. You are not afraid of me. You are not afraid to speak your mind."

"Why would I be afraid?" I shrugged.

"Because I am a king." He stated.

"And I am Fae." I replied.

"True. If you wanted you could probably kill me right now and there would be little I could do to stop you."

I tilted my head. "Then you'll be pleased to know that I don't make a habit of killing kings."

"No. But you do not care much for manners either." He smirked.

"Have I been rude?" I asked seriously because I didn't think I had been intentionally so.

"No, not rude. But you are not like other women. You refuse to curtail to anyone."

"And should I?"

"I think you have earned the right to speak your mind."

I smirked then. Admittedly, part of me was starting to like this King despite myself.

"So, Prince Fain…" He began again.

"Why do you care?"

"Because the Prince I knew hated magic. Almost hated the Magi too."

"I know. He told me."

"And you somehow won him over?" He said.

Ellie Sanders

"I wouldn't say I won him over." I replied, feeling awkward and embarrassed about even discussing it with him, a man I'd only just met, and a Lesser King to boot.

"The rumours are that he is with you only on the orders of his brother…"

"What?" I snapped, coming to a complete stop. "Who says that?"

He shrugged. "So, it's not true then?"

"No. Fain would never have done something like that." I said.

He narrowed his eyes as though he was trying to see something in my face, as though he was trying to see the lie in my words.

"Are you satisfied?" I asked him, all but staring him down.

He grinned back at me. "For the moment."

We walked on in silence. Though it felt neither peaceful nor awkward. In my gut it felt like this King had something else to say, something else he wanted to bring up with me only he kept whatever it was to himself.

As we came full circle I saw the palace looming ahead.

"It is late." Rette said. "And while I want to make the most of our time together, we should go to bed."

My body reacted, my heart went into panic, I stepped back as he stepped forward, his face twisting into one of concern. Surely he didn't mean what I heard? We'd only just been discussing Fain, surely he didn't think I'd what, behave like that?

"Perhaps I should have chosen my words more carefully." He said quietly as I stared down at the ground. "Not all the Lesser Kings are like him."

I nodded still avoiding his gaze, with my face feeling hot enough to fry an egg on.

"Look at me." He said gently and I forced myself to obey. "I will not hurt you. I will not touch you. And I am loyal to the High King. I swore an oath to him that I take very seriously."

"What do you want me to say? That I am sorry?" I asked confused and embarrassed.

"No. You don't need to apologise. But I want you to understand, in this palace, in my Kingdom you are safe. No one will touch you. No one will harm you."

I shook my head. "You say that but you cannot promise that."

"No but you can. You are Fae. When Yannis took Temoor, you were not in full control of your powers…"

"How do you know if I was or not?" I snapped.

"I am not stupid, Alice." He replied calmly. "You did not have the power you have now, anyone can see that. If the same thing were to happen today I don't doubt that it would end very differently. But you need to realise the power you have and stop allowing people to have control over you."

"What does that mean?" I asked.

He smiled again, "Think on it. Figure it out."

Thirty-Seven

ALICE

The following day Rette announced we were going to go on a hunt. Apparently he wanted to treat me to a days' entertainment and this was the best he could come up with. I'd smiled and acted like I was honoured when in reality, the thought of chasing down some poor animal was far from my idea of fun.

King Rette's hunting grounds were thankfully not far from the palace. I stuck close to Guillaume as we rode through the woods and was more than a little thankful when the stag we were chasing got away before anyone could kill it, not that I voiced that opinion out loud. The King's men spent a whole hour trying to corner the poor beast but, right at the last minute, it had jumped free of their trap and made a successful bid for freedom.

King Rette then called the whole hunt off and had food put out for everyone to enjoy as if this sort of thing was a regular occurrence.

I was careful to look happy, to be enjoying it, and though I was, a part of me was thinking about the other Fae still stuck out a few hours ride from where we were, literally waiting on our return.

And a part of me was thinking of Fain too. God only knew how far we were from Temoor and, after the way I'd left, the need to return felt like it was becoming unbearable.

I picked at my food, not overly bothered about eating despite my hunger. King Rette watched me with that amused look on his face that I was starting to expect.

"What's so funny?" I asked him after a moment and he shook his head.

"I thought you didn't like King Callin, but you don't seem to mind his ledenberries."

"I'm not going to not eat these because of my opinion on King Callin. Besides, I like King Callin now." I replied.

"But he put you in an iron cage, did he not?"

"Yes..."

"So, you've forgiven him then?" He teased.

"For the cage yes, not so much for the dresses he forced me to wear." I stated and he laughed more.

"King Callin's lands are hot, and their women like to make the most of it."

"Well, where we were was not hot, so there was no excuse."

He smirked before looking across at Guillaume who was seated like yesterday, just down from me but too far to easily converse with. He was sat in silence, eating his food as if he was intentionally ignoring everyone.

"Your bodyguard is quiet, isn't he?"

I shook my head. "Do I have to say it again?"

He laughed. "No. Although I'm starting to think he might be your advisor more than your protection."

"What makes you say that?"

"The communication thing you both do. The weird talking without talking."

"It's not that weird. I do it with Prince Fain too." I said before I'd stopped to think and I screwed my face up at the potential stupidity of that admittance.

"Interesting." King Rette replied taking in my reaction. "Why are you hiding it if it is not so weird then?"

"I'm not hiding it. It's just complicated."

"Sure it is." He replied before taking a bite of his apple and giving me a smug look.

"I did want to show you more of my kingdom." He said deliberately changing the subject. "But there is nowhere we can properly ride to in the short timeframe you've allowed me."

"Perhaps another time then." I murmured.

"Are you threatening to come back to my lands?"

I let out a laugh. "Only if the High King permits it."

"And what about me? What if I don't?"

I shrugged, like his opinion didn't even matter. "The High King out ranks you and you said it yourself, I'm Fae, so you can't stop me."

He grinned more before take another bite but we both looked around at the sound of horses. At the sound of someone riding fast in our direction.

Rette frowned, getting to his feet and walking away from me as four riders approached. One practically jumped from his horse before bowing to the King and whispered quickly in his ear. He narrowed his eyes at the man's words before he glanced back at me with a look on his face that I couldn't read.

As I watched them I knew something was up. Something had happened. It felt like my gut suddenly twisted. Was it the other Fae? Had something happened to them despite their promises? Was it Atran? Had he escaped? Had more Magars found them?

King Rette beckoned me to him and I got up, walking as calmly as I could. "What's happened?" I asked as soon as I was in front of him.

"We need to return to the palace. I'm sad to say our time together has come to an end."

"Why?"

"There is someone there who wishes to see you."

"Who?" I asked confused. Who even knew where I was right now? I doubted even Jelric did, despite his vast network of spies.

"It will make sense when we are back." He replied before nodding to the servants to start packing up.

Rette took my arm, steering me to where the horses were, while Guillaume rushed to catch up with us.

His main guard sprung up around us, though in that moment I couldn't tell if it was less about protecting their King and more about keeping me subdued.

I didn't speak but I kept glancing at the King who was making a point now of not looking at me once.

WE RUSHED THROUGH THE CORRIDORS, ME FOLLOWING RIGHT BEHIND the King but keeping pace with his steps. He stopped in front of the closed double doors to the same room he had first met me in and he turned to face me.

I frowned, tensing at his strange expression.

"I am sorry, Alice. I have been misleading you somewhat." He said quietly.

I gritted my teeth. "What are you talking about?" I asked him feeling my stomach start to twist. Was this some trap after all? Was this all some ploy that I'd walked right into? The fact that Guillaume was here, right beside me gave me some comfort but not much. If he planned this right he could have us very easily bound in iron and locked in his dungeons.

"Please understand I had my reasons for it." He said and then he pushed the doors open.

I braced myself for whatever horror this was, whatever fight I now had to face and I looked from him to the figure stood obviously waiting for me.

My jaw dropped. I blinked, feeling like my eyes were playing tricks. "What are you doing here?" I asked.

Nela half ran to me, throwing her arms around me in an embrace that squeezed the air from my lungs. "Where have you been? I've been looking for you everywhere." She half-hissed.

"Why, what's happened?" I replied, looking from Nela to the King who was just stood there, hands by his side, placid and yet clearly on edge. "What's going on?"

"What does she know, your Highness?" Nela asked King Rette.

He shook his head slightly. "She knows nothing. I have told her nothing." He stated.

"Told me what?" I asked raising my voice.

Nela sighed. "The High King has been poisoned."

My eyes widened. "What? How?"

"They don't know."

"Is he okay?" I asked.

"No. They don't know what the poison is so they cannot treat him." She stated.

I screwed my face up at that. It made no sense. "What does that mean?" I asked looking from Nela to the King. Both gave me a look I didn't like. "They must be able to do something. Surely Jelric can do something."

"That's not all…." Nela said quietly.

I gritted my teeth ready for whatever else Nela was about to say.

"High Prince Rillon is back."

"What?" I gasped, feeling like I must have misheard her. That there must be some mistake. How was that even possible?

"As in the one that tried to…" Guillaume started to say before he glanced at King Rette.

"Yes." Both Nela and I replied almost at the same time while King Rette frowned.

"Tried to what?" He asked looking between us.

I shut my eyes and stepped away, suddenly needing space to breathe. Space to think too. What the hell was going on? How was he back? How had he somehow escaped his banishment? Had the Council just welcomed him back because Uther was indisposed? Why would Fain have let that happen?

"What did he do?" King Rette asked me again.

I turned my head, stared back at him, for once not feeling the shame but the anger about what had happened. "He was like Yannis." I said quietly. "Exactly like Yannis."

"There's more…" Nela stated.

"What more?" God, what else could possible have happened? Surely we hadn't been gone that long?

"Rillon has declared himself Regent. He has taken the city with the help of King Ide and half the Council and he has Prince Fain locked in the dungeons on a charge of treason."

"What?" I snapped before turning to look at the King again. "You knew about this?"

"I did."

"And you said nothing?" I hissed.

"I had my reasons."

"What reasons?" I demanded. What could possibly justify him keeping that from me?

"Prince Rillon claims you and the Prince conspired together to poison the High King and steal his crown." He stated.

"What? That's absurd. Why would we have?"

"Who doesn't want to be High King?" King Rette asked watching my face that same way he had since I'd arrived. Studying it for my reaction, only know I knew why.

I shook my head disgusted. "Have you learnt nothing about me over the last day?"

"That's why I kept quiet." He murmured. "I wanted to see what you did and didn't know. To judge if you were guilty of what they said or not."

"You shit." I replied before I could stop myself and Nela gasped in shock, looking at King Rette as if she feared he might lock me in chains but in that moment I didn't care. All I could think was that Fain was in danger. Fain was in trouble and this man had kept that from me. "You knew. You knew the High King was in danger. You knew they had Prince Fain locked up. How could you say nothing?"

"I had to see for myself. I heard what Prince Rillon was saying. He sent an envoy here. He has declared himself High King in all but name. But I had to be sure before I acted.

"Sure of what exactly?" I snapped.

"That you weren't involved."

"How could I have been? I have been here, in your Kingdom this whole time."

He tilted his head, sighing. "I know that. But it would have been an easy cover."

"You really believe I would have poisoned him? Poisoned the High King?" I persisted.

"No. I said I wanted to get the measure of you. To see the real Alice and I wasn't lying about that. I knew what everyone said about you. About your beauty, about your powers, and I listened when Rillon's envoys came to tell me what you had supposedly done but I didn't make my mind up until after we had spoken at dinner."

I drew in a deep breath, closing the distance between us. "And what did you decide?" I asked not caring how my tone sounded, not caring if I offended him.

"What do you think?" He snapped back. "I told you before I was loyal to the High King. That hasn't changed. I told you I wanted to see beyond the lies, beyond the rumours about you and that hasn't changed."

"Fine. So, you believe me or not?"

"Of course I believe you." He replied.

I gulped, blinked, stepped back as it sunk in that for once someone was on my side. I turned to Nela who was stood watching us both like she didn't know what to do. "I have to help him. I have to help Fain."

"There's nothing we can do. Rillon has the whole city locked down." She stated.

"I'm not going to leave him there. Not in Rillon's hands. He hates him. He's always hated him."

Nela shook her head.

"I have to try." I said. "If you can get me in I can get us out."

"You want to risk it?" King Rette asked breaking between the two of us. "If you try to save him it will only look like you are the conspirators Rillon is portraying you as."

"I don't care what it looks like." I half cried. "I don't care what anyone thinks. I'm not leaving him there."

"You really do love him, don't you?" Rette murmured.

I narrowed my eyes, staring him down once more. "Did you think that was a lie too?" I asked him coldly and he smirked.

"Not anymore."

"If you're as loyal as you say you are then you have to help."

"Alice…" Nela said quietly but I ignored her. I knew I could push him now and I knew I had to.

"What are you suggesting I do?" He asked, ignoring Nela as well.

"Go to Nind. The Crown Prince is there. If Rillon has taken the throne then Prince Hal needs to be protected."

His eyebrows rose. "You want me to start a war with Prince Rillon?"

"No. If he is simply acting as Regent then you are simply protecting the heir to the throne. There is no issue. You are an ally to the High King. There is no war." I shrugged.

His lips curled at my words. "I think too many people have underestimated you." He said quietly.

"If they have then that's their mistake."

He nodded back at me. "It will be." He said.

I didn't know how to respond to that so instead I turned to look at Guillaume.

His face was one I'd seen only too often and I knew what he was going to say. Those same old lines about not having to always be fighting these battles. That Prince Fain wouldn't risk himself for me. And yet he had. When we'd left Temoor that's exactly what he'd done, he'd stood up to Uther, he'd shouted at him about my freedom.

"I have to go." I said before he could speak.

"I know."

I paused, surprised by his tone. "You're not going to try to persuade me otherwise?"

He shook his head. "What would be the point? Besides, he's your mate. Of course you would do everything you could to save him."

"My what?" I replied.

He glanced behind me, no doubt to where Nela and Rette were stood, able to hear every word.

"He's your mate." He said. "That's why you have this bond between you. That's why you were able to make him half-Fae in the first place."

I frowned, shaking my head slightly. What the hell was he talking about?

"Go," He said. "When you come back I'll explain it. I'll explain everything."

"So, you knew?" I gasped, my confusion turning to anger now.

He drew in a deep breath, placing his hands on my shoulders. "Be angry with me by all means. But right now, there are more important issues at hand."

I nodded, knowing he was right and turned to face the King once more. "Guillaume needs to return to the other Fae."

"I will have my men escort him." He replied glancing between us.

"What other Fae?" Nela asked.

"It's a long story. I'll explain on the road." I said quietly.

"I'll have horses and provisions readied for you both." Rette said.

I inclined my head. "Thank you, King Rette."

"Be careful, Alice." Rette warned. "King Ide is no fool. There will be spies everywhere. They'll be looking for you."

"I know how to hide and I can protect us both." I stated.

"In that case, I'll see you at Nind." He murmured, bowing to me before motioning his arm towards the door.

Thirty-Eight

ALICE

We rode out of the city and away as fast as our horses would carry us. I was back in my Fae armour but I kept my cloak around me, with my hood up, and my eyes ahead, as if I expected an ambush at every turn.

We made camp only when Nela forced us to stop and even then I grumbled about it.

"You can't ride all night." Nela said as she passed me some food.

"I can." I huffed.

"Well, the horses can't. If you tire them too much they'll be no good if we need to make a quick exit out of Temoor."

I gritted my teeth, knowing she was right but it didn't make it any easier. I wanted to be there now, hell I would ride the horses the whole way and not care about the consequences if it meant I would get to Fain quicker.

He was my mate. My mate.

I still didn't fully understand what those words meant but every time that word echoed in my head our bond seemed to stir. Seemed to repeat it like a song. I guess if I'd known more about Fae Lore, if I'd understood myself and my magic better, then all of this would have made more sense.

But it was too late for regrets, too late for anything.

I shoved a mouthful of food in, trying not to think about what was happening to Fain at that very moment. I wouldn't have put it past Rillon to have hurt him, to have tortured him even and I mentally tried to come to terms with that. That right now he could be in pain, he could be injured and I couldn't do anything to stop it.

"Who are the other Fae?" Nela asked.

I blinked, coming out of my head. "They were in hiding but the Magars found them and had them all collared. Guillaume and I went to rescue them."

"How many?"

I shrugged. "Over a thousand."

Her eyes widened. "A thousand?"

"It's a Fae army." I jested with a wry smile.

"And Uther wanted you to bring them back to him?" She guessed.

I winced. "Not exactly. We argued about it. He let me go but I don't think he wanted anyone to know where I was headed in case I came back empty handed and it made him look weak."

Nela nodded and let out a deep sigh.

"What?" I asked.

"It just explains it. All the secrecy."

"What secrecy?"

"The High King told the Council he'd sent you off on a mission but not what it was. They didn't like being kept in the dark. And because no one knew where you were, Rillon used it to convince everyone that you must have been behind the poisoning and that you had someone made Prince Fain disloyal."

I scowled at her words. "How could they believe him? After everything he has done and everything I have done?"

"They didn't. No one does. But Rillon has King Ide and his cronies backing him. They have taken the city with force and most of the Council is under guard and can't do anything to fight him."

"What of Jelric? No one's even mentioned him." I said.

"I don't know but I suspect they've bound him with iron. He's too much of a threat to Rillon not to."

I ran my hands over my face, sighing. "I can't believe he has managed all this."

"He's clearly been planning it for quite some time."

I knew she was right. He had to be. And so did Ide. God, what I would do to them when I got my hands on them both.

"So, are you bringing the Fae to the High King?"

"Yes. But it's complicated…" I began.

"How?"

"I'm not bringing them back to merely become slaves, to become more weapons for his precious war." I half growled.

"Then what are you doing?"

I grinned, feeling like speaking these words, confirming them made it more real. "We're claiming our freedom." I said. "All of us, together. We are going to make him and the Council recognise us and grant us protections under the laws of this land."

She blinked at me for a second. "Were." She said quietly.

"Excuse me?"

"You were going to claim your freedom from Uther. But Uther is dead, or as good as. He cannot grant that to you now."

I paused, gulping, wondering how true that was. How much this turn of events changed things.

Had Guillaume realised this too?

Was he already telling the other Fae what had happened, and worse, were they even now deciding that this whole saga had been a mistake, that it would be better for them to turn around now and flee back to the secrecy of the Fae realm?

Would Guillaume even return to Temoor or would he leave too? I guess I couldn't blame him if he did. He'd more than paid the price for agreeing to teach me.

"How did you find out what was happening?" I asked. As far as I knew Nela was meant to be far away, training.

"Jelric managed to get a messenger to me and warn me what was happening after Rillon shut the Council down."

"But you haven't heard anything since?"

"No." She confirmed. "But I also made sure no one could find me. Everyone knows I'm loyal to Fain, I doubt they'd let me walk around free."

"You think they've put a price on your head?"

She shrugged. "Wouldn't you if you were them?"

I grunted back. Yeah, I would do exactly that. I'd eliminate every threat there was including Prince Hal and Cait too. Though I didn't voice those fears.

"Tell me, did you finish your training? Are you a General now?" I asked trying to distract myself.

"Yes but technically I'm not a General until the High King's Commander awards it." Nela said.

"So, we have to save him for you too then." I stated.

Nela smirked slightly. "When you put it like that…" She half muttered, staring at the flames.

Three days. Three days of hard riding and little rest. Even I felt sorry for the poor horses when we got close to the city.

"We should probably leave the horses here." Nela said as we stopped in a small copse.

"We're that close?" I murmured peering out.

"Not exactly but they'll be on the look-out and two riders will be easier to spot than two people on foot."

"By foot will be too slow." I stated.

"Alice, we have to be strategic." Nela pointed out.

"And we have to be fast." I replied.

"So quit arguing and get off your horse." Nela said.

I rolled my eyes but reluctantly did as I was told. As we tethered them to a tree I placed a charm around them to conceal them from any view.

"You sure you'll be able to find them on the way back?" Nela asked and I nodded.

"Yes. I've put a tie to the magic. It'll be easy for me to find them but no one else will be able to feel it."

She stared at me for a second. "What the hell has happened to you since I left?"

"What do you mean?"

"Your magic, even the way you're carrying yourself."

"I don't know what you mean."

"It's like you've grown up." She stated. "Like you've grown into your powers."

"Thanks?" I replied laughing as we quietly started making our way out. We had a good few hours of walking ahead of us and that was all with the hope no one realised we were coming.

"Have you tried healing anyone else?" Nela asked.

"No. The Healers don't think I can. They think it's just me I can heal."

"Well, that sounds very selfish of you."

I laughed. God I'd missed Nela. When it was all over there was no way I was letting Fain send her anywhere again.

From behind us we heard a twig snap and both froze. Nela turned her head in the direction of the noise while we waited to see if it was anything more than just wild animals.

Another twig snapped. A bigger one. We tensed, looking at each other.

Nela pulled her sword silently out of its sheath and I pulled my magic, ready to attack should I need to.

"What do we have here?" Someone said behind us.

We both jumped, turning as a soldier stood eyeing us up. More footsteps shuffled around us and as we looked we could see the soldiers circling us from all sides. I stared at the sigil on their armour. A boar on a white shield. I knew I'd never seen it before.

"Who's men are you?" I asked taking a step towards them.

"Not so fast." The man closest to me said pulling his sword, pointing it in my direction like it was an actual threat.

"I said who's men are you?" I repeated louder.

"The High King's." He replied.

"And which High King is that?" I asked because the sigil they had sure as hell wasn't Uther's.

"The only High King that matters." He replied with a smirk. "High King Rillon."

I narrowed my eyes, letting the magic spark from my fingers. "There is no such King." I snapped just as Nela aimed the sword.

I swung my arms, sending a blast of light through the air, knocking every soldier except the main one to the ground. Nela's blade swung past me and took care of the final man and he cried out as it buried itself in his chest.

"What did you do to them?" Nela asked.

"I knocked them unconscious." I replied grabbing my shield and chucking it over my shoulder so that it protected my back.

Nela eyed the bodies for a second before she moved to untie the horses. "We need to move." She stated. "There'll be more of them on their way."

"I thought you said we had to go on foot?"

"We don't have much choice now do we?" Nela replied.

I sighed, realising this entire plan was now going to shit. The sun wasn't even close to setting and I doubted we'd get within a hundred yards of the city walls before someone spotted us. Unless...I frowned, looking up at the sky,

"Do you ever get eclipses here?" I asked.

Nela frowned at the strange word. "What is that?"

"When the moon covers the sun." I explained.

She shrugged. "Not often. Every ten years of so maybe but everyone gets really funny about it, even the Magi do. It's not a good sign."

I smirked. "Perfect." I said, pulling my magic to me and mentally stretching out as far as I could.

Nela screwed her face up in confusion as she watched me but I did my best to ignore her. To focus solely on the task ahead.

All around the world suddenly shook, as though the very air was being moulded, changed. I opened my eyes staring up at the sun even though I knew I shouldn't. I could feel it, feel the world around us changing and bit by bit a dark slither started to cover the brightness.

Nela gasped beside me.

The air started to cool. The lightness started to fade. The birds stopped singing and it felt like an eery silence was all around.

"Fucking hell." Nela spluttered. "How the hell did you do that?"

I grinned back at her. "You said my magic had grown…"

"I didn't mean that much."

"Come on. They'll know we're here now. Let's not keep them waiting."

"You sure you want to do this still?"

I looked back at her with what I hoped was a look of determination. "I'm not walking away now."

We kicked the horses into a gallop, riding down to the city as fast as we could. It wasn't like it mattered now because the sky was so dark it was hard to see anything.

We skirted around the city walls and I couldn't help but glance up looking at the soldiers on the walls but it was like we were invisible now.

We dismounted and secured the horses before Nela led me up the rickety path.

"I didn't expect it to be this bad." I muttered.

"It's worse when you're trying to escape down it." Nela warned.

"That's definitely noted for later." I replied.

We snuck in through the tiny passageway that linked into the Upper Castle. If Fain was in the dungeons then we had to make it across half the damn building before we'd even get to him.

As I walked, I adjusted the hood covering my head. Sure, they knew I was there but that didn't mean I needed to make it easy for them.

We walked quietly, stealthily, through the corridors. The whole castle felt odd. Silent. As though Rillon had placed the entire city under a spell. I gritted my teeth and kept going but then something made me pause.

A whisper of magic. A murmur of something dark. Something twisted. I looked at Nela and she frowned back at me.

"What is it?" She whispered.

"I think it's dark magic." I replied.

"Are you sure?"

"Not exactly. It's strange. It doesn't feel right…"

"Do you know where it's coming from?" She asked.

I closed my eyes, trying to isolate it, to locate it and my stomach dropped when I realised. "The High King."

"What?"

"It's his rooms." I stated.

"The poison?"

I shrugged. "Could it be?"

"I'm not Jelric. I don't know."

"We need to get Fain and get out of here." I stated.

"You can't fight it?" She replied.

"Not like this. It's too risky." I didn't want to admit that the pattern, the feel of it felt like pure death. Pure destruction.

Nela nodded and we walked on, picking up pace, practically racing through the corridors now.

When we finally reached the dungeons I threw my magic out, using it to sense what was beyond the door.

"There are soldiers there." I whispered.

Nela nodded, pulling her sword but I held my hand out to make her stop.

"Let me. There's a whole garrison."

"You can take them out?"

"I'll only knock them out." I stated. "I don't want to kill them unnecessarily."

"They want to kill you, Alice." She pointed out, like I didn't know it.

"Then let's be the bigger people here." I said, hiding my true reason. "If we kill everyone we meet, we'll only be feeding into the lies that Rillon is spewing."

Nela nodded. "Fine. Do it your way." She replied moving aside so that I was in front and she was now protecting my back.

I closed my eyes, pulling my magic and blasted the doors off their hinges. I wanted to scare them. I wanted to show them all that I wasn't messing around.

The minute the door went down an arrow came shooting at me and I only just ducked in time to avoid it. As I narrowed my eyes another came at me, hitting the armour on my arm and bouncing right off.

I sent a wave of magic, watching as the entire room full of armed soldiers collapsed as if a tsunami had poured through them all.

"After you, General." I said holding my hand out and Nela rolled her eyes.

"What did you even need me for?" She muttered.

"That's not true. You know I couldn't have done this without you." I replied as we walked to the second, larger, more secure door.

"Sure. Keep telling yourself that." Nela muttered before I blew the second door of its hinges.

Another series of arrows came at us, at me. I snarled annoyed as one almost took my head off. In a flash, I quickly dealt with the second set of soldiers, and Nela gave me a smirk as we heard them thump to the floor.

But through the darkness I saw movement. I paused, tilting my head, and my eyes connected with his.

For a second it felt like the entire world stopped spinning.

It felt like everything stilled.

And that bond, that connection, it burnt fiercer, brighter, stronger than ever as I stared at the man, as I lost myself in the mesmerising eyes of my mate.

Thirty-Nine

FAIN

I was up the minute I'd felt her magic. The sky had darkened, I could see it from the tiny window of light that had shone into the cell. I frowned not understanding it but I knew she was behind it.

Then the soldiers had come.

I thought Rillon had sent them to kill me at first. And though I wouldn't have put it past him, Rillon wasn't smart enough for that. Wasn't tactical enough to think that far ahead. No doubt he'd figured that a few soldiers would be enough to stop Alice and I smiled, realising how little Rillon understood her power.

He still thought of her as the scared girl he had pinned down and attacked in the gardens when she had no control. But now she was so much stronger than that. Now, she was going to show him what she could do.

When the first door smashed off its hinges, I held my breath. The soldiers all shifted though, all reacted as if they already understood this wasn't a fight they could win.

When the second door smashed off its hinges, I stepped back, my eyes daring to believe that it was really her, that this was happening.

She sent her magic like a wave, sweeping them all off their feet. And then our eyes connected. That bond inside me whispered despite the iron still firmly wrapped around my wrist. Perhaps it was the human part that allowed it but I didn't care. I didn't stop to consider it. Everything in my head, in my body, all of me focused on her.

"This is a dream." I murmured.

She stepped up to me, staring through the bars that separated us.

"It's a bad one if you're in the dungeons." She stated.

"It's never a bad one when you are in it." I replied and she rolled her eyes before leaning through the bars and kissing me.

Gods, for a moment I lost myself. Forgot myself. I could have died here, right now, and I would have died happy just to have had this one last kiss.

"Alright love birds. We're in the middle of a prison break, remember?" A familiar voice said.

Alice laughed turning round to look behind her and I frowned. "Nela?"

"Who else could have helped her?" Nela replied.

I looked between them. "How…?" I began but Alice shook her head slightly.

"Step back." She ordered. "I'm going to break the door but I can't promise where it will fall."

I nodded, moving to the back wall of the cell, feeling that cold stone against my back.

The metal rang out as the lock broke and the whole thing swung open.

"Well, that was anticlimactic." Alice muttered more to herself before walking up to me. She took my hand, examining the darkened flesh. "They bound you with iron." She spat, and for the first time I truly understood her hatred of it.

"Can you get it off?" I asked.

She grinned at me. "Of course I can." She said almost as the damned metal snapped in half.

I gasped as that horrific grip on my insides suddenly eased. As the world returned to colour. As the magic I'd barely noticed inside me suddenly roared like a thing possessed.

I grabbed Alice then, pulling her into my arms, holding her tightly as though I needed to prove to my own body that she was real and that she was really there.

Reluctantly I let her go, reluctantly I let her slip away.

"We need to hurry." Nela stated.

"We need to find Rillon." I growled.

Alice shook her head. "Not today."

"I'm not leaving." I said.

"What are you talking about?" She asked him.

"Rillon did this. He poisoned my brother. He planned this entire thing."

"I know." She placed her hands back on my chest, calming me. "But you have to think tactically, we can't fight him and win today. We have to get out of here and regroup."

I opened my mouth to argue but she cut me off. "We have to get to Nind and to Prince Hal."

"What about Uther? We can't just leave him here." I persisted.

"He'll be under guard. We won't be able to get close." Nela stated glancing at Alice who nodded.

"We can't win today, Fain. If you want to save your brother then we have to leave and come back. It's the only way."

"We have to go. Now." Nela said and we both heard the urgency in her voice.

We rushed from the room but we only made it as far as the corridor before more soldiers swarmed us. Alice stepped forward and quickly knocked them out of the way and into a heap of bodies.

And I felt it, every twist of her magic, all the power of it, as it flowed from her. Gods, she was breathtaking.

She grinned back at me as if she could read my mind and Nela tutted at us once more.

When we reached the final corridor, the guards were hot on our heels. We climbed down those rickety steps as quickly as we could and as soon as our feet touched the ground, Alice pulled her magic collapsing the entire frame behind us and stopping anyone else from following.

The sky was still dark. The moon was still covering the sun and that eerie silence still hung around in the air. Nela climbed on her horse and I climbed on Alice's with her sitting behind me.

As we turned to ride away we heard the sounds of horses and knew that Rillon had sent more soldiers.

"I've got this." Alice said. "Ride and don't stop."

She wrapped her arms around my waist as I kicked the horse into a gallop. Beside me Nela's horse kept neck and neck with mine.

I wrapped an arm around Alice's, holding her in place. I didn't know what she was going to do but I felt the magic, felt the pull of it and the way the earth shuddered.

A wall of dirt shot up behind us.

The guards yelled out in surprise.

But we didn't stop. We just kept going, kept galloping onwards, while that wall kept what felt like the entire world from off our backs.

Forty

RILLON

The chair shattered to pieces as I threw it against the wall. "How is this possible?" I asked turning to look at the soldiers stood uselessly in the doorway.

"We couldn't fight her. Her magic was too strong."

I shook my head at the bullshit. "I gave you enough men. I gave you more than you asked for…"

"And she beat them."

"She is one girl." I yelled. "Yannis had her beaten and on her knees surrendering to him." Hell, I had her pined against the ground, way before that.

"Your Highness…" A soldier rushed in and bowed quickly. His face flitting from panic to something else entirely.

"What now?" I half shouted.

"They're rebelling…"

"Who are?"

"The people, they've broken the curfew. They're out in streets…"

"What?" I snarled turning rushing out to the balcony, staring below at what looked like a hoard of people. All out. All where they had no permission to be. "What is this?" I muttered.

"The girl saved this city." Highflynn said beside me. "I warned you if she came back, they wouldn't just let it go."

I narrowed my eyes, feeling that hate and that bitterness swirl inside me. "How are they loyal to her over me?" I asked, not that I wanted an answer. Not that I needed one. I would make them loyal. I would beat it into their very flesh if that's what it took. "Shut it down." I ordered. "Kill them if you have too. This is my city. If I cannot have their loyalty then their fear will be enough."

As the soldiers dashed from the room, my eyes fell on him. He was leaning against the desk all but smirking as he watched me. Sure, he'd been the architect of all of this, he'd been the one to spring me from my shithole of a prison, but I was still the High Prince, no, I was more than that now, I was High King in all but name and this man had the audacity to stand before me, as if I were still in chains.

"What do you want?" I snapped before I could stop myself.

He shrugged lazily back at me. "I have no needs at present."

"You have nothing to say about the girl?"

"What would you have me say?" He replied, as those eyes of his glowed. "I told you she would come, I told you to be prepared for it and you failed."

I snarled. "I didn't fail."

"Then she is in your dungeons now, is she?" He asked so coldly I couldn't stop the shiver that ran through me. "She is collared and chained as you promised me?"

I shook my head slightly.

"No. She is gone. And Prince Fain with her." He stated. "You failed. Admit it."

"I DIDN'T FAIL." I yelled, grabbing the nearest thing to me and lobbed it as hard as I could against the wall.

He didn't move. Didn't react. Just continued to sneer at me. "I gave you your chance, Rillon." He said.

"You will use my title." I spat.

"It makes no difference to me. Your human titles are a concept lesser men make to validate themselves because they have no real power."

"I have power." I stated, clenching my fists. I was the High King now. I had more power than anyone else in this cursed land.

He laughed then. "A man who has power does not need to state it."

I narrowed my eyes, sick of his bullshit. Somehow I'd have to work out how to rid myself of him when the time came. "What do you want?"

"As I said, I gave you your chance. When they return, I will deal with the girl."

"She is mine." I stated taking a step towards him. "It was part of our agreement."

"And yet she slipped through your grubby fingers just like the last time…"

"She will be mine." I clenched my fists.

"Then leave her to me." He said getting up to go.

"If you let me down…" I warned.

He threw his head back and laughed. "Do not presume to threaten me, boy. I put you where you are and I can just as easily remove you."

I scowled, knowing he was right. Deep down I knew it. For all the power I had, this man had more, this man could destroy me with barely a moment of thought, but what choice did I have? I needed the throne, hell, I deserved it, and I deserved the girl too.

And this man would ensure I had both those things.

I just had to play this game carefully. Watch my moves. And when everything was within my grasp I could rid myself of this inconvenience too.

Forty-One

FAIN

We stopped only when we felt we'd gotten far enough away. And even then it was only for a few hours rest. I didn't know how long that wall Alice created could last but I hoped that even now it was there, protecting us, shielding us.

Nela set about making a small fire while Alice walked the perimeter, creating a shield to hide us.

My skin tingled with the feel of her magic. My heart seemed to dance at the taste of it. As if being bound by the iron and now free had suddenly changed something inside me. Had ignited the magic Alice had given me.

And all the while I sat there, clenching and unclenching my fists. Trying to make sense of it all. Of how any of this could have happened.

"What are you thinking about?" Alice asked quietly, moving to sit beside me.

"My brother." I replied.

"Which one?"

"The one that matters." I stated lifting my eyes from the dirt, looking at her.

"I'm sorry." She said.

"For what?"

"For not being there. For leaving."

I shook my head. "You didn't know what was going to happen. And you had to help the Fae."

"I'm still sorry though."

I gave her a small smile, taking her hand, relishing the feel of just her skin against mine.

"What happened?" She asked. "How did you end up in the dungeons like that?"

I winced. "Uther and I were talking. And then he collapsed. Cait…" I trailed off remembering that look on her face, those words.

"What about Cait?"

"She was the one who had me arrested." I stated. "It all happened so fast."

"What?" She gasped. "Why would Cait think you'd do anything to harm your brother?"

I shook my head because the only logical conclusion made no sense. There was no way Cait was working with Rillon, conspiring with him. What would she have to gain from it? She was already married to Uther, to the man she loved, why would she turn on him? I knew they had their moments. I knew they argued but not enough for her to want him dead.

Alice sat there like she knew I needed space to think. She didn't speak. She just let her presence alone be a comfort. Across from us Nela set about roasting a rabbit she must have caught while I'd been lost in my own head.

I lifted my hand to stroke her face and her eyes fluttered shut at my touch. "Tell me about the Fae. What happened with them?" I murmured.

"Oh." Alice said before biting her lip, clearly hesitating.

"What?"

"Well, it was the Magars. They collared them. Collared them all."

"How many?"

"Just over a thousand." She said as if it were nothing.

My jaw dropped. "A thousand Fae?" I repeated shocked. Where on earth had such a mass been hiding? My stomach twisted as I realised the Magars now had this power at their disposal.

"It gets better..." She smirked. "Guillaume and I found the survivors and we managed to track down the ones they took..."

I watched as she explained what had happened, seeing her face change with emotion as she mentioned the collaring and some arsehole Magi she now had captive.

"How did you break it? Your collar?" I asked.

"I twisted the magic around and turned it on itself. In my head it made sense though I imagine it might blow Jelric's mind when I try to explain it to him."

I laughed. "When it comes to you, every bit of magic you do blows his mind."

Nela passed us both some meat and we all started eating in silence. My stomach growled in appreciation and I tried not to think about the last decent meal I'd had. The guards had given me stale bread once a day, and I'd had to pick the mouldy bits off it.

"Has Alice told you her grand plan?" Nela said.

"What plan?" I asked seeing the way Alice winced at her words.

"It might not happen now." She murmured. "Not now your brother is..." She trailed off as if she didn't want to say the word we were all thinking.

"Tell me." I replied.

She huffed, throwing Nela a look she deliberately chose to ignore it.

"The Fae wish to return with me. Or at least they did."

"What?"

She jerked her head in defiance. "I was going to force Uther to grant us all our freedom."

My eyebrows rose, I glanced from her to Nela to see if this was some sort of joke but clearly it wasn't.

"I don't want to argue with you." She said quietly. "Not with everything going on right now."

"I'm not going to." I replied. "But if you want to do it, if you want to fight, then I will stand beside you."

She nodded, "Seems like a moot point considering."

"We don't know that yet." I said taking her hand.

"We should probably talk about you too, about your powers."

I nodded. Now that that iron was gone I could feel it more than ever, simmering under my skin, almost desperate to be let out. "Not tonight." I said. "Tonight we should just rest."

She pulled a face like she wanted to argue with me but then clearly thought better. "Fine. But once we get to Nind we're having this discussion."

"Nind?" I repeated confused. "Why would be going to Nind?"

Her lips curled. "Did you really think I would leave Hal unprotected?"

"Ridley is there." I stated. "Ridley is meant to protect him."

She shook her head. "You know as well as I, Rillon will go after Hal. He has to. It's the only way he can rule."

She was right. I knew it. Logically, I knew that was the case. But the thought of Hal injured, of him dead. That memory of him back at Heatherly, of me storming that castle, fearing the worst, convinced that they'd butchered him in his bed.

"So who is there?"

"King Rette."

My eyes widened. "What?"

"I told him to go. To protect the Prince."

"How, when did you meet him?" Rette was one of the few Lesser Kings that I actually trusted. Besides Callin, I wasn't sure any of them were safe around Alice.

She shrugged taking another bite of the rabbit leg in her hand. "We had to cross his lands to get the Fae. So I made sure he played his part."

I shook my head, half mesmerised by the way she said it, the way she acted like what she'd done was nothing.

She gave me a quizzical look, her lips hinting at a smile. "What?"

"You never cease to amaze me." I said almost breathless.

"Stop it, Prince Fain." She replied but she let me pull her in and hug her anyways.

Gods, to feel her, to feel her warmth, her strength, just her. That bond between us soared, my heart thumped like it had never known joy until this moment. I stared down at her face, completely, utterly enraptured by her.

"We should get some rest. We need to be moving in a few hours if we want to stand a chance of making it to Nind before Rillon's henchmen catch up with us." Nela stated.

"Since when do you make the decisions, Nela?" I joked, tearing my eyes from the beauty in my arms.

"Since you made me a General." She quipped and we all laughed.

We curled up, Nela pointedly the other side of the fire from us and Alice close to me, but not as close as I'd like. When I pointed it out, she murmured about not wanting to make it weird for Nela who said loudly that that ship had already sailed.

We'd put out the fire. The night was cool but thankfully not cold.

I lay there, my head spinning. My thoughts relentless. Now that the iron was gone it felt like a fog had lifted, that my mind had cleared and I could finally think straight.

"I get it." I said quietly.

"Get what?" Alice whispered.

"The iron. What it does."

She blinked at me through the darkness. "Your magic is growing, Fain. We have to get it under control. No more pretending it isn't."

My lips curled up. "Just like you did?"

She nodded. "If you can use it, then you can fight."

"I like my sword thank you very much." I stated.

"You'll like magic better." She promised. "And you'll find it's far more effective than a mere blade."

I wanted to scoff, to dismiss that comment but I knew it was true. If I could fight with magic I would be so much more of a warrior than I was right now.

"Sleep, Prince Fain." She whispered. "Tomorrow will be a long day."

Yeah it would. And so would all the days after because something told me this nightmare was not going to end anytime soon.

Forty-Two

ALICE

We got up before the sun. Rode as far as our poor horses could go before we sought rest. Day after day. Night after night. We pushed further onwards.

Only once did we encounter any soldiers on the road. They tried to ambush us but before either Nela or I could register the attack Fain destroyed them with his magic.

No, not destroyed them. Obliterated them.

I'd gulped and exchanged a look with Nela but neither of us said anything.

Fain and I still shared one horse. I rode up front, almost in his lap and the proximity was not lost on me. Not for a second. Every dip in the track, every move the horse made caused my body to shift against his. Could he feel it? Was it affecting him the way it did me? He certainly wasn't showing it if it was.

And all I could think about, all my mind kept focusing on was that we were mates. Mates.

I made up my mind to find out what that meant because clearly my magic understood it. Even Fain's magic understood it.

"Where did you get that armour?" Fain asked quietly as we made our way down what looked like an almost familiar track. But then every track looked familiar.

"It's Fae armour." I said. "I got it back where the Fae were hiding. There was a whole armoury full of it."

"Is it magic?"

"Sort of. It will protect me from attack but only where the leather is."

He nodded before running his hand across my thigh and, while my heart skipped at the contact, I told myself not to show it, not to react.

"I like it on you." He murmured into my ear and I rolled my eyes, forced myself to focus on the path ahead, fighting the heat that suddenly burnt in me. That practically exploded.

But as I stared I realised suddenly that I did know the road, I knew the landscape too. We were almost at Nind.

I let out a sigh, one of relief. We had made it. We could rest now. Plan. Figure out a counterattack and a way to stop Rillon.

And more importantly we would know for certain that Hal was safe.

Fain looked at me, with a knowing grin on his face. "We're almost back…" He half whispered in my ear as if it were some sort of promise of love.

"To Nind." I said. Trying not to fidget, not to rub my body against his.

"Do you remember the last time?" He asked me quietly.

"The spectral?"

"No, the rest…" He said.

My face flushed, a vision of us, of everything we had done last time we were hear flashed in my head. How had I not even thought of that?

"Urgh." Nela muttered.

I burst out laughing and as Fain joined in, it broke whatever spell seemed to have befallen us.

"I'm sorry, Nela." I said meaning it. I didn't want to make her feel uncomfortable. "It's Fain's fault."

"Well, thank the Gods we're here because now I can get a little space from you too."

I smirked catching Fain's eye before forcing myself to look ahead once more.

I could see the soldiers now. Hundreds of them. They'd set up some sort of blockade and as we approached I felt Fain tensing, no doubt expecting this to turn into another fight. But when they saw us, they all seemed to fall over themselves to get out of our way.

"Apparently we've been expected." Nela said.

"Apparently so." I replied as we kicked our horses on for the final few yards.

Once we reached the castle, all we could see were more soldiers, tents, what looked like utter carnage. I stared in disbelief but my mind registered the different sigils.

"Can you see what I see?" Nela murmured.

"Yes." Fain said before I could.

It wasn't just Rette's army here. No, what looked like half the High King's army were amongst them. And as I stared more I saw the unmistakable sigil of King Callin too.

"They've all made a beeline for here." I whispered.

"This is good." Fain said in my ear. "This is very good."

I didn't need him to confirm it but the fact he did made me relax more. If we had numbers, if we had two Lesser Kings on our side then perhaps we stood more of a chance of beating Rillon.

We dismounted quickly, ensuring our poor horses got the rest they deserved.

As I walked beside Fain I stared up at the battered walls of castle. Gone was the pure white stone. Gone was the majesty.

It was encircled by trebuchets. And even now the soldiers were slinging rocks at it. Each one pounded the stone, shaking the very earth beneath us.

How it was still standing I had no idea.

My eyes fell on what was undoubtedly the command tent and inside, bent over a table was King Rette himself. He looked up, met my scowl with a smirk and then his eyes cast behind me to where I knew Fain was following.

"You." I said, pointing my finger. "You destroyed my castle."

Rette rolled his eyes. "Always so dramatic." He replied.

Fain looked between us like he couldn't quite tell what was going on.

"I asked you to protect the Crown Prince not smash the place in." I stated.

He sighed, nodding, and I saw it then, the weariness in his face. "Your plan was a little more complicated than you led me to believe, Alice."

I paused at those words. "How so?"

"Come. I'll explain." He said walking back in the direction of his tent and leaving us to follow.

The three of us walked in together and the few Generals that occupied the space fell silent. As I looked around I noted that Callin wasn't there. That Rette was the only king.

"What's going on?" Fain asked.

"The Castle is under siege, High Prince Fain." Rette replied.

"I can see that but why? I left Lord Ridley in charge."

"He is not anymore. Your brother sent King Ide to secure the castle for him and no doubt take the Crown Prince into his custody. We arrived just after the castle fell to Ide."

Shit. Shit. Shit. Shit.

If I'd thought about it sooner, if Rette had been quicker then Ide could have been smashed against the walls the way those rocks were currently being obliterated.

"So, Ide is in there?" I asked.

"Yes and Lord Ridley and Crown Prince Hal too."

All of them. Locked in that castle together. I clenched my fists walking to the entrance of the tent and stared up at the place Fain had offered me so long ago as a home.

"How long can it hold?" I murmured.

"I'm not sure." Rette replied. "They've already endured one siege so their supplies can't be great but it's hard to tell. They've certainly got enough soldiers in there to put up a good fight though."

"Have you seen Prince Hal?" Fain asked.

"No. We've seen no one except an envoy they sent out." Rette said in a tone that hinted at some insult he'd born.

"And what did they say?" Fain asked.

"Oh exactly what you'd expect." He said. "That they are there to keep the Crown Prince safe. That they are under the orders of High Prince Rillon etcetera."

Fain scowled before looking across at me. "Can you do anything?" He said quietly but they all heard it and I felt them watching me for a response.

I shrugged. "Maybe. I don't know where the Prince is, and Mira and Ridley are in there too. I don't want to do anything that might put them in danger."

He nodded turning back to the King. "If you agree, for the moment we should hold this position."

"I agree Prince Fain." Rette said.

"And the other soldiers, who are they reporting too?" Nela asked stepping forward from where she'd stood beside the other Generals.

"Me. Prince Frederic is here but he is taking my command. Prince Rillon has King Callin under guard, and there was no one to lead any of the High King's soldiers who fled Temoor..." King Rette stated.

Under guard? Callin was under guard? I gritted my teeth, forcing myself not to consider what might be happening to him. He was a Lesser King after all, perhaps Rillon might be more respectful of him considering his status.

"I will take command of them now, King Rette." Fain said.

Rette bowed his head before turning towards me. "And I assume you will take command of yours as well?" He asked.

I frowned, with no idea what he was talking about. And then it hit me. "They came?" I said half gasping. God, I'd thought they'd cut and run. I'd thought they'd turned and headed for safety now that our plan had fallen apart.

"Your bodyguard brought them for you." King Rette replied I laughed at that same old jest.

"Bodyguard?" Fain repeated.

"Guillaume brought the rest of the Fae." I explained seeing his eyes widen as he realised what I was saying. That we had over a thousand Fae, right here, at our disposal.

"Where are they?" Fain asked Rette.

"In the woods. They weren't as keen to fully mingle with my soldiers yet, at least not all of them."

"I will go to them." I said before rushing out the tent, anxious to find them, anxious to prove to myself that this was real.

Forty-Three

FAIN

Rette stared back at me. No, scrutinised me. But I hadn't missed the bow he'd made to Alice, the gesture one would make to a royal, to a queen.

"Thank you, King Rette." I said after a moment.

"It's not me you need to thank." He said glancing out of the tent and then back to me. Hinting at what we both knew was true.

"Well, I thank you all the same."

He smiled. "She is very persuasive."

"She can be." I replied. "She's also incredibly stubborn too."

"I think I've seen that." King Rette said pouring two drinks and passing one to me. "I wasn't sure she was going to do it..."

"Do what?" I asked taking it from him.

"Get you out."

"She is stronger now, stronger even than I realised."

"I wouldn't want to go against her and I haven't even seen her use her magic." Rette replied before taking a sip of his drink.

"How are you here? I know she asked you but I don't understand how you two even came to meet." Sure, Alice had told me they'd been in his lands but that only felt like half the story.

"She and the other Fae were in my lands. Prince Rillon sent an envoy claiming you were both traitors. I wanted to see for myself before I simply handed her over to him."

"It's probably best you did." I stated. "She wouldn't have gone without a fight."

His expression told me he knew that to be true. "That wasn't the only reason if I'm honest Prince Fain."

I paused, narrowing my eyes. "What other reason did you have?"

"I have heard enough rumours about her to make me curious." He shrugged. "It's not every day you meet a Fae, at least not in my case, and after the audience with Yannis…"

That audience. Even now, even just the memory made my anger flash. I knew it wasn't her and yet the way she'd been, the way she'd stretched herself over Yannis. My magic flared. I felt the heat of it under my skin, right along my fingertips.

"You know that wasn't her, right?" I said.

"Yes. But I was still curious. Added to that were the rumours about the two of you…"

That put my back up more. I knew enough were talking. I knew Ide had spread as many lies as he could, twisting what we were, turning it into something dirty, something salacious. "Why did that matter to you?"

"I have known you for most of your life, Prince Fain in one way or another. I know how you feel about magic, about the Fae in general, and yet this girl managed to change all that, to win you over…" He shook his head. "I had to see it for myself."

I blinked, realising that his curiosity wasn't from that same malevolent place as everyone else's seemed to be. "It wasn't hard. I loved her from almost the moment I met her."

Rette smiled at my admission. "Well, I can't blame you for that, putting how she looks aside, she's definitely one of a kind."

I laughed. "Yes she is."

"And I know she is loyal to Uther." He added.

"What makes you say that?" I replied.

"I asked her. In my own way I was testing her, trying to see if she knew about the poisoning."

I tilted my head, curious myself to know how she'd convinced him. "What did she say?"

"Probably what you already know, she doesn't like being his possession..."

"I know that."

"But I think she feels safer with him than the Lesser Kings."

I felt my face harden. "She has not had it easy." I said.

"No, and I know we Lesser Kings are to blame for that, although it sounds like Prince Rillon was not so kind to her either."

I scowled then. "She told you?"

"She alluded to something but not what exactly."

"She is the reason he was banished." I stated not wanting to go into any more detail. It wasn't my secret to tell and she'd gone through enough of an ordeal when it had happened. I wasn't about to open up old wounds on top of the ones she was still dealing with from Yannis.

"I see." King Rette said before finishing his drink. "Well, I for one would support her being free. I think it's about time too."

"What?" I said shocked.

"Does it not make sense? She is loyal to the High King, she is no more of a threat to him than any of us kings, and less so seeing as she doesn't hold any lands."

"She has a Fae army now..." I said before I could stop myself.

Rette grinned. "Exactly Prince Fain. Don't you think that would be a useful tool for negotiation?"

"Uther is dying." I replied. "I doubt now is the time to..."

"Now is the perfect time." Rette cut across me. "Now, when the world is on fire. And I urge you to be ready. To make your move. Rillon may have the advantage at present but when the time comes, you need to make sure this ends favourably for her."

"That's exactly what I intend to do." I said, hearing the edge to my voice.

"Then we are agreed." He smiled. "However this plays out, Alice will get her freedom."

"The Fae will get their freedom." I replied, knowing that Alice would only be happy with that outcome. Would only truly settle for that.

Forty-Four

ALICE

I could smell the woody scent of the trees. The pollen of the first spring flowers as they scattered the ground. The last time I'd been here I'd been on death's door.

And Guillaume had saved me.

I paused, remembering that night, that pain, that fear.

I'd drawn the Fae to me, had beckoned them, and they'd answered as if they owed me their fealty. How strange it felt to be back here, and to be back with them too. It felt like a homecoming, despite the desperate circumstances.

Ahead I could see the tents, the people, all of them buzzing around. Amongst them I spotted Guillaume and made a beeline for him.

His eyes widened when he saw me.

"They came." I said, still almost not believing it.

"Of course they did." He replied. "You promised we'd get our freedom, remember?"

I tried not to wince. Was that even possible now? Could it even be done if the High King was dead?

"I take it you succeeded in getting Prince Fain out?" He asked.

I nodded, "Did you expect any other outcome?"

"Not from you." He replied.

I laughed back and then saw his face turn serious.

"Are you angry with me?" He asked.

"About the mate thing?"

He nodded.

"Sort of. I guess you had your reasons…"

"I did. And if you will listen I'll explain them."

"I don't understand it. What it means." I said, folding my arms, watching a group of Fae about my age, though it was hard to tell. They were busy making arrows, tying feathers to the end and then putting them in a pile. Apparently they were already mucking in with this war. Helping in whatever way they could.

"Anna could explain it better." He stated. "It would be easier, more comfortable for her."

"Right." I sighed. "So, everyone knows?"

"The Fae do. As soon as they saw your magic in him, they knew."

"So, you can only pass magic onto someone if they're your mate?" I asked. No wonder Jelric didn't understand it. No wonder he'd said it was a complex piece of Fae Lore. Did he know about mates? Was that new information to him too? I couldn't decide if I wanted to divulge that or not, but then everyone knew Fain and I were together, would it make any difference to know we were mates too?

"Speak to Anna." He said just as she spotted us and came rushing over.

"I take it you turned the sky black?" She said grinning.

"I had to move quickly and it seemed the most logical thing at the time."

She smirked. "To block out the sun?"

"You know me." I replied. "I like to be dramatic every once in a while."

We all laughed at that.

"How have they been while I've been gone?" I asked.

"Good." Anna replied. "I think some of them are still adjusting, still getting used to be out and being seen by everyone but there has only been one incidence."

I tensed up, narrowed my eyes, "What incidence?"

"A soldier wanted to try his luck…"

"In what way?" I asked but I could already guess.

"In the way you'd expect." Guillaume replied and I felt a flash of anger.

"What happened?"

"The girl is fine." Anna stated. "She sent him packing with his tail between his legs."

"Whose solider was it? What sigil did he bear?" I could hear the anger in my voice as I spoke. In my head I'd feared the Fae would be collared. That that was their only threat. Not that.

"King Rette's." Guillaume said. "He handled it himself too."

My eyebrows rose. "Enough to be a punishment?"

"Enough for Meg to be satisfied." Anna said which I guessed was enough.

We started walking through the camp, making our way to where Guillaume had set up a tent for me. As we passed by Fae would stop and smile, and welcome me back, and in truth it made me feel like a returning hero, even though I knew I wasn't one.

I glanced behind me, at where the tops of Nind skimmed the clouds, far above the trees. God knows what Mira and Ridley were dealing with right now. God knows what hell Ide had already put them through. And Hal, I could only pray that he was still alive and that Ide hadn't already slit his throat.

"Why the look?" Guillame asked me.

"I need to figure a way of breaking the siege." I said.

"Can the soldiers not do it?"

I winced. "I'm not sure we have the time. Ide is not a good man, Indi told me some horrible stories about what he used to get up to in his kingdom. I don't want to leave them at his mercy for any longer than we have too."

"I'm sure you'll think of something." He said.

"I have an idea I'm just not sure how it would actually work." I admitted.

"Are you going to block the sun again?"

I laughed. "No, but it's along similar lines. I'm sick of all these people with no magic trying to intimidate us and I think flexing my own muscles every so often and showing what we are capable of wouldn't do them any harm."

"Now you sound like a Fae queen." He teased and I laughed again.

Forty-Five

ALICE

I stood staring up at those walls, up at my beautiful Nind, and wondering where Mira was, and Hal, and Ridley too. If Ide had hurt any of them then I was going to make sure he pay for it.

God, it felt like the tower all over again. Me on the outside. Helpless to do anything.

Except it wasn't was it? There was one significant difference.

I smirked, half cursing myself for not thinking of it sooner.

In my head I spoke to Guillaume, gauged his opinion of my plan, after all, I needed the Fae's buy in. I needed all their help to ensure it worked.

When his voice rung in my head, confirming that enough of them were ready and willing I knew this was it. That this was a showdown.

Fain, and Nela, and Rette had been hauled up in their tent, no doubt planning and strategizing about the siege. Trying to figure their own way to break it. Part of me had wondered if I should have been in there too.

I turned on my heel, stalking back through the treeline and to where the soldiers were.

I could feel their eyes watching me, looking over me in my armour as I walked. It had taken me a long time to realise that I couldn't stop their looks, couldn't stop the rumours either, but none of it mattered really. They could say what they wanted, look at what they wanted because in the end I was going to be myself now, irrespective of their opinions, irrespective of their thoughts on the matter.

As I walked into the command tent, it felt like everyone instantly fell quiet, staring at me.

King Rette bowed and I thought the frown at the gesture. I could see Fain glancing at him sideways before looking back at me. I inclined my head, acknowledging his show of respect the way I'd seen Uther do so many times. And then Prince Frederic followed, as did almost everyone else except for Fain, bowing to me as if I were someone of importance.

"Pull your soldiers back from the walls." I said looking from King Rette, to Prince Frederic, and then finally to Fain.

"What are you going to do?" King Rette asked.

I smirked. "You'll see." I said before turning and walking back out.

"Alice..." Fain called, quickly following after me.

"Relax, Prince Fain." I murmured as he came up right beside me. "I'm not going to damage the castle."

"Our castle." He said forcefully.

I stopped, turning to face him. "You mean our home?" I replied and he tilted his head at the amusement in my eyes. Could he tell that I was teasing him again even now, even in this moment?

He was right within touching distance from me. I could smell his scent in the air. I could see the way his magic sparked in his eyes.

He glanced at my lips, slightly parted, and I swore for a minute he was going to kiss me, devour me, right here, in front of everyone.

That bond twisted, it tightened. A gasp escaped my mouth as I felt it.

"If they weren't watching us right now…" Fain said.

I clenched my fists, fighting back the blush that threatened to give me away. I could feel all the eyes on us both, everyone in the tent was out now, seeing the two of us, even the soldiers around were watching this display too.

"What would you do, Prince Fain?" I murmured so that only he could hear. His gaze devoured the curves of my body beneath the leather of my Fae armour.

And in that moment it was like it was just the two of us here, that no one else mattered, no one else even existed.

"You already know." He said taking a step nearer, closing that distance and I knew what he wanted, what his body and mine were practically screaming for. For a second I considered letting him do it, letting that feeling consume us entirely.

Only now was not the time.

I put my hand on his chest, stopping him mid-step, but not taking my eyes from his face.

"I'm taking that castle back first." I said before turning around and walking away without looking back.

I GLANCED ACROSS AT GUILLAUME. WE WERE STOOD, ALL OF US, spread out all along the moat, encircling round the walls of the castle. The air was thick with Magic and something about it made me feel alive, like part of my soul was right there surrounding me.

I'd ditched both my sword and shield. It seemed pointless to take them, pointless to weigh myself down when my magic was going to be more than enough for this.

I stood just in the Fae armour I had on, facing the gap between the moat and the raised drawbridge beyond.

I took a step forward, focusing on that drawbridge with all my might. The other Fae were doing their part. I could feel it even if no one else, none of the soldiers, could. Now, it was time for me to do my bit.

Slowly, the drawbridge began to drop as if the castle itself was opening up just for me. As I raised the portcullis, I heard the gasps of the soldiers behind.

All of them had stood, watching as we spread out, as we created the circle. It must have looked so strange to see us doing nothing, no perceivable magic but the soldiers, even King Rette and Prince Frederic had no idea what the rest of the Fae had just done.

As I began to walk towards the opening, Fain's voice rang out in my head. *'Be careful.'*

I paused, looking back across the distance to where he was stood. *'I will.'*

And then I crossed the bridge and walked unchecked into Nind.

THE COURTYARD WAS SILENT. ALL AROUND I SAW THE SOLDIERS, slumped over, hunched over, clearly they'd been watching too. Until the magic had hit them and they'd fallen asleep.

The corridors were silent too. More soldiers were there, all bearing King Ide's sigil. As I saw the mess they'd made I felt a flash of anger. How dare he? How dare Ide even have the audacity to go there, to our castle and trash the place as he had.

I resisted the urge to head for the dungeons. To find Mira, and Ridley, and Hal.

That wasn't my part of this plan.

No, I was here for Ide. I was here to make that man pay.

Once the castle was secure I could look for my friends. Fain had taught me that. Do your duty first, then follow your heart.

Guillaume had taught me that too in his own way. It had been a hard lesson to learn but now I'd got it.

I walked up the great staircase, searching from room to room until I found him, sat in the same chair Uther had sat in, as though he had the right to occupy it.

Another flash of anger hit me but I forced it back down.

I clicked my fingers, watching as the man's eyes opened. As slowly, he woke up.

He blinked, jerked, sat bolt up right staring at me with wide, and I was pleased to note, shocked eyes.

"Hello, King Ide." I said as he gripped the arms of the chair as if in support.

"How...?"

"Your soldiers are sleeping. Everyone is sleeping. I've taken my castle back."

He got up. One swift, smooth movement that brought him towering over me. I'd forgotten how tall he was. How much his presence had always overshadowed me and used to make me shrink back into myself with every word he uttered.

Used to, anyway.

"Not so fast." I said pulling a little magic to force him to stop.

"You're a fool if you think you can beat us." He said.

I smiled. "But I already have. Look out the window. My Fae have you surrounded." I replied calmly back to him.

"What Fae?" He snarled.

"Take a look for yourself..." I held my hand out, releasing the magic that held him and he hesitated before walking to the window and looked down.

His eyes widened, his body grew impossibly still, as it dawned on him exactly what he was up against.

"The way I see it you've got two choices." I said.

"And what are those?"

"You either surrender to me now and we walk out together..."

"Or?" He cut across me.

"Or I drag you out like a dog." I said.

He sneered, folding his arms. "You think I'll simply surrender to you, girl? You think it'll be that easy?"

"You are many things, King Ide, but an idiot is not one of them. Take your chance now, walk out with me and I will see you are treated fairly."

"Lies." He spat. "You would have those soldiers execute me the moment I cross that moat."

I rolled my eyes. "On what charge?"

He smirked. "You want me to say it?"

"You don't need to." I replied. "We both know what you are. What you've done. You conspired with Prince Rillon to steal the High King's crown."

He took a step towards me, obviously trying to use his weight to intimidate me. Only that wouldn't work anymore.

"Either you knew, or your did nothing after High King Uther was poisoned, and you came here to make sure the Crown Prince wasn't a threat. What were you going to do? Kill him?"

"I would have done no such thing." He scoffed. "Prince Hal is a child."

"But he was a threat to Prince Rillon. You knew he'd die eventually, it was the only way Rillon could have kept the throne."

He shook his head. "I wouldn't have let that happen."

"Don't pretend to be noble now." I snarled.

He laughed. "You have grown very big for your boots, haven't you, girl?"

"No, I just finally realised what I was capable of and I'm not going to put up with it anymore…"

"Put up with what?"

"You and Prince Rillon, and every other person that thinks they can control me, tell me what to do, try to intimidate me, like you have any power over me." I said, feeling those words in my bones.

"I am a King." He half shouted.

"Then decide, are you going to walk out of here now as one or am I going to drag you out like a traitor?"

I pulled my magic, just a little, just enough to make him feel fear, to feel intimidated, to feel every moment he had made me recoil, made me flee away from him. Every moment he had enjoyed making me squirm under his gaze too. I let the flames fill my hands, that same blue, electric flicker that I'd produced almost ritually since I'd gotten free of Yannis's grasp.

He narrowed his eyes and I saw the defeat written there.

We walked back in silence. I had nothing to say to him and I didn't care to hear any words he had. He kept glancing around, staring at all his men, still snoring under the enchantment. Every step, every movement echoed around us in the eery silence.

But as they got to the Courtyard I saw him hesitate.

Just for a moment.

Because we could see them now, all the soldiers, all King Rette's army, and Prince Frederic's and the High King's too. They were still stood, watching and waiting and not understanding anything that had happened from the moment I'd disappeared.

"Why did you not just send your soldiers in?" He asked. "You dropped the drawbridge. You could have fought it out instead of choosing the cowards option."

"I'm not like you." I replied. "I don't see the point in killing people if it can be avoided."

"Even my soldiers?" He sneered, before glancing at the ones not far from him.

"Even yours." I said. "They were simply following orders. Why should they have to die just because the man who leads them is a traitor?"

He looked disgusted, as if I was somehow weaker than him because I wasn't willing to see people die. And then he looked back, seeing King Rette, Prince Frederic, and then Prince Fain stood all waiting for him.

"Walk." I ordered as he glared. "Walk or I will drag you."

He shook his head, spat on the ground in front of him and then walked, holding himself up as though what he had done was something to be proud of.

I let him go ahead. Waited, poised to react but there was nothing he could do. He had no army now. He had nothing. I'd stripped him of everything, and soon, very soon we'd strip him of that crown still perched on his head.

He crossed the drawbridge alone. King Rette nodded for two of his soldiers to seize him and King Ide didn't even put up a fight.

'Do you want us to stop?' Guillaume asked. I shook my head looking across at him.

'Not yet. I want to take their weapons first. I don't want any fighting if we can avoid it.'

He grunted in agreement.

And then I turned to look at the others, all waiting for me to tell them what to do.

"Send them in." I said. "Everyone is asleep. Take away their weapons, disarm them and then we will wake them up."

King Rette nodded before looking to his men. "You heard her. Get on with it." He commanded and I saw as they all sprung up and rushed into the castle.

"That was very impressive." Rette said after walking up to me.

"Thank you, King Rette." I replied.

"Will you do the same at Temoor?"

"No. It's not possible with Temoor." I stated, my mind flickering to that dark magic, to whatever the hell was there, in Uther's rooms.

As Fain stalked towards me I lost my trail of thought.

"You…" He said, shaking his head and that tension, that spark flared once more.

"We have to find Prince Hal." I said.

"Lead the way…"

"It's your castle, Prince Fain, I think you should go first."

He took my hand, squeezed it, and together we walked back inside.

Forty-Six

FAIN

We found them in the dungeons. Mira, Ridley, and somehow Cait too.

But Hal wasn't among them.

My fear spiked when I realised that. When it sunk in that he wasn't here.

Ridley was badly beaten, Mira had a nasty cut along her arm from what they could see and Cait had a bruise across her face but it looked older, as if it had happened days before.

There were other people there, all crammed into the small cells that Nind had, all of them still fast asleep under the magic that the Fae had cast over the castle.

I glanced at Alice, frowning.

"What?" She asked me.

"Why have you not woken them up?"

"We need to wait until the soldiers are all disarmed." She stated.

I shook my head slightly. Hal was missing, he was out there, somewhere, and the best chance we had of finding him was speaking to the very people drooling at our feet.

"What?" She asked.

"Sometimes you need to accept that you cannot save everyone." I said.

Before she could answer a soldier came rushing in and we both turned. "King Rette sent me. He says it is done."

"They are disarmed?" Alice asked and he nodded.

"Yes, your Highness." He replied before bowing again.

Alice swallowed. I glanced at her, seeing the shock on her face and she brushed it off as if it were some sort of mistake.

"Get some Healers." She ordered and he nodded, bowed, and left.

Within seconds I felt the magic around us fracture. Felt it shatter like a tiny web that had scattered into the wind.

"Can you feel it?" She asked me.

"The magic stopped." I replied.

She smiled as we heard the sound of movement, of everyone starting to wake up.

Alice rushed to Mira, hugging her tightly before moving aside so that the Healers could see to her arm.

As she turned to Cait, I pulled Ridley aside. I didn't care that he was hurt. I didn't care that he needed a Healer more than anyone. "Where is Hal?" I asked.

His face was so badly bruised he could barely open his eyes. But I saw the despair, the anguish.

"They took him. We fought as best we could."

"Where is he?"

He could barely speak beyond a whisper, could barely utter the words but I heard them anyway.

I rushed from room, rushed up the damned stairs and through the castle. My heart pounded in my chest, my body screamed in protest as I forced myself on and on. As I raced to find him.

The door slammed against the wall. Evidently the soldiers here had remained hidden enough that no one had found them and they'd simply woken up along with everyone else.

The first came at me, sword raised and in my anger I grabbed the blade with my bare hands. Magic poured from me. It poured into that metal and snapped it in two.

The man stepped back spluttering.

But the second decided to take his chances. I threw my hand out, mimicking that action I'd seen Alice do back in Temoor. It had felt so easy, the magic had felt so simple and to my surprise a blast of power shot out, knocking him clean off his feet and turning him to ash before he hit the floor.

The first man ran for the door. I didn't care to chase him. I didn't give a shit if he lived or died.

My eyes landed on the tiny form in the corner. The unmistakable shape of a body hidden beneath a blanket.

"No," I cried, sinking to my knees, crawling to where he was.

I yanked the blanket off, saw the pale, deathly colour of his skin.

"No," I growled, grabbing him, holding him to me. "Not Hal, please not Hal."

I couldn't take it. I couldn't take that he was dead. A boy barely old enough to have lived. My hand cupped his head. I could feel the blood all matted in his hair. They'd smashed his skull in.

But as I held him I swore I heard a whimper. Small. Almost insignificant.

I released my grip, staring at his face.

Gods, he was breathing. Somehow, by some miracle, he was still alive.

"Healer." I bellowed, stumbling back to my feet. "I need a Healer."

I raced out of the door, with him in my arms, yelling over and over.

Hal didn't make another sound, didn't even seem to register the noise.

"Prince Fain?"

I blinked staring at the stranger before my head kicked in.

"Help him." I growled. "Help him."

The Healer nodded, pulling a crystal and while I cradled him in my arms, he set about trying to save Hal's life.

Forty-Seven

ALICE

I crouched down beside Cait. She had a nasty bruise on her face and the way she was holding her wrist made me think she'd hurt it too.

"How are you here?" I asked. I didn't want to sound harsh but I remembered what Fain had said, that she had been the one to have him arrested.

"Rillon threw me out of castle. Out of Temoor." She said. "He said I wasn't married to Uther, that I was nothing to him and he threatened to give me to his soldiers."

"What?"

She screwed her face up as the tears streamed down them. "I don't know what happened. I don't understand any of it."

"What do you mean?"

"Uther. Everyone says he was poisoned but how?"

I narrowed my eyes at those words. "You were the one who accused Fain of doing it. You had him arrested."

"What?" She gasped, staring at me like I was mad.

"You were there, you called him a traitor."

"No," She shut her eyes, shaking her head as if it were filled with something she needed gone. "I don't remember that. I just remember finding Uther, in that cramped room. And then Rillon…"

I frowned, studying her face. "What do you remember before that? Before the poisoning?"

She shrugged. "Nothing of note, I'd been out for a walk, when I returned there was a Magi waiting for me, but I didn't know why. Then everything goes hazy…"

My stomach dropped. God, it had been so simple. So easy hadn't it? "You were glamoured." I stated.

"What?"

"Glamoured." I said glancing to where Mira was. Remembering that same trick they'd pulled with her, spelling her mind so that she did what they wanted.

"What does that mean?" She asked.

"They bewitched you, Cait. Rillon must have had it planned."

She sobbed, covering her face with her hands. "He wouldn't let me stay with him. I begged him. Begged Rillon. Only he wouldn't listen."

"When you did see him, did he seem odd to you?"

She frowned. "In what way?"

"I don't know exactly…"

Her hand gripped my wrist tightly as she seized upon what I was asking. "What do you know?" She gasped.

I winced. "I can't explain it but when we were there, getting Fain out, I felt something. It was coming from the High King's rooms."

"What was it?" She asked, her face so fearful.

"Dark magic."

"Are you serious?" She hissed and I felt half the people turn to look at us.

"Don't say anything." I said quietly. "Not yet. I've not told anyone but you and Nela."

"Not even Fain?"

"No."

"Is it Rillon? Is he in league with the Magars?"

"I don't know." I replied. "But it has to have something to do with the High King. No one could figure out what he was poisoned with…"

"You think it is dark magic they poisoned him with?"

"I don't know. But we need to get to Temoor. The longer we wait…"

"Don't say it." Cait said quickly.

But I already feared it was too late. Far too fucking late.

Forty-Eight

ALICE

I didn't know where Fain was. I heard whispers as I searched the castle that Hal had been found. That he'd been taken back to King Rette's tent and was being looked after by the Healers.

I'd put Ide in the dungeons. And locked Atran in there with him. Creating a wall of magic that kept them isolated and ensured no one could break either of them out.

As I made my way through one damaged room into another I could sense him, could sense the magic I'd shared inside him.

I turned, walking right along the corridor and up another staircase before standing in front of the door I knew he was behind.

When I pushed it open I saw him stood there, in the middle of the room with his back to me. For a moment I just watched him, hiding in the doorway, my eyes running over the rippling muscles beneath his shirt.

And then he turned, his eyes brightening momentarily as they fell on me. "Why are you here?" He asked.

"I came to find you."

"Oh." He replied before turning back around and surveying the mess once more. Apparently even our rooms hadn't been safe from the destruction that Ide and his soldiers had wrecked on our home.

"How's Prince Hal?"

"I don't know. The Healers are with him now. There was nothing more I could do."

"You found him, Fain, that is enough."

He shook his head like he thought otherwise but he walked towards me, placing his hands on my shoulders and that simple touch seemed to light a fire inside me. "Today you were a true warrior." He said. "A queen."

My eyes widened. He must have known what that word meant, how calling me that was a risk.

"Don't hide from it. Don't turn your back now." He growled.

"I'm not hiding." I replied.

"Even if Uther recovers, everything will change. You understand that, right?" He said searching my face for the answer.

I frowned, hearing the seriousness of his voice. "The Fae still want their freedom." I stated.

"And they will have it." He murmured, "With you as their queen."

"No,"

His fingers landed on my lips, silencing me, silencing those protests. "Claim it, Alice. Claim what you were born to be. What your blood marks you as."

I winced. "I thought you didn't believe in things like bloodlines."

"This isn't about me, this is about you."

"And making me a queen." I half whispered.

"My Queen." He said before planting an almost chaste kiss on my lips. One that disappeared far too quickly. One that left me desperate for more. "And what a queen you will make."

"Why are you still talking?" I asked.

"What would you have me do?"

"Shut up and fuck me already." I replied.

His eyes flared, his hands pulled my hips right into his and he captured my lips in a devastating kiss. I moaned, wrapping my arms around his neck to deepen it but clearly that was not what he wanted right now. He pushed me back enough to look at my face, to no doubt check that I was not having second thoughts, or freaking out, or anything else and then his hands were tearing at my armour, clawing at it to get it off.

He slipped my top up over my head and I kissed him once more as he carried me from what had been our beautiful sitting room and into the now trashed bedroom.

My hands scrambled to undo his breeches, to get them off and, as he lay me onto the bed, he was the one who yanked them down.

I stared at his cock, at the glistening bead of precum right at the very tip. He fisted himself, watching my face again, clearly hesitating.

"Alice,"

"I said fuck me." I half-ordered, cutting across him. I didn't want to have this conversation; I didn't need to. I was so far beyond all of that right now. What I needed was him, this, us.

That bond twisted and we both reacted, both moaned as it seemed to coil tighter and tighter.

I pulled him down, spreading my legs wide and, as he buried himself inside me, I couldn't help the gasp.

His arms cradled me, his mouth claimed mine once more as he began sliding so deliciously in and out. I rolled my hips, I met every single one of those thrusts, feeling like this moment was more than just physical, that both of us were reclaiming something.

"Is this what you wanted, my Queen?" Fain murmured into my ear.

I couldn't respond. I could barely formulate words as my eyes rolled right back in my head. I moaned, I writhed, I lost myself in not just his touch now but the memories, the history, what we'd been before and what we truly were.

Mates. We were mates.

As I stared back at him, I knew he deserved to hear the truth, that he deserved to understand what all of this meant. Only right now I didn't want to face it. Right now, I just wanted to lose myself in the physical, lose myself in the feel of his touch, his love.

"Stop thinking." He whispered, sliding his hand between my thighs. "It's just you and me right now. That's all that matters."

I gasped as his fingers began to circle my clit, as more pleasure than I thought possible rushed through my body.

I buried my face in his neck, inhaling that deep, heady scent that I'd loved and missed so much.

I could feel my orgasm building, I could feel from how Fain was thrusting inside me that he was getting close. I wrapped my arms around his neck claiming his mouth once more as I whispered the words 'I love you' over and over.

When it finally hit me it felt like an explosion. Like a gift of mercy too. It felt like everything inside me, every fear, every concern, every moment of torture I'd lived through and tried to forget was gone, forgotten, erased.

We slumped against the sheets. A tangle of sweaty limbs and panting breath.

I shut my eyes, revelling in the fact that we had this back, that I had this back.

His hand stroked the few strands off my forehead. I sighed, leaning into him. "We should get back." I murmured.

He tilted his head, "Is that what you want?" He asked in a tone I knew only too well.

I bit my lip, shaking my head, wanting to ignore the voice of reason but saying it anyway. "Fain,"

His hands snuck down, they teased along my skin, and though I should have been more than satisfied with how he'd fucked me, the promise of this, of more, had me spreading my legs again.

His lips curled. His eyes stared right between my thighs. "You command me, now." He stated. "And as my Queen, my sole focus is to ensure you're satisfied."

"Is that right?" I said breathlessly. Desperately too.

"Tell me what you want," He said as those fingers slid right where I needed them. "Tell me you want to go back and I will stop."

"No," I practically yelled the words as he withdrew his touch. "No,"

"My Queen wants more?"

"I need it." I clung to him, my nails digging into his skin as I begged with my eyes for him to continue.

A soft rumble echoed from his throat. He twisted his body, laying so that his mouth was barely an inch from my pussy and his hot breath was already there, promising so much. And he placed his hands on my thighs spreading them wider still.

"My Queen," He said planting a kiss right on the part of me that made me melt. "Mine,"

I shut my eyes, arched my hips as his tongue began to lick, to tease, to slowly, delicately taste me as if we had all night and there wasn't an entire army waiting on us.

Forty-Nine

FAIN

Gods how I'd missed this. How I'd missed the feel of her, the sound of her pleasure, but most of all the taste of her. I ran my tongue between her folds, tasting her heat, savouring each delicious drop.

My hands scooped under her ass, raising her hips so that I could properly tongue fuck her.

And her eyes bulged as I did it.

If I wasn't so caught up in this I would have teased her, taunted her for how much she was riding my mouth but I was too focused on the endgame, to focused on ensuring she got what she was so clearly desperate for.

I speared one finger inside her and then another. Her warm, slick heat, welcomed them, suctioned around them as I began to pump slowly away.

"Fain," She gasped. Her hands grabbed the sheets, she screwed them up, twisted them as though she was trying to keep herself from flailing.

"Come for me," I said. "Be a good girl and come all over my hand."

She whimpered, she mewled, she panted as I curled right onto that spot I knew she loved.

"Oh fuck, oh fuck, of fuck,"

"That's it," I murmured watching her struggle, watching that release building and how she was fighting it, how sweat was once more beading right along her brow. "Come apart for me, Little Fae, show me how much you need me."

"I do need you." She gasped. Her legs, kicked, her back arched so far I thought it might snap and then she was screaming, coming hard enough that her inner walls gripped around my fingers like a vice.

"So fucking beautiful." I said watching her. "So fucking perfect."

She slumped again, her cheeks flushed, and her breasts heaving. And then she crawled back into my arms, wrapped herself around me as she kissed me.

"I love you." She said quietly. "I'm so sorry it took me this long to get back here."

"Don't," I replied, placing a finger gently on her lips. "You needed this time. We both did."

She sighed, pulling a face like she wanted to say more and I kissed those words away, kissed those thoughts away. We were back. She was healed. That was all that mattered. If I'd had to wait an entire millennium to get to this I would have, I would have waited forever just for one more kiss.

We got dressed slowly as though we still weren't yet ready to be leaving this space. Weren't yet ready to be around anyone else but just each other. She stared at me, as I walked around collecting our clothes from where we'd discarded them in our haste.

But as she bent down to pull hers on I froze, seeing all those scars, all those horrific memories etched out in her skin. I know I'd seen some of them but I didn't realise how much more there were.

"They're all over your back." I said quietly.

She gulped, turning to look at me and nodded a little.

"If I had known…" I began but she shook her head, walking back to me.

"It's over." She said. "All of it is over."

I cupped her face, kissed her gently and she pulled away as if she was afraid I might just rip her clothes off and devour once her again.

"Come on. Before King Rette sends out a search party." She muttered.

"He wouldn't dare." I replied as she laughed.

Fifty

ALICE

We walked across the drawbridge still hand in hand. With every step we took, hundreds of eyes followed us. In the distance I spotted Guillaume stood, obviously waiting for me.

'Everything okay?' I asked him.

He nodded. *'Just waiting on my Queen.'*

'Get something to eat, Guillaume. King Rette is being demanding of our company tonight.'

Guillaume nodded, bowed, and disappeared into the treeline.

"Can you communicate with him too?" Fain asked me after Guillaume had gone.

"Yes. I can communicate with all the Fae in my head now and the Magi too when I choose it."

"So, we're not special then?" He said.

I paused, "Why do you say that?"

"If you can do it with all the other Fae…"

"But you're different. You're not Fae. Not full Fae." I stated, and that word echoed in my head. I needed to understand what it meant. And more importantly I needed to tell him.

"But we do need to talk." I said quickly. "About us. There are things I've kept from you. Things you have a right to know."

His face reacted, his eyes darkened. "What things?"

I went to answer but someone was suddenly there calling us both, beckoning us to where clearly everyone was waiting.

When we walked in, everyone stood. I tried my best not to cringe and hoped I succeeded as I took the empty seat that King Rette was gesturing to beside himself. Fain sat across from me, next to Cait, and as the room returned to normal, our eyes connected.

'*Can we talk after this?*' I thought to him.

'*Of course.*'

I smiled at him, half-wishing we could just leave right now and continue our conversation.

"Thank you for finally joining us." Rette said beside me, drawing my attention away.

"It's almost like you missed me, King Rette." I quipped and he laughed.

"Not me but everyone else insisted we had to wait for you. Apparently, they are all quite enamoured with you." He replied.

"Why would that be?"

He looked at me like I was having him on. "After what you did today..." He said and I sighed before taking a sip of my drink, realising that that feeling steadily growing inside me was guilt. If I'd come up with my plan sooner, if I'd acted faster than maybe Hal wouldn't have been so badly hurt.

Servants started weaving through the tables, placing food in front of us. Great steaming dishes that admittedly made my mouth water. I smiled at them and murmured my thanks before taking some.

"I trust you and Prince Fain got suitably reacquainted?" Rette asked quietly.

I half choked on my drink while he openly laughed.

"Careful, King Rette, I warned you before…" I muttered.

He rolled his eyes. "You don't scare me anymore, Alice."

"You mean I did once?"

"Perhaps. But now I know better." He replied before his eyes shifted back to the Prince. "I think you are good for each other." He said quietly.

I shook my head, deliberately not looking at Fain in case I blushed and gave myself away. "Why are you so interested in our relationship?" I asked him.

He shrugged. "What else do I have to concern myself with?"

"Maybe the fact that your High King is mortal peril?" I stated.

"You are always so serious, Alice. Besides there is little we can do about it tonight. You have won Nind back for us. King Ide is confined to a dungeon and best of all, you haven't had to shed one drop of blood to achieve any of it…"

"That almost sounded like a compliment." I teased.

"It was meant to be."

I sighed taking a mouthful of food. "How is Hal?"

He winced, glancing at Fain before back at me. "In truth, not good."

"You don't think he will recover?" I whispered.

"Pray to the Gods that he does." He said. "Because if we lose both the High King and his heir, it will certainly end in civil war."

"Not if I can help it." I said, clenching my fists.

"Let's focus on Temoor first. On ridding ourselves of Rillon."

"Amen to that." I replied raising my glass.

He frowned. "What does that mean? 'Amen'?"

I let out a sigh. "It's an expression from my world. A way that we pray, I guess."

"I see." He murmured, holding his glass up. "Amen."

Apparently he took the entire gesture to be the prayer. I bit my lip, deciding there was no point in correcting him.

He took a long swig of his wine, like he thought it was actually blessed and then he placed it back on the table. "Have you forgiven me yet?"

"For what?"

"For tricking you, for not telling you sooner about the High King and Prince Fain?"

I paused, thinking about it. "I was annoyed but I understand why you did it."

"You called me a shit."

I laughed, remembering the shock on Nela's face. As Rette started laughing too everyone looked up at us.

"You were." I stated.

"I guess so, but my intention was good."

"Before you opened those doors, for a second, I thought it wasn't…" I began.

"You thought I had betrayed you then…?" He said studying my face.

"Yes." I admitted. "Can you blame me?"

"No. I think it was a logical conclusion to make, based on what you've been through."

I gritted my teeth, shutting down that memory, that reminder that threatened to overwhelm me. "I wish everyone would stop referring to it."

He glanced at the scar across my cheekbone as if he knew how I'd gotten it. "I think you should be free, Alice." He murmured.

"What do you mean?"

"I mean of the High King. You have done enough. You have been through enough."

"Careful, King Rette." I said quietly, looking around and feeling like we were suddenly in very dangerous territory with so many people about. So many ears to hear our conversation.

"I spoke to Prince Fain about it too." He continued.

My eyes widened. I looked across at him seeing that he was busy talking to Cait, comforting her from what I could see. He hadn't said a word. Hadn't mentioned it. But then when had we had the time?

"I believe, in the right circumstances, we could force High King Uther's hand." He stated.

"What do you mean?"

"The Lesser Kings could."

"Why would you do that?" I asked.

"Partly because we owe it to you and partly because it makes sense. You are no more of a threat than any of us."

I shook my head. "He won't see it like that."

He tilted his head, looking suddenly every inch the king he was. "Then I shall make him see it."

"Why? Why would you do that?"

"Is that not what friends are for?" He asked.

"Is that what we are? Friends?" I replied.

"I would like to think we are. You asked for my aid and I came."

"I didn't mean to force you into something though…"

He held up his hands, "There was no forcing. I came because I wanted to."

I frowned, trying to figure out if this was all some game, some trick he was playing on me. Since when did any of the Lesser Kings ever view me as anything other than a thing to use?

"See it for what it is, Alice, at face value." He stated. "Don't always see mistrust and betrayal, especially where there is none."

"You claimed I was an enigma but now I think it is you that is one." I said.

He laughed. "I like the sound of that. I've never thought myself clever enough to be one."

I laughed with him. "Maybe you are cleverer than you realise then." I observed before dropping my voice. "But you know, all of this means nothing if Uther does die."

"That is where you are wrong." He said leaning right over, ensuring no one could hear us. "If Uther dies, then you need to be ready to move."

"Excuse me?"

"If there is no High King then the power struggle that will engulf this land will likely kill all the Fae unless you get yourself and them free."

I gulped, seeing the way his face had gone from mirth to hardness in the blink of an eye.

"I mean it, Alice. You need to be prepared to act. And you need to make sure you do not hesitate."

"I won't." I said.

And I wouldn't. Not now, not when my freedom, when all our freedom might actually be within our grasp.

Fifty-One

ALICE

I saw Fain get up and leave. I saw Cait follow right after him and I knew where they were headed. That they had gone to check on Hal.

When the meal was done, I slipped away as best I could too, only I didn't go after them even though I wanted to.

No, instead I went to find Anna. If Fain and I were going to talk then I needed to have answers first.

She was back in the Fae Camp, sat by the fire, with Stephen and a few others whose names I hadn't yet learnt. I smiled at them all and then they left us to it as if they knew I needed a private conversation.

Anna fixed me with her gaze as I sat on the log beside her. "You want to know what it means, don't you?" She said.

I nodded, guessing that Guillaume had already spoken with her.

She smiled, rubbing her hands together in a slow circular pattern as though she were trying to warm them up. "Finding your mate is a wonderful thing." She murmured.

"Does everyone have one?" I asked.

She pulled a face. "I'd like to think so. It would make more sense if that was the case but not everyone finds their mate."

"Are some Fae?"

"Yes." She replied. "It is far more common to have a Fae mate than a human one."

I nodded, storing that information. So, Fain and I were doubly rare.

"But what does it mean?" I asked.

"It means the Gods matched your souls. The universe put you two together."

I blinked, feeling like that sounded too far-fetched. The universe? It was hard not to laugh at the absurdity of it.

"Your souls are drawn to one another. Your destiny is tied to each other." She explained. "That is why you made him half-Fae, because you can live for a thousand years, a human cannot live a fraction of that, and when ones mate dies…"

"What?"

"It is an awful thing, a horrific thing. More painful than losing your magic, more painful than the sharpest blade against your flesh. Most Fae do not survive a year after their mates passes. Their soul withers and dies without them."

I winced, wondering how true that might have been, how many times I'd come close to death, had wished for it, not knowing I was wishing that for Fain too.

"He has magic." I said quietly. "He cannot control it. It comes in bursts, mainly when he is angry."

"That's because you have not finished the mating." She said simply.

"The mating?"

"If you leave him as he is, his magic will eventually burn out." She stated. "He will live far longer than a human but to truly be mated, you have to turn him fully Fae."

"That's a thing?" I gasped. "How, how do I do that?"

She took my hand, and murmured softly the ritual, the words, everything I had to do to fully change him. When she finished, I sat there staring at the fire, wondering how it would feel, how our bond might change if I did that.

"Does everyone know about this? About mates? About what Fain is to me…" I screwed my face up feeling annoyed at my own ignorance. How long had I been in this world and yet still I knew so little of my own kind.

"Yes." She said honestly. "We all know. It is something we teach newcomers, all the parts of Fae Lore."

"But I know nothing of it." I said feeling exasperated. "I know nothing of my history, my family's history, any of it."

"I can teach you, I can answer any questions you have." She reassured me. "And I have that book still."

I nodded, sighing, clenching and unclenching my fists as I considered everything I'd learnt. "Would you do it?" I asked her. "If you were me, and Fain was your mate, would you turn him fully Fae?"

Her eyebrows rose in surprise. "It isn't for me to say." She said before holding her hands up to silence my interruption. "He is your mate. He is the one who would change, perhaps the question isn't for me, or even you, but for him. Would he want to become fully Fae?"

I bit my lip, realising that she was right. I'd been looking at this all wrong. I'd been selfish, thinking only of me, my wants. But this was about Fain, his life, his future.

I rose to my feet, murmuring my thanks, knowing what steps I needed to take.

Fifty-Two

FAIN

I slipped away from the meal early. Alice had been deep in what looked like a serious conversation with Rette and both Cait and I wanted to check on Hal.

When we reached his tent, I saw guards posted outside, all along the perimeter.

Cait tensed, but I took her arm, reassuring her, and led her inside.

He looked so impossibly small. So fragile. Laid out on the bed, with a blanket thrown over him and a bandage wrapped around his entire head so that none of this thick hair was on show.

The Healers had said they'd done all they could and now we just had to wait. But I felt useless, helpless, pathetic.

I sunk to my knees, taking his hand, silently begging him to wake up. Beside me, Cait was crying. In many ways she'd become a real mother to him and I knew this was tearing her up as much as it was me.

"He will make it." I said. "He has to."

She nodded but she didn't take her eyes from his face, as if she was afraid looking away from him might seal his fate.

WHEN I GOT BACK TO MY TENT, I FOUND ALICE WAITING FOR ME. SHE turned, her green eyes sparkling almost with mischief and I ran my eyes over that delicious body of hers before my mind even registered that I'd done it.

"Are you always going to do that?" She asked.

"Do what?"

"Look like you're undressing me with your eyes?"

My lips curled, despite my inner torment. "It's hard not to when you look like that."

"I'm hardly dressed inappropriately…"

I grabbed her waist, pulling her hips towards me. "That armour clings to every curve of you."

She narrowed her eyes. "It's meant to protect me." She stated.

"Not from me it's not." I said.

She rested her head against my chest, sighing, "I've missed this." She said quietly.

"I've missed you." I replied.

"How is Hal?" She asked.

"Still unconscious."

Her face reacted. Something akin to guilt flashed there.

"You weren't responsible, Alice." I said quickly.

"If I'd acted sooner…"

"No," I said, wrapping my arms around her. "Don't do this. Don't blame yourself. You didn't know."

"He's going to be okay, isn't he? He's going to make it?"

"I hope so." I replied. But deep down it felt like every second that passed his life ebbed away more. Not that I voiced that.

I cupped her cheek, staring into her face. She'd said we needed to talk and there was plenty that I had to say too. Secrets I'd been carrying that needed to be spoken.

"Fain…"

"Let me speak first." I said cutting across her.

She frowned like she didn't understand and I guess there was no way she could. I led her to the couch, motioning for her to sit and she gritted her teeth, clearly expecting the worst.

I sat beside her, taking her hand in mine. "Right before Uther was poisoned, we talked about you, about your freedom." She chewed her lip, pulling a face. "He said he would let you go on the condition that you agreed to marry me."

"What?" She snapped, standing up like she'd just been shot.

"I told him it wasn't a choice." I said quickly. "That he wasn't giving you an actual option."

She narrowed her eyes watching me for a second. "He really said that?"

"Yes. I didn't want to say anything but I'm not going to keep secrets from you, no matter how unpalatable they are."

She stared at me, shaking her head, clearly processing it.

"Say something." I said gently.

"I don't know what to say." She admitted.

"I won't do it." I stated, getting up, moving to close the distance between us.

"Which bit?" She asked laughing slightly, which I'll admit threw me.

"Why is it funny?"

"Is it not?"

"I thought you'd be furious…" I began.

She pulled a face. "Who says I'm not?"

"You're laughing."

"Do you not want to marry me, Prince Fain?" She teased making me laugh now.

"Alice..."

"So that's how you left it then? The discussion about my freedom?"

"Yes. If you want to, for your freedom, then I would..."

She shook her head. "I don't want to. Not like that." She said cutting across me. "Besides, that wouldn't give the rest of the Fae theirs, would it?"

I hadn't considered that. Selfish as I was, I'd only considered her needs. Her life. "What did you want to say?" I asked.

She took my hand as her whole expression seemed to change. "I found out something."

"Tell me."

She dropped her gaze to our hands, "There's a reason we have this bond. A reason I was able to share my magic with you. A reason I made you half-Fae."

I frowned confused. She'd said it hadn't been intentional. She'd always maintained that. But now it sounded like she'd done it on purpose. Had she been lying all this time?

"What reason?" I asked.

She gulped, like whatever the next words out of her mouth were going to change everything. "We're mates."

I stared at her, not understanding what that meant but that bond, that connection seemed to fully comprehend it. It flared brighter than ever. It wrapped itself around me, around my heart and I almost gasped out at the intensity.

"It means our souls matched. That magic and destiny put us together." She said.

"How," I stammered, getting to my feet and something inside me seemed to fuse. "How did you learn of this?"

She got up, taking my hands once more. "A Fae can only transfer magic to non-Fae if they are mates. That's why it happens. Because Fae can live for hundreds of years and humans cannot."

My eyebrows rose in surprise. "So, I can live that long?"

She gave me a wry smile. "Only if we finish the transformation."

"What…?"

"I only did one part of it. There is a second part. A part that means you will turn Fae. You will become Fae."

I blinked, staring at her, seeing the way that magic glowed in her eyes, the way it illuminated her skin. What would I look like if I became fully Fae? Would my skin shimmer the way hers did?

"Do I have to do it?" I asked.

She shook her head. "No. You can remain as you are but eventually this magic inside you will burn out."

"Will our connection go with it?"

"No, Fain." She smiled. "Nothing can destroy that."

I breathed a sigh of relief that she was mine, that she would always be mine. My hand cupped her cheek, that magic inside me rippled like water as our skin connected.

"You decide Fain. I won't pressure you either way."

"I want to do it." I said.

Clearly she didn't expect that. Clearly she thought I'd want to think about it, to consider it. But why would I? I'd spent so long now caught in this grey between human and Fae. And this way I would be with her, by her side, exactly where I belonged.

"I want to do it." I repeated.

"Okay."

"Now."

Her eyes widened. "N, now?" She half spluttered.

"Is it possible? Do we need to be somewhere special?"

Her lips curled. "Not exactly. But we can't do it in this tent."

"Then take me wherever we need to go."

She bit her lip, kissing me quickly, before pulling me through the entrance and out into the cool, dark night.

Fifty-Three

ALICE

My head whirled. My heart seemed to think it was in some sort of race. With every step I took I tried to calm myself but how could I? Fain was my mate and tonight, together, we would complete this.

We walked in silence, out of the camp, and into the trees.

I stole glance after glance at him and when he caught me, he gave me a reassuring smile.

"Where are we going?" He asked softly.

"Do you trust me?"

"I trust you." He replied. "And I will follow you wherever you go."

God, if that bond wasn't already molten it would be after that.

I felt my cheeks flush, felt my magic stir along my skin as if it was desperate to get out, desperate to meld with the magic I'd given Fain.

The wind whispered through the leaves. Far behind us were the lights of the Fae camp. While I knew we could technically have performed this ritual anywhere, I wanted seclusion, I wanted intimacy, and with thousands of soldiers around us, neither Fain's tent, nor mine would provide that.

When we finally came to a clearing that felt far enough, I stopped.

Fain scanned the area, looking for something that explained why we were here of all places.

"Once we do this there is no turning back." I warned.

He nodded, his face as serious as my tone.

"I can speak the words but I need you to repeat the magic I create."

Again, he nodded.

I drew myself up, breathed in that sweet spring air deep into my lungs. Though Anna had told me what to say only hours ago, I already knew it by heart. Had repeated it over and over so that when the time came I was ready. I guess I just didn't expect it would happen tonight.

I took his hands in mine, creating a circle with our arms. As our skin touched, that bond bubbled and fizzled, as if it too understood what we were about to do, as if it knew the step we were taking.

"In the realms where the stars embrace the night, where moonlight weaves its silvery light, there our love blooms full of grace. A bond that time cannot erase."

Fain held his breath, tensing, barely blinking as he watched me, as he heard the song.

I pulled my magic, weaving it in between our hands, twisting it around us. As Fain did the same, I gasped, feeling the way our souls suddenly turned to flames. The way our love melded into something tangible. Something you could reach out and physically grasp.

"In every touch, a spark ignites..." I managed to say, though how I could speak I didn't know. "A flame that burns through endless nights. Two souls entwined, forever bound, in love's pure magic, we are found."

Light. Searing light erupted.

I shut my eyes, I screamed but I couldn't tell if it was from shock or from ecstasy as wave after wave wracked through my body. Fain gripped my hands, refusing to let go, and as that light fused, the pressure eased.

I blinked, looking up, registering at the exact same time that Fain did, that that light was rising, twisting, floating above our heads.

It looked like a star, created solely from our bond.

It rose higher and higher, rapidly increasing in speed before it came to rest, far above our heads, like a real star, twinkling in the sky. I blinked, wondering if that's what all of them were, all those stars. That every Fae who found their mate created one.

When I looked at Fain I almost cried out in shock. His ears now bore that distinctive point. His brown eyes sparkled with amber magic. And his skin glowed the way mine did.

Though he'd always been beautiful to me, his features had altered, his cheekbones were higher, more chiselled, his jaw was broader, and I'd put money on him having somehow developed more muscle.

Gone was his human form.

He was all Fae now.

"Alice," He said quietly, only I didn't let him say more. Something carnal overtook me. Something desperate clawed at my heart.

I launched myself at him, half tearing his shirt. Half clawing at his trousers to get them off.

His growl told me that he was as desperate in this moment as I was.

"My mate." He said, yanking my clothes off, "My mate," He repeated as he lined himself up, "My mate," He practically yelled as he buried himself inside me.

"Fuck," I gasped, wrapping my legs around his waist to hold myself up, to get some sort of anchor.

I rolled my hips, I gyrated against him as he cradled the weight of my back with his strong arms and thrust so deliciously into me.

"Your mine." I said staring into those amber eyes. "And I am yours."

"Forever." He agreed.

I grabbed his jaw, feeling that stubble prick my fingertips and I kissed him as if I wanted to taste those words. My tongue wrapped around his, they danced.

And all the while he sent me closer and closer to heaven.

"Fain," I gasped.

"Mine," He growled back, "All mine."

I shut my eyes, I wrapped my hands around his neck wanting to feel every inch of his skin pressing against my own. "Mine," I replied.

That magic, that bond we'd created so long ago, twisted, it locked together and I felt the heat of it as it seared the skin of our arms, as it flared enough for us both to see.

Fifty-Four

FAIN

I was Fae. I *was* Fae.

I stared at myself in the tiny mirror but I didn't need the glass to confirm it. I could feel it. I could feel how different everything was.

My body felt stronger, faster, more agile.

And the world felt alive, vivid, more real than my human form had every understood. Every gasp of air that blew in the wind sounded like a song. The leaves on the trees, the dew, hell, even the clouds, everything felt different, looked different, was different.

But none of that mattered because the only thing I could think about was our bond, that constant, beautiful reminder of what we were.

Along my skin, I could see that twisting pattern of magic. That permanent, physical sign of what we were to one another.

Beside me, I could hear Alice sleeping. For a moment I watched her, more enchanted than ever and then I forced myself up. Forced myself out of her tent and back to my own.

Alice had ripped my shirt in half and I hastily yanked on a new one.

When I passed a group of soldiers they glanced at me, looked away, and then glanced back in surprise. I couldn't tell if they knew who I was but I guess the whole camp would learn of this soon enough.

That bond seemed to soar at the notion.

At the fact that from now on everyone would see that Alice was mine and I was hers. That no one could ever deny it.

When I approached Hal's tent, the guards moved to block me, but they fell back quickly when they realised it was me.

I grunted to them, slipping inside, and saw Cait curled up, half asleep on the floor beside Hal's still immobile body.

I grabbed a blanket from the side, placing it over her and she frowned for a second before she started to stir.

"Sleep." I murmured. "I'll watch over Hal."

She groaned, forcing herself up anyway and then half shrieked when she saw me. "What did you do?"

I guess I should have expected that. Should have anticipated that most people would not react with joy at my new form.

"Alice is my mate." I said. "And last night we completed what she started so many years ago."

Cait blinked, reaching out to touch my face, studying my skin like a work of art. "What does that mean? What is a 'mate'?"

"It means our souls were destined for one another."

She smiled, nodded, though I knew she didn't really understand. "Then you are happy?" She said.

Happy, Gods, I don't know what I was feeling but joy, happiness, pure undeniable euphoria wasn't close to describing how I felt but saying that here, with Hal as he was, it felt like sacrilege. "We are what we were always meant to be." I stated.

Cait took my hand, squeezing it before her eyes cast back to Hal. He hadn't moved an inch, he barely looked like he was breathing.

I frowned, staring at his chest and then I realised with horror that he wasn't.

I yelled for help, scooping him up. His body went limp in my arms. So horrifically limp. Beside me Cait started sobbing, tearing at her hair once more.

When the Healer rushed in, I held him out, begging once more for my nephew to live.

"I'm sorry." The Healer murmured.

"No." I growled. "No."

"He's gone."

I didn't believe it. I couldn't believe it. Hal wasn't meant to die like this. He was meant to live, to rule, to grow old and marry and die in his bed with his wife beside him and all his children crowded around.

Not like this.

I pulled my magic, forcing it into him but I didn't know the spells. What spells could bring someone back anyway? The Healer tried to stop me but I shook him off. What good was magic, what good was any of this if I couldn't save Hal?

Cait collapsed at my feet, and my legs buckled.

I sunk to the floor, both of us cradling his tiny body as those tears fell and fell and fell.

Fifty-Fife

ALICE

I woke alone but I knew where Fain was. That he'd gone to watch over Hal.

As I rolled over, under the soft fur of the blanket, I breathed in the last hints of his scent.

I could see that twisting swirl of magic imprinted almost like a tattoo along my arm, telling any Fae that cared to look that I was mated. That Fain and I were.

I smiled, feeling for the first time at peace.

That frantic, spiralling chaotic state that our bond had existed in almost from the start was now gone. Finally, now, it had settled.

My mind flickered to what Rette had said at the feast, and to how everyone seemed to be treating me. I knew my blood technically made me a queen but I didn't want to just assert myself, to act like I was suddenly in charge if the other Fae didn't want that.

I got up, yanked on some clothes, and decided to go find Guillaume, to speak to the other Fae, to figure out some sort of order to what we were, what we wanted to be.

As I walked the perimeter I found Guillaume sat with Stephen and Anna.

He smirked when he saw me as if I'd been up to no good. "Are you sneaking back to our camp?" He teased.

"I'm not sneaking anywhere." I laughed.

"Sure you're not." He said.

I glanced from him, to Stephen, to Anna. "I'll be meeting with King Rette in a few hours to come up with a plan of attack for Temoor." I stated. "I think it might be good to sort ourselves out first."

"Meaning?" Stephen asked narrowing his eyes in what I took to be suspicion.

I drew in a breath of air. "We need a leader." I said. "We need to get properly organised. If we even want to stand a chance of getting our freedom we have to present ourselves as a force to be reckoned with."

Guillaume nodded.

"I agree." Stephen said getting to his feet.

"You do?" I don't know why but I expected him to argue with me, to point out how wrong I was, how stupid I was.

"Yes." He replied. "Naturally it would make sense for you to lead us."

My jaw dropped. I thought Stephen hated me.

He glanced at my face and let out a chuckle. "I'm thinking strategically, Alice. The humans all know you, you've earnt their respect as well as their fear. And with your blood it means they'll recognise your position without too many questions."

"And the Fae?" I asked.

He shrugged. "We need a leader. Your magic is strong. Whether I like it or not your magic commands ours. That puts you in charge."

I gulped. He made it sound so logical. "I don't want to just assume…"

"We are happy to have you lead." Guillaume said.

"Fine." I sighed. "But I want to establish some sort of Council. We can vote in the members. I don't want to be a dictator. I want everyone to feel like they have a say."

"I think that's a good idea." Anna said smiling.

"Queen Alice." Guillaume said.

"Stop it." I muttered.

"No, we should use your actual title." Stephen argued. "We're up against kings, nothing less than a leader of that rank will suffice."

I bit my lip, silently agreeing while also feeling like I was so out of my depth. Queen? How on earth could I be a Queen?

"I'll speak to the others." Guillaume said. "We'll organise some sort of vote and go from there."

"Fine." I smiled, pretending this was okay and that I wasn't silently panicking at the very idea of it.

Three hours later we walked into Rette's tent. Me first, followed by Guillaume and Stephen. Rette bowed low to me and I smiled, returning the gesture.

By the table Nela was hunched over what looked like a map of Temoor. As I moved to get a better look I saw that it was new, updated, with all the ruinous parts from Yannis's siege marked out in vivid detail.

When Fain walked in, the entire tent reacted. Guillaume quickly hid his surprise, as did Stephen.

Fain smirked, but his eyes promised bloody murder as he moved to stand beside me.

"High Prince Fain." Rette murmured before glancing at me. "It appears you have undergone some sort of transformation."

I tilted my head, studying that tight, angered expression on Fain's face. *'What's wrong?'*

He looked at me and a twist of pain, of grief passed through our bond. It clutched at my throat. It strangled me with its fury.

"No," I said out loud.

He nodded, confirming everything I already knew.

"When?"

He drew in a deep breath, practically staring everyone down as he spoke. "Crown Prince Hal passed a few hours ago."

I gulped at the tone. At the fury in it. At the pain still vibrating through our bond. My hands gripped the table in front of me and my knuckles turned white with the pressure.

"My deepest condolences." Rette said inclining his head.

Nela looked away, obviously fighting back tears.

"We make Rillon pay for this." Fain growled. "We make him pay for murdering my nephew and poisoning my brother."

"We will." Rette said before anyone else could.

"Then we leave today." Frederic stated.

I glanced at Fain who shook his head. "We bury Crown Prince Hal first."

"If you need help…" Frederic began but Fain cut across him.

"He was my nephew. This was his home. The least I can do is dig his grave."

I watched as he left. As he disappeared through the door without glancing back.

For a second I hung my head, fighting the grief that threatened to overwhelm me. And then I forced myself to bury it, to compartmentalise. "There's something else." I said. "When I was at Temoor, getting Fain out, I sensed something. Magic. Dark magic."

Guillaume narrowed his eyes. Stephen's back went ramrod straight and Rette, he stared at me for a second as if he thought he'd misheard me.

"What does that mean?" Frederic asked. "That Rillon is in league with the Magars?"

"Possibly." I shrugged. "At the very least we need to be prepared for an attack. Any kind of attack."

"You think he'd stoop that low?" Frederic replied.

"He murdered his own nephew." I stated. "I doubt there isn't anything he wouldn't stoop too."

"I agree." Rette said. "And our Magi will be ready."

I nodded back. "In that case we should be making preparations." God knows how long it would take the Fae to be ready.

As I walked out, I asked Guillaume to see to it, wanting to find Fain, wanting to be beside him, even if it only gave a little comfort.

Fifty-Six

ALICE

We buried Hal beside the trees, in a sunny spot surrounded by flowers. I stood in silence, with Cait beside me, watching as Fain drove a spade over and over into the dirt, covering himself in the process.

They'd washed his body. Wrapped it in silk. Given it every honour worthy of his rank.

And I couldn't look at it. Not for a second.

It hurt too much to think he was gone. To think that I wouldn't hear him terrorising the stable boys, that I wouldn't see him riding his favourite horse, or cursing at his watchers when they annoyed him.

The tears streamed silently down my face and I didn't bother to wipe them away.

It wasn't enough to get justice. It wasn't enough to make Rillon pay for what he'd done. I wanted Hal back. I wanted him alive.

And I knew I'd never have that.

Cait picked up his body, handing it to Fain and together they placed him into the grave.

Silently Fain began filling it. But as the seconds went by I realised he was muttering under his breath, cursing Rillon, cursing everything that he'd done.

We didn't have a headstone. Nothing worthy to mark the grave of a Crown Prince. Fain left a wooden marker that I knew he'd replace as soon as this war was over.

But still it didn't sit right that that was how we'd left him.

Alone in the dirt.

Alone without anything to state his name.

Alone when he should have been riding with us, laughing with us, on that dapple grey horse that he'd loved so much.

When we finally left, the entire army seemed to share that grief.

I rode beside Guillaume, at the head of what was now being referred to as 'the Fae Army.' Fain rode alone, with his head bowed and I knew he needed time. Needed space.

For days we rode, and ate, and slept as if we were robots. As if the world no longer mattered.

I slept beside Fain but we did no more than hold each other and often I would wake to the sound of my own weeping as he soothed me.

We left Cait with Mira at Nind. Though they'd fully recovered it made little sense to drag them halfway across the land when they wouldn't be fighting. We left Ridley too. Left him to watch over Ide and Atran and ensure neither of them could escape.

But as we drew closer to Temoor, as it's great mass started to stretch itself upon the horizon we saw something else between us and it; an army large enough to rival our own numbers.

I looked across at Guillaume and he shared the same concerned expression.

Technically, with so many Fae, we didn't have much to worry about but I knew not all the Fae wanted to fight. Afterall, they'd come on the promise of freedom, not for the cry of blood.

A messenger came riding up. I recognised his sigil as being Rette's and I kicked my horse forward to meet his.

"What is it?" I asked.

"King Edda and King Hayes have answered King Rette's summons." He said quickly. I tried not to react, not to show that this was the first I'd heard about any summons. "They are requesting an audience."

"Of course they are." I muttered. These Lesser Kings seemed to love a bloody audience, didn't they?

"Your presence is needed, your Highness," He bowed as low as he could considering he was sat in a saddle.

"I'll ride with you." Guillaume said quietly.

"They probably won't let you inside." I warned.

He grinned at me. "Then I guess I'll be playing your bodyguard again."

I snorted, kicking my horse onwards. If they wanted to talk then we might as well get it over with.

King Rette was stood waiting for me just beyond a hastily thrown up tent. I dismounted, throwing my reins to the nearest guard.

"They want to talk?" I said.

He nodded. "You may not find them as amenable as I have been." He warned.

"When is a Lesser King ever amenable?" I retorted.

He smirked, before putting his arm out to stop me from walking. "Before you go we also need to correct something."

I frowned, seeing the hint of something in his eyes.

"What?"

He clicked his fingers and a servant came rushing forward. I stared at the cushion in his hands, at the object sparkling on it.

"A crown?" I gasped

"We will need to procure a more suitable one when all this is over." Rette said

"I'm not wearing that." I replied. "I have no need for false presentations of power."

He shook his head, "Do not be a fool, Alice. You're about to walk in there and face off against two kings who will undoubtedly be looking to subjugate both you and the rest of the Fae. You need every bit of help you can get."

"And a crown helps, does it?"

"A crown symbolises what you are. Do not forget they wear one too. To dismiss yours would be dismissing their own power."

I swallowed, letting his words sink in. I'd never been good at this game of politics. Jelric had told me that time after time. Perhaps now was the time to start learning. Perhaps now was the time to play by their rules instead of expecting them always to adapt to mine.

"Fine." I said relenting.

Rette picked up the almost delicate looking twist of metal and placed it on my head.

"A true Queen." He murmured while I bit back the sarcastic words on the tip of my tongue.

We walked into the tent together. I could hear the murmur of chatter from the outside but as soon as we entered they all fell silent.

My eyes darted from Hayes to Edda, two kings I'd only ever seen through Rebecca's memories.

Edda's lip curled as he stared at me, pointedly looking at my Fae armour and then at the crown on my head. King Hayes managed to keep his face impassive except for his mouth that seemed to be trying to form coherent sentences despite no words actually leaving his throat.

"King Edda, King Hayes…" King Rette said obviously amused by their reactions. "May I present to you Queen Alice, the real Alice."

"Why is she wearing a crown?" King Hayes asked after finally finding his voice.

"She is a queen. All queen's wear crowns do they not?" He replied and Edda's jaw dropped.

"How is she a queen?" He asked.

I took a step forward, out of Rette's shadow. I'd be damned if they saw me as passive in all of this. "I am Alarin." I said. "My family have ruled over the Fae for the last thousand years."

Hayes let out a sound so high pitched you could mistake it for a squeal.

King Edda turned almost purple. "How is this possible?" He growled.

"The High King will not have it." King Hayes stated.

"Enough." I snapped. "We are not here to discuss my bloodline or my right to rule. We are here to take back Temoor. To save High King Uther."

"Alice is right. We are here to save my brother." Fain said walking in and if my crown hadn't been enough to rile them then his new appearance seemed to send them over the edge.

"Fae." Edda spat like it was curse.

"So, it is true, you did trick him…" Hayes raised a pointed finger at me.

"There was no trick." Fain said. "Alice and I are mates. We were fated for one another."

Half the room seemed to shift. I knew they didn't understand what those words meant but it didn't matter. The mark on our skin, the binding of our souls was what counted.

We knew. Fain and I.

"We're not here to debate what Fain and I are." I said. "We are here to discuss Rillon and how we are going to hold him accountable for his crimes."

Edda tilted his head. "Prince Rillon claims that you poisoned him. That the both of you sought to steal his crown." He paused as if he was trying to sound as dramatic as possible. "Considering what state we've found the Prince, I'd say that evidence is pretty strong."

"Have you seen High King Uther? Has Rillon allowed anyone to check on him?"

"The man is dying. You think he should be exhibited for the entire of Herani to gawp at?" Hayes asked.

"Are those your words or Rillon's?" I snapped back.

"Why would I poison my brother?" Fain said. "I have served him my entire life, both as a soldier and then as his Commander."

"Perhaps you grew tired of serving him." Edda replied.

"If that is what you think then why are you here, King Edda?" I asked.

"You expect me to believe you, girl?" He asked quietly.

"I don't care what you believe." I retorted. "I came here to save the High King. I came here to get this city back and to make Rillon pay for what he has done. Now you can help me or you can get out of my way because I am not leaving until that city is in our possession and until the High King is back on his throne."

He narrowed his eyes, looking across at King Rette. "You believe her? You believe she and the Prince are innocent?"

"I know they are." He said. "And I know Rillon is responsible for murdering Crown Prince Hal."

Edda's eyes widened at that revelation. Hayes glanced sideways at him then whispered, "The Crown Prince is dead?"

"Rillon sent Ide to do his dirty work." Prince Frederic spat.

I could feel the way the mood changed as that bombshell sunk in.

"If you are convinced then so am I." King Hayes said.

"Fine." Edda murmured before fixing those sharp eyes back on me. "But watch your mouth girl, you may be Fae but I am a king."

Before I could reply King Rette snarled. "She is a queen and you would do well to remember it."

I looked between them both. "I thank you King Rette for your chivalry but I do not need anyone to defend me or my honour. King Edda, I do not care if you think I am a queen or not. It bears no relevance on me or my people. But I will treat you with the same courtesy you treat me. If you are disrespectful to me, if you are insulting, then I shall be the same back to you. And if you hurt me or any of my Fae, I will make you pay without hesitation."

I let my magic spark, let it show in my eyes and prove that I wasn't just hot words and no action.

He glared at me, obviously swallowing whatever insults he wanted to say. "Fine. I will be respectful." He muttered.

Fain walked over to the map strewn out across the table. Quietly he started asking questions, strategizing. Edda seemed less than forthcoming in his replies but Hayes was quick to answer with whatever information he could.

I kept back, letting him take charge, letting his experience and years as Uther's Commander benefit us. Afterall, what did I know about planning a battle? The few I'd ended up in felt less like strategy and more like complete and utter chaos.

As I watched him, it was hard not to notice how everyone else responded, how they let him take charge. Even Edda and Hayes' Generals seemed to respond to him as he were their Commander.

When he looked across at me I had to bury the heat that hit my cheeks. Now was not the time.

"I think it best if you focus your army on any Magi's, any magic that they may use against us."

"Agreed." I said feeling both King Hayes' and Edda's eyes now firmly back on me.

"Why can't they simply take the city for us?" Edda asked.

"There are too many civilians." I replied. "Too many people would die if we did that."

"But you brought down King Yannis's walls all by yourself, could you not do the same here at Temoor?" I could hear the challenge in his voice. The taunt too.

"Temoor is three times the size of Caraden and it's a city not just a castle. If I bring down these walls it will crush half the city with it, not just the soldiers inside but our own too. Rillon may be our enemy but not everyone else in there is." I explained, keeping her voice steady, keeping her voice calm.

"We may not have a choice." Fain said and I knew what he was thinking, what he wanted to say, that I couldn't save everyone. That sometimes casualties were necessary.

"If it comes to it, then I will." I replied. "But it can't be our first course of action."

"You made everyone sleep at Nind, is that not possible here?" King Rette asked.

I shook my head, wishing that was a solution. "It was only possible because we surrounded the castle, we reflected our magic off of each other. We cannot do that here because of the size and the proximity to the sea. It's a tough city to attack."

I shot Fain a look at the last of my words. Afterall, that was the reason Fain had chosen Temoor in the first place. For those very virtues. Only they were biting us in the arse right now.

"I'm open to suggestions if you have any but I won't risk lives if we don't have to." I added as if that was my only fear.

"Not even for your King? Your High King?" King Edda asked with a tone I knew was meant to goad me.

"We think High King Uther has been poisoned with dark magic, if he has then I will be the one that needs to take that magic from him." I stated. "To purge him of it. To do that, I will have channel it into myself, King Edda…"

I felt Fain react from across the table, as if he could understand the magic I was talking about, as if he could already guess the potential consequences.

"…You have never felt dark magic, have never had to let it into you. The last time I did, a spectral almost killed me. Whatever is in the High King will be stronger, more powerful, much worse than a mere spectral. So you ask if I will risk lives for my King, and I can tell you I will do more than that, because there is a high chance that to save him, I have to sacrifice myself."

I heard the sharp intake of breath. I felt the way everyone around me reacted. As my eyes found Fain's across the room I silently dared him to question me, dared him to shout out that he wouldn't let me, that he was going to lock me away, just like he used to, that he was going to stop me from fighting just like before.

"Why did you say nothing of this before?" He asked almost calmly.

I shrugged. "I knew what it was. I knew it would come to this. There seemed little point in ruminating over it before we needed to."

He narrowed his eyes. *'You didn't even share it with me…'*

'I knew what you would say.'

He sighed.

'I have to do this.' I stated. *'If you want to save your brother…'*

"I know." He said out loud and I felt all that anger, all that fight that had been gearing up inside me ease.

"This is the only way to save him and ensure this world doesn't turn to chaos." I said.

He nodded before his eyes darkened and he looked back at everyone else. "See to your armies. Tomorrow we will take this city back."

Fifty-Seven

ALICE

I made my way through the Fae camp checking in on as many of them as I could. Tomorrow they'd be fighting and I didn't want to think about how many might be injured as a result. Fighting for a king they'd never met. For a king that only wanted to own them, to possess them, that saw them as just a thing to own.

Guillaume walked beside me and as every day had passed I felt more and more like he was my right-hand man in all of this, guiding me and supporting me when I needed it.

As we sat down with our newly established Fae Council, it felt both exciting and somewhat unnerving. With everything we had planned, we were anticipating a long siege, and for all we knew by tomorrow we could have taken the city and already be free.

But if Uther died, if he didn't make it...I gritted my teeth trying not to think about that outcome.

Around me a discussion grew about where we might go, where we might live once we were granted our freedom. I knew for me, with Fain as my mate, that I couldn't leave Temoor, that I couldn't leave his brother. That until the Magars were defeated we would have to stay and fight.

At the sound of approaching footsteps, the Council fell silent. I looked up and saw Fain stood, frowning at us all as if he was trying to figure out what exactly he'd walked into.

And I could tell from the looks on some of the Fae's faces that they either didn't know who he was or were shocked by the fact he was now Fae.

"This is High Prince Fain." I said, "Prince Fain, this is our Fae Council. You've just walked in on our meeting." I added with a slight smirk.

"Apologies. I wasn't aware you were busy. I'll come back." He said and I went to nod but Guillaume held his hand.

"Stay if you wish, Prince Fain." He said. "Now that you are Fae, you are one of us and you have every right to be a part of this."

Fain looked across at me, hesitating. "What do you want me to do?" He asked.

"Stay if you want." I said. Guillaume was right, he was Fae now and I needed to start acting like it, start treating him like it too.

When the meeting came to a close I beckoned Fain to follow me. So far we'd spent most nights in his tent, and I'd sneak back in the early hours and see to the Fae while he was seeing to Uther's soldiers.

As he walked in, I could feel him looking around, assessing it.

I poured out two drinks, and passed him one.

"You created a Council?" He said.

"Yes, it felt right. I wanted us to be a democracy."

He raised an eyebrow but didn't say anything so I took another sip of my drink. Waiting.

He looked around the tent again as if taking in the sparseness of it.

"What were you expecting?" I asked.

"A little more comfort." He replied.

I laughed. "I don't need comforts, Prince Fain. Besides we are at war. A tent and a bed is all that is needed."

"Spoken like a solider not a queen." He said.

"Can I not be both?" I teased passing him his glass.

"No." He said as he took it, closing the distance between us.

"Maybe when this is all over I can look for some comforts, I can look to fit out my space as a queen should."

"If you live." He said.

And I heard it then, that edge, that anger. I looked up meeting his hardened gaze. "Fain…"

"Why didn't you say anything?" He asked.

"Because it wouldn't have changed it. I have to do this."

"Can Guillaume not do it?"

"What? Of course he can't and even if he could I wouldn't ask that of him." I snapped back at him.

"You are a queen. That's exactly what queen's do."

"I won't be like that. I won't ask anyone to take my place." I stated. "Besides it has to be me. The other Fae's magic is not strong enough."

"And you think yours is?"

"You think it is not?" I challenged him.

"You said it yourself back at that Audience. You said that there's a high chance you might die."

"There's a chance I might live too." I stated.

"What chance? What are the odds?"

I shrugged. "I don't know. It's not like I've ever tried something like this before."

He snarled, shook his head, and muttered, "Not good enough," under his breath. I downed my glass and went to pour another, turning my back to him before I spoke.

"You can't stop me in this, Fain. You said it yourself I am a queen and this is my decision alone."

"I still command the High King's army."

"But you do not command me." I said turning round to face him once more.

He snarled, crossing the distance between us and all but pinned me against the cabinet.

"Do you want to save your brother?" I asked him quietly.

"Stop talking." He said, lifting his hand, grasping my jaw.

"I thought that's what we were doing? Discussing this like adults." I murmured.

His thumb skimmed along that silver scar on my cheekbone then down across my bottom lip.

"Fain…" I half whispered, half gasped.

"I cannot tell you what to do." He said. His face contorted into one of pain, of anguish. "I cannot command you…"

"Yet you would try."

"No. Guillaume said it himself earlier, I am Fae too, now. That makes you my queen as well as theirs."

My eyes widened. My breath seemed to catch in my throat. "What are you saying then?" I asked, my voice barely more than a whisper.

"That I understand it even if I don't like it. That I can't stop you and if you don't come back to me, I will never forgive you." He said before his lips crashing against mine and his need took over.

I wrapped my arms around his neck, pulling him tighter as my tongue drove into his mouth returning the urgency of his kiss, the desperate, almost crazed frenzy of his lips against mine.

He grabbed at my clothes, wrenching them off me while I clawed at his like a madwoman.

When he thrust into me, I groaned at the force of it. I locked my legs around his waist, dragged my nails down his back, desperate for more, desperate for him to devour me completely.

He wasn't being gentle. He wasn't being soft. He was taking right now. Claiming me. Domineering me in a way he'd never done before. But I knew this part of him, I recognised it in myself.

That Fae instinct took over us both and we lost ourselves to it.

His mouth worshipped my flesh. His hands held me like I was precious and as he drove us both to our end that pleasure built and built until all I could see, all I could think about was him. Us. This bond.

He came groaning, with his hands digging into my skin and I knew I'd be covered in bruises. I clung to him, not wanting to let him go, not wanting to let his skin off of mine.

"I love you so much." I said.

"I love you more than you know." He replied.

Fifty-Eight

ALICE

This was it. Judgement day.

I woke up, safe in Fain's arms and I knew from the moment I left them that all that peace, that love, that safety would be gone.

That this day would bring death, and destruction, and I only hoped that when the sun came down, it was us on the winning side. Us the victors.

I rode with the Fae Army while Fain returned to lead the High King's. I wasn't sure how they felt about being led by a Fae but they knew Fain, had served under him for years, I guessed that loyalty overrode all other thoughts.

As I joined the other Kings, I saw the mass of soldiers, the sheer numbers we had. We'd already surrounded the walls and that only too familiar silhouette of war engines littered the landscape.

I wondered what Rillon was thinking, what he was doing. Was he afraid? Did he think he could beat us still?

Temoor had fallen easily to Yannis. Too easily. But then they'd had insider help. Would we have the same stroke of luck? Was it possible that someone inside might be willing to turn tail and let us in?

This new city we'd built was bigger, stronger, more unyielding and I wondered how long we would be waiting outside its walls before we finally broke through. It made my gut twist because the High King didn't have time. Even now magic would be working its way through his system, freezing his blood and paralysing him second by agonising second.

And where was Jelric? Still, no one had mentioned him, had even thought of him. Did Rillon really have him bound in iron? I couldn't see any other alternative because he wouldn't be helping him. He wouldn't still be inside if he knew Fain and the other Kings were mounting a defence.

He wouldn't just stand by while Uther slowly died.

It felt weird to be on this side, to be looking at Temoor and laying siege to it when not so long ago I was stuck within its walls, trying to defend it from the very thing I was about to do.

'*Are you okay?*' Fain's voice echoed in my head.

I looked across at him and nodded. '*Yes. I just don't like battles. Or sieges.*'

'*No one does.*' He thought back with a small smile. I rolled my eyes at him and looked back at those damned walls.

And then the gates opened.

King Rette spotted it first. They were sending an envoy.

As the riders approached my jaw dropped when I recognised who it was.

Lord Highflynn rode up to us with four soldiers surrounding him. Two carrying banners bearing that same strange sigil I saw last time I was at Temoor.

When he saw Fain, his eyes practically bulged out of his head. His lips turned up in a sneer. And then he turned his head, fixing his gaze on the three Lesser Kings.

"I am here on behalf of High Prince Rillon. He orders you to stand down and submit to his Regency."

"Prince Rillon has taken the throne by force." Rette snapped. "We will do no such thing."

"You would defy your Regent? You would be a traitor as well, King Rette?" Lord Highflynn asked him.

Rette threw his head back and let out a loud mocking laugh. "The only traitor here is Prince Rillon and neither you nor any other of his followers will convince us otherwise."

Highflynn jerked on his horses reins, and the poor beast reared up on its back legs. "You sit beside the true traitor. All of you do. Prince Fain poisoned his brother. We have a signed confession that says so."

"That is a lie." I said before I could stop myself and Highflynn finally looked at me.

"Don't be a fool girl. Despite the lies and promises Prince Fain has whispered in your ears, you belong to the High King and while he is indisposed, you belong to his Regent. To disobey him now would be a mistake."

"Is that so?" I replied.

"You have a chance to come with me now. Beg Prince Rillon for forgiveness and he may surprise you with his generosity."

"You think I would do that? Just hand myself over to him." I snarled. "He is the one that poisoned the High King, he is the one that sent an army to Prince Hal's home. Do not think we are stupid."

"You are if you think you can defeat him. He has more allies than you know. He will destroy you all with very little effort."

My magic sparked at his words, I felt it suddenly rage and I felt Fain's react beside me.

"You dare to threaten us?" King Hayes growled.

"It is not a threat, King Hayes. You have one hour to pull your soldiers back. One hour to submit or you will feel the full force of Prince Rillon's wrath."

"Rillon's wrath?" Fain repeated in a voice I barely recognised. "He thinks he can fool us? He thinks he can steal Uther's crown? And you," He snarled. "You aided him, you supported him."

"Rillon is my Prince." Highflynn said loudly, throwing his voice enough that the soldiers around us could easily hear. "Rillon is the rightful heir to the throne. To stand against him is treason. To stand against him is death."

Rightful heir? Did they know then that Hal was dead? Had some spy or other whispered that fact into their ears? I glanced around, wondering how much weight his words might have, whether the soldiers might change their minds and suddenly switch sides.

But a ripple of magic, a flash of something so fierce it stole my breath, made my head spin. I knew what had happened before I saw it with my eyes.

I knew Highflynn was no more.

Fain seethed, flexing his hands, and I could feel the magic he used still vibrating between his palms.

"Rillon *is* death." Fain snarled. "And soon, Rillon *will* be dead."

No one spoke. No one replied. We just turned our horses and left his burnt, charred remains as an answer to Rillon's demands.

I PACED THE GROUND, FEELING LIKE AN INVISIBLE COUNTDOWN WAS over our heads. I wasn't afraid of what Rillon might do but I knew Uther was running out of time. Fain and Prince Frederic poured over the map we had of the city with Nela and the other Generals, adding their thoughts here and there.

King Hayes sat in talk with King Rette, while King Edda stood by the doorway staring at the city, scowling.

It was almost an hour since Highflynn had ridden out with his ridiculous demands. Whatever Rillon had planned, it felt like we were about to see it. To see another play of his hand.

"Come here." King Edda said to me, jerking his head.

I narrowed my eyes before walking to stand beside him, waiting for him to say whatever it was he clearly had on his mind.

"You could break this siege." He said quietly.

"It's barely even begun." I replied. I could feel the others glancing at us, watching us, though I doubted they could hear the words we spoke.

"But you could do it. You have that power don't you?" He asked and somehow it didn't feel like a question.

"If it comes to it…"

"Then why do you wait? We all know what Rillon is. And the High King, your King, is right there, dying as we speak."

"Do you think I don't know that?" I muttered, trying to keep the edge out of my voice.

"You could walk into that city, even now, you could walk right through, killing anyone that came near you and you could save him." He said.

I flinched, feeling that magic in my soul, even though I hadn't cast it. "You don't understand it." I replied.

"Then explain it to me."

I scowled. But then maybe he was right, maybe I should explain it and then he might start to understand. "How long have you been a King?"

"Longer than you have been alive."

"And how many people have you killed?"

"Enough."

"With your own hand?" I asked.

"When it was necessary." He half-growled. "I fought in the Great War."

"So, you know what it feels like to take someone's life. But to do it with magic, it is something else entirely." I stated.

He dropped his gaze, staring me up and down like he was trying to see the lie. "How is it?"

I shrugged, looking away from him and back to the city. "When you use magic, you pull that essence to yourself. It becomes part of you. Each tiny bit, each tiny pattern of it. It builds inside you, at least it does with me. I have used magic before to kill, and it stayed in me. It consumed me like a poison though I didn't realise that was what it was doing then."

"So, you're saying you're afraid to use magic to kill?"

"No, not that. I am afraid of what I would become if I did what you asked." I admitted. "If I use my magic in that way, it may well consume me and then I will no longer be who you see. I will no longer be a force for good."

"You would become like the Magars?" He guessed.

I sighed. "That's what I think anyway."

"So, you don't know for sure?"

"No. I would only know if I walked down that path and by then it would be too late."

"And you're saying you won't risk it, even for your King?"

I stared at him for a second. "Did you not hear…?" I began but then my head turned in horror. My body reacted on instinct.

"What is it?" Fain asked and I knew he could feel it too, that foul taste of magic.

"Spectrals." I said but before the words were even gone from my mouth I was running.

Sprinting.

Racing to where the Fae were.

Guillaume was already riding towards me, with my horse right beside him. I practically threw myself up into the saddle, my hands grasping the reins for dear life.

"We have to fight them." I yelled.

"We're already on it." He said as we turned around and headed to where the mass of dark magic was.

I could see the Fae already fighting them. I could feel the beauty of their magic against the filth of the spectrals. In a way it was awe inspiring. Breathtaking. To witness it, to see that pure magic and so much of it. One by one my Fae destroyed them before they got close to the human army.

Only Rillon sent more. More spectrals. And dybba's too.

Hour after hour, he bombarded us as if he thought it might wear us down. As if Rillon believed our magic might tire and fade.

As night fell he tried a new trick, unleashing thousands of burning arrows on us all. The Fae threw up a shield to block them and while we were momentarily distracted, they opened the gates and a swarm of dybba unleashed themselves on the humans.

Their screams cut through me as I once more raced to the heart of the battle. I knew Guillaume was beside me and I also knew the other Fae were right on my tail.

I threw my magic out, sending blast after blast but it didn't feel enough.

As I drew closer to the city walls I could feel it, the change, the way the air hissed, the way the wind howled.

Guillaume gave me a look of horror and I knew my own was contorted into a similar one.

"What spell is that?" He gasped.

Only I didn't know the answer. I didn't want to know.

The magic was too dark, too twisted. It made my head spin. It made my stomach twist.

"We have to stop it." I screamed as I saw it seeping out, weaving between the soldiers, eating their very souls from their chests.

"We have to find the source." Guillaume replied and I knew he was right. We'd spent too long being distracted, too long playing Rillon's games, fighting spectrals when there was a bigger monster to take out.

"Alice,"

I turned at his voice, seeing Fain there, like a beacon amongst the chaos. That bond sparked, my magic flared as if it had been reborn. He was too far to touch and yet that's all I wanted to do, to reach out, to prove that he was real. That there was something more than just this horror around me.

"We have to get inside." I cried over the mass of bodies.

He winced, like he understood that doing so would put us all in the line of fire. "Then we breach the walls."

I nodded, burying the guilt because I knew people would die. Innocents would die. But what choice did we have? They would die anyway. Our entire armies would be decimated if we didn't stop that magic from spreading. Right now, I was playing god, deciding who would live and who would die and I hated every second of it.

I drew in a deep breath, spread my hands, and as I pulled the air from every particle around me, as I wrapped it around, creating a gust of wind strong enough to rival a tornado, I sent it forward, directed it right at the stone in front of me.

I heard the crack. I heard the rumble as the wall took the full impact of it. Like a river cutting through the earth, we saw the way the wall split, the way it spread and the way it turned into an avalanche of rubble.

As the dust poured down I knew the moment was now and I kicked my horse, urging it forward, and jumped through the chaos into the city.

'I'll find you.' Fain's voice rung in my ears. *'I'll find you.'*

I gulped, forcing the wave of emotion I felt down, forcing myself to focus on the now, on the battle, on the fact that at that very second countless soldiers were racing to attack me.

I sent them flying, knocking them over like skittles, and continued onwards.

Behind me, I knew the others were fighting their way through and the sound of clashing metal filled the air like a symphony of horror.

When I reached the castle, I kept charging onwards, riding up the stone stairs and down each corridor, using my magic to fight anyone who tried to stop me.

Only when I reached the Royal Chambers did I stop.

Fifty-Nine

FAIN

The moment those walls fell I knew she'd be gone. That she would seize the opportunity and use the dust cloud as cover. But as she rode, as she jumped that mountain of destruction she still stole my breath. And under my skin, that swirling mark fizzled.

When she disappeared from view it was hard to fight the fear that that was it, that she would fight whatever Magar was conjuring that magic and then she would continue on, she would search for Uther and when she found him everything we were would end.

She would sacrifice herself, give up her last breaths for a man who I knew would never consider doing the same for her.

I snarled, clenching my fists, desperately hoping against hope that her magic was strong enough, that she was powerful enough to defeat whatever had hold of my brother and survive it.

And as the mass of soldiers around me began to surge, I knew that I had to focus on me, on now, on this battlefield right here or I'd end up with a sword in my belly and all my fears for Alice would be for nought.

So, I fought, I butchered, I cleaved a path right through the onslaught, forgetting that I had magic at my disposal. Forgetting that I was now Fae. My warrior instincts took over, and I reverted back to the soldier I'd always been. The soldier Uther had made of me.

But as I cut down one assailant after another I realised the ones fighting us weren't that. They weren't fighters. They weren't even fully grown adults. They were boys, teenagers, barely old enough to hold a sword. And most of them would be dead before sunrise.

My gut twisted in anger. I knew Ide preferred to use untrained peasants as his fighting force, not seeing the benefits of wasting his treasury's gold on a professional army but to see it up close, to witness the true brutality of it, was something else entirely.

When I finally reached the steps of the Lower Castle I was almost relieved to see real soldiers. A real fight.

We made slow progress then, cutting our way, limb by limb until we overcame everyone that stood against us and we finally breached the doors.

Behind me the mass of soldiers swarmed inside, rushing from room to room. There was little resistance, very few who still fought back.

I left them to it, left them to secure the castle because my fight, my focus was on one thing only.

"Rillon," I shouted his name, racing from one corridor to the next. Wherever he was, I would find him, wherever he was hiding, I was going to hunt him down like the worthless piece of shit he was.

I crashed into the Council Chamber, smashing the doors right off the hinges. All about where strewn pieces of paper, as if it were all confetti. Half the tables were overturned and most of the chairs were lying on their backs or had been smashed to pieces as though someone had had a full-on paddy.

The room was empty. Deserted.

I narrowed my eyes, turning, trying to sense where Rillon might be. If I had to search all night, if I had to search every cursed room, then I would.

But as I walked out the door something flew at me. I turned, striking back, instinctively using my magic to repel them and I blinked in shock when I realised who it was.

"She turned you." Niseri spat, still waving the blade in her hand as if she could hurt me. "That bitch was foolish enough to do it."

I let out a laugh, pinning her against the wall. "I should have guessed you'd be here, mixed up with all of this." I said. "Was it your nasty little friends that conjured all that dark magic?"

She screwed her face up, twisting about as if she believed she was strong enough to get free but all it did was loosen her grip on the blade enough that she dropped it. "You'll know soon enough." She stated.

I turned on my heel, ripped the curtains and used them to tie her up. Only, I didn't have time for this. I needed to find Rillon.

"He's dead." She screamed at me. "Uther is no more. I put the knife in his chest myself."

I paused, lowering my head, soaking up that piece of knowledge. Even if she hadn't done it, she'd been close to him, right when he was at his most vulnerable. If Alice hadn't had stripped her of her ability to channel magic I would have believed she was responsible for all this chaos, all this dark magic. "If that's the case then I will see you hanged for it." I stated.

"No, you won't." She cried back. "He will save me. And he will burn this castle to the ground."

I didn't know who 'he' was but that didn't stop me from turning back around and hauling her up with my bare hands by her throat.

"Alice was right to have stripped you of your abilities." I said. "Look at you, you're everything you despise now. You're weak, powerless," I tilted my head, seeing the marks on her face that I knew were from bruises delved out way before this battle. "I could drag you out of here, throw you off the tallest tower and there'd be nothing you could do to fight me."

She glared back.

"But I won't do that." I said grinning. "I'm going to keep you alive, I'm going to lock you in the very dungeons you broke all those years ago. And I'm going to take great delight in breaking your bones, in cutting up your flesh. In ensuring you suffer for the rest of your very long, miserable life."

I slammed her back into the wall, knocking the air right out of her before I dragged her out, down to where the dungeons were.

When I walked in, I could sense someone was there. I paused, scanning the darkness as Niseri struggled in my grasp. I'd shoved a torn piece of fabric into her mouth to shut up her curses but that didn't stop her muffled protests.

Beyond the door at the end, were the dungeons. My plan had been to throw her into one and deal with her once everything else was sorted but I realised now that that wouldn't be how this played out.

The only light came from the last remnants of the fire. I knew the brightness of the corridor would have made me little more than a silhouette and yet as I saw the two figures across from me, it was obvious both who they were and who I was as well.

"I knew you would come."

"Is that so?" I growled.

He smirked, twisting the blade, turning it against Jelric's flesh. To his credit Jelric didn't even flinch. He just stood there, still as a statue, as if the iron around his wrist had made him immune to pain.

"I knew you'd come look for your pet Magi."

I tossed Niseri, shoving her hard enough that she slammed into the wall and to her credit she was smart enough to stay where she fell.

And then I drew myself up, holding my hands out as if in surrender.

His eyes twinkled with amusement at the gesture.

"Do you know how long I have dreamt of this? How long I have planned this Fain? To get my revenge, to ensue the entire world knew that I was the worthy one, not you."

I didn't reply, I just stared at those manic eyes.

"Uther always preferred you." He spat. "From the moment he brought you back from that village, he always favoured you. But it was me who deserved his love. Me who sacrificed everything for it."

"What did you sacrifice?" I scoffed. He'd spent his entire life being pampered, while I'd spent mine being turned into something useful, something to benefit Uther, not that I minded. He'd saved me after all, the least I could do was return the favour, and besides, I liked being a soldier. I was damned good at it.

"I sacrificed." Rillon snarled. "Every day I had to watch you, I watch how you squirmed your way in, how you manipulated our brother the way your whore of a mother manipulated our father…"

"She wasn't a whore." I bellowed.

He let out a laugh. "She sure knew how to spread her legs like one."

I let the anger flood me, let it mingle with the magic. As my skin tingled, as my eyes blazed with fire, Rillon narrowed his, realising for the first time what he was seeing through the darkness.

But it was Jelric that said it. Jelric that spoke the words out loud. "You're Fae."

I nodded, keeping my gaze on my so-called brother.

"She did that?" Rillon hissed, taking a step forward and dragging Jelric with him. "She gave you that?"

I knew the 'she' he meant was Alice. The hate, the jealousy, the desire in his voice sent something through me, something animalistic, something feral.

"She is my mate." I growled.

"She was mine." He yelled back at me. "She was mine."

I saw the movement. I saw the way his hand lashed out and the knife caught the crimson light. Jelric groaned as the blade came down and Rillon buried it in his side.

I raced forward but Rillon jerked back, holding that now bloodied edge against Jelric's throat. "On your knees." He ordered.

I glared at him, met Jelric's gaze, then dropped to them.

"You think you've won, don't you?" I murmured.

"I have won." He retorted. "By sunrise you'll be dead, Uther will be gone, and the throne will be mine."

"You forgot about Alice." I said as my lips curled.

"Oh no I haven't." He said back. "She'll be exactly where I want her, broken, collared, and begging for my mercy."

I let out a laugh. "You think you can collar her?" I asked. "You think anyone can collar her?"

"She is Fae." He spat like the word was trash.

"She is more than that." I said, "She is Alarin."

He frowned, obviously confused by the strange word and the knife dropped a fraction of an inch. "What?"

I pulled my magic, sending it, not at Rillon, but at Jelric. He groaned, crumpling as the weight of it forced him from Rillon's grasp and onto the hard stone floor beneath him.

Rillon snarled, trying to lash out, stabbing wildly at the air but none of his blows could land with the shield I'd thrown up.

I rose to my feet, taking each step so deliciously slowly as I closed the distance. "You haven't won, Rillon. You were never going to win."

He slashed that blade, bringing it inches from my face and I grabbed his wrist, snapping it clean in two as he hollered in pain. "You cannot beat us." I stated. "You cannot beat her."

He thrashed, jabbing, trying to throw me off as I wrapped my magic around him like a coil of chains. I'd never been one to toy with my enemies, to inflict pain for pain sake but as I stared at him all I could see was that garden back in Montefore. The way he'd had her pinned down. The terror in her eyes. And that horrific sound she'd made as he'd overpowered her.

All these years, all this time I'd still held myself responsible for that first attack. I'd known what Rillon was. I'd known what his intentions had been and yet I'd failed to protect her when she'd been at her most vulnerable.

I was going to make him pay for that. I was going to make him pay for every second of her fear. For every disgusting word he'd ever uttered to her. For every filthy desire he'd ever dreamt of. For every look, every torment, all of it.

So, I let that brute inside me out. I let that monster that had overcome me so many times in Yannis's lands. I embraced it entirely, as I snapped bone after bone in his body. As I crushed his joints, and shattered his limbs. And when I could crush him no more I ripped the very flesh from his back. I tore it from his chest, I clawed every bit of his skin until he was nothing but a bleeding mass.

And all the while Jelric watched, Jelric witnessed it with his hands clasped to his side, and his eyes widen with shock at what I'd become. What I truly was now.

When that last breath finally slipped from his mouth I grew still. I stopped. I fell to my knees, not out of exhaustion but out of relief. He was dead. He was gone. The man who had been responsible for so much pain was finally gone.

I blinked, turning my gaze to the Magi, and I dropped the protective shield. "You're hurt." I said.

"Pleased you finally remembered that." He snapped.

I huffed, wondering if I should have been more considerate, should have been more concerned about his wounds.

"It's nothing a Healer can't fix." He stated.

"Good."

I offered him my arm and he shook his head. "Fae and Magi cannot touch." He stated.

"What?" I frowned confused.

"Our magic won't allow it."

Some distant memory stirred, that first time Jelric had spoken with Alice, when he'd demonstrated her powers and she'd finally accepted she was Fae.

But a shuffling caught my attention. Reminded me that there was someone else here, someone else I needed to deal with. I stalked back across, grabbing Niseri as she tried to kick out and as quickly as I could I locked her into a cell.

When I came back out I faced Jelric again. "Your magic is bound by iron." I replied glancing at the band still burning around his wrist. "That means I can touch you, right?"

He huffed, shaking his head. "I am fine." He said taking a step forward and practically stumbled onto his face.

"Come here, old man." I growled as he protested and I threw his arm up over my shoulder, half crouching from the height distance between us. Slowly, carefully, I walked us out in search of a Healer.

"I don't need to be carried like a baby." Jelric huffed but clearly he was in a lot of pain and I wondered how much of a brave face he was putting on.

"Worried the rest of the castle will see?" I teased.

He glared at me, muttering under his breath but I'll admit I was more than a little relieved when we did find a Healer. As Jelric pulled back his robes, he revealed a nasty ragged, gash but it didn't look as deep as I feared it was.

"Were you bound in iron this whole time?" I asked him.

He grunted. "And locked in my rooms."

"Maybe it was for the best." I replied. At least he'd not been murdered as I'd feared.

"The best?" He repeated, staring at where the Healer was waving their blue crystal over his wound.

"You're still alive aren't you?" I stated.

He paused, studying my face. "Where is Uther?"

"I don't know. Alice went to find him."

He tilted his head as if he couldn't understand my tone of voice.

"Hal is dead." I said quietly. "Rillon sent Ide to Nind to ensure he wouldn't be a threat."

His eyes widened, for a minute I thought he might breakdown and start crying, but before I could say anymore I felt it, a flash of fear, of panic, of sheer utter terror through our bond.

"Alice," I growled as my head snapped in the direction of where I knew she was.

"Where is she?" Jelric asked.

I stepped back, letting that Fae part consume me once more.

I didn't reply.

I didn't say a word.

Those black wings tore from my back, they ripped right out of me and as I sprinted for the nearest window the only words in my head were that I had to find her.

I had to help her.

Sixty

ALICE

I expected a fight. I expected Rillon to have packed these rooms with enough Magi to be a threat even to me.

And yet there was none of that.

I walked from room to room, seeing the unbelievable, ostentatious display of wealth. The gold painted furniture, the beautiful silk paper on every wall, and those great chandeliers that hung with what had to be more than a thousand diamonds far above my head.

But as I moved I could feel it, that growing, throbbing, consuming pull of dark magic.

As much as my body wanted to run, as much as my instincts told me to get the hell out of there I forced myself onwards, following it's trail until I found myself in front of an almost bland door.

I drew in a long breath, steeling myself for the horror of what would lay beyond this wood and then I pushed it open, quickly, before I could change my mind.

I stepped inside, noting the stark difference between this room and all the ones I'd already been in. How plain it was. Beyond the bed itself there was nothing.

But on that bed, laid out, surrounded by a swirling haze of magic was Uther.

"What the…?" I muttered as I took a step nearer but I stopped before I got too close.

I'd experienced enough dark magic in this world but this was something else. Even the pattern looked different, as though the person who'd created it wasn't Magi, wasn't Fae, was something else entirely.

Despite the horror, he looked peaceful. As if he was simply having a nap. But how could he be so peaceful with all that magic twisting inside of him? He had to have been in agony, trapped, locked in his own body, unable to escape.

I took a deep breath, mentally trying to prepare myself only what could I do to prepare for something like this?

When I pulled at that magic, it ripped into me like a thousand razor blades tearing at my flesh. I screamed, fighting the urge to let it go, fighting the urge to release it and simply run.

I pulled more, feeling it tearing into me, feeling it twisting and snarling as it seeped into every pore. Fear erupted in me, my body trembled but I didn't stop. I couldn't stop. I just had to hope that I could survive this.

Around me I could see that haze changing, it started spinning, rotating manically as if my actions had caused it to be unstable.

I pulled again, allowing more inside me.

My knees collapsed beneath me. I fell hard onto the floor, panting as that magic took over. Of all the times I should have died, all the times this world should have killed me I wasn't going to just give in and let them win now.

I could do this. I knew I could.

I gritted my teeth and pulled again. That magic tore through me and I screamed. I screamed and screamed until my throat went hoarse and no sound left my lips.

I collapsed as that magic overtook me. As it twisted inside me now. As it smothered my own.

I couldn't move.

I could barely breathe.

I gasped, hearing a rattling in my chest as if the spectral were back laying claim to my body once more.

I don't know how long I lay there.

It felt like forever.

As if time itself stopped.

As if the very laws that governed day and night had broken.

And all the while that dark magic made itself welcome inside me, melting into every cell of my body, tainting it.

As a hand reached down and strong arms scooped me up, I managed to gather some sort of strength. I forced my body to obey me. I forced my eyes to blink and my hands to curl themselves into fists.

But my magic was silent. My magic was still.

As I looked up at the stranger, I realised with horror that he wasn't a stranger at all. That I knew his face. He was Fae, just like me.

"You," I gasped.

He glanced down and those purple eyes sparkled back at me.

"I told you I would return for you." He murmured.

"Put me down." I said.

He tilted his head, tutting slightly. "You are weak. I doubt your legs can carry you."

"I'll manage."

He chuckled, but he ignored my request and carried on holding me in his arms. And only then did I realise he was walking, carrying me out of that room where Uther had been and to god knows where.

"Where are we going?" I asked.

"I told you that before as well. I told you I would take you away from these humans."

"No," I snapped. "No, I don't want to…" I began jerking, wriggling in his arms, trying to get him to drop me.

"You'll hurt yourself if you're not careful." He warned.

"I don't care. Put me down."

He sighed as though my behaviour was an inconvenience to him but he did it anyway, smirking when I staggered back, almost overcome by my own weight.

I grabbed hold of the railing, clung to it, as the freezing night air whipped around me. When I'd left the battlefield it'd only just turned to night. Now the stars shone brightly above my head.

I blinked, taking it all in, seeing that far below that fight was still raging. Was Fain amongst them? Was Nela there? And Guillaume too? I could sense the magic, sense the Fae even from this distance.

"You were stupid to take that magic in." The man said.

"I had no choice." I sighed. "How else could I save him?"

He tilted his head, pulling a face of disgust that marred his beautiful features into something ugly, something grotesque. "Why would you want to do that?" He snarled.

"Because without Uther this world will turn to chaos." I snapped back.

He let out a laugh. A cold, bitter laugh that sent a chill right down my spine. "On the contrary, Alice, without Uther this world *is* a far better place."

"Is?" I repeated with a sinking feeling in the pit of my stomach.

"Uther is dead." He said.

I blinked, shaking my head. "No, he can't be, I pulled the magic from him, I…"

"You were too late." He said taking a step closer and instinctively I leant back, feeling my heart thump, feeling my body react the way one did when they knew a predator had them caught and captured.

My eyes flickered past him, over his shoulder, realising that right now we were on the very tops of the castle. Could I make it past him if I wanted to make a run for it? Would my legs even carry me that far?

He must have seen where my eyes went because he stepped in front of me, shaking his head. Tutting once more.

"Who are you?" I half snarled.

"My name is Dray." He said almost softly, as if he meant to lure me with just that knowledge.

"Dray?" I repeated, feeling like I'd heard that name before only I couldn't recall where.

"You were meant to be mine, Little Queen." He said.

"Excuse me?"

"You were meant to be mine. That was the promise. The deal we made."

"What deal?" I snapped. What the hell was he even talking about?

He grinned, leaning in, pinning me in place with both his arms. "Our family. We were going to tie our bloodlines together, unite the Alarin line."

I narrowed my eyes. "But you're Alarin too."

"We are not so closely related to make it incompatible." He murmured as if such a thing didn't matter.

I snarled back at him in disgust.

His hand reached up, he cupped my face as I tried to jerk back. "But how can I trust you after everything you've done?"

"What do you mean?" I whispered.

"You joined them. Our enemy. You helped them. You fought for them." He stated, his voice turning more into a growl with every word he uttered.

I glared back at him unsure how to answer without goading him more and in my weakened state I knew that would be a mistake. A big one.

"You let him fuck you too." He said grabbing my jaw roughly in his hand. "Prince Fain of all people." He spat. "You let him touch you, claim you."

"He is my mate." I replied.

His eyes widened. His whole body reacted to that. I knew the blow was coming. The way his fist slammed into me told me his power, his strength far outweighed mine in this moment. He stepped back, letting me crumble to the floor at his feet.

"You will not speak of it." He growled. "You will not speak of what he is."

I grasped my cheek, feeling the way it was already bruising, but my magic seemed to come to life, finally, after feeling like it might stay dormant forever, finally it seemed to wake up. I just had to keep him talking, had to keep him distracted long enough that I could use it.

"You have betrayed us. Betrayed us all." He shouted.

"How have I?" I snapped back.

"You joined with them. You fought alongside them."

"Why do you care so much?"

"Because they collared us. They had us bound in their dungeons. And when they couldn't break us, they had us butchered like we were cattle."

"Who did?"

"The man you claim is your mate." He spat.

"Fain would never have…"

"But he did." He sneered. "I was there. I watched him. I only escaped because of Niseri. She saved me."

"What are you talking about?" I cried. None of this made any sense.

"He killed them. All the other Fae. He had them collared and locked in the dungeons and then he killed them one by one."

"It was you." I gasped, suddenly realising everything. "You killed Elynn."

"Who?" He frowned.

"The soldiers. You brought the walls down."

"I did what I had to survive. They killed everyone. Every last Fae and I vowed my revenge…"

I shook my head, trying to control my panic. This wasn't happening. This couldn't be happening.

"…and you joined them. They captured you, showed you what they were, and you still let him fuck you." He shouted so loudly his voice echoed around us.

"You're wrong. He's not like that. He didn't…"

"I was there. I saw it." He cut across me with such venom in his voice.

I covered my face with my hands, trying to think, trying to breathe. That dark magic was still twisting inside me and it made my head spin. "What do you want with me?" I gasped.

"I want what's mine. What was promised." He said, grabbing my arm, yanking me up off the wall that had been my support. "I want my throne, I want my kingdom and I want you beside me."

"What?" I spluttered.

"You are mine, Alice. From the moment you entered this world and before that too, you have belonged to me. Not the High King. Not any King. Not Prince Fain, but me." He shouted.

I yanked my arm back, my magic flaring at those words, and I landed once more against that brick wall.

"I am not yours." I cried. "I will never be yours."

He tilted his head, his anger flashing in his eyes. "I didn't want to resort to this," He muttered before sending a wave of magic at me.

How I deflected it I don't know, but I hissed, pulling my own, hitting him right back.

He let out a chuckle as if this were some sort of a game. "Don't make me hurt you," He said quietly.

"Like you haven't already." I said pointing to the bruising on my face.

He drew himself up and I could feel the power he summoned. "You're coming with me even if I have to drag you the entire way."

"Not while I'm here, she's not." Fain snarled, landing between us with those great wings of his flapping as if he'd been flying his entire life.

My eyes darted to him, I whimpered, both relieved at his presence and so fearful of what might happen now. How he might be hurt. I knew he could do some magic but I also knew he didn't have the skill to fight this Fae.

God, how stupid I'd been in not teaching him. I'd left him vulnerable. I'd left him almost defenceless.

"Go," I cried to Fain, desperately hoping he would listen. "Go."

"I'm not leaving you." He said back, moving to put himself between me and Dray. "If you want her you have to go through me."

Dray grinned, barring teeth that looked almost razor sharp. "Is that so?" He said. "I get to destroy you and keep her?"

Something evil, something twisted, erupted from his hands. I screamed, feeling the magic, feeling the destruction of it as it slammed into Fain sending him flying, slamming into the wall with the impact.

He groaned, trying to get back up while I scrambled over to where he lay, cupping his face in my hands. He blinked at me, obviously dazed. But I could still feel him trying to pull his magic, trying to do something, anything to continue fighting.

"Perhaps you should have taught him how to actually use that power you gifted him." Dray taunted.

I glared up at him. "Go to hell."

"Enough of this. Come with me now." He ordered.

"No." I snarled.

His lip curled, he glanced back at where Fain was trying to get up and I knew what he was going to do.

I snatched at the air, snatched at the fire within it, forcing myself to my feet. "He is my mate." I screamed. "And you will not touch him."

I sent that blast out, channelling every last bit of anger, of love, of power I had left and as it felt like the world exploded, my knees buckled, my legs gave way and I collapsed beside Fain, praying that it had been enough.

Sixty-One

FAIN

That magic exploded from her. It erupted.

The sheer force of it stole my breath.

And the brightness forced me to throw my arms up to shield my eyes.

When I dropped them, I saw that we were alone. That the other Fae had fled and was gone.

My body felt battered, my wings felt like someone had trampled all over them. I crawled to where she was laying.

Her eyes were shut tight, her hands were balled up and she was curled into herself as though all that magic had depleted her entirely.

"Alice," I murmured.

She didn't move. She didn't make a sound.

I stroked her hair from her face, fearful that all that energy had stolen her life but to my relief I could see her chest rising. I could feel it too, in our bond, I could feel that she was still here, that she hadn't gone.

As carefully as I could I picked her up, I cradled her and I forced those wings of mine to respond. She rolled into my chest, her head resting against my heart while the faintest hint of a moan escaped her lips.

I braced my legs, flapped my wings and soared up into the air, up into the night sky.

The wind flickered around us. The battle far below seemed to still and I wondered if it was over. If all of this was now finished.

Rillon was dead.

Whoever that Fae had been, he'd fled.

And Uther, I knew Uther was gone too.

I didn't know what would become of Herani now. We had no High King. No one to govern the Lesser Kings. Could they rule in harmony without one? Or would they turn to war too? Would this escalate, would this spread, would all of Herani be on fire as each king sought to gain the greater title?

"Fain?"

My eyes dropped to her face, I saw hers blink, then slowly open.

"Where are we?" She asked.

"In the air."

Her eyebrows furrowed. She glanced about and then she gasped as she realised it was true. "We're flying?"

My lips curled as the surprise. "It felt the safest option at the time."

She let out a snort. "Were you trying to steal me away? Make some grand romantic gesture?" She teased.

I let out a laugh and Gods did it feel good. "Something like that." I murmured.

She grinned, nodded and then her expression fell. "Is he gone?"

"He's gone."

"He…"

"Not now." I said cutting across her. Whoever he was, whatever his involvement was, we had to focus on the now. "We need to find Rette, and Callin too if we can."

"Why?" She asked.

"Uther is dead, we have four Lesser Kings here, I'd be very surprised if one of them didn't make a play for the throne."

She jerked in my arms. "That's possible?"

"Anything is possible with them."

"But you're…" She paused as if she didn't want to say it. "You're Uther's brother. Are you not able to take the throne?"

"No." I shook my head. "A bastard cannot rule and nor would I want to. Besides, I'm Fae now, my place is beside you now."

Her lips curled at those words. "Is that so?"

I couldn't help the smile that spread across my face, nor the way I claimed her mouth, just for a moment. "You are my mate." I said as if it were a treasured secret. "My life is with you."

"We could just leave." Alice whispered. "We could just fly away and leave these kings all to it."

I'd considered that. I'd contemplated just whisking her away, disappearing. But I knew the consequences of that. "We have friends here." I said. "If we leave, many of them will get hurt."

She nodded back, her face going so serious. "Then I guess now is the time to fight for our freedom." She replied.

Our freedom. I guess she was right, now I was truly Fae my life hung in the balance as much as hers and all the others did.

We dropped down, lower and lower, while I scanned the horizon trying to make out the different factions, trying to place where Rette might be. Where Prince Frederic might be too. But it was hard to see when everyone around us was a soldier, and everyone was either covered in dirt or blood, or the gods only knew what else.

When we landed, I helped Alice to her feet. She seemed better now, stronger, as though all that energy drain was long past.

"We need to get moving." I said, stilling my wings, folding them back in on themselves.

"You're not going anywhere." A voice snarled behind us and we both turned just as the lances dropped. As the soldiers rushed to circle around us as though we were caught in a snare.

I took a step forward and Alice moved, pulling me back. "Iron." She whispered staring at the weapon almost taking my eye out.

King Hayes stepped out between his men, glaring at us. "You really thought we'd just let you both go?" He said. "You really thought this wouldn't end any other way?"

"And what way is that?" Alice asked.

He smirked, holding up the glinting metal in his left hand and I knew, I could feel it, I could sense the magic that swirled around it. The horror of what it was whispered into the air.

"Collar them." Hayes barked and those lances, those iron tipped spears held us in place as his Magi quickly moved to follow his instructions.

I stared at Alice, I pulled her to me, wrapping my arms around her to try to keep her safe. But as those spears pierced my skin, as I felt the iron stealing my magic, I growled, feeling the futility of this, the inevitability.

I couldn't fight them.

I wasn't strong enough and, as that damned Magi got closer and closer, I couldn't see how we'd escape this time.

Sixty-Two

ALICE

Fain's arms wrapped around me like a fortress. I could see the iron, I could see the collar too.

Only I wasn't afraid. Not this time.

I kept my eyes on Hayes, on that smug look on his face because he thought he'd won. He thought tonight would be his victory and from now on we would be his little playthings to use and abuse.

"Are you claiming Uther's throne?" I cried out. "Is that what this is, you collar us and then make a play for being High King?"

His eyes confirmed it. His grunt told me enough.

"If you behave, perhaps I'll let the two of you share a cell." He taunted.

I glared back at him, shifting in Fain's arms. The Magi was right there, in front of us both now. He held the collar up as if we would just lower our necks and accept it. As if we had no fight in us whatsoever.

"You fool." I hissed. "You utter fool."

All that fear, all that concern about using my magic to kill was forgotten. What did it matter if I became a villain? What did it matter if I turned into something dark when the very people I was supposed to be helping were happy to sell me out and use me? I pulled my magic, twisted it, taking the time I knew I had to conjure something truly horrific, no longer caring about the consequences, about how it might taint me, change me.

And I sent it blasting into the man, into all of them, the Magi and the ring of soldiers as well. They didn't just erupt, they exploded.

They vaporised, turning the air into a red mist.

I heard Fain react. His arms loosened as if he knew he no longer needed to fight.

Buti felt it inside me too. I felt that silent, slithering change. The way so much death seeped into my bones. I gritted my teeth, acknowledging it, accepting it. This was what this world made of me. This was necessary, to live, to survive.

I sent another blast of magic, this time down to the earth beneath our feet and I projected us both up, into the air.

I elevated us as though we were gods and this king was nothing but an insect beneath our feet.

"Poor King Hayes," I taunted, as he stumbled back in shock. "You thought you would be High King." I cried out loud enough for all the soldiers, for all his army to hear. "You thought you could control me?"

I laughed, feeling as my magic wrapped around me, as that anger, and that fury changed me. As it remoulded me into something dark. Something truly Fae. My nails turned to talons sharp enough to rival any blade. My teeth turned to fangs that I knew could rip a throat right out.

I drew myself up, I channelled that magic, letting it burn, letting it boil the very air.

"Kill her." Hayes hissed. "Kill that bitch."

Fain tried to move, tried to block me, as if I needed his protection, but I was quicker.

Hayes' soldiers rushed forward. Hundreds of them, all moving in unison, all obeying their King as if they were robots. As if they had no thoughts of their own.

I threw my magic out, I threw it far enough that it surrounded all of them, all his men, and himself included.

And as I took a deep breath I misted them all. I turned them to nothing.

Fain gasped but I couldn't tell if it was from shock or pride.

As we sank back down to the ground, he grabbed me, spinning me around in his arms.

"You," He murmured as those eyes flared with magic. His hand reached up to cup my cheek. He kissed me as if my lips were the very elixir of life. "You are magnificent."

I let out a laugh, relieved that he hadn't felt that magic and rejected me for what I'd done. "Did you doubt me?"

"Not for a second."

I gave him a wry smile because I'd felt it, his fear, his desperation when he'd thought we were bested. My hand skimmed up to his side, to where those soldiers had pierced him with iron and I channelled my magic, healing those wounds.

At the sound of rushing footsteps, at the sound of what could only be another army we turned, prepared to fight again. Prepared to kill.

King Rette yanked on his horse's reins. Beside him, King Edda openly scowled.

I blinked, seeing the other riders, King Callin, Prince Frederic, and two kings I knew only from Rebecca's memories; King Morre and King Gant.

So, they were all here. Every Lesser King had come.

I narrowed my eyes, daring them to take a step forward. Daring them to challenge me.

"Queen Alice." King Rette said pointedly.

Gant, Morre, and Edda all stared at him in disbelief.

I tilted my head as the ghost of smile crept across my face. "King Hayes is no more." I stated. "He and his army have been decimated."

"You will pay for that, Fae." Edda spat.

"No," I replied, letting my magic flare enough for them all to really feel it. "This is how it stands from now on; you come for me, you harm me or any of my Fae and you will suffer the same consequences."

"The Fae belong to the High King." Edda snapped back.

"High King Uther is dead." Fain stated.

"And the Fae belong to themselves." I added.

Edda exchanged a look with Morre. Before they could argue, before they could try to turn this around I set my magic out, letting it spark in the air. "We are not your possessions. We are not your weapons. We will not be collared. We will not be cowed. We are stronger than you, we are more powerful than you, and it is time you humans learnt that fact."

Gant gulped.

Edda continued to glower but he looked like he thought better than to argue.

And Rette, he pushed his horse forward. "The Fae will be recognised as a people." He declared.

"But where will they live?" Morre spluttered.

"Wherever the hell we want." I replied, taking Fain's hand and together we turned our back on those humans. Fain flapped his wings, scooping me up, and as they stared at us, we flew up into the darkness of the night sky.

Somewhere on this battlefield the other Fae were nursing their wounds. I had to find them. I had to tell them. Because we had done it. We had won our freedom.

No longer would we be hunted.

No longer would we be viewed as merely objects.

From now on, we would make sure Herani understood our power and that they feared it and respected it in equal measure.

Sixty-Three

ALICE

It'd been weeks since the battle. Weeks since I'd killed another Lesser King. Weeks since we had gained our freedom.

We held a great funeral for Uther, before burying his body beside his son at Nind. The journey there and back had been heartbreaking and it felt like I had cried the entire way, though I'll admit my tears were far more for the boy than the King.

Did I feel relief that Uther was gone? In so many ways he had been my jailer, and yet all that bitterness, all that anger that had once raged in me, had eased. Now, I felt pity for him. Pity for what he had become and for the awful way he had died.

Perhaps becoming queen had given me an insight into where his head was at. I certainly felt the weight of that crown now that I was responsible for so many lives.

For a moment, as I lay there, halfway between sleep and consciousness, I wondered if this was all just a dream but I could see from the drapes around my bed that I was in my new suite. A royal suite. One fitting for a queen, at least that was according to King Rette.

Beside me, Fain was fast asleep and I could hear the soft, gentle, easiness of his breathing.

And then that stabbing, sharp pain twisted through me. My breath faltered. My body tensed. For a second I became a statue, frozen under the clutches of a magic too dark to fathom.

When it released me, I slipped from the bed, snatched up a blanket and walked out into the main room.

Quietly, I opened the double doors onto the balcony and stepped out.

The wind was chilly, brisk and I pulled the blanket around me, staring up at that beautiful night sky. Somewhere amongst those stars was our star. Our constant beacon burning as brightly as the bond between us.

I felt my tears trickling down my cheeks, only I wasn't sure if they were from joy or relief. Pain or happiness. It was finally over, all the torment, all the loss of control at being treated as little more than a slave. My mind flickered to the other Fae, to their faces when I'd told them that they were free, that they were protected now under the law and I smiled.

But the other Fae was out there somewhere. Plotting. I shook my head, feeling a momentary flash of fear because I knew it wasn't over. That he was behind it all; the Magars, the spectrals, all the attacks.

He had orchestrated all of it and I still had to tell everyone why.

That tightness, that pain twisted inside me and I pushed it back down. I knew what it was, that my body was now caught in a battle, constantly fighting the dark magic inside me. I just didn't know what it meant, what my future would be. Would it eventually burn through me? Would it kill me, and possibly Fain with me? Or would I be strong enough to defeat it?

As I stared out, I heard the sound of footsteps behind me.

"Fain," I whispered just as his arms wrapped around me.

"Why are you awake?" He asked softly.

"I couldn't sleep."

He turned me around, a frown ghosting that beautiful face. "Is it the magic?"

"Yes. It was fighting with me." I sighed.

"Can you stop it?"

"It is calming now." I stated. "It's like a dragon, when it is calm and sleeping then I am okay but every so often it wakes and it roars."

He frowned. "What is a dragon?"

My lips curled and I let out a chuckle. "It's a winged creature, covered in scales. They breathe fire from their mouths."

He nodded as though what I'd said was perfectly normal and he planted a kiss on my forehead. "Then I will sit with you and we can wait for the dragon to sleep together."

I smiled, leaning against him, glancing over his shoulder, out to the moonlit water beyond. "How much did you hear when I was out on the battlements?"

"Enough." He said before adding. "He killed Elynn."

"He is behind it all." I replied. "The Magars, the attacks, everything."

"Then we will fight him."

"It won't be that easy." I stated.

"Perhaps not but we won't let him win."

I nodded, gritting my teeth. He couldn't win. I wouldn't let him but with this magic inside me I wondered how strong I was to fight him.

"I need to teach you." I said. "It is time you learnt to truly use your magic."

His lips curled into a smile. "You mean you aren't enjoying what I can do so far?"

I let out a laugh as he swept me up into his arms. "You know I hate it when you do that," I whispered.

"Do what?"

"Carry me like I weigh nothing." I stated.

He tilted his head, planting a kiss on my lips and, as I felt the air move around us, I knew we were flying with the castle suddenly below us.

That those great wings of his were carrying us far away.

"But you do weigh nothing." He teased as we soared up to what felt like the very heavens themselves.

And those stars, those bright, beautiful beacons of light, twinkled more and more as we rose.

The End

A Place Of Crowns & Chains

BOOK FIVE

ALICE IS A QUEEN NOW. THE FAE QUEEN.

And more than that, she's secured freedom and security of all the other Fae too.

But the other Alarin is out there and he doesn't just want his crown, he wants Alice as his queen.

With the war taking a deadly new turn, can Alice protect her people while still helping the rest of Herani?

Can she and High Prince Fain beat this deadly new foe?

Can she survive with the dark magic still twisting inside her?

And when all out war finally erupts, with Fae fighting Fae, human fighting human, do Alice and Fain have what it takes to finally bring peace to the Herani?

Sneak Peek

ALICE

Every step echoed down the corridor as I walked. I pulled a little magic to sober myself up and, as that drunken haze lifted, I became more and more aware of how vulnerable I felt. How on edge, despite the magic at my disposal.

The moonlight shone through the crystal windows and turned the shadows into something menacing.

I paused, glancing back, convincing myself that this was all in my head.

That I was being silly.

No one was there.

It was just me.

But a hand reached out, wrapping around my mouth, stifling my cry, as I was pulled back into the darkness and that only too familiar feeling spread over me, numbing every defence I had.

"Where are you going my Little Queen?" Dray hissed into my ear.

I jerked, wrenching to get free as his arm slid across my shoulders to pull me in tighter. I whimpered, hating the way my body responded, the way it melted, as if I desired his touch, as if I wanted it.

But my mind, my mind screamed at me to move, to fight.

"Get off me." I cried.

He laughed, nuzzling his face against my hair, against my neck, as if he was sniffing me like an animal.

"You smell so good." He murmured.

"Let me go." I snarled, forcing my head to take charge, to override whatever the hell he'd done to my body.

"If I had my way, I'd never let you go." He replied, moving his hands, pressing further into my softness and while my body was responding my mind was screaming out against it.

"I hate you." I gasped. "I hate you."

"No, you don't, Alice." He said stepping back, turning me around to face him while he smiled as though this were a game between us.

"You killed all those people at Tyburne. You murdered them." I hissed.

"No, Alice, you killed them." He replied, "I warned you. I told you to watch your words but you didn't. You thought you could just speak of your love like it doesn't matter to me. Like there wouldn't be consequences. You needed to learn."

"That wasn't me. That was all you. You're a monster." I stated.

"Perhaps you haven't learnt well enough." He snapped. "Perhaps you need another lesson?"

"I hate you." I said before I could stop myself.

He scowled, those purple eyes darkened with anger as his magic swirled. "You haven't learnt at all have you? I told you to watch your words and still you don't."

The pain hit me so hard I doubled up. Stumbled back, collided with the wall behind me. My knees buckled, my entire body turned, twisted and convulsed with it.

"I took away your pain, Alice." Dray said, stepping closer as though he wanted to savour every moment of my agony. "I wanted to help but if you don't want my help then you have to accept the consequences. Every one of them."

I collapsed onto the stone, gasping as wave after wave of darkness coursed through me.

He sighed, sounding almost disappointed. "I was trying to help you, Alice. I didn't want you to suffer. Accept my help, accept my love."

He crouched down, holding his hand out in front of my face like this was all perfectly reasonable. Like I would just lift my own and take it.

I shut my eyes, balled my hands into fists, refusing to give in. "I don't want you." I gasped.

"Then you choose the hard path." He stated stepping back, glaring at me.

Another jolt of dark magic surged. I shut my eyes but that didn't stop the scream that rung from my lips. It didn't stop the way my back arched around enough to break. It didn't stop the tears that streamed down my face.

He stood there, watching, as I curled up, further and further, immobilised, paralysed.

And then he vanished.

Only I couldn't move. I couldn't do anything but stay here, in this agony, waiting for this to pass.

Get the final chapter in the Fae Girl series, 'A Place of Crowns & Chains' here

Ellie Sanders

ELLIE SANDERS LIVES IN RURAL HAMPSHIRE, IN THE U.K. WITH HER partner and two troublesome dogs.

She has a BA Hons degree in English and American Literature with Creative Writing and enjoys spending her time, when not endlessly writing, exploring the countryside around her home.

She is best known for her series of spy erotica novels called 'The BlackWater Series' as well as standalone novels, 'At The Edge of Desire', and 'Good Girl', and 'Vendetta: A Mafia Romance'.

For updates including new books please follow her Instagram, TikTok, and Twitter @hotsteamywriter

Other Books by Ellie Sanders

Printed by Amazon Italia Logistica S.r.l.
Torrazza Piemonte (TO), Italy

52258366R00241